A Stardance Summer

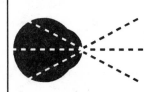

This Large Print Book carries the
Seal of Approval of N.A.V.H.

AN ETERNITY SPRINGS NOVEL

A STARDANCE SUMMER

EMILY MARCH

THORNDIKE PRESS
A part of Gale, a Cengage Company

Farmington Hills, Mich • San Francisco • New York • Waterville, Maine
Meriden, Conn • Mason, Ohio • Chicago

LIBRARY OF CONGRESS CIP DATA ON FILE.
CATALOGUING IN PUBLICATION FOR THIS BOOK
IS AVAILABLE FROM THE LIBRARY OF CONGRESS

ISBN-13: 978-1-4328-5093-7 (hardcover)

Published in 2018 by arrangement with Macmillan Publishing Group, LLC/St. Martin's Press

Printed in the United States of America
1 2 3 4 5 6 7 22 21 20 19 18

Because He bends down to listen,
I will pray as long as I have breath.

Psalms 116:2

Welcome to the world, JD.

*This book is dedicated to all the readers
who loved the Callahan brothers and
asked me for more. I hope you enjoy
camping with the Callahans!*

ACKNOWLEDGMENTS

I want to thank St. Martin's Press for the fabulous support of all things Eternity Springs. Jennifer Enderlin, Anne Marie Talberg, Monique Patterson, Kerri Resnick, Tom Hallman, Marissa Sangiacomo, Justine Sha, and Jennie Conway make writing for SMP a pleasure. And to my editor, Rose Hilliard, what can I say other than thank you, you were wonderful to work with and I'll miss you!

I must also thank Dixie Taylor and the GG's for introducing me to the world of glamping. You inspired me from the moment I arrived at the campground and continue to do so to this day. Thanks for inviting me into your lives.

To my dear friends and plot partners Nicole Burnham, Christina Dodd, and Susan Sizemore, thank you for the constant support and creative suggestions that keep each of these books different — even this far into the series. And to Mary Dickerson for always being there to say, "You'll get it done. You always do." I love you all.

PROLOGUE

Norman, Oklahoma

On a Wednesday afternoon in October at the tennis center, nine-year-old Liliana Howe batted a tennis ball at a backboard and fumed. Boys were such jerks!

It was bad enough that after a summer of lessons and dedicated practice she'd totally embarrassed herself in her very first match of her very first tennis tournament. She'd been so nervous. Not only had her mother left work to watch her, but middle school football practice had been canceled that day, so her older brother, Derek, had been there to see her humiliation, too. Derek and his best friend, Mark Christopher.

After spying Mark sitting in the bleachers, she'd double-faulted six times and lost in straight sets.

Liliana shuddered at the memory. He was such a hunk. He had dark hair that he wore a little long and dark-green eyes framed by

9

long, thick eyelashes. She coveted his eyelashes. Her mom wouldn't let her wear mascara yet. Mark was the tallest boy in eighth grade and superathletic. She'd never seen a single zit on his face. He'd already gotten his braces off.

She thought about him all the time.

She whacked the tennis ball hard. Derek and Mark had been best friends since third grade, and in fourth grade they'd built a clubhouse in Mark's backyard. A tree house. It had two stories, because they'd needed a deck on the roof for a telescope to watch the stars. Derek said that Mark knew all the constellations and all the stars and that you could see the stars real well from the top of the tree house.

Lili wouldn't know. She'd never been up in Mark Christopher's tree house to look at the stars. They said it was only for boys. They even had a sign that said No Girls Allowed.

She didn't think that was nice or fair. One time when she knew the Christopher family was on vacation, she sneaked into their backyard and checked out the tree house. She didn't get to see the stars, however, because she couldn't trespass at night. Doing so in the daytime had been wicked enough. But sneaking out of the house at night would have crossed the line.

Lili never crossed the line. She was a good girl. She didn't misbehave.

But she'd always wanted to see the stars from the top of the tree house. She used to beg Derek to let her go up there just once. He always said no. That he couldn't take her because No Girls Allowed was the number one rule. He and Mark had made a blood oath.

And in the four years since they built the tree house, they'd never changed their minds. For four years, Lili always had been left out.

That's why she was fuming now.

After her disastrous tennis match, Lili watched the singles match being played on the center court. Golden-haired, blue-eyed, big-boobed, and athletic Tiffany Lambeau versus plain, skinny, flat-chested Melissa Levin. Lili rooted hard for Melissa. Tiffany had a mean streak and Lili couldn't stand her.

She destroyed poor Melissa on the court.

After the match, Lili saw Mark talking to Tiffany. Flirting with Tiffany. Smiling, giggling, golden Tiffany.

When she heard Mark tell Tiffany to meet him at his tree house at ten so they could watch the fireworks show from a special

11

event at Owen Field, Lili had tripped over her own feet, fallen down, and skinned her knee.

Her brother had noticed and laughed at her, of course. She wanted to claw his eyes out, though not because of the laugh. She wanted to scream, *What about the blood oath?*

But she didn't. She'd watched Mark and Tiffany leave the tennis center holding hands.

Recalling that moment, Lili hit the tennis ball so hard she broke a string in her racket.

No Girls Allowed. Blood oaths. "Come watch the fireworks with me," she mimicked.

Lili stewed and steamed about it the rest of the afternoon, through dinner, and while she did her math homework. She was excellent at math, so she finished quickly. She brooded about it when she took her bath, and for once she couldn't concentrate during her thirty minutes of free reading before lights-out.

She lay awake in the dark, drumming her fingers against the sheets. There wasn't a cloud in the sky tonight. Mark Christopher was going to show Tiffany Lambeau the stars. Fireworks.

It just wasn't fair.

Not fair at all.

Hadn't Lili been the one who used her allowance money to buy the stronger telescope lens for Derek for his birthday? Wasn't she the one who asked Mom to make ginger cookies instead of chocolate chip for after school snacks because she knew that Mark liked ginger cookies better? Wasn't she the one who kept her lips zipped when she knew that Derek was sneaking out of the house to go hang with Mark?

Why does Tiffany get to go?

Lili's throat got tight. Tears pooled in her eyes and she fiercely blinked them away.

Not fair. It wasn't fair. *It should be me.*

She glanced at the clock. Read 9:56 p.m. and a burst of anger propelled Lili out of bed. She threw on her clothes, pulled on her sneakers, and did something she'd never . . . ever . . . done before.

She crossed the line.

Sneaking out of the house, she crept into the alley and slinked her way from garbage can to garbage can until she reached the Christophers' backyard.

The gate hung open already. Had Mark left it open for Tiffany or was she already there?

Stealthily, Lili slipped into the yard. She crept toward the huge old oak tree where the tree house had been built. At the base of the ladder, she paused and listened.

From above, she heard a giggle. *That* giggle. Lili winced. Mark murmured something and softly laughed. More giggles and then a long, long silence. And a feminine sigh.

Then something fluttered down from the trees and fell at her feet. Lili stared at it, her eyes widening, her stomach sinking.

A baby-blue bra.

That's the moment that Liliana Howe finally accepted that she'd never see the fireworks with Mark Christopher.

Quiet as a mouse, she'd sneaked below the tree house and scooped up the blue bra. On her way back home, she tossed it into a garbage can.

Chapter One

Twenty years later

I won't cry. I absolutely, positively will not cry.

Liliana Howe silently repeated the mantra as she rang the doorbell of her parents' home in Norman, Oklahoma. She still had a key to the house, but her arms were full with two large white paper bags of her father's favorite Tex-Mex from the taqueria over by Oklahoma University.

Brian and Stephanie Howe met at home for lunch every day, but it was rare for Lili to join them. She usually worked through lunch. But then, today was not a usual day, was it?

Her father answered the door. His gray eyes rounded in surprise. "Lili? Did we forget a lunch date?"

"No, Dad. I was in the neighborhood. Thought I'd surprise you with lunch from Miguelito's."

"Well, that's nice." He opened the screen

door. "Come on in. Let me help you with those bags."

He led her through the house back toward the kitchen. "That smells wonderful. This is a real treat, Liliana. Your mother doesn't let me have Mexican too often."

"It's been too long since I've seen you guys."

They walked into the kitchen to find her mother seated at the table staring intently at her computer. Typical Stephanie Howe. Always working. Without looking up, she said, "Stevenson has the best rating, but —"

"Look who's here, honey," Lili's father interrupted.

Stephanie Howe finally glanced up, her thoughts obviously somewhere else, because she gazed at Lili as if she didn't recognize her. Lili waved her fingers. "Surprise."

"Oh." Stephanie gave her head a little shake. "Lili. Hello. Did we forget a lunch date?"

Inwardly, Lili sighed. "No. I was in the mood for Mexican and I thought of Dad."

"It's not good for his cholesterol."

"No, but once in a blue moon won't hurt him. Dr. Derek told me that himself."

She unloaded the bags, setting tacos, cheese enchiladas, refried beans, guacamole, and tortilla chips in the center of the table.

Her mother brought plates and silverware from the cabinet. "Nevertheless, it's nice to see you. It's been too long. How are you, Lili? Have you recovered from tax season?"

"It's definitely behind me," she replied with a wry twist of her lips.

They all filled their plates. Not anxious to spill her own beans, Lili took an extra spoonful of refried and asked, "So, what do you hear from Derek?"

Her parents spent quite a bit of time talking about their renowned heart surgeon son. Nerves caused Lili to make a pig of herself on chips and guacamole, and she didn't miss her mother's judgmental frown.

Finally, after extolling Derek's most recent peer recognition award, her father asked Lili what was new with her work and the moment was at hand.

She sipped her water, wished it were a beer, and summarized the sequence of events that had led her to this crisis point. Then she waited for them to react.

And she waited.

And waited.

Her parents shared one of those long, hard-to-read looks that made Lili's stomach do a bit of a sick flip. Her father cleared his throat. "It's an incredible tale."

Her mother nodded. "Unbelievable."

Lili sucked salt off her bottom lip. She hadn't expected them to jump to their feet and vow to make the villains pay, but she'd thought they'd be angry on her behalf. Not . . . reserved.

Deep within her, despair kindled to life. They were her parents. She was counting on them. Nevertheless, she pressed ahead, calmly and logically laying out the approach she wanted to take and the assistance she needed from her mother and father.

Again, her parents shared one of those inscrutable looks. Lili's heart began to pound.

"I don't know, Liliana," her father said, rubbing the back of his neck. "It would be hard to fight them. They're powerful people. I hate to say it because it's not the way this country was supposed to work, but if a Normal Joe tries to go up against powerful people, most often he loses.

"I don't want to see you get involved with making a charge against the police. That could turn nasty real fast. This cop . . . you said you think your bosses might have threatened him, too? He might be in an even tougher position than you."

"But he lied, Dad! He falsified records."

"But you have no proof of that, do you?"

"Just my word." *Isn't that enough, Dad? At*

18

least for you?

"Maybe you should let things lie for a while. Give it some time. See how things work out. I think it's simply too soon to call the governor and ask for a personal favor."

That, Lili knew, was a no. A no and a verbal punch to the gut. After her father's heroic efforts during Central Oklahoma's most recent tornado outbreak, hadn't the governor given Brian Howe her direct phone number and instructions to call if he ever needed help with anything? Lili could think of only one reason why he denied her request, and it made her want to toss her guaco.

"Maybe later on when everything settles down we can look at the situation again."

He didn't believe her. He didn't believe *in* her. Neither did her mother. Lili's heart twisted. She knew her parents. They wouldn't come right out and say it, but she saw the significant looks they'd exchanged. Noticed the way they wouldn't meet her eyes.

They believed she'd been driving drunk last night and the DUI was legit. They did not believe that she'd been set up.

They thought she'd lied.

Lied!

Hurt like nothing she'd ever known

washed through her. Lili had never been a liar. Even as a child she'd been frightfully honest. Hadn't that been her way of attempting to gain favor with her parents? Her brilliant older brother spun stories that had fooled her equally brilliant parents, but eagle-eyed little sister often knew the truth. And tattled. But always with the truth.

Always.

Yet now, they doubted her? They believed her so irresponsible that she would climb behind the wheel of a car after she'd been drinking, thus risking her life, the lives of others, and her license to practice her profession?

Good grief, did they think she'd embezzled money from senior citizens, too?

Lili swallowed hard. Inside, her heart was bleeding. *I will not cry. I will not cry.* She couldn't believe this. What was she going to do now?

The only thing she was certain of was that she needed to leave. Immediately. Before she lost her enchiladas all over her mother's Italian tile.

But Lili couldn't make herself stand up. Her knees were too weak.

"I think your father is right." Stephanie Howe reached over and patted Lili's hand. "You know, dear, maybe this is for the best.

You haven't been happy in your work for some time now."

"You never liked accounting," her father added helpfully. "Perhaps it's best that you look on this event as an opportunity."

An opportunity? For what? Prison? Hysterical laughter bubbled up inside her, but Lili swallowed it down.

Lili's mother rose from the table and removed a glass pitcher of iced tea from the refrigerator. She topped off her husband's glass and changed the subject.

Lili didn't really care about the plans for their next-door neighbor's upcoming retirement party. Nor did she give a fig about OU football recruiting rumors. She spent the rest of the meal in a distracted fog.

Finally, having cleaned his plate — twice — Brian Howe set down his fork, wiped his mouth with a napkin, then checked his watch. "I've gotta run. I have a one o'clock conference call."

Standing, he leaned over and pressed a kiss against Lili's hair. "It was nice to see you, sweetheart. Don't be such a stranger."

Minutes later, he walked out the door and Stephanie was preparing to follow. "I hate to rush you, Lili, but I have office hours before my two o'clock lecture."

Stephanie Howe taught advanced mathematics at OU.

"That's okay, Mom. Why don't you go on? I'll stay and load the dishwasher."

"Thank you. You'll lock up when you're done?"

"I will."

Her mother ducked into the master bedroom and returned a few moments later with her hair and teeth brushed and wearing new lipstick. On the way out the door, she paused. "Lili, things happen for a reason, and often, we don't know what that reason is. Sometimes you simply need to give it a little time."

She gave a little finger wave, then exited the house. Lili stood in the center of her parents' kitchen, her arms hanging limply at her sides. She heard her mother's car start, then back out of the driveway. Lili was alone. Alone and . . . lost.

Her parents didn't believe her. Why not? What had she ever done to earn this lack of faith?

Nothing. She might not have been the smartest Howe sibling, but she'd made it a point to be the one who never screwed up. Derek the Favorite couldn't say that. The time her brother had come within a phone call of getting an MIP, he'd deserved one. He and his trouble-magnet best friend had celebrated the no-hitter Mark had thrown in the regionals of the state baseball tournament by buying a fifth of bourbon with fake IDs and drinking themselves silly in a public park. Neither had gone near a car, but still.

Derek's good luck was that their father's administrative assistant's husband was the chief of police. Dad had called the chief on Derek's behalf and worked out a deal. Derek would pay the required fine and do the required community service, but it wouldn't go on his record. Gotta protect the college applications, you know.

He'd called for Derek.

He won't go near the phone for me.

Pressure filled Lili's chest. It reminded her of that achy feeling she got when reading a novel where the protagonist discovers that her loved one has betrayed her. At that point in a book, Lili invariably skipped ahead to read the ending.

Lili needed happy endings. Satisfying endings didn't work for her. She wanted happy-ever-after.

Once she knew the book was a safe read, the emotional grief she experienced eased. Then she invariably read the rest of the book backward. She was weird that way.

She'd never expected to be the wronged character in a real-life novel. Not with her parents cast as the betrayers, anyway. She wished she could skip to the end of this story. Maybe then she'd discover that her parents had believed her and believed in her all along and they had a really good reason for doing what they'd just done.

Yeah. Right. And I'll win the next season of Who's Got Talent *because of my spreadsheet expertise.*

Ordinarily, pity parties were not Liliana's style. Today as she picked up her father's plate from the table, she had a star-studded gala going on.

Mom and Dad didn't believe her.

She took two steps toward the sink, then abruptly stopped. She dropped the plate.

Actually, she threw the plate. With both hands. Hard.

It smashed against the floor, shattering into dozens of pieces. Next she threw his glass and her mother's plate and her own plate and glass. And Liliana realized she was panting as if she'd run five miles. Tears pooled in her eyes, but she blinked them away.

Then, because she was Liliana, she got a broom and dustpan and cleaned up her mess.

About the time her mother would be pulling into the faculty parking lot at OU, Lili exited the house and locked the door behind her. Then she removed her parents' house key from her key ring and dropped it through the mail slot in their front door.

As she walked down the sidewalk toward the slate-gray sedan she'd parked at the curb, the soon-to-be-retired neighbor drove into his driveway. They exchanged waves and Lili extended a trembling hand toward her car door. "I absolutely, positively won't cry."

Maintaining her composure, she slid into the driver's seat and calmly buckled the safety belt. She started her engine, shifted into drive, and slowly pulled away from her childhood home. She wouldn't cry. She wouldn't curse. She wouldn't break any more dishes or squeal her tires in a fit of temper.

Lili wasn't reckless. She didn't act rashly and seldom lost control of her temper or emotions. She was logical and deliberate and controlled.

And honest. Totally honest.

Just the way a good accountant should be.

The faintest of sobs escaped her at the thought.

She'd broken her mother's Fiesta. And yes, she had goosed the gas on her practical sedan, though not enough to squeal the

25

tires. She wasn't certain that her engine even had enough power to do it.

Her landlady's voice echoed through her mind. *I think this car's get-up-and-go got up and went before it ever left the showroom floor.*

"I bought it used," Lili had defended.

Patsy Schaffer clicked her tongue and shook her head. "Oh, honey. Of course you did."

Buying this car had been a good decision, Lili told herself now. A practical purchase. Cars lost value the moment they were driven off the lot. The last thing she needed was a big car payment.

Especially since as of today, she didn't have a job.

She sucked in a shuddering breath. *What am I going to do?*

"Fight."

That's what she needed to do. That's what she'd come to her parents' house to do. To gather her resources. To prepare for war. This injustice could not be allowed to stand!

So fine. She'd go into battle by herself. Work from the bottom up instead of the top down. She could do it. She was a grown-up. She didn't need her parents to fight her battles. She was accustomed to doing things alone, wasn't she?

She'd go back to the office. Today. Now.

What could it hurt? They couldn't fire her again. She'd demand to speak to Fred Ormsby, the other founding partner. She'd outline her case and demand that the situation be investigated by an independent party. Then she'd go to the police and do the same thing with them.

She could do this. She was strong.

She was scared.

By the time she pulled onto I-35 headed north to her office building in downtown Oklahoma City, she'd lost the battle to hold back tears. Soon she'd soaked four tissues and was on to drowning her fifth.

Then, just as she signaled her intention to take the upcoming exit, a motorcycle screamed by, passing on the right. Only by the grace of God did she avoid hitting him.

In that instant, the blaze of Lili's temper evaporated her fears. If she'd had another dinner plate, she'd have thrown it at the fool. She was furious that the rider had endangered himself by riding recklessly without a helmet. She was incensed at her former friend and mentor in the firm and at his criminal connections in the police department who were able to create false DUI charges out of nothing.

And her parents . . . Lili swallowed hard. Her parents. For them, she had no words.

Downtown, she found a parking spot two blocks from her building, so she took it. She grabbed a fresh tissue, flipped down the visor mirror, and wiped away mascara tracks. She blew her nose, put on fresh lipstick, and pinched some color into her wan cheeks.

Drawing two calming, bracing breaths, she stepped outside and prepared to go to war.

Lili marched up the street. *You can do this. You can do this. Right is on your side. Justice will prevail.*

She was halfway to her building's front door when the problem occurred to her. They'd taken away her credentials. She wouldn't be allowed upstairs.

They'd taken her credentials. They'd taken her reputation. They'd taken her license. A great yawning sense of despair opened up inside her. *I'm powerless.*

The door to her building opened and her former mentor and the firm's other founding partner stepped outside. *Okay. Okay.* Her luck was turning. Here was an opportunity. Approaching them on a public street wouldn't be her first choice, but the fact that they'd come out of the building right at this particular moment was a sign, was it not?

She took one more step forward, then

stopped abruptly. A third person had joined them. A third person smiled and laughed and flirted up at the two men old enough to be her father.

Tiffany Lambeau.

Lili's nemesis.

When Tiffany had followed Mark Christopher to the University of Hawaii, Lili had hoped Norman, Oklahoma, had seen the last of her. Instead, Tiffany had come home with an MBA and a "broken" heart quickly healed by a prominent banker. Now Tiffany was on the prowl again, and she'd started working at the firm late last year as a consultant. She knew everyone of consequence in town — maybe the entire state — and she'd quickly weaseled her way into visiting the corner offices. Often.

Lili watched the trio turn the other direction and stroll up the sidewalk, arm in arm, and she had no doubt that she was looking at Ormsby, Harbaugh, and Stole's newest partner.

The guacamole in Lili's stomach made a threatening rumble. "Oh yes," she murmured. "Talk about a sign."

She could possibly face the powers that be at the firm. She might even be able to hold her own while presenting her case to the cops. But Tiffany Lambeau? Forget about it.

Some parts of high school a girl simply couldn't leave behind.

Lili pivoted and returned to her car. She thumbed the lock, opened the door, slid inside, and calmly fastened her seat belt. She sat with her hands on the wheel for a full five minutes, the events of the day running through her mind like a bad movie. How many times today had she asked herself, *What am I going to do?*

Now, finally, at — she glanced at the clock on her dash — 2:27 p.m., she knew the answer. "That's it. I'm done. I quit."

Lili switched on her ignition, shifted her car into drive, and spoke her life-changing decision aloud. "I'm going to join the Tornado Alleycats."

CHAPTER TWO

Brick Callahan sat at his desk in the office of the Stardance Ranch RV Resort just south of Eternity Springs with the phone on speaker, massaging his temples while he listened to his adoptive mother's scolding. "It's a high school reunion, Mom. I didn't go to the tenth. I have no desire to go to the fifteenth."

"But you were Homecoming King. And Student Council president. You should support these types of events. There will come a time in your life when relationships from your youth will matter to you again, and if you don't keep in touch . . ."

"I can always find 'em on Facebook."

"Now, honey."

"Mom, I appreciate your concern. Truly. But I do keep up with the people who matter to me. I talked to Derek Howe earlier this month. He's not going to the reunion, either, by the way."

31

"That's a shame. He was class president."

"And he's got bigger fish to fry nowadays, Mom. Did you hear that he did the heart part of the surgery for those conjoined twins from Brazil last month?"

"Yes, it was in the newspaper." Cindy Christopher sighed. "I just hoped to get you home again, sweetheart."

"I run a summer business, Mom. It's simply not practical for me to take time away in the middle of June."

There was a long pause that had Brick bracing himself. He knew his mother so well.

"As long as you're not staying away because of that woman."

Bingo. "You've seen what I'm building up here, Mom. I'm in the tourist business. It's tourist season. Which reminds me . . . you and Pop are coming up for the Fourth this year, right?"

"Oh, definitely. We wouldn't miss it. In fact, I had a conference call with Annabelle and your aunts last week to make plans. I've always loved the Fourth of July holiday, but being able to help make it such a fun and special day for the Rocking L campers takes it to a whole new level."

"I know."

Local philanthropists Jack and Cat Davenport had established the Rocking L to give a few weeks of fun, adventure, and respite to children who had had suffered a significant loss. Brick's good friend Chase Timberlake was in his first year as camp director and he was doing a great job lining up locals to help make the session the best it could be.

"So how are the Callahan women doing?" Brick asked, happy for the conversation to shift in a different direction. They discussed his birth family for a few more minutes, but when his persistent mother tried to bring the subject back around to a visit home Brick was relieved to see his foster brother Josh Tarkington arrive early for his shift.

"Guess who just walked into my office, Mom? Here, say hello to Josh." He shoved the phone at his brother and mouthed, *Be back in a few minutes.*

Brick decided he might as well make a tour of the camp and see how today's arrivals were settling in. His business had welcomed a windfall this summer when a large camping club chose Stardance Ranch to be their summer headquarters. They'd bought out the entire camp for fifty-three nights and the vast majority of his available seventy-five spaces for the balance of the summer.

He'd been able to add two more full-time employees, which freed up his time and allowed him to concentrate on his other project — Stardance River Camp.

He climbed into one of the golf carts he used to get around the RV park and made a slow circuit, waving to those guests who were obviously busy, stopping to chat with anyone who looked as if a chat would be welcome. He'd just finished an entertaining conversation with two sisters from Louisiana in a thirty-one-foot Dutchman who were out exploring the camp with their miniature dachshund, Elle.

"Brick! Hold up a moment, will you, dear?"

He turned to see the head camper herself, Patsy Schaffer, hurrying toward him. The woman just made him grin. She wore fire-engine-red hair cut short and styled spiky on top, a white cotton blouse with the club logo on the pocket, Capri jeans, and sneakers. Bright red lipstick framed a smile as bright as sunshine. "What can I do for you, Patsy?"

"I know we don't have the activity center booked for tonight, but I wonder if it might be free? We've a new member due to arrive later — Jana cleared the reservation for us earlier this morning. I always like to have a special welcome to our new members. So if no one is using the center, may we impose?"

"It's open. You're welcome to it."

"Oh, that's just wonderful. Thank you so much."

"No problem."

Brick finished his route and returned to the office to find Josh ringing up a sale of laundry detergent for a guest. "You owe me," Josh said.

"For what?"

"Backing you up with Cindy. You could find time to go home for your high school reunion."

Brick scowled at his foster brother. "Did you tell her that?"

Josh snorted. "Yeah, right. I like this job. I don't want to lose it."

"Smart man."

Smirking, Josh returned to the computer, where he had the accounting program open and the stack of receipts Brick had left for him in a manila folder beside it. "What's this cash receipt from the lumberyard? From January?"

"I sent my sport coat to the dry cleaners yesterday. Found it. Had that meeting with the Marriott reps."

Josh shook his head. "You need to be more careful with receipts, Bro."

"Yeah . . . yeah . . . yeah. I know." They both turned when the door opened. Brick straightened and prepared for problems when he spied the unhappy frown on the face of his guest up at Stardance River Camp. "Mr. Beyhan. Is there a problem?"

"Other than the fact that I've been married two whole days and I may never get laid again?"

Brick and Josh shared a cautious look.

"The tree house is fabulous. It's luxurious and has everything a guest could wish for. The views are breathtaking."

"And the problem?"

The young man sighed heavily. "My wife thought she heard a bear last night. I think it was something smaller. Probably a rabbit. Nevertheless, I followed the directions you have posted and scared it away. We got back to sleep and I thought everything was cool, but today she's been chewing on it. She's scared. This is not the honeymoon I'd hoped for."

Brick started thinking. Moving them to the tents at River Camp wouldn't be any better. He'd send them into town to the honeymoon cottage at Angel's Rest except it was currently booked. That's how they'd ended up at River Camp.

"Do you have anywhere else we could

stay? It doesn't have to be fancy. Just . . . not so isolated?"

It was an issue Brick hadn't previously considered. A problem like this wasn't really his problem — guests knew exactly what they were getting when they rented at Stardance River Camp. That said, he was selling five-star service. So . . . he needed to provide it. And he had one option to offer.

"I do have something. It's a different experience, but it's definitely luxurious and it's parked here at the Ranch. It's a large RV, a motor coach. Has a king-sized bed and a custom interior. It's definitely not as rustic as the tree house but —"

"I'll take it!" Relief infused the honeymooner's voice. "Thanks, man. You may have just saved my marriage."

"Don't you have a horseback ride scheduled for this afternoon?"

"Yes."

"We'll move your stuff down to the RV during your ride. Check with Josh, here, when you're done and he'll show you to the motor coach."

"Okay. Great. This is great. Thanks so much. I need to go tell Elizabeth so she stops calling her mother."

The young man rushed out of the office and the door banged behind him. Josh arched a curious brow. "You're renting out your grandfather's coach?"

"Hey. He's a partner in River Camp. And a businessman. He'll understand."

"Are you going to tell him?"

Brick hesitated. "Afterward. Maybe. No."

Josh laughed. Brick shrugged and added, "It's their honeymoon. Will you hold down the fort here? Branch doesn't keep a lot of personal items in his coach, but it'll take me a while to deal with what's there."

"Sure."

Another trailer pulled into the park as Brick got back into his golf cart. Josh exited the office to greet the new guests and Brick headed back through his camp, returning waves and asking after his guests' comfort. When a woman from New Mexico called out her praise of the shower room, he thanked her and drove on toward his grandfather's motor coach, his spirits high. *What a friendly group.* That gave him a good feeling about the summer.

When he'd first received the query through his website from a female-only camping club, he wasn't exactly sure what to expect. Would they be inexperienced campers? Complainers? Prima donnas who'd expect the staff to do all the physical work of setting up a campsite in an RV park?

Not that it mattered. The reservation numbers Patsy Schaffer had rolled out to him in her initial e-mail had taken his breath away. No way could he turn down that amount of business — even if they did prove to be guests from hell.

He'd done a little Internet sleuthing of his own, and after reading their website he'd felt encouraged. Women primarily in their fifties and sixties whose organized activities included bingo, bunco, and a book club didn't sound like prima donnas. In his subsequent e-mail exchange with Patsy she'd included a few photos of their most recent campout along with a list of the club's rules: no drugs, alcohol only in moderation, and campgrounds and fellow campers must be treated with respect.

Brick had processed the reservation immediately.

And today the Tornado Alleycats were descending upon Stardance Ranch.

CHAPTER THREE

Lili figured if somehow, by the grace of a merciful God, she made it safely to the bottom of Sinner's Prayer Pass she'd need a crowbar to pry her fingers away from the steering wheel of her new Ford pickup truck.

Considering that she was only one-third of the way down and she'd already come way too close to sliding off the narrow road at one of the switchbacks, she figured chances were good that the crowbar would be the coroner's problem.

Lili had never driven a truck before this trip. Never pulled a trailer of any kind. What had made her think she could safely tow a fifth wheel to the end of the world called Eternity Springs? Doing it through the flatlands of Oklahoma was one thing. Climbing the Rocky Mountains was something else entirely!

Obviously, she'd been out of her mind

four days ago after witnessing Tiffany Lambeau strutting her stuff downtown on the heels of the debacle at Lili's parents' house. She'd definitely been angrier than she'd ever been in her entire twenty-nine years of life.

Thinking about it again today made her hands shake. That and the sheer drop-off below her. "What's the deal? Is there a guardrail shortage the media has ignored?"

Directly ahead at the U of a switchback, she spied a wide spot in the road marked Scenic Overlook. She pulled into it, shifted into park, and breathed a sigh of relief.

She seriously wondered about her sanity. Never before had she been this angry. Never before this scared behind the wheel. She switched off the engine, climbed down from the cab of the pickup truck, and shouted out at the vast mountain vista before her. A lot of nevers. "What the heck am I doing?"

The words that echoed back trumpeted through her mind: *Looking for a life.*

It was true. Here she was with her thirtieth birthday churning toward her like an F5 tornado. She had no boyfriend or social life or even a pet because she'd worked seventy hours a week playing keep up with the over-achieving sibling and trying to earn the approval of her uber-successful parents.

And what had that gotten her as a result? *A clean balance sheet? Clean bedroom sheets? To heck with that.*

"If this is what being good gets me, then I'm ready to be bad."

Liliana wanted a life. She wanted to have fun, to be adventurous, to do things she might actually live to regret.

I want to grow up and be like Patsy!

Liliana had been renting a garage apartment from Patsy Schaffer for three years now. It had been a humbling experience to discover that Patsy's life was about a million times more interesting than hers. The former exotic dancer had married a divorced oilman ten years her junior when she was forty-one. They'd had "twenty-two and a half blissful years followed by six months of misery" before she lost him to liver cancer. She'd traveled the world with her "Billy-luv," published a truly frightening serial killer novel, interviewed three former First Ladies for a magazine article, and never missed a Sunday in church if she could help it. Now in her seventies, Patsy had a social calendar that would make someone half her age sigh with exhaustion. And she was off to a summer in the mountains with a couple hundred of her closest friends.

Lili envied Patsy her extensive friendships. She had a handful of friends, but they were all in some way connected to work. Wonder what they thought of her now? Wonder what gossip was going around the office about her?

Even if Lili's friends believed in her innocence, they wouldn't want anything to do with her. Just the whiff of fraud was enough to make anyone persona non grata at the firm. In their shoes, Lili would have felt the same thing.

She'd bet the Saint Christopher medal on her visor — the one she'd bought at the Catholic church gift shop after navigating her first mountain pass — that if their situations were reversed Patsy's friends would rally around her. Lili really needed to work on finding a new group of friends.

"And that's what you're doing. Right?" Surely out of a camping club of five hundred women Lili could find a few ladies with whom she shared something in common.

Five hundred. Not for the first time, Lili shook her head at the number. Patsy had founded her female-only camping club five years ago, and she'd regretfully capped membership just last week because organizational logistics had become a nightmare. Of course, not every member made every trip, but they always had a crew of at least eighty show up for the weekend events. Thirty-seven of the Alleycats had booked a campsite for the entire summer in Colorado along with Patsy. Another fifty-seven had booked more than a month. Dozens and dozens of others campers planned to come and go as time would allow throughout the summer.

No, not campers, Lili corrected herself. *Glampers.* The Tornado Alleycats went glamping.

"It's a fusion of glamor and camping," Pasty had defined in answer to Lili's question when the older woman brought home a new Airstream trailer two years ago. "Glamping involves traveling in comfort, if not outright luxury, in order to get off the beaten tourist path and immerse oneself in authentic local culture or environment."

Lili's only experience with camping had been related to advising a client that no, he couldn't deduct his RV payments as research for the book he hoped to write someday. Lili had never gone camping as a child. Her parents weren't fans of the outdoors and the summer camps they'd sent her to were educational ones, usually set on college campuses.

She'd done a lot of those kinds of camps.

Physics camp. Weather camp. Math camp. Engineering camp. Biology camp. By the time she actually arrived on campus at UNC as a freshman, she was an expert on dorm rooms.

She did have the opportunity to go camping once. A guy she'd dated in college offered to take her tent camping at a state park, but the whole peeing-in-the-woods thing had turned her off.

Patsy's style of camping was a long way away from sleeping on an air mattress and peeing in the bushes. After a month of decorating her travel trailer in order to make it "perfectly Patsy," Lili's landlady had given her the grand tour. The task took less than two minutes, but it had been enough to give Lili trailer envy.

Not that she'd been able to do anything about it. She'd had that seventy-hour work-week going on, after all.

She had thought about that trailer tour the day of the debacle as she had sat at a red traffic light on the edge of downtown Oklahoma City. The previous day, Patsy had left for her summer in Colorado. She'd begged Lili to steal a long weekend away from work and join her at some point during the summer. Lili had promised to try.

45

After partnerships had been announced, of course.

When the traffic light had switched to green, she shifted her foot from the brake pedal to the gas and pulled slowly forward. Too slowly, apparently, for the guy behind her had bumped his horn and sped around her. She'd ended up in the lane next to him at the next red light. He'd revved his engine and flipped her the bird. Her vision had gone as red as the traffic light. She'd turned right just to get away from him.

And fifteen minutes after that, she'd ended up headed west on I-40. Clueless as to why.

Now, four days later, two death-defying miles away from her destination, she knew that had been a lie. Four days ago in Oklahoma City, Liliana had made a choice. A totally reckless, impulsive choice. Reckless, impulsive, and totally out of character.

Fight-or-flight. She'd been ready to fight, but then her parents had thrown the first punch. Seeing her nemesis on her former mentor's arm had knocked her flat.

So that had left flight.

And that's what she'd done. Wearing a suit and heels with a half gallon of milk and leftover curry in her refrigerator, she'd exited I-40 without using her blinker and turned into a Ford dealership. The one right next to RV World.

She'd fled Oklahoma like Thelma in search of Louise in a heavy-duty Ford pickup towing a thirty-two-foot fifth wheel, headed for a place called Eternity Springs.

Lili stared down at the little town nestled in the valley below. She spied church steeples and Victorian houses and a main street right out of an 1880s mining-town photograph. The place looked sort of charming from here. It certainly was isolated. Probably a good place to hide. What were the chances she'd run across anyone who knew her here?

She lifted her face to the sun, filled her lungs with sweet mountain air, then exhaled heavily. She eyed the cab of her truck. She could do this. She had this. All she had to do was avoid death while descending the balance of Sinner's Prayer Pass.

Then she could begin her new life.

Brick sprawled facedown across the king-sized bed inside the home he intended to use for the summer, the prototype tree house he'd built before settling on the final design for the two he'd constructed up at Stardance River Camp. He came awake with a start. "What the . . . ?"

Living at the edge of a mountain forest, he was accustomed to unusual sounds in the night: the creepy, baby-like cry of a fox, the grunt of a bull moose looking for love, the scream of a mountain lion and crash of a falling tree. This was the first time — and he hoped the last time — that he'd ever awakened to the god-awful noise of 1970s disco.

He lifted his head from his pillow and scowled at the glowing red numerals of his bedside clock. *Two twenty-seven? Seriously?*

The Alleycats hadn't looked like troublemakers, he thought as he pulled a plump feather pillow over his head in an attempt to drown out the Bee Gees' "Stayin' Alive." They'd looked like . . . grandmas.

Hearing another blast of music from the direction of the campground — *Gloria Gaynor, shoot me now* — he wondered if he'd been fooled by false advertising. Maybe they might be more aptly called the Tornado Troublemakers.

He wasn't the least bit surprised when his camp phone rang a minute later. Branch's motor coach. The honeymooners. Great. "Callahan," he said when he answered the call. The new husband sounded a little desperate.

"Yes. . . . Yes. I heard. I'm sorry." Rolling

out of bed, he added, "I'm on my way to take care of it right now."

Brick switched on the bedside lamp, then pulled on his jeans, yesterday's flannel shirt, and his boots. He grabbed his pack, then took the walkway to the ground and his golf cart.

The distance between the RV campground and River Camp was over ten miles by road. However, he'd cut a trail over the ridge dividing the two and built this particular tree house at a spot where he could tend to both places. Maybe someday if River Camp proved to be as successful as he hoped he'd build a cabin near this spot and finally set down permanent roots. Or maybe not.

When it came to housing, Brick was a wanderer. He'd never owned a home. Never really wanted to. Since moving to Eternity Springs, he'd lived in a rental apartment, in a trailer, on his uncle Luke's houseboat on Hummingbird Lake, in his dad's house at the Callahan compound, the North Forty, and, for now, in this tree house. The lifestyle suited him just fine.

Solar lanterns illuminated the trail that led him down the mountain toward the campground in the flats. Brick didn't need the lights in order to navigate his way. He knew this land like the back of his hand.

He'd coveted the property from the moment he'd first laid eyes on it. Three years ago while negotiating on behalf of his grandfather for the purchase of a four-hundred-acre section of land from the owners of one of southern Colorado's largest ranches, Brick had topped the eastern ridge on horseback, gazed down into the picturesque valley, and lost his heart. Brick was fiercely proud of his independence, and he'd thought long and hard about entering into any sort of partnership with family — especially his domineering grandfather — but the pull of the property wasn't to be denied.

Branch Callahan, the wily, interfering old coot, had scented blood in the water.

So Brick had hired Mac Timberlake, an attorney even craftier than his granddad, to structure a deal that Brick's pride could abide and his bank account could manage. To help sell the deal, he'd enlisted the help of Aunt Maddie — the one person on the planet consistently able to influence Branch. The day they'd signed the papers ranked right up there with the best days of Brick's life.

He'd moved a trailer onto the property and begun building his dream on a shoe-string, taking it slow in an effort to do it right. He'd had some setbacks and the lean times had yet to fatten up, but he was encouraged. He now had a full-time staff of ten, counting himself, and he loved the work.

KC and the Sunshine Band blared out through the darkness and Brick winced. Of course, every job had its drawbacks.

The trail Brick followed evened out as he exited the trees and made his way toward the lakeshore and the RV and tent campground. Raucous laughter drifted across water. He didn't try to hold back his sigh. Sound carried through the nighttime forest. Bad disco carried louder than almost anything.

This was not a good start to the summer. With so many new guests, he shouldn't have skipped making his usual final round of the Ranch before going to bed. He'd been so blasted tired after the horrors of the evening that he'd been lazy.

He shuddered at the memory. The sights. The sounds. The scents. *Holy Moses, the scent.* The helplessness and horror that he'd felt.

Nothing like learning that "sympathetic vomiters" do exist while driving over Sinner's Prayer Pass with three wailing urchins in the back of your two-week-old extended-cab pickup.

That's what he got for doing a favor for family. He loved Uncle Gabe's kids; he truly did. But he'd think twice before volunteering to play chauffeur to all three of the little puke monsters again after a pizza parlor birthday party.

"Disco Duck" screeched out across the night. "Speaking of puke," Brick muttered.

He grew closer to the campground. Three separate campfires burned along the bank of the lake. Gales of laughter, bone-chilling screams, and numerous splashes told him the ladies were indulging in a midnight swim. Despite his irritation, Brick snorted in amusement. What had they expected from a lake full of snowmelt while the calendar still officially read "Spring"?

However, experience told him that the late-night dip would make his break-up-the-party efforts easier. Nothing made a man — or granny — want to crawl beneath the bedcovers like being frozen to the bone.

Whistling beneath his breath — oh, hell, a KC and the Sunshine Band earworm was not a good thing — he approached the lake just as the full moon broke from behind a cloud and illuminated the scene before him.

He slammed his foot on the brake. He turned his head and squeezed his eyes shut, but not before the sight burned into his brain.

He'd expected swimsuits, but they were skinny-dipping! They were . . . *ah, jeez* . . . naked grannies.

Brick appreciated a peep show as much as any other man, but this was just wrong. He seriously wished he hadn't seen that. But even as he tried to scrub his memory, a new song entered his head. One from *Sesame Street.*

He'd heard it early this evening when he'd delivered the stinking kids to their parents. Gabe's wife, Nic, had plopped the baby down in front of the TV to distract him while she cleaned up the twins. On PBS, Bob and Susan had been singing "One of These Things."

"One of those things," Brick murmured.

One of the female bodies standing beside the lake had been toned and taut and sleek as a mountain cat, with full breasts and curvy hips and legs worthy of a 1940s pinup girl.

"Most definitely, not like the others."

With all the noise they'd been making, they hadn't heard him approach. He briefly considered fading back into the trees without making his presence known, but "Disco Duck" reminded him of the honeymooners and potential TripAdvisor reviews.

Keeping his head turned away, he called out the warning he sounded when he went into the ladies' restroom or shower room to fix something: "Man on the premises."

After a moment's silence, someone called, "Thank God."

Laughter exploded from the gathering, and Brick knew right then and there that he was in for a long summer.

He counted to thirty, then stepped forward, making a cautious scan as he approached. Naked skin had disappeared beneath towels and T-shirts and cover-ups, thank heavens.

And then he spied her.

Legs.

He dragged his gaze slowly up her towel-clad body to her face. Something niggled at him. A sense that he'd seen this woman before.

He had not checked her into camp. He was certain of that. However, at least half of today's arrivals had checked in after his shift had ended. Maybe she'd been in town for a day or two and he'd seen her there. If that was it, she hadn't been wearing shorts when he saw her. He'd remember legs like those.

He forced his attention to the matter at hand. "I'm sorry, ladies. I hate to be a buzz-kill, but I need to enforce our noise policy."

Patsy Schaffer placed her hand on her chest, her fingers widespread. She batted her lashes and spoke in a tone syrupy with innocence. "Oh? Stardance Ranch RV Resort has a noise policy?"

He couldn't help but laugh as he stepped forward into the firelight. "Yes, ma'am."

He heard a gasp, and then Legs said, "Mark?"

Mark was his given name. He rarely used it anymore. The Callahan clan had christened him with the nickname Brick a few years ago, and it had stuck. He narrowed his eyes and studied her.

"Mark Christopher!"

Christopher. His adoptive family's name. Not Mark Callahan or "Chris" Callahan as he'd been known to the family for a time, but Mark Christopher. For Legs to know him by that name, she had to be someone he knew in his youth.

He gave her another swift once-over, and truth dawned.

No. No way. She couldn't be Derek's sister. Brick's childhood best friend's uptight, nerdy, overachieving, good-girl little sister must have a doppelgänger. Liliana Howe would *never* skinny-dip in public.

And yet . . . she'd always been tall. *Those*

legs. But she'd been skinny. *She's not skinny anymore!*

Somebody abruptly switched off the music. Into the sudden silence, Brick said, "Freckle-Sticks? Is that you?"

CHAPTER FOUR

Freckle-Sticks.

Lili had been mortified when she realized that whoever called out from the forest had undoubtedly seen her accept Patsy's skinny-dip dare. She'd figured the "whoever" was likely the studly campsite owner whom the Alleycats had been chattering about. Brick Callahan. A stranger. She'd met a few people named Callahan through the years, but never a Brick. A peculiar name like that she'd have remembered.

So Lili was in no way prepared to be caught with her pants down — literally — by a blast from her past.

But then she'd recognized him, and she'd spoken his name — the name she'd known him to use — without thinking. Why the heck hadn't she kept her big mouth shut?

Freckle-Sticks.

Suddenly Lili was a child again. Tall and skinny, flat chested and freckled, and hopelessly secretly crushing on her big brother's best friend.

Not that he'd ever noticed her. The glands-driven idiot had been too busy mooning over Tree House Tiffany.

The pair had been an item for over ten years before she dumped him for somebody else. Cheerleader and captain of the baseball team. Homecoming Queen and King. Both intelligent. Both good students. Mark had been a bit of a wild child, but Tiffany . . . she'd been a two-faced Queen of Mean. Always sweet and polite to adults, but a bully to other girls.

Not to boys. Never to boys. Ol' Tif was smarter than that. But Mark, Derek, every other boy in the school, they all thought she'd hung the moon.

Patsy and the 'Cats are right. Guys are stupid. All guys. All the time.

And *this* stupid man had just seen her naked. *Finally, I have something in common with Tiffany.*

Her instinct was to turn and run, but that would only cause her grief with the Alleycats. She forced herself to stand her ground. "Seriously? Did you seriously just call me by that horrible nickname?"

"So it *is* you." His gaze trailed slowly down her towel-clad body and locked on

58

her legs. "I almost didn't recognize you. You've put on some weight."

Outraged gasps sounded from the Alleycats. Obviously realizing that he'd stepped right into the hoo-ha, Brick quickly clarified. "In all of the right places, Liliana. You look good. Really good."

She wanted to melt into a puddle of embarrassment. Not for the first time, either, where Mark Christopher/Callahan was concerned. Hadn't he witnessed the most horrifying event of her entire life?

Oh, now that's a wonderful place to let your brain go right now.

Fighting off the humiliating memory, Lili wrapped the beach towel more securely around her body. This was ridiculous. She shouldn't be embarrassed because Mark Christopher had seen her naked. She definitely shouldn't be humiliated. He'd said she looked good, hadn't he?

So quit hunching your shoulders, stand up straight, and show off the girls! You have good girls!

He'd never call her Freckle-Sticks again.

He might call her just plain Freckles, though. She still had freckles. Not that he would have seen them in the moonlight. Lili recalled that Mark had shown every sign of liking the freckles on Tiffany's shoulders.

59

He'd nibbled on them enough.

Lili called on her newly christened inner Alleycat, straightened her spine, and lifted her chin. "What are you doing here? I thought you moved to Texas after college."

"I did for a little while. Then I moved to Colorado. Stardance is my resort."

"Oh. You manage it?"

Pride rang in his voice. "I own it."

Lili rolled her tongue around her mouth. She hadn't seen much of the facility beyond the campground, but the accountant in her couldn't help but do a quick mental inventory. *Bottom line? Big bucks.* Resentment washed through her. "That's right. You came into money, didn't you?"

Firelight clearly illuminated the way his mouth flattened into a displeased frown. Flatly, he said, "Not exactly."

Lili remembered now. The whole daddy's-money thing had contributed to his breakup with Tiffany. Lili felt snotty for having brought it up.

He shoved his hands into his pockets and shifted his attention back to Patsy. "As I mentioned, Stardance has a noise policy, ma'am. It and a handful of other policies are printed in the booklet I gave you at check-in. Please review them, and if you have any questions, feel free to ask. The goal is for every guest to enjoy his or her visit with us."

"Of course," Patsy said, her tone repentant. "I do apologize. As I mentioned this afternoon, we're celebrating the addition of a new member to our club. I thought we were the only people here tonight, so we could kick up our heels a bit. I should have realized that staff spent the night onsite and we'd be disturbing you, too."

Mark shook his head. "We have some honeymooners here tonight. They are way over at the edge of camp, but I'm afraid your music woke them up."

"You don't sleep on the premises?" Patsy asked, her voice filled with innocence.

Sharon Cross sniffed. "It's only a little past two. What are honeymooners doing sleeping this time of night, anyway?"

That question set off a flurry of off-color speculation. Mark made a show of slapping his own head. "And to think I expected an all-female camping club to be nice, quiet ladies who'd talk about books and roast marshmallows over the campfire."

"Book club is tomorrow night," Patsy said. "You're welcome to join us. We're discussing *Fifty Shades of Grey.*"

He exhaled a combination sigh and laugh. "It's gonna be a long summer, isn't it?"

"Oh, I certainly hope so," Patsy said.

"A long, *hot* summer," another Alleycat called out.

"Think I'd best toddle off to bed now. You ladies have a good night."

"Good night, Brick," Sharon called. "Sleep tight. Don't let the bedbugs nibble on your . . . knees."

Considering the minimal amount of light, she couldn't be certain, but Lili thought he might have blushed.

Then he turned around, waved good-bye, and disappeared into the forest. The Alleycats pounced.

"How do you know Camp Director Dreamboat?" one of them asked.

Another said, "I thought his name is Brick. Why did you call him Mark?"

"Yes, what's the deal with his *name?*" asked a third. "He's not in witness protection or something, is he?"

"I can't believe you already know him. Will that make our plan easier or more difficult, I wonder?"

Lili whipped her head around toward the last speaker. "What plan, Patsy?"

"You need a summer romance."

"With Mark Christopher?" Lili squeaked. *Yes!* shouted her inner bad girl. Or maybe it was her inner twelve-year-old. "Like I need a skunk in my trailer."

Sharon Cross asked, "Do they have skunks in the mountains? Somebody hand me my phone. I want to Google it."

"Camp Director Dreamboat isn't a skunk," someone said. "He's more of a mountain lion — sleek and strong. Bet he can . . . run . . . for hours."

"I think he's an elk. Big and strong. And horny."

Now it was Lili's turn to do a face plant in her palm. "You women are wicked!"

"I'm so glad you noticed, dear. We do try."

A giggle escaped Lili at that. She loved these women already. She truly did. "I'm cold. I'm tired. It's obvious I'm going to have to train in order to be fit enough to hang with the Tornado Alleycats." She slipped her bare feet into the flip-flops she'd left beside the water. "Except for the play-list, it's been fun, ladies, but I'm headed for my trailer."

"Sleep well, Lili dear," Patsy said. "I'll see you in the morning for our walk."

"You still want to walk?"

"Of course."

"Same time?"

"Yes, of course. Don't be a slugabed."

Lili swallowed a groan. She'd made a promise, but 6:00 a.m. would come very early. "All right. See you then."

"You can tell us all about CDD tomorrow at happy hour," Sharon added.

Camp Director Dreamboat, Lili interpreted.

She retrieved a flashlight from the backpack she'd brought with her to the party and headed toward her trailer. The fifth wheel and pickup she'd purchased sat parked at the far end of the Alleycats' row of reserved slots. As she walked toward her new home, she reflected on the evening's big surprise.

Mark Christopher. Aka Mark Callahan. AKA Brick Callahan. She couldn't believe it. "Wonder if he has any other names?"

Leave it to her to screw up running away from home. She wouldn't put it past Mark to call Derek and report on her first thing in the morning. *I'd better silence my phone before I go to sleep or Derek might wake me up at the crack of dawn.*

Her brother wasn't happy with her. He'd phoned almost immediately after she'd sent a brief group e-mail to her family explaining that she'd chosen to take an extended vacation. She'd realized right away that her parents hadn't shared the facts about her new circumstance. Lili had almost poured out her troubles to her brother at that point, but fear had held her back.

64

Had Derek reacted like her parents, she couldn't have borne it.

So she'd rolled out vague excuses that he didn't buy. Then, tired of being pestered, she'd spent three hours composing another e-mail meant only for her brother. In it, she promised to check in once a week. She hadn't admitted where she was going or who she was going with, and while she had not directly lied, her carefully chosen words had made it sound as if she'd finally found romance and was traveling with a lover.

"Three hours of creative effort wasted, most likely," she muttered. Mark would surely call Derek and let him know that she'd run off with a group of grannies instead of a tall-dark-and-handsome hottie.

Which brought her thoughts right back to Mark Christopher. Man, had she crushed hard on him for years. The angst of teenage unrequited love. Looking back on it, she wondered why she'd done that to herself. She'd never stood a chance with him. He'd never noticed her. Not as anything more than Derek's little sister, anyway.

Even if he hadn't been stuck on Tiffany, he'd always been out of her league — Mr. Popular, the two-sport letterman with the very real possibility of a major-league baseball career in front of him. He'd earned scholarship offers from a number of Division 1 schools. He'd chosen Hawaii, Lili remembered, because he'd "liked beaches, bikinis, and the baseball coach."

And of course, Tiffany had chosen to follow him there.

Derek had been bummed about his best friend's choice. He'd been headed to Cornell, and he'd hoped that Mark would take one of the offers he'd had from schools on the Eastern seaboard.

Her parents had been not-so-secretly relieved to see Mark on the other side of the country from their golden boy. They blamed Mark for the fact that Derek had swung and missed on admission to both Princeton and Harvard. After all, her parents had believed that Mark had been the instigator of the brawl he and Derek had participated in their senior year — the lone smirch on Derek's high school record.

Mark had thrown the first punch, but her parents hadn't known the whole story. Lili did. The fight had erupted because of *her* on what had been the most humiliating day of her life.

Two weeks into her freshman year in high school, on a school bus headed for a debate club competition in St. Louis, Lili restlessly tapped her foot. She was excited, but anxious

66

about the competition. She'd had a nervous stomach all day.

As vice president of the club holding court in the back of the bus, Derek had banished her to the front. She didn't care. She was thrilled her brother hadn't forbidden her to come along.

Lili was the only freshman on the trip. The two sophomores were boys who sat across the aisle and one seat behind her. She thought maybe one of them — Johnny Brewster — might like her, because he kept stealing glances at her.

She didn't have a boyfriend. She'd never had a boyfriend. Too many freckles. Boring blond hair. Boring blue-green eyes. No boobs or butt. She'd just about given up on ever getting them. She was the only girl she knew who had yet to have her first period.

She glanced over her shoulder and caught Johnny at it again. Only she realized then he wasn't looking at her. He was sneaking looks at the girl in front of her.

Beautiful auburn-haired, doe-eyed Tree House Tiffany with the curvy hips and boobs that now measured a D. She'd flounced up to the seat in front of Lili about thirty miles ago after getting into a snit with Mark. Now she lay on her back with her legs propped up on the seat in front of Lili. She even had pretty feet.

Of course Johnny was looking at Tiffany, not Lili. He was looking at Tiffany's legs — like every other guy on the bus.

Maybe that was why Mark sauntered up the aisle. He lifted Tiffany's legs by the bare ankles and slipped into the seat beside her. For the next half hour, Lili got to listen to their murmured bickering. Tiffany had given Mark back his senior ring. He was trying to cajole her into taking it back.

When Tiffany broke into "tears," Mark made soothing shushing noises and soon apologies spilled from the very same lips that earlier in the same conversation had claimed that he had nothing to apologize for. Lili rolled her eyes. Clueless guy. She'd thought Mark Christopher was more savvy than that, but apparently not.

Despite being in full view of everyone on the bus and their teacher if he'd bothered to glance over his shoulder, the pair in front of Lili began cuddling and kissing, so Lili turned her head and stared out the window.

She was beyond ready to get off this bus. Her nervous stomach gave another cramp and nauseated swirl, and she feared she might throw up. When Mr. Bronson stood up and announced they would be stopping soon at McDonald's for lunch, she breathed a sigh of relief. She needed off the bus. She needed fresh air. The moment the bus pulled into the parking lot, Lili hopped to her feet.

Johnny Brewster exclaimed in a loud voice, "Hey, new girl. You need to change your tampon!"

Lili felt all the blood drain from her face. And, oh no, pool between her legs.

Oh no. Oh no. Oh no. No. Please don't let this be happening. Please, God. Please.

She rushed blindly toward the exit door, vaguely aware of laughter and the buzz of cruel comments. Of course, the door wasn't open yet and she had to stand there and die.

"Here," said a gruff voice behind her.

Lili felt something against her shoulder. She glanced down and saw a letter jacket and a large male hand no longer sporting a senior ring. Though she wouldn't have believed it possible, her humiliation grew.

Nevertheless, she took the jacket, wrapped it around her waist, and fled the bus the moment the door opened.

She didn't even think about her purse until she'd made it to the bathroom, shut herself in a stall, and hung Mark Christopher's letter jacket on the door hook. Her bag. She'd left her bag on the bus. Her bag with the emergency supplies she'd carried for three whole years in anticipation of this moment.

Great, just great. What was she going to do now?

Sit on the commode and cry, that's what. She'd sob big, fat real tears, unlike those little fake glimmer sheen things that Tiffany managed to work up. She'd sit and cry and never leave the bathroom.

On top of all the humiliation, her stomach hurt and she still thought she might throw up.

The door opened. Derek's girlfriend, Terri Lane, said, "Liliana? I brought your purse and your backpack."

When her bags plopped over the top of the stall door, relief melted through Lili. Not only supplies, but a change of clothes also. "Oh, thank you. Thank you, Terri."

"Are you okay?"

No. I'll never be okay again. "I'm fine."

"Okay. Good. Well. I'll . . . um . . . I need to go order my lunch. Mr. Bronson said we have a thirty-minute stop."

"Okay." Lili waited until she was alone in the ladies' room once again to tidy up and change. Then she tried to work up the nerve to leave it by lecturing herself.

This was the most embarrassing moment of her life, but it could have been worse. It hadn't happened in the school cafeteria in front of two hundred people. And this was high school.

Not middle school. Everybody knew that girls menstruated.

Hey, new girl.

Lili closed her eyes and breathed in a shuddering sob.

Hinges squeaked as the bathroom door swung open. Tiffany swept in and stopped right in front of Lili. Her brown eyes blazed and her voice vibrated with fury.

She drew back her hand and slapped Lili hard. "You stupid b. You've ruined everything."

Lili gasped, fell back a step, and covered her stinging cheek with her hand. "What . . . ?"

"It's not enough that you humiliated yourself. You had to go and spoil my entire weekend! The only reason I came on this stupid debate trip was to be with Mark. Now he's being sent home and it's all your fault!"

"What?" Mark was being sent home? "Why?"

"Because he got in a fight, that's why. Because your brother mouthed off at those sophomores who were only saying what everyone else was thinking after you leaked all over yourself. Then the shoving started, and Mark just had to get involved. Had to stand with his man. Now they're both getting sent home and it's all your fault and I hate you."

Oh no. Her parents would kill her and Derek both.

71

"Give me Mark's letter jacket. We're back together, so it's mine, and I'll need it to keep warm tonight since Mark won't be there to do it."

Her head spinning, her cheek stinging, and her heart hurting, Lili moved to retrieve the jacket she'd left folded over her backpack. Without speaking, she handed it to Tiffany.

The girl held it out in front of her and started to slip it around her shoulders. Then she winced. "Oh, gross. This is just great. You stained it."

Tiffany threw the letter jacket back at Lili. "Get it cleaned. If the stain doesn't come out, you need to buy us a new one."

Lili clutched the jacket to her chest, closed her eyes, and wished she would die. Right here. Right now. Just . . . go away.

Instead, when the announcement was made to load up, she got onto the bus. No one spoke to her, thank goodness. She returned to her window seat, slumped down, and pulled the letter jacket up over her head, pretending to be asleep.

She smelled cologne. A guy's scent, though she didn't know its name. Derek wore Axe. This was different. It smelled nice. It smelled . . . older. Kind of dreamy. Warm and comforting.

Lili sank into the jacket, sank into the scent,

and let her mind go blank.

Fifteen years later, with the memory of the most horrible day of her youth fresh on her mind, she wondered if Mark Christopher still wore that Armani cologne.

It had taken her weeks after what she'd personally termed the Incident to identify the scent, primarily because she started searching the fragrance counter at drugstores. It wasn't until she graduated to trying the men's fragrance samples at department stores that she found it. If she'd entertained a vague idea to purchase a bottle to use as calming aromatherapy, it evaporated at her first glance at the price tag.

Nevertheless, she never smelled that particular fragrance without thinking of Mark Christopher.

Wonder if he ever thought about her? He'd treated her no differently in the wake of the Incident. In fact, the only reference he'd ever made to it was a brief "Thanks" when they passed in the hallway between classes two weeks later, the day after she'd sent the replacement letter jacket she'd purchased to his house.

Not that she saw very much of him after the debate trip from hell. It wasn't difficult to avoid him at school. He and Derek remained good friends, but since Mark had thrown the first punch in the parking lot fight, he'd become persona non grata around the Howe house. On the rare occasions he did come around, Lili made herself scarce. Then Mark's birth father found him, and even Derek didn't see much of him for a while.

Lili's freshman year passed in a miserable blur. She quit the debate team, of course. Her grades dropped — little wonder since she mentally checked out from just about everything in the wake of the Incident. As a result, she'd taken a hit to her class rank from which she never completely recovered. Unlike her brother, no Ivy League for her.

It's a wonder her parents had waited until now to basically disown her.

As for her unrequited love issue . . . the Incident had managed to crush her crush. If she and Mark had exchanged more than two dozen words between that day and tonight, she'd be surprised.

She'd seen him only once since he'd graduated from high school. It had been . . . what . . . four years ago? Maybe five? They hadn't spoken that night, either. In fact, she didn't think he even noticed her. She'd been dining with a client.

Lili noticed the familiar figure seated in the

steakhouse's bar area when she smiled up at the waiter who'd set her order on the table. He sat alone, a highball glass with three fingers of amber liquid in front of him, and he stared broodily out the window.

Mark Christopher. Wow, now there's a blast from the past.

She couldn't help but steal glances toward him throughout her meal, and when her client excused himself to visit the restroom, she'd taken the opportunity to study her brother's old friend at her leisure.

Maturity looked good on him. It didn't surprise Lili that he'd grown even more handsome in the years since she'd seen him last. His frame had filled out. He wore his dark hair military short. Dressed in faded denim jeans and a white cotton sports shirt with the cuffs rolled up, he had a pair of Ray-Bans hanging from a cord around his neck. A waitress approached, tried a flirtatious hip waggle and grin on him as she asked a question. Lili had read his lips. "Another Jameson's. Neat. Another double."

He spoke without taking his gaze off of . . . what?

Lili followed the path of his stare to the street where a horse-drawn carriage waited outside of First Presbyterian Church. "Oh," Lili murmured aloud. Now it made sense.

Her mother had mentioned that Tiffany Lambeau was getting married that weekend.

To somebody other than Mark Christopher.

Lili felt like a voyeur as she watched Mark watch the front of the church. It was hard to put a name to the expression on his face. Maybe because that expression was expressionless.

She could easier define what he wasn't. He wasn't happy. He wasn't sad or somber or visibly miserable. But neither was he uninvested. The best word she could come up with was "intense."

Lili wondered if he'd had come here to crash the wedding for the "if anyone knows a reason why not" moment. If so, he must have decided against it.

Her dinner companion returned, and for the rest of the meal Lili struggled to keep her mind on business. Despite her best intentions, her attention continued to stray toward the man in the bar.

She was discussing a potential tax strategy with her client when Mark froze with his drink halfway to his mouth. She lost her train of thought as emotion flashed like lightning across his face, there and gone in an instant, but so intense that it burned into her memory.

Lili didn't need to glance over her shoulder to see that the church doors had opened and the bride and groom were hurrying to their waiting carriage.

Tonight as Lili reached her campsite, she recalled that flash of emotion that had blazed across Mark's face that evening. Such love. Such grief. Such heartache.

"Such an idiot," she murmured, opening the door to her trailer.

And yet Tiffany Lambeau had fooled a lot of people for a long time. Pretty girls could do that. Pretty girls with Academy Award–worthy acting talent could take it all the way to the bank. Or, in Tiffany's case, the banker. And now to the accounting firm.

Kudos to Mark for getting out of the relationship before doing so involved lawyers. Or child support. The banker hadn't been as lucky. His prolonged custody battle with the Queen of Mean had been the talk of the hair salon where both women had their hair cut — and Tiffany had hers colored. (Guess that auburn Mark had liked so much had been fake from the start.)

Lili wondered if Mark knew the truth about Tiffany's hair color. She wondered if he knew about the divorce or about Tiffany's new position at the consulting firm where Lili had worked.

The day that Tiffany had sashayed into the office with the head of HR and a brand-new title Lili had to stretch to maintain her professional composure. The old saying about it's not what you know but who you know had never been more true. For almost six months she'd had to put up with twice-weekly meetings with the Queen of Mean.

The best thing about running away from home had been leaving those meetings and that particular coworker behind. What sort of cosmic joke was it that Lili had fled the frying pan only to land in Mark Christopher's fire?

Actually, his lake. Naked.

Well, at least she wasn't on her period.

CHAPTER FIVE

Despite the late-night sleep interruption, Brick was up before dawn the next morning. He had a full day ahead of him that included a meeting with his banker, a teleconference with his marketing guys, and lunch with the woman who helped him with his books. He was afraid he already knew what the last was about. The rumor going around town was that the Bartons had split up and Donna was moving to Denver. Donna Barton helped a dozen businesses in town with their books. If there was something to this rumor, he wouldn't be the only person looking for help. Since finding it in town this time of year when everybody already had everything they could handle was tough, Brick wanted to get a jump-start on the process and get his dibs in ahead of everyone else if necessary.

First, though, he needed to make a run into town to load up a breakfast basket with warm cinnamon rolls at Sarah Murphy's bakery. He planned to tuck a gift certificate for a couples massage at the Angel's Rest spa in the basket with the rolls and leave it for the honeymooners as an apology for last night's disturbance.

He sauntered into Fresh Bakery just as the sky began to lighten in the east and was surprised to discover the town's veterinarian behind the counter instead of her mother. "What's the deal?" he asked Lori Timberlake. "You having to moonlight to keep the lights on in the kennel these days?"

"Not hardly." Knowing her friend, she poured Brick a cup of coffee. "Based on the hours I've been working of late, we have more pets than people here in Eternity Springs. And by the way, rumor has it that Donna Barton might be leaving town."

"I heard." Brick gave the aroma wafting from the cup an appreciative sniff. "This almost smells as good as the cinnamon rolls. Your mother is a goddess, Lori."

"I know."

"So what *does* bring you to Fresh this morning? That husband of yours jonesing for cinnamon rolls?"

Lori laughed. "Always, but he left for the Rocking L before the rolls came out of the oven today. Campers arrive this morning."

"Ah. Bet Chase is excited."

"Excited and nervous. He talked Mom into donating cookies for the welcome reception, and since I was awake anyway, I figured I could put in a few hours here to help her. She's been working her fanny off getting the house ready for the prodigal son's return."

"Devin's coming for a visit?"

"Actually, I'm not sure," Lori said, her expression turning speculative. "He hasn't come right out and said anything, but when he was home for Christmas I got the sense that he might be thinking of moving back."

"Your parents would love that. Might put a crimp in my style, though."

Lori shot him a puzzled look and he further explained, "Your brother has that Aussie accent that makes the ladies swoon. He's serious competition for me. I might not —"

She interrupted him with a snort. "As if you have a hard time getting a date. Is there a single, single woman in town who you haven't dated at least once?"

Brick made a show of pursing his lips and rubbing the back of his neck. "Celeste won't go out with me. I've asked her a dozen times."

Lori rolled her eyes. "Celeste is at least

forty years older than you."

"Hey. I don't age discriminate." He paused a beat, then asked, "Does she have a daughter, do you know? Or a granddaughter?"

"Brick," Lori chastised.

"How old do you think Celeste is, anyway?"

"Who knows?" Lori said. "Somewhere in the seventies, I'd guess, although she has the energy of a twenty-year-old."

"I hear you. I could barely keep up with her on that Hike to the Heavens fundraising climb up Murphy Mountain that she and your dad organized last weekend. By the way, how successful was that project? Did they meet the goal?"

Lori's green eyes brightened. "Exceeded it by twenty percent. They raised enough to replace all of the pews at Saint Stephen's and resurface the parking lot."

"Excellent news. Your family does a lot for this town, Lori."

"They're not the only ones. Chase told me that your family has offered to host the campers at the North Forty for the Fourth of July again. That's wonderful."

The North Forty lay along the shore of Hummingbird Lake and was the first piece of Colorado property the Callahan family had purchased after the reconciliation between Branch Callahan and his four sons — Matt, Luke, Brick's father, Mark, and the youngest, John Gabriel, who went by "Gabe" in Eternity Springs.

Names and the Callahans were a fluid thing.

Gabe lived in Eternity Springs year-round with his wife, twin daughters, and infant son. Branch and his other three sons all had built vacation homes on the North Forty property for their families. They visited often and most summer weekends found at least one family group in attendance. It had become a Callahan family tradition for the whole clan to spend the Fourth of July in Colorado and officially host Eternity Springs' fireworks show over Hummingbird Lake. Last year they'd invited the Rocking L campers down for a picnic and the event had proved to be a roaring success for family and campers alike.

"We're glad to do it," Brick replied, perusing the contents of the bakery's display case. "The family has as much fun as the campers. Besides, entertaining the kiddos gives my dad a good excuse to make the fireworks show even bigger. The man loves making things blow up."

Lori grinned with appreciation. "Last

year's show was ridiculous."

"This year's will be even better. He's got a lead on a company out of Louisiana that supposedly does a spectacular job — and will let him help."

"I heard rumors about a homemade ice cream contest."

"That's my aunt Torie's project," Brick said, distracted from the bakery case as Lori's mother swept into the room carrying a tray of muffins fresh from the bakery's oven. "She's been in a panic ever since word hit town that Jared Kelley wouldn't be reopening the Taste of Texas creamery this summer. Good morning, Sarah."

"It's a justified panic," Sarah Murphy observed. "Good morning to you, Brick."

"Whatcha got there?"

"Blueberry pecan muffins. Want one?"

"Hmm . . . I'd better take a couple dozen. No, make that three dozen. And three cinnamon rolls, please."

"Hungry this morning, Callahan?" Lori asked with a grin as she topped off his coffee.

"After the night I had, you'd better believe it. In fact, I'll have one of those cinnamon rolls to eat now if I may."

Brick laughed aloud when mother and daughter's eyebrows flew up in an identical show of interest. "Ladies, please. It was completely innocent. On my part, at least."

He summarized the events of the early-morning revelry, describing his guests in general terms but leaving out the fact that he had a previous relationship with one of the Tornado Alleycats. So to speak.

Liliana Howe. Now there was a blast from the past. He talked to her brother occasionally — usually during the Series — but they seldom, if ever, talked about family. From what Brick knew of her and the Howe family, the last place he would have expected to find Liliana was camping with an all-female club. At his campsite.

The arrival of new customers, tourists headed for a morning of trout fishing, interrupted his tale, so Brick carried his cinnamon roll and coffee to one of the half-dozen small tables available for dining inside of Fresh. He took a bite of a roll and savored the flavor of cinnamon and yeast and sugar for a reverential moment. He was lifting a second forkful to his mouth when the front door opened and another large group of customers filed inside. At the back of the line, a mixed group of locals and tourists, he spied his friend Claire Lancaster.

Brick grinned at her. "Good morning, Mrs. Lancaster."

"Good morning to you, Mr. Callahan." The owner of the town's holiday shop, Forever Christmas, beamed a smile as brilliant as sunshine reflecting off the snowcap on Murphy Mountain.

Brick did a double take. He'd always thought that Claire was an exceptionally pretty woman — he'd had a thing for redheads all his life — but this morning the woman positively glowed. If she'd been a man rather than a woman, he would have made a joke about getting laid. She was still a newlywed, after all, having married this past Valentine's Day. But he sensed her mood involved something more than a lusty roll in the hay with the town's talented handyman.

He folded his arms, tilted his head, and studied her. "Okay, Claire. What gives? I'd ask if you won the lottery, but since you're already rich as Midas I don't think that's it. What has you beaming so bright I need shades?"

If anything, she only glowed brighter. "It shows?"

"Something shows."

She strolled over to his table, swiped a bite of cinnamon roll, then popped it into her mouth. "I'm pregnant."

"Claire!" Grinning like a wild man, Brick

stood and picked her up by the waist. He twirled her around, laughing, then kissed her hard on the mouth.

She giggled like a schoolgirl as he set her down and dipped his head, touching his forehead to hers. "I'm so happy for you and Jax and Nicholas. That's a great family you're growing there, sugarplum."

"I know. I'm so blessed. Nicholas is beyond excited."

He kissed her once again, then observed, "Another Maternity Springs baby. I think the city council really should post a warning on the city limits sign."

"You're not the first person to say that." Claire glanced over her shoulder toward the line that had shrunk to only two people during her interaction with Brick. "Ooh. Let me go, Callahan, so I can get in line. I'm starved and there's another group of people about to come inside."

Brick followed the path of her gaze and through Fresh's plate-glass window, his stare collided with another's. Lovely Liliana. Judging by the sour look on her face, she woke up on the wrong side of her trailer this morning.

"Some things never change," Lili said to Patsy as she saw Mark in a lip-lock with a redhead.

"Why do you say that, dear?"

"Our summer landlord." Lili nodded toward the window and the couple inside. "When he was a teenager, he couldn't keep his hands off of a redhead."

Patsy reached for Fresh Bakery's front door. "Hmm . . . maybe before we head back to camp I'll stop by the drugstore and buy some hair dye to touch up my roots."

Lili couldn't help but laugh as she followed her friend inside the bakery. She was tempted to throw her arms around Patsy and give *her* a kiss. She had a way of making everything seem better.

Lili had been cranky as a bear when the alarm went off this morning, but she'd dragged herself out of bed, thrown on her running clothes and sneakers, and exited the trailer to meet Patsy at the spot they'd designated the previous day. She'd been both surprised and amused when Patsy said she wanted to make a pit stop at the bakery in town before taking their walk.

"I like to walk off my meals rather than exercise," she'd said. "So sue me."

Hitting a bakery for breakfast was just the sort of decadent thing Lili would never have done in the past, so she was particularly game for the idea. Leave it to her rotten luck to begin her day with "sugar" that had nothing to do with calories.

Lili knew better than to hope that they could get in and out of Fresh without interacting with redhead-ready Romeo, so she braced herself as he turned to them and said, "Well . . . this is a surprise. I expected you ladies to sleep until noon."

"Not us." Patsy waved a dismissive hand. "Life is too short to spend it in bed. Unless you have somebody with you, of course. And you're doing something much more fun than sleeping. You're up early yourself, CDD. I hope that means you share the same philosophy."

The redhead looked at Mark. "CDD, Brick?"

"It's nothing," he was quick to say.

"Now, Brick." Patsy slipped her arm through his and announced, "We've dubbed him 'Camp Director Dreamboat.' "

The redhead laughed, as did the two women behind the bakery counter. Lili quickly lifted her hands in surrender. "Not me. I have nothing to do with this."

"Camp Director Dreamboat," repeated the redhead. "It fits you, Brick."

"It does," the younger woman behind the counter added. "Although loyalty makes me say that it fits my husband better. Chase *is* an actual camp director, after all."

"And he is a dreamboat, too," the redhead added. "But you're pretty dreamy, yourself, Brick."

"That's enough. Let me introduce you to two of Stardance Ranch's guests, Patsy Schaffer and Liliana Howe." He gave a brief explanation of each local woman's occupation, then added, "Patsy is one of the campers here for the whole season, so I imagine you'll see her from time to time. Liliana, how long are you staying with us?"

She hesitated, unwilling to commit herself to anything considering that the circumstances had changed the moment she recognized Mark Christopher. Derek hadn't called her yet, but that didn't mean anything other than Mark hadn't called her brother first thing this morning. Finally, she said, "My plans are flexible."

Patsy reached over and patted Lili's arm. "She's going to stay the summer. She just hasn't realized I've talked her into it yet."

Lili gave a noncommittal smile and a shrug. Mark informed the local women, "Lili and I went to high school together."

"Oh?" Lori asked, her eyes lighting with interest. "Now that's interesting news. You can give us the whole scoop about the pre-Callahan days. What was his name again?"

"Christopher. Mark Christopher." Lili glanced from Lori to Mark, then back to Lori again and asked, "I'm curious how he came to be known as Brick."

The three Eternity Springs women shared a look and a laugh. Lori said, "If you're around town much this summer, you will likely meet one of the Callahan brothers. Ask them how he came about the nickname. Or if you really want to be entertained, wait until his grandfather comes to Colorado for the Fourth of July holiday and get him to tell the story."

"Hey, can't I get a little respect around here?" Brick glanced at Lili. "Since my dad is named Mark, I tried going by 'Chris' for a while. When one of my uncle Luke's kids said my name, it sounded more like 'Brick' than 'Chris.'"

"That's not what his grandfather will tell you," Sarah Murphy said with a wink. "All the Callahan men have nicknames. Brick's dad, Mark, is Devil. His uncle Luke is Sin. And since the older generation in his family thinks Brick's stubborn and hardheaded . . ."

"A head as hard as a brick?" Patsy asked, amusement in her tone.

Brick rolled his eyes and Sarah nodded.

Lili didn't try to smother her grin. "I

suspect my brother, the Christopher family, and most everyone else in Norman would agree. Mark, remember that time you got stopped for speeding and —"

Mark interrupted. "It's too early in the morning for dirty laundry, Liliana. Could I bribe you with a cinnamon roll to keep your mouth shut? It's a good deal, I promise. Sarah's cinnamon rolls are sinful. My treat — for both of you ladies."

Lili wanted to crow. He didn't know it, but he'd just presented her with the perfect bartering opportunity. "As much as I'd love to try one, I'm afraid I'd better not indulge myself."

"I'm going to indulge," Patsy said. "However, I'll buy my own. Those rolls are why I'm here, in fact. I've read the reviews on your Web site, Sarah, and I knew I'd have to try them early in my visit. This morning seemed like the perfect time. I thought I'd take a couple back to camp with me, too." She showed the women a sheepish smile and added, "I'm afraid our group got a little rowdy last night. I want to give a little peace offering to the honeymooners."

"Great minds think alike," Mark said with a laugh. "I had the same idea."

"Let me do it, please. We were the trouble-makers. And I truly do want to beg your pardon for disturbing the peace last night. It will not happen again. I'm afraid we got caught up in the first-night giddy, and once Lili made her announcement we all just went a little crazy with excitement."

"What announcement?" Mark asked.

Lili knew she'd better put a stop to this right now. She took a step forward, placing herself between Mark and Patsy. Frowning at her friend, she said, "Patsy, may I remind you, what happens in the trailerhood . . . ? Maybe you should place your order so we can get back and finish our walk before we meet the girls to go shopping."

"Yes." Patsy patted her arm. "Of course. What was I thinking?"

"What announcement?" Mark repeated.

Lili ignored him and smiled at the red-head. "So, Mrs. Lancaster, you own a Christmas store? It's open year-round?"

"Call me Claire, please. And yes, Forever Christmas is open daily, with the exception of the usual holidays. If you're shopping in town, I hope you'll stop by. We're on Cottonwood and Third."

"Thanks. I'll do that."

"Liliana," Mark began.

"You know what I just thought of?" she told him. "Do you remember that time you and my brother prank called —"

"Liliana!"

Lori Timberlake laughed out loud. "Oh, this is gonna be a fun summer."

Mark gave an exaggerated sigh, then addressed Sarah. "Is my order ready?"

"It is. Are you paying or shall I put it on your account?"

"My account."

"You have an account at the bakery?" Lili asked, thinking it unusual.

Sarah explained, "He's in here all the time without his wallet."

Mark shrugged. "It's the halfway point on my run. A man has to refuel."

"With muffins?" Patsy laughed. "Now, that's my kind of exercise."

Mark took the white bakery bags Sarah Murphy handed over, thanked her, then exchanged a few softly spoken private words with Claire Lancaster before saying a general good-bye and exiting the bakery. As Lili followed Mark, she heard Lori say, "So, do we get to know what that hug and kiss was all about, Miss Christmas?"

Lili did a bit of dodge-and-dance with a group of four headed into the bakery as she exited, so Mark had rounded the back end of a white pickup truck and was approaching the driver's side door, "Mark? May I have a word with you?"

He halted and glanced over his shoulder, an easy smile gracing his lips. "You might as well go ahead and call me Brick, Lili-fair. My dad is in town enough that if you say 'Mark Callahan' everyone will be thinking of him."

Lili-fair? Despite herself, Lili's stomach did a warm little flip. *What happened to "Freckle-Sticks"?*

"So, what is it you want to ask me?"

Now that the moment was upon her, she didn't quite know what to say. Despite his talk of dirty laundry, she knew she, on the one hand, couldn't embarrass him with tales of his past. He, on the other hand, could destroy her. Fifteen years hadn't dulled her mortification regarding the bus incident. Not that she thought he'd actually bring it up, but the fact that he could took the teeth out of that bartering idea she'd had.

She blew out a quick breath and decided to lay it on the line. "I have a favor to ask you."

"Sure. What can I do? Is there a problem with your campsite?"

"No. It's fine. Actually, what I've seen of Stardance Ranch so far is very nice. I'm looking forward to my time here."

He waited. She tried to search beyond the twelve-year-old living inside her to find the confident twenty-nine-year-old she was before her parents ripped the rug from beneath her.

"Liliana?"

"Don't call Derek," she begged.

He leveled a steady look upon her that silently demanded further explanation.

"Please. Don't tell him I'm here. The family knows I'm safe, but they don't know where I am. I'd like to keep it that way. I'm almost thirty years old. They don't need to know where I am every minute of every day."

Mark folded his arms and leaned against his truck. "Having a little family conflict in Leave-It-to-Beaver-Ville?"

Lili blinked in surprise at the mention of the old TV show, unable to recall the last time it had come up in conversation. She was a fan of old sitcoms. She watched *Leave It to Beaver* reruns embarrassingly often. In fact, whenever current events took a grim turn Lili found she gravitated toward 1950s-era television for her entertainment escape. Beaver Cleaver had been the youngest member of a quintessential suburban family, the stories told heartwarming and refreshingly innocent.

Snapping her fingers, she said, "That's who you reminded me of, Mark. Eddie

Haskell."

"Sleazy Eddie? Seriously? Obsequious to June and Ward but a troublemaker when he hung with Wally? I must have misheard you, then. I thought you just asked me for a favor."

Liliana grimaced. "Oops. Sorry. I apologize."

Actually, she'd always thought Mark was more the heartthrob Robbie from *My Three Sons.*

"Yes," she quickly continued, "life has become a bit stressful in . . . what town did the Cleavers live in . . . May-something?"

"Don't remember. Let me Google it." Mark pulled out his phone and a moment later said, "The town is Mayfield. No mention of the state."

"In that case, let's say it's Mayfield, Oklahoma. I'll bet you didn't know that Wally and the Beaver had a sister, did you?"

Mark made a show of rubbing the back of his neck. "Quiet girl? Tall and skinny?"

Dryly, Lili said, "With freckles."

"Yeah. I remember her. Heard she grew up lookin' good. Real fine. So what . . . Ward and June aren't happy with her these days?"

"Not much." Despite the spurt of pleasure his compliment gave her, a sudden lump of emotion formed in Lili's throat and she swallowed hard. "She's disappointed them."

Mark snorted. "It took her this long? As I recall, Ward and June set a ridiculously high bar. So what happened?"

She shook her head. "It's not a story for a street corner."

"A campfire, then."

She hesitated. "Perhaps. In the meantime, can I count on you to respect my privacy?"

He frowned and considered the question. "Is Derek gonna call me looking for you?"

"No. Definitely not."

"Then I don't see a reason I'd need to volunteer anything. Do you?" he asked with a shrug.

"Not at all." She touched his arm, her smile sincere. "Thank you, Mark."

"You're welcome." He took her hand and squeezed it. "Although I figure it counts as a favor, so you owe me."

"Fair enough." She glanced down at their hands. He hadn't let it go. *He's holding my hand!* Lili dragged her thoughts back to the favor. "I won't tell anyone in Eternity Springs about the time you put shrimp into the hubcaps of the principal's car."

He laughed. "Oh, man. I haven't thought of that in years. Remember how it attracted all the stray cats in the neighborhood? Good times, good times. Derek and I were . . . what . . . thirteen? Fourteen? The principal deserved that, you know. I don't care that he graduated from the University of Texas. The principal of an Oklahoma public school can't go around town saying he's pulling for the Longhorns on Texas–OU weekend!"

"You have a valid point."

"Damn skippy." He casually brought her hand up to his mouth, kissed it, then released it and opened the door to his truck. "Don't fret, Freckle-Sticks. Your secret is safe with me. Now, I'd better get moving. I have a full day on my docket."

He was in the truck with the engine started before she managed to say another word. Behind her, the door to Fresh opened and Patsy stepped out into the brisk morning air.

Lili watched Mark Callahan's truck turn a corner and grumbled, "I like 'Lili-fair' a whole lot better."

CHAPTER SIX

Brick hung up his office phone and spoke into the empty room. "This I gotta see."

His friend and one of Eternity Springs' leading citizens, Celeste Blessing, had just requested a campsite for this evening. Never mind that she owned half the property in the county, including Angel's Rest Healing Center and Spa, a resort that included a handful of RV campsites of its own. Luckily, one of the Alleycats due to arrive today was running a day behind, so he had a spot for Celeste.

Apparently, she was joining the Tornado Alleycats for their book club discussion. Brick murmured, "They must have been lying about the title they're discussing."

Though he could be wrong. Probably was. Just because he couldn't picture Celeste reading mommy porn didn't mean it wasn't something she enjoyed. And who was he to judge, anyway? He wasn't an unenlightened, old-fashioned Neanderthal of a man who wanted his lady's biscuits in the oven and her buns in bed.

Well, most of the time, anyway.

Wonder what sort of books Liliana reads?

Don't go there, Callahan.

Maybe he'd find out if he made his evening inspection a little earlier than usual. He could stroll over to the activity center around seven o'clock. Just to check on things, of course. Do his job. And, see what sort of trailer Celeste was pulling, while he was at it.

He'd met a lot of interesting people in his life — especially since the day his dad walked into his world — and Celeste had a secure spot near the top of the list. The Carolina native still had a bit of mint julep in her voice, and she could put a person firmly in his place with a "Bless your heart" and a smile. She displayed a joie de vivre that was both contagious and inspiring. How many times had he heard one of his female friends in town say they wanted to be Celeste when they grew up?

In some ways, she reminded him of his grandfather. The word "character" described them both. Independent. Intelligent. Fierce in defense of those they loved. Branch would kill for his family. Celeste had created a family here in Eternity Springs — shoot, he figured she counted most of the town as family — and Brick knew she'd go to the wall for any one of them if necessary.

In temperament, they were polar opposites. Branch Callahan was a mean old cuss. Celeste Blessing, a kind and gentle angel.

Who may or may not read mommy porn.

And who'd given Brick a ready-made excuse to show up at tonight's book club meeting.

You don't need an excuse. They invited you, Camp Director Dreamboat.

Brick grimaced and groaned aloud. He shouldn't go anywhere near that building. He'd been thinking about Liliana Howe all day long, and not in any way he should be thinking about a best friend's little sister.

But in Brick's defense, growing up had treated Liliana damned fine. He was a guy, after all. Of course he'd notice. How could he help but notice? The image of the naked woman with the water of Hummingbird Lake sluicing off her creamy skin in the moonlight would be burned into his brain until the day he died.

Which would arrive sooner than anticipated if he ever acted on the fantasies that had drifted through his mind today. Derek

Howe had always been fiercely protective of his little sister. He'd whip Brick's ass just for thinking what he'd been thinking.

Wonder what she'd done to bring down the wrath of Ward and June upon her lovely shoulders?

That flash of vulnerability he'd seen travel across her face this morning had struck him hard. He'd always been a sucker for damsels in distress.

Need to be real careful here, boyo. Hadn't that been one of the reasons why Tiffany had kept her claws buried in him much longer than she should have?

The ringing of his business line interrupted his musings. He checked the caller ID, halfway expecting it to be a number he recognized. If Celeste was coming to camp, he wouldn't be surprised if one or more of her "besties" decided to join her. He picked up the phone. "Stardance Ranch, can I help you?"

"Hey, bro. How they hanging?"

It took a beat or two to place the voice. "Courtney?"

"None other."

Well, holy crap. Brick propped a hip on his desktop and shook his head in wonder. Two blasts from the past in the same week?

"It's nice to hear from you, Court." He

meant it, too. He hadn't talked to Courtney Gibson in five or six years. A grade behind him in school, she had lived with the Christopher family on and off during their elementary and middle school years. His parents would have adopted her, too, had her drug-addicted mother ever given up her parental rights. Instead, Courtney had bounced in and out of the household while her mom bounced in and out of jail. It was a story that happened all too often. "How are you doing?"

"I'm doing all right. I'm living in Denver these days."

"Oh yeah? I'm in Colorado, too. But I guess you know that since you called me."

"I talked to Cindy last week. She told me you had settled in a little town up in the mountains. A real out-of-the-way place."

"Eternity Springs."

"Yeah. That's it." Courtney paused almost imperceptibly before adding in a studiously casual tone, "I was thinking I might stop by for a visit next weekend if you're going to be around."

Brick's antennae went up. "What's wrong, Court?"

"Nothing. Really. Nothing."

Understanding the power of silence, Brick simply waited.

"Okay. Maybe I'm feeling a little low. I've been with a guy for a year now and we broke up recently. It's . . . hard."

Brick gave a sympathetic nod. "I get that. I'd love for you to visit, Courtney. Did Mom mention that Josh Tarkington is working with me up here?"

Since Josh, too, had bounced back and forth between his legal guardian and his foster home, Brick didn't instantly recall how often Joshua's and Courtney's paths had crossed, but he knew they'd spent some overlapping time at the Christopher home and that Courtney had known him.

"She did. She said he needed time away from storm country for a while."

"Yeah. He's feeling snakebit where tornadoes are concerned."

"I imagine so. Cindy told me that he's lost his home more than once. How many times has he been hit?"

"Four hits in three storms. He lost both his home and business in the last tornado, his car in one before that. The worst was the first storm, though. His house took a direct hit from an F4. He was inside with his girlfriend and her kid. They both died."

"That's terrible. I'd have moved away after that," Courtney observed. "What sort of work does he do for you?"

"A little of everything, but he mostly works in the office. He's taken the paperwork off my hands, for which I'm grateful. And of course, he fixes everything that breaks."

"He always liked to tinker with engines. I remember him being a detail person. Unlike you."

"Hate details. I'm definitely a big-picture guy."

"It'll be nice to see you both."

"Do you already have a place to stay? If not, you're welcome to a bed in the bunkhouse where some of my seasonal help stay. I'll warn you up front, it's nothing fancy. My fancy accommodations I reserve for paying customers."

"Cindy said you run a campground for high rollers, that you get a stupid amount of money for renting out tree houses and tents that have bathrooms."

"Stardance River Camp is a separate facility, but yeah, it's stupid expensive. But at the RV campground we have a section for tent camping, too. My guests can visit on the cheap or in total luxury. Now, let me tell you how to get here."

Brick gave his foster sister directions, and they spoke for a few more minutes before ending the call. He walked out of his office just in time to witness Celeste's arrival.

He laughed out loud.

"Oh, glory be, look at that," Patsy said. "I'm in love. Just head over heels in love. I *need* one of those!"

Lili looked up from the butterfly she was coloring in the adult coloring book Patsy had given to her in time to see a vintage Shasta trailer enter the campground. Though the vintage trailers were well represented among the Alleycats and other camping clubs, this was the first time she'd seen one being pulled by a vintage car — a fire-engine-red land yacht of an automobile. The wings of the car's taillights matched the Shasta's trademark wings. "What is that?"

Reverently, Patsy said, "A Caddie. A Coupe de Ville. Early sixties, if I don't miss my guess."

"Is this one of our girls arriving?" Lili asked, using the term Patsy used for all of her club members.

"No, that's Celeste."

"Ah." Lili set down her colored pencil. "Which explains the custom paint job on the Shasta. I've seen stripes and polka dots before, but this is the first trailer decorated in angel wings."

Celeste Blessing was the guest author for

tonight's book club meeting. She'd published a gift book titled *Guidelines for Aspiring Angels* that was filled with inspirational sayings, examples, and advice. Lili had been captivated by the content in the small book. The illustrations made it a work of art. "You said the illustrator is coming tonight, too?"

"Yes. She'll be here later. When Celeste called me earlier to ask about overnighting with the club, she told me that Sage Rafferty would join us but couldn't stay overnight. She has young children."

"I'm looking forward to meeting them both."

Lili would never consider herself an aspiring angel, but she'd found Celeste's commonsense advice to be both a comfort and an inspiration. Sayings like "Angels let slights roll off their feathers" and "Don't be afraid to test your wings" seemed to have been written just for her.

Celeste pulled her trailer into the slot next to Lili, and by the time she'd killed the engine and opened the driver's door an admiring crowd of Alleycats had gathered around.

"What a fabulous rig you have!"

"What year is she? The trailer. Well, actually, the trailer and the car."

"What's her name?"

"I can't wait to see what you've done inside. You will give us a tour, won't you?"

"Girls! Girls!" Patsy exclaimed. "For heaven's sake. Give our special guest some breathing room. My friends, this is Celeste Blessing. Celeste, meet the Tornado Alleycats."

The attractive woman perhaps a little older than Patsy smiled brilliantly as she exited her car. Laugh lines framed twinkling sky-blue eyes. Gold earrings shaped like angel wings dangled from her ears and peeked from beneath a stylish silver bob. She wore a bright red cotton blouse with wings embroidered on the pocket, jeans, and red canvas sneakers. She glowed, and just looking at her brought an answering smile to Lili's face.

Celeste waved a hand dismissively. "Don't worry. Y'all aren't crowding me one little bit. Of course I'll be happy to show off Angelique once I'm all set up. That's part of the fun of owning vintage, isn't it?"

"Most definitely," replied Sharon, who owned a 1965 Spartan.

Celeste continued, "I'm so excited to join you all tonight. This is my first official book signing ever!"

"We're thrilled to have you," Pasty replied. "Do you need any help setting up?"

"That would be so kind. I learned long ago not to turn down help when it comes to an extra pair of hands."

"I volunteer!" Lili said, waving hers. She stepped forward and extended her hand. "I'm Liliana Howe, Ms. Blessing."

"Oh, call me Celeste, dear." They shook hands, and then Celeste added to the group, "I mean all of you, too."

Patsy stepped up then and shooed the group away, reminding them not to forget to bring their books to the meeting in order to get them signed. "And of course, remember to bring your cash or credit cards. Celeste's book will make a fabulous gift."

As the crowd dispersed, Celeste turned to Lili. "It's a pleasure to meet you, Liliana. Don't you have the loveliest eyes? They remind me of the color seafoam on a 1961 Shasta trailer. I had such trouble choosing between that color and this lovely red for my Angelique. Both were just so beautiful. But the red matched my car and a girl does like to coordinate, doesn't she?"

"That she does," Lili replied, grinning. "What can I do to help?"

"Let's wrestle the outdoor rug out of Angelique first and then we can tackle the canopy."

"Absolutely not!" sounded a deep, familiar

voice from behind Lili. "I'm not letting you set up, Celeste."

Appalled, Lili whirled on Mark Callahan, her hands fisted on her hips. "And why not? She's an invited guest and we have room for her."

"Pax, Lili-fair. I'm not letting her do it because I'm doing it for her."

"Now, Brick," Celeste protested. "I'm perfectly capable —"

"I know you are, but both my moms would whip my butt and take away my gentleman card if they got wind that I let you set up on your own."

"You have a gentleman card?" Lili couldn't help but ask.

He narrowed his eyes at her. "Is that sarcasm I hear in your voice, Freckle-Sticks?"

"Oh my." Celeste turned an appalled expression toward Mark. "I know you have the Callahan fondness for assigning nick-names to people, but honestly, Brick. Did I seriously hear you say that? What in heaven's name are you thinking?"

He didn't look the least bit ashamed. "I called her that before I became a Callahan."

Celeste offered Lili a sympathetic smile, then arched a brow at Mark. "So you've been a fool for some time."

Lili snorted a laugh and Celeste winked at her. "You've known our Brick for quite a while, then?"

"I was in elementary school. He and my brother were friends."

"Her brother helped me build my first tree house and she had a crush on me."

"I did not!"

"Derek said you did."

"Oh, he was such a liar," she lied. Lili decided a change of subject was in order. "Don't you have a rug to haul?"

Celeste laughed and opened the door to the trailer she'd named Angelique. Soon they had all the comforts of home set out — and then some. Obviously, Celeste knew how to go camping with the girls.

Her color palette was red and white with complimentary gold accents. Her outdoor rug was a red-and-white checkerboard inside a band of gold, and ribbons printed with angel wings trimmed the edges of her tent canopy. She parked a red bicycle beside her door, hung window baskets with live red geraniums, and set out vintage red suitcases decorated with beads and Scrabble squares that read: "When you are lost, listen to your inner angel and she will help you find the right road."

When setup was finished, Celeste offered

Lili and Brick a cold drink. When she stepped inside of Angelique, Brick turned to Lili and said, "She's wrong, you know."

"Celeste?"

"Yes."

"About what? I can't picture her being wrong about much of anything."

"Your eyes. They are lovely. Seafoam works as the color, but not the comparison to a trailer. That's just wrong."

Lili went still. Did Mark Christopher just compliment her eyes? First a hand kiss and now an eye compliment? Was this bizarro world or what?

Fumbling for a response, she gestured toward Celeste's campsite. "Trailers can be cute."

"Your eyes aren't cute. They're beautiful, Liliana. Alluring. You have a siren's alluring seafoam eyes, the kind that can lure a man to death. Just like a mermaid. You have mermaid eyes. Mermaid . . . attributes."

Oh holy Moses.

"It's not difficult at all for me to think that last night . . . this morning . . . I spied a mermaid who'd just found her legs." He flashed a wicked grin and added, "You were certainly dressed for the part."

Lili felt her cheeks flush. She opened her mouth to speak but could find no words.

Before she could conjure a response, Celeste exited her trailer carrying a tray containing three cups of iced lemonade. In keeping with her theme, she served the drinks in red Solo cups.

Mark thanked Celeste for his drink and said something about needing to fill up the soft drink machine. Then with a, "See you later," he strode blithely away — as if he hadn't just turned her world upside down.

When Lili finally dragged her gaze away from him, she saw that Patsy had joined Celeste. The two women watched Lili with knowing looks in their eyes.

"He is quite the doll, isn't he?" Celeste asked.

Patsy nodded enthusiastically. "We've dubbed him Camp Director Dreamboat. So give us the dish about Brick, Celeste."

"Why don't we sit down?" She gestured toward the folding table and chairs Brick had set up before departing. "Patsy, may I offer you a cup of lemonade? Fresh squeezed."

"That would be lovely, thank you." When Celeste returned a few moments later with another red plastic cup, Patsy asked, "So, tell us, Celeste, is he seeing anyone?"

"Other than the redhead we caught him kissing in the bakery this morning?" Lili wanted to bite her tongue the minute she heard the bitter note in her voice.

"Hmm . . ." Celeste pursed her lips. "I don't know who that might have been."

Patsy said, "I think her name was Claire. She runs the Christmas store."

Celeste waved her hand, her expression brightening. "Oh, I know what that was about. Claire and Jax announced today that she's having a baby. She and Brick are good friends. I expect it was a congratulatory kiss."

"On the mouth?" Lili asked, unwilling to quite give it up.

"Yes, well, it's his way. The men in his family are quite friendly." Lili managed to stop herself from rolling her eyes as Celeste continued. "Brick dates often. He is very popular with the single ladies in the area."

Patsy sounded a little disappointed when she observed, "So he's a player. A heart-breaker."

Some things never change.

Celeste shook her head. "No. Not at all. From everything I've observed, Brick is quite careful in that respect. Word around town is that he never dates the same woman more than three times. If anything, he's everybody's friend."

"Ah . . . he's the heartbreak-ee," Patsy said.

Celeste pursed her lips and nodded. "I sense that the walls around his heart are tall and thick. He's won't admit to it, but I'm certain he's had a broken heart of his own in the past."

Lili could no longer remain silent. "He dated a girl through high school and college. I don't know what caused their breakup, but she married someone else."

"The Homecoming Queen."

"You know about Tiffany?"

"I didn't know her name, but I know there was a long-time girlfriend his family didn't care for."

"Oh, really?" Lili perked up at that. She had never met anyone who didn't think Tiffany was just sweet as pink cotton candy.

"Brick's stepmother, Annabelle, has nothing nice to say about her." Celeste sipped her lemonade. "Have you met the Callahans, Lili?"

"No. I think my brother has met his father, but I never did. I do know the Christophers. Paul and Cindy are very nice people."

"Yes, they are. They've been guests at Angel's Rest a number of times, although now when they visit Brick they stay at Mark

116

and Annabelle's house at the North Forty. The two families have become great friends. I'm sure they'll be up for our Fourth of July extravaganza."

"That's nice for everyone," Patsy observed. "Blended families of any type can be a challenge. For adoptive parents and a birth family to get along . . . Brick is lucky."

"In many ways, he is," Celeste observed. "He has a lot of love in his life, but not that piece that makes a person's life complete. He needs that."

"Isn't that handy." Patsy clapped her hands. "So does Lili."

"Stop." Lili tried to ignore how her heart went thud-a-thump at the thought. "Just stop right there, Patsy."

"Did he lie when he said you had a crush on him?"

"I was in middle school!"

"Young love," Celeste observed, her blue eyes twinkling over the top of her cup. "It's something to be celebrated."

"Arrgh! I had crushes on the Backstreet Boys and Orlando Bloom, too!"

"Legolas was a favorite of mine." Patsy said.

"I'm more an Aragorn girl," Celeste replied. "Vigo Mortensen. Yummy."

Patsy patted her hand over her heart. "Oh

my, yes. When you first see him in the tavern in *Lord of the Rings* . . . I swear I got goose bumps. Legolas is pretty — and the way he used that bow was sexy as sin — but Aragorn is so manly."

Celeste folded her arms and thumped her index finger against her lips. "Our Brick is a nice combination of Legolas pretty and Aragorn manly, don't you think?"

"Perhaps." Patsy pursed her lips and considered. "I haven't seen him without his shirt, yet, so . . ."

"Enough!" Lili closed her eyes. "You ladies sound like teenagers."

"And I hope that never changes," Celeste observed.

"Amen, sister."

The two women clicked Solo cups, shared a smile, and caused Lili to laugh out loud. "All right, then. Something came up last night, and I'm compelled to ask. Have either of you ladies read *Fifty Shades of Grey*?"

Chapter Seven

Brick had already decided to accept the Tornado Alleycats' invitation to the book club, but when Celeste asked him to take a few photos for her social media efforts during her presentation he was happy to have something to do there. He owned a copy of Celeste's book, of course. Most everybody in Eternity Springs did. He'd given copies to Annabelle and his mother and all of his aunts for Mother's Day, and he had flipped through it to check out Sage Rafferty's illustrations, but he couldn't say he'd done more than scan it.

A man could take only so much wisdom from a woman before spiders began to crawl up his neck. Even a woman as fabulous as Celeste.

The women in his world had loved *Guidelines for Aspiring Angels.* Based on the buzz in the room, the women here tonight did, too.

He took a dozen or so photographs when Patsy introduced Celeste. When the applause died down, Celeste handed out giveaway bookmarks for the audience to pass back. She didn't use a microphone, but when she began to speak her voice carried easily to the back of the room where Brick stood.

"I'm here tonight to talk to you about angels, and the first thing I'll say is that angels mean different things to each of us depending on our personal spirituality or religious beliefs. Whether you're a believer or not, I suspect you probably have a mental image of what guardian angels look like. Take the example of the painting by Plockhorst that depicts a guardian angel hovering protectively over two little children approaching an abyss. Do most of you know that work?"

In the gathering of about forty, 90 percent of them nodded.

"Good. Now for tonight's purpose, I want you to wipe that image right out of your mind. Because you see, the advice in my book doesn't pertain to guardian angels. I want to talk to you tonight about guiding angels."

"What's a guiding angel?" an Alleycat observed. "I've never heard the term."

"Not a what. A *who*. Guiding angels are those people in your life with good hearts who teach life lessons. They are the people who prove to you that it's okay to trust — yourself and one another. They are those who show us how to determine our own destinies. They are the persons — male or female — who prod you into action, patiently allow you to make mistakes, and help you pick yourself up again when you fall or fail."

A thirtysomething woman near the back of the activity hall raised her hand. "You're talking about everyday people."

In an unusual moment of self-reflection, Brick thought it sounded like Celeste was talking about his mothers — his birth mother, his adoptive mother, and Annabelle, his stepmother.

Celeste beamed a smile at the Alleycat. "Everyday people who are doing an angel's work. They are women — and men — who have a single agenda when it comes to their relationships. Anyone know what that agenda is?"

Someone called, "It's in your book. Page forty-three."

Celeste laughed and folded her hands atop the lectern. "So it is. And it's what aspiring angels need to keep in mind as they work toward earning their wings. At the root of every angel's agenda is love."

The crowd broke into applause.

Brick reflected on Celeste's words later after he finished taking pictures and made his evening walk-through of Stardance Ranch. He had an 82 percent occupancy rate tonight — not bad for the middle of the week. He was fully booked on weekends right up until the Fourth of July.

He was one lucky son of a gun. He wouldn't be where he was now if he hadn't had a full slate of guiding, guarding, and aspiring angels in his life from the git-go.

"Penny for your thoughts," came a voice from out of the shadows.

He looked over his shoulder and smiled. "Lili-fair. Is the book club over?"

"No. The second title of the night is a thriller I haven't read. It sounds like something I might like, though, so I left before spoilers. Besides, I do have a book I started this afternoon and I'm anxious to get back to."

"Oh yeah? What are you reading?"

"The first of the Lord of the Rings trilogy."

"Interesting choice."

"I was inspired." The wry note in her voice intrigued him, but before he could follow up with a question she continued, "So, what did you think of Celeste's talk?"

"I guess 'inspired' is the word of the night. She does have a way of filtering through all the white noise to get to what really matters, doesn't she?"

"She does. When she talked about cutting the strings that bind our wings I thought she was talking directly to me."

"You feeling earthbound, Lili-fair?"

Following a long pause, she said, "It's been a tough month."

"Since you're on radio silence with June and Ward, I figured as much."

"Don't forget Wally. I'm not talking to him, either."

"What did he do? Give you a bad stock tip? Run a boyfriend out of town? Kick your dog?"

"I don't have a dog," she replied with a definite whine in her voice. She shoved her hands into the back pant pockets of her jeans and lifted her face toward the sky. "I'm rethinking my positions."

He waited a beat. "Horizontal or vertical?"

"Well now, that's an interesting way to put it." As she spoke, the moon moved from behind a cloud and a silvery light illuminated her face. Once again, she reminded

Brick of a siren in the night. "Did you stay for the question and answer session?"

"No. I left right after Sage talked about the illustrations."

"Someone asked Celeste about expectations. She spoke to how important expectations are to achieving your dreams, but also acknowledged the burden they present."

"Your parents always had sky-high expectations of you and your brother. It wasn't a bad thing, though. Look at how much you've achieved."

Brick didn't miss the sour look that crossed her face. "You gonna tell me what's eating at you, Liliana?"

"No, I don't think I will. Oklahoma and the things that happened there are in my rearview mirror. I'm not looking backward, not more than a little glance now and again, anyway. I came to Colorado to sharpen my scissors and slice those strings and jettison the ballast of my family's . . . of my own . . . expectations. I needed a few days to adjust to my new reality, but enough is enough. It's time for me to quick stalling and act."

What's she gonna do, go skinny-dipping in a mountain lake?

Brick felt a little frisson of unease. She sounded just a bit too brittle for his peace of mind. "What's wrong with Oklahoma?

What's wrong with our hometown? People are friendly. They're good, salt-of-the-earth sorts. Except for the tornadoes that blow through way too often, it's a great place to live."

"You don't live there. You went away to college and never came back."

"I visit." Once. He'd gone home once, when Tiffany married her banker. "I just never moved back. But I had a whole new family to get to know." And an ex-lover to forget. Was that what this was about? "Did you have a bad breakup, Liliana?"

"Depends what sort of breakup you're talking about." Her soft laughter held a bitter note. "I haven't been in a relationship for a while. All work and no play and all of that."

She removed her hands from her pockets and squared her shoulders. "I'm done with that. I'm done letting negativity and resentment rule my days. I'm through with the ugliness of office politics. I'm through being a hamster running on a wheel in pursuit of . . . whatever hamsters pursue. Nothing that truly matters, that's for sure."

"You sound bitter."

"I *am* bitter. For too long I've spent all my energy positioning myself to take advantage of opportunities that I was told I

125

wanted. I totally ignored my own instincts, my own wishes and desires. It took a bomb going off to get my attention."

A bomb? "What kind of bomb?"

She plowed right ahead as if he hadn't spoken. "I've learned my lesson and heard the message. Life is a gift too precious to waste. Time is a resource too valuable to squander. Celeste said that sometimes all an aspiring angel really needs to fly is to take a running start. Well, tonight I'm putting on my running shoes."

She turned to him then and, despite the fact that her face was cast in shadows, he recognized the intensity of her focus.

"I don't have to be anchored to or by my past. You're the perfect example for me. You're not Mark Christopher anymore. You're Brick Callahan. If you can change your name, I can darn sure learn to fly."

Then she did something he never would have expected from Liliana Howe. She grabbed hold of his shirt just below the neckline and pulled his face down to hers. Just before her lips took his in a sizzling kiss, she demanded, "Show me how."

Lili drifted off to sleep that night right with the world. She'd all but knocked Mark Christopher's feet — no, Brick Callahan's

126

feet — right out from under him. She'd kissed him senseless, then sashayed back to her fifth wheel as if she were Queen of the Campground.

Only maybe she didn't sashay. Maybe the kiss had snapped enough of those strings binding her wings that she had flown to her trailer on a breeze of self-confidence. Stranger things had happened. Maybe not to her. Not before now, anyway.

But hey, she was a changed woman. She was a Tornado Alleycat. She'd heard Celeste Blessing's advice and acted upon it in a big fat check-it-off-your-bucket-list manner.

Not that she had a bucket list. Yet. She needed to take care of that. First thing tomorrow. Tonight she'd drift off thinking about something she'd dreamed about for years. His lips. The taste of him. And hadn't his arms just instinctively wrapped around her and held her tight against him? All that muscle. The physical work he did had made him hard as a . . . Lili giggled softly . . . Brick.

Take that, Tiffany.

It was Lili's last conscious thought before drifting off to sleep.

Unfortunately, she awoke the following morning to a phone call from her mother, which not only changed the atmosphere but also managed to retie a string or two around Lili's feet. Derek had just received yet another Top-Doc award. Her mother had been asked by Mrs. Richie why Liliana had left the firm.

One step forward and two kicks in the butt back.

In the space of one short conversation, the self-confidence in Lili's manner disappeared and her mood turned heavy, still, and oppressive. The quiet before the storm. What she'd known all her life as tornado weather.

It made her just a little bit crazy.

Three minutes after ending the phone call with her mother, she went online and booked the skydiving trip that three of the more adventuresome Alleycats had scheduled for that afternoon.

Maybe it hadn't been at the top of her yet-to-be written bucket list, but if she intended to fully embrace her independence she needed to think outside the box. Jumping in tandem with a professional was safe enough. Lili knew that.

But when it came time for Lili to jump out of a perfectly good airplane, she chickened out.

On the way back to Stardance Ranch, she told herself that if she had wanted to skydive bad enough, she'd have gone through with it. The problem in this case wasn't cowardice, but lack of desire. She needed to figure out what she really wanted from this summer of discovery. She needed to define her own goals, dreams, and desires.

That's why she spent that evening working on her bucket lists. Plural. She created one for her summer in Colorado and one for her life. The two lists had a limited amount of overlap, and it was with a certain amount of glee that she marked off an item on her Colorado list: Kiss Brick Callahan.

After serious debate, she decided that she had not met the qualifications to mark off a somewhat similar item on her life list: Kiss Mark Christopher.

Might as well space these things out.

Over the next week, she marked six items off her Colorado list and two off her life list. She went zip lining and rock climbing and fly-fishing. She lounged in a hammock on a sunny afternoon and binge read a classic historical romance author.

She turned off her phone and disconnected from the Internet for twenty-four hours straight. Cutting strings meant cutting all sorts of strings.

She enjoyed that so much that she wanted to do it for a second twenty-four hours.

Guilt stopped her. What if there was a family emergency of some sort? A real emergency? She'd never forgive herself if her family truly needed to contact her and couldn't.

She solved the problem by having all of her calls forwarded to an answering service to whom she gave strict, emergency-only instructions and the number of the burner phone she purchased in town. Then she went offline and out of touch again and enjoyed the experience immensely.

Liliana didn't see much of Brick that week. The fact that most of the other Alleycats mentioned seeing him from time to time caused her to surmise that he was avoiding her. When she first realized it, she experienced a twinge of hurt, but after a bit of consideration she decided to be amused. And encouraged.

She'd surprised him. She'd acted out of character and shocked his socks off. Good for her, the reinvented Liliana Howe. When Saturday arrived, she decided that the time had come to work on another item on her list.

Romance.

So at the regular Alleycat morning gathering at the campground's activity center where members met and arranged plans for the day, she spoke up. "I intend to go out on the town in Eternity Springs tonight. Would anyone care to join me?"

"Sure," Sharon Cross said. "You know me; I'm always up for partying."

That much was true. Sharon was definitely the party girl in the club. After three of her besties expressed a desire to join in the fun, Sharon added, "Where are you thinking of going?"

"I'm open to suggestions. Murphy's Pub in town has a great patio. I saw a sign saying they have live music on the weekends."

Sharon nodded. "That would work. There is also a place called the Bear Cave. I'm told it's a dive, frequented by locals mostly, but a new owner is trying to clean it up and the jukebox has a great playlist. A place like that can be a lot of fun as long as you go in a group. Depends on what you're in the mood for."

"I want to dance," Lili declared. She hadn't gone out dancing since college. The last time she'd danced at all was last fall at a friend's wedding.

"There's a nice dance floor at Murphy's, but I'm told it stays packed this time of year," Patsy observed. "It's a tourist-friendly spot. You might have better luck at a honky-tonk."

Honky-tonk. The term gave Lili a little shiver of excitement. Honky-tonks were common in Oklahoma. Common and a little trashy and not anything she'd ever been brave enough to try before. In the spirit of reinventing herself, Lili stood tall. "I vote for the Bear Cave."

The other Alleycats shared a look and a shrug. "Bear Cave it is," Sharon said. "Want to do dinner in town first? We could grab a burger at Murphy's, listen to the music a bit, then head out honky-tonkin' after that."

"Sounds perfect."

"In that case, ladies, unpack your party shoes. It's gonna be a hot time in the cold mountains tonight."

Brick sauntered into Murphy's on Saturday night with a smile on his face and his mouth watering for one of their half-pound burgers with fixings and fries. He was hungry because he'd managed to miss lunch. He was smiling because he was going to dinner with his siblings.

Mom and Pop had always taught the children who lived with them — the two they'd officially adopted and the dozen or so foster kids who'd been in and out of the house — to consider themselves to be brothers and sisters. They'd been a family and that had meant a lot to the children who called the Christopher house home.

It still meant something to Brick today. His dad and Annabelle had given him brothers and sisters, and he loved the little guys dearly. But he was twenty years older than Tanner and Emma and Will. Courtney and Joshua and the others who'd shared the Christopher home were Brick's age. To one extent or another, they'd shared his childhood. Those were strong ties not easily broken.

When he'd answered Courtney's knock on his office door this afternoon, he'd experienced a wave of remembrance and familiarity that had warmed his heart.

Brick regretted that in the wake of the personal earthquake that had occurred when Mark Callahan walked into his life he'd failed to tend to his Christopher family ties as much as he should have for a while. He didn't beat himself up over it. The Christophers had been totally supportive of him. His actions and reactions had been understandable for someone who had grown up with absolutely no idea of his genetic history at the time when he was making that giant leap to adulthood.

With an avalanche of new family upon his world, he'd spent his free time becoming a

Callahan, and yet a part of him always would remain a Christopher. He arrived at Murphy's Pub tonight an Oklahoma boy with the siblings he'd walked to school with and whose beds he'd short-sheeted on more than one occasion.

"This is a happening place," Courtney said. For the first time since her arrival, the accompanying smile actually reached her eyes.

Courtney Gibson wore her hair in a short, spiky style, dyed red with purple tips. Big gold hoops hung from her ears. Her brown eyes looked tired, and the shadows beneath them were darker than Brick cared to see. She was thin. Too thin. She'd lost probably thirty pounds since he'd seen her last. Twenty of those were too much. She definitely needed one of Murphy's cheeseburgers tonight.

Brick hoped he was seeing the aftereffects of the breakup, not an illness. "You feeling all right, Cort?"

"I'm fine. Just tired from the drive." Her gaze swept around the pub and then her smile widened. "There's Joshua! Whoa, his hair is longer than mine. What happened to Mr. Preppy?"

"He's embraced his inner mountain man."

Courtney called, "Josh!"

134

Josh Tarkington sat at the bar with a glass of water in front of him. At the sound of his name, he straightened. The ends of his black hair brushed shoulders almost as wide as Brick's as he turned around. His mouth spread in a huge smile and his gray eyes lit with pleasure. "Courtney! I couldn't believe it when Brick told me you were coming for a visit."

"Brick?"

Josh smirked. "His new name. Fits him, doesn't it?"

"Yeah. It seriously does."

"Hey," Brick protested. "No ganging up on Big Brother allowed."

The two younger siblings locked gazes and snorted. Then Josh opened his arms wide. "Hello, stranger. If you're not a sight for sore eyes. C'mere and give me a hug."

Courtney went into Josh's arms and Brick heard her softly laugh, but when she pulled away from her brother's embrace Brick saw tears in her eyes.

Well, hell.

Noting the tears, Josh frowned. "What's this, Courtney?"

"Nothing. Never mind. I'm just . . . I've missed you guys."

"Missed you, too, honey. Let's go sit down and you can tell us what you've been up to.

I reserved a table for us out on the patio."

"I'll put in our order. Burgers and beer all around?"

"Iced tea for me," Josh said.

The owner of Murphy's Pub, Shannon Garrett, was working tonight, and Brick visited with her while she saw to their drink order. "Lookin' good, tonight, Mrs. Garrett."

"Thank you, Mr. Callahan."

"How's our birthday girl doing?"

Shannon lit up like the sun. "Brianna is fabulous. You have to see the photos Chase gave us. Best first birthday portraits ever."

"The man is talented with a camera — and kids. Word around town is that this summer's session at the Rocking L is going well."

"Lori says Chase is a happy man." She set the second mug of beer and the tea on a tray.

"It's nice to see," Brick observed.

Shannon set a numbered order marker beside the drinks, and he carried the tray out to the patio. Josh was telling Courtney a story about his first encounter with a moose not long after his arrival at Stardance Ranch. Brick passed out the drinks and they spent the time until their meal arrived discussing their past and avoiding all mention of current situations. Brick figured he'd get a good meal in Courtney first, then they could find somewhere more quiet and talk.

He sipped his beer and listened with a faint smile on his lips as his brother and sister traded quips over the memory of a water gun battle that had lasted an entire summer.

It was nice to see a smile on his brother's face, too. While Josh and Brick had never been particularly close, Brick cared about him. Josh'd had a helluva time the last few years, a run of bad luck like Brick had seldom seen. He'd been glad to be able to help Josh.

They were a lot alike, actually. Proud, competitive, only a few months apart in age. Stubborn. Josh hadn't accepted Brick's help after the first tornado. Or the second. He wouldn't have this last time, either, but Brick had caught him at a low point with his offer.

It had worked out well for Brick, too. Josh was an organizational wonder and a mechanical whiz. When he'd come to work for Brick shortly after the beginning of the year, he'd taken over the detail work Brick despised and freed him to focus on building and bringing his dream to life.

He tuned into the conversation. Courtney

was saying, ". . . job in a bookkeeping service. Decent work. Not exciting or anything, but it was steady and paid well. Then I had a blowout and wrecked my car. Hurt my back. Missed a lot of work and ended up losing my job."

"What a lousy break," Joshua said. "How long ago was the accident?"

"About a year ago."

"Are you better?" Brick asked. "All healed up?"

"For the most part, yeah. My back is better, anyway. I'm working again. My heart . . ." She shrugged. "Some guys don't do well with illness."

"Prick," Josh declared.

"Tell us his name and we'll go beat him up for you."

"My heroes." Courtney's smile went a little wistful and she said, "No. As much as the idea appeals, I know I'm better off putting that all behind me. It's just so . . ." Her voice caught. A sheen of tears filled her eyes.

Seated beside her, Brick put his arm around her and pulled her close for a hug. Courtney dipped her head onto his shoulder at the same time Murphy's front door opened and a half-dozen happy, chatting women swept onto the patio.

Liliana wore a fitted yellow polka-dot

sundress and strappy heels better suited for the sidewalks of Beverly Hills than those of Eternity Springs. *Wow.* Brick thought she looked like a million bucks.

She met his gaze, noted the position of his arm and Courtney's head, and turned away. Across from him, Josh slowly lowered his drink to the table. "Looks like the Alleycats have arrived."

"Who are they?" Courtney asked.

"Camping club. Staying at Stardance for the summer. Excuse me. I think I'll go be hospitable and say hi."

Josh was up on his feet and sauntering toward Lili before Brick managed to end his hug with Courtney. Something ugly stirred in his gut as he watched his brother switch to charmer mode and chat up the campers. Josh was a friendly enough guy as a rule, but no way would he have bolted to say hello to campers if all six of the women were fifty and above.

He was hitting on Liliana.

And Brick didn't like it one little bit.

CHAPTER EIGHT

Lili didn't know why she was surprised to find Brick Callahan in a bar with his arm around a redhead. So what else was new?

She told herself she didn't care. She'd gotten her Colorado bucket-list kiss. Now it was on to other items. Like romance.

So when the sexy guy who'd checked her into Stardance Ranch rose and sauntered over toward her table, she offered up a bright, determinedly confident smile when he tipped the straw cowboy hat he wore and said, "Hello, ladies. Looks like you decided to skip the big bingo game at the activity center tonight."

Lili nodded, idly wondering why he looked familiar. "We did. The five of us decided we needed a night out on the town."

Sharon Cross stepped forward and offered her hand. "I've seen you at the camp, but we haven't met. My name is Sharon."

"I'm Josh. Nice to meet you, Sharon. Are

you enjoying your visit to Colorado?"

"I'm loving it so far. Josh, have you met the rest of my friends here?"

"Ms. Howe and I met when she checked in. Likewise for Ms. Hernandez. But these two ladies . . ."

Sharon introduced Mary-Ellen Carkin and Corrine Swain, then invited Josh to join them.

"I'd love to, but I'm having dinner with family. Maybe afterward?"

"I'm afraid we're not staying," Mary-Ellen informed him. "We're going to a place called the Bear Cave."

His eyebrows lifted. "That's an interesting choice."

"Lili wants to dance," Sharon added. "I do hope the Bear Cave attracts some single men who like to dance."

Lili wanted to kick Sharon under the table for being so obvious. At the same time, her gaze checked out his left hand. Ringless.

Lili's wasn't the only mind that went in that direction, because Patsy tossed a look toward the table where Brick and the red-head sat. "So, family, you say? Your wife?"

Lili swallowed a groan. Patsy made Sharon look like an amateur.

"Our foster sister. She's visiting Stardance Ranch for a few days."

Then it clicked for Lili. "I know you. You lived with the Christophers."

Josh's brow furrowed and he studied her intently. "I'm sorry . . . I'm drawing a blank."

"Mark — or I guess I should say Brick — and my brother Derek are friends. They played baseball together in high school. They built the tree house in the Christophers' backyard."

"Oh yeah. I remember him. Forgot his name, but the tree house is legendary. Brick is still building them. So your brother is Derek. Derek Howe. He's a big-deal doctor, isn't he? A surgeon?"

"Yes."

"And you're from Norman. Funny, Brick hasn't mentioned a local connection." Josh's smile turned flirtatious. "Guess he wanted to keep you all to himself."

Liliana laughed at the absurdity of it. "Not hardly."

Josh noted the waiter approaching his table with what appeared to be his order. "Our dinner is here. I'll try to drop by the Bear Cave later if I can manage it."

"That would be just lovely," Sharon said. "Wouldn't it, Lili?"

Embarrassed, Lili gave up trying to pretend that her friends weren't being obvious.

142

She rolled her eyes and sighed. "Sorry."

He grinned and winked at her as he tipped his hat once again before returning to his table. Lili narrowed her eyes and frowned at her friends. "Seriously? Could you be a little more obvious?"

Sharon clapped a hand over her heart in a gesture of innocence. "What?"

Mary-Ellen snickered. "He *is* cute. Not as cute as CDD, maybe, but if sometime this summer I decided to go the cougar route he'd certainly be on my to-do list."

Everyone at the table laughed at the absurdity of that. Mary-Ellen was the devoted wife of a Methodist minister who was in South America this summer on a mission trip with their two sons. She led grace before every community meal and organized a morning devotional for those club members who wanted to attend.

Their own orders arrived and Lili turned her attention to her mushroom-Swiss burger. The musicians took the stage at one corner of the patio just after the burger baskets were cleared and orders for desserts had been placed. The ladies at the table shifted their chairs to make it easier for everyone to see and in doing so gave Lili an unimpeded view of Brick.

She tried not to stare at him. She tried

very hard. But the man was a magnet for the eyes.

Maturity looked good on him. So, too, did the mountain man flannel shirt, jeans, and hiking-boots look. Funny, whenever she'd thought about him she'd always pictured him in an Italian suit and tie.

He caught her looking at him, and their gazes held for a long minute. Then the woman at his table said something that garnered his attention. Lili studied her.

She didn't remember her at all, but that wasn't surprising. The Christopher family had a lot of kids in and out of their home. Lili's own parents had been torn between admiration for Paul and Cindy Christopher and disapproval of their revolving front door.

Dessert arrived — three kinds of pie from Sarah Murphy's bakery — and the Alley-cats dug in and began discussing favorite pie recipes. When the guitarist concluded his first set, they paid their tabs and gathered up their things to leave. The Alleycats all waved a good-bye to Brick's table, and when the other girls indicated they wanted to make a stop at the ladies' room before they left Lili stepped outside onto the sidewalk to wait for them. She had her head down, tucking her wallet back into her purse, so she didn't notice Brick's approach until he said her name. "Lili, tell me y'all aren't really going to the Bear Cave."

Her chin came up. "We are."

"It's not a good idea. It's a rough place."

"I'm told a new owner has changed things."

"He's trying, but that's easier said than done. Some hard characters have been going there for years. They don't change their habits easily. There's been some trouble at that dive in the past couple of weeks. You and your friends need to stay away from there."

Another time, in another place, if he were another person, Lili would have listened to him. Tonight she wasn't in the mood. "I appreciate your concern."

He scowled at her. "You're going anyway, aren't you?"

That put her on the spot. Maybe better sense would have prevailed once she no longer stood beneath that disapproving frown of his, but faced with the challenge Liliana couldn't very well back down. Not the new and improved Tornado Alleycat Lili. "Well, yes."

He muttered something about stubborn women, then retreated back inside Murphy's Pub.

Lili mentioned Brick's concern during the drive out to the Bear Cave, but the older women dismissed it. "I asked about it today while I grocery shopped at the Trading Post," Jana Hernandez said. "Everyone assured me we'd be just fine."

The dozen or more motorcycles parked outside of the bar when the Alleycats arrived almost gave them second thoughts, but Sharon pointed out that they were high-dollar rides. "I'm sure they're fine. Motorcycle clubs are all the rage nowadays, you know. This time of year, this is probably a club of doctors and lawyers from Texas."

Sharon was close to being right. The riders belonged to a university alumni club from Houston on a charity ride raising money for MD Anderson. Not that they weren't a rowdy bunch. Within five minutes of the Alleycats' arrival, it became obvious that Lili would have the opportunity to dance her sandals off if she so desired. But the men were gentlemanly in their rowdiness and they invited all the women to dance. Mary-Ellen revealed herself to be a pool shark when she challenged one of the riders to a game of eight ball with the loser making a donation to the youth group of the winner's choice.

Because she'd grown up with an older

brother, Lili wasn't the least bit surprised when twenty minutes after her group arrived at the Bear Cave the door opened and Brick, his brother, and his sister walked inside.

Waltzing across the dance floor like the belle of the ball, Lili admitted to being just a little bit thrilled to see Brick Callahan.

Brick was not at all happy to be at the Bear Cave. He'd anticipated a nice, relaxing evening catching up with Courtney. Instead, he was nursing a serious case of indigestion after watching Joshua go hound dog on Liliana.

At least now Josh had some competition. A lot of competition. The motorcycle club guys were all at least ten years older than Liliana, but that didn't stop them from swirling around both her and Courtney. Shoot, they didn't leave the other ladies alone, either. Tonight the Bear Cave was a regular pickup bar. Nothing like mixing men, women, drinking, and dancing to get the juices flowing.

And what the hell did Liliana think she was doing? Dancing and laughing and flirting outrageously. Was she looking for a hookup with a married guy from Houston? Or was she too naïve to realize that was the vibe her actions telegraphed?

Brick sipped his beer and scowled as his brother cut back in to dance with Liliana. "Come dance with me, Mark," Courtney said as she returned to the dance floor after ducking outside for a few moments to cool off.

"Thanks, but I don't —"

"Don't argue," she interrupted. "And don't tell me you can't dance. As I recall, you had some pretty good moves."

Brick did like to dance. He just wasn't in the mood for fighting his way through a throng to dance with Liliana. So he danced with Courtney and Jana and Sharon and Corrine and waited for just the right time to cut in on Liliana.

When the first strains of an old Johnny Cash song rose from the jukebox, Brick decided he'd waited long enough. He cut in on the dance and Lili gave him a breathless smile. "Admit it, Callahan; you were wrong and I was right. The Bear Cave isn't dangerous."

"I admit there's a safe enough crowd in here right now. That could change at any time."

"If it changes, we can leave." Her long blond hair swirled around her shoulders as he twirled her. "I love this place. It's fun!"

She certainly appeared to be having fun. Her eyes sparkled. She laughed readily. He tried to picture the young girl who used to give Derek hell over their tree house rules. His memories of the child were hazy. He recalled the teenager more easily. Freckles and legs. Braces, too. She'd always been quiet, though. Quiet and shy and seldom noticeable.

He twirled her again and she threw back her head and laughed. "You have changed, Lili-fair."

Josh, blast him, smoothly cut into the dance. "Good one, Bro. It fits her."

Outmaneuvered, Brick watched his brother dance Liliana across the dance floor. Trying not to scowl, he threaded his way toward the bar and ordered another beer.

He lifted his gaze toward the television hanging in one corner and tried to care that the Rockies were tied at three in the bottom of the ninth. Brick was a baseball guy. He was passionate about pennant races. To-night, although he kept his gaze on the game, his attention remained somewhere else entirely.

He had no business casually flirting with Derek Howe's little sister. He had a firm personal rule against mixing business with pleasure. No hookups between him and campers. After the break-up with Tiffany, he'd gone through his phase of banging everything in a skirt. That got old pretty quick. Nowadays, he dated because he genuinely liked women and enjoyed their company, not because he was out to get laid.

And never because he was looking for a relationship. That was one road he had no desire to travel a second time.

Behind him, one of the Alleycats discovered the karaoke machine, called for a round of umbrella drinks for the house, and soon the party atmosphere had risen another notch. One of the Alleycats was doing a decent rendition of Carole King's "You've Got a Friend."

Brick kept his gaze on the baseball game until the Rockies' left fielder hit into a double play that ended the game. From the corner of his eye, Brick noticed a flash of yellow exiting through the bar's back door.

He scanned the bar, looking for Liliana. No yellow sundress anywhere. She'd gone outside.

With whom?

Not your concern, Callahan. Not your business.

Unless that person was Joshua. He shouldn't be hitting on the Stardance Ranch guests, either. It was against company policy. Had to be in the employee handbook.

Well, it would be if Brick had an employee handbook.

"Something for the to-do list," he muttered, searching the room for his brother.

Josh was nowhere to be seen.

Not your business. Not your concern.

Nevertheless, his feet carried him toward the door.

The cool mountain air felt refreshing after the stuffiness of the bar. Once the door closed behind him, the quiet of the evening settled around him like a warm, soothing blanket. The Bear Cave was far enough from the center of town that traffic noise didn't intrude, close enough to Angel Creek that he could hear the rush of white water bubbling over the creek bed. On the one hand, Brick loved that sound. He found it peaceful.

On the other hand, the lack of sound coming from either his brother or Liliana disturbed him.

Male voices from around the side of the building caught his attention. *Joshua.* Brick followed the voices and discovered his brother admiring the club members' bikes. Another time, Brick might have joined them

151

— he liked a powerful ride as much as the next guy. But tonight he spied a glimmer of yellow in the moonlight. Liliana sat all alone atop a picnic bench beside the creek. A string of solar lights hung from the tree above silvered her hair and cast her in an ethereal light. Brick was powerless not to go to her.

"Needed some fresh air?"

"Thought I'd better leave before I got dragged into karaoke. I'm not much of a singer."

"I have a good voice," he told her, teasing rather than bragging.

"I remember." Her voice was glum. "Is there anything you don't do well?"

"Hmmm." He pretended to consider it. "No. Nothing that I can think of."

To his alarm, the noise that escaped Liliana sounded a little like a sob. He rested his hand on her thigh. "Liliana? What's wrong?"

"I should never have had that strawberry daiquiri."

"Not at the Bear Cave, no."

"Rum goes to my head faster than anything. I get . . . weepy."

I shoulda stopped with Joshua to talk Harleys. "Are you . . ." He paused and searched for a substitute for the word "drunk." ". . . sick?"

"At heart. I'm sick at heart."

Ah. Now he had a glimmer. *Bet she's coming off a heartbreak, herself.*

"I never wanted to be an accountant."

Okay. That one caught him by surprise.

"Had to pick a profession to please my parents. Something deserving of the Howe family name. Something that required an exam. A doctor. A lawyer. An engineer. Of course, Derek already had the doctor box checked. And let's face it. He's brilliant. I'm . . . adequate."

"Liliana . . . ," Brick began.

"You'd better go back inside, Brick. Or go talk to the motorheads. I'm having a pity party and no one should have to listen to it."

"Keep talking, Lili-fair. I'm hanging on your every word."

"I made a mistake when I picked accounting over architecture. I think I actually might have enjoyed that. But I was good with numbers, you know? Numbers come easy to me. But they bore me."

"So quit them." She'd turned her face so it was hidden by the shadows, so he sensed rather than saw her sharp gaze. "Life is too short to do work that you don't enjoy."

"I know. I'm trying to tell myself that. I need to look at this disaster as an opportunity. And I am. I do. It's the darned rum."

Disaster? "What happened, Liliana?" He waited a moment and when she didn't respond took a guess. "Did you get fired?"

Her laugh was as bitter as burned coffee. "Oh yes. I definitely got fired."

"Why?"

She folded her arms. "Promise you won't tell Derek?"

"I promise."

"I mean it." She shook a finger at him. "Your solemn oath."

"My solemn oath."

"If you break it . . . hmm . . . okay . . . if you break it you'll bring a curse down upon the Sooners. They'll never win another national championship for as long as you live!"

"Pretty good one, Liliana. Except I didn't go to OU. I went to Hawaii. Remember?"

"Oh. Well." She shrugged, weaving a little. "Doesn't matter. You grew up in Norman, Oklahoma. You can't ever leave OU loyalty behind."

"Sure I can, but that's not a concern. You have my word that I won't tell Derek."

She let out a little giggle. A little semi-hysterical giggle. "They say that I embezzled two hundred twenty-seven thousand dollars. And sixty-seven cents."

Brick took half a minute to try to make sense of what he'd just heard. Liliana Howe a thief? Yeah. Right. And Celeste Blessing was undoubtedly her accomplice.

Lili held her breath. She wasn't exactly sure why she'd spilled her guts, but she'd sobered up the minute the *e* word tumbled from her lips. She was afraid to look at him, but at the same time she couldn't look away. Her heart was in her throat. *Believe in me, Brick.*

"Well, hell, Freckle-Sticks," Brick drawled. "I'd have figured you'd be smart enough not to go for that last sixty-seven cents."

The smile started in her heart and bloomed like a sunflower as he finished the nonsensical comment. He'd found the perfect way to convey that he didn't believe it for a second.

"So what's the story?" he asked as the Bear Cave's door opened and Sharon stepped outside, looking around for Lili. At the same time, Joshua turned away from the motorcycles and stepped toward them.

"It's long and this isn't the time or place," Lili replied with a measure of regret. She'd had just enough rum that she would have liked to share the whole ugly story tonight.

155

Brick shocked her when he said, "Tomorrow's my day off. I'm going hiking up in the high country. Come with me."

Before she could answer, Josh said, "A man turns his back just for a moment and what happens? His brother tries to horn in on his date. How's that for brotherly love?"

"Buying me one umbrella drink does not a date make, Josh," Lili said with a laugh.

"Details. Come back inside. I want to dance with you again."

Sharon spied Lili and waved. "Honey, Pauline danced one too many times. Her arthritis is paining her. You about ready to head back to camp?"

"I'll take you back later," Josh offered.

Brick didn't say a word, but he watched her very carefully. It had been a fun night, but Lili was ready to go. Nothing like ending the evening on a high note, too. Lili was just tipsy enough to be able to imagine that both of the Christopher boys were flirting with her.

"Thanks, but I'm ready to call it a night."

"You're breaking my heart," Josh said.

She laughed and gave him a quick, friendly hug. "Thanks for the drink and the dances."

She turned to Brick, but the idea of reaching out for a friendly hug wasn't quite the same. He took the decision out of her hands by leaning over and kissing her cheek. He spoke softly into her ear so that only she could hear. "I'll pick you up at eight."

"But your sister came to visit. I can't interfere with —"

"She has plans tomorrow. Eight a.m."

Lili floated back into the Bear Cave to get her purse and say good-bye to the bikers who were traveling on the next day. The ladies piled into their designated driver's truck, and Mary-Ellen drove them back to Stardance Ranch.

Lili's head spun pleasantly as she drifted off to sleep.

CHAPTER NINE

Brick lay awake long into the night chewing on the little bombshell that Liliana had dropped outside of the Bear Cave. At the time, he'd reacted to the defensive light in her eyes and the pugnacious tilt of her chin and the way she obviously braced for a blow.

And he'd known. Somebody had let her down.

Who? Somebody she respected? Somebody she trusted? Somebody she loved? All of the above?

Judging by her reaction, he'd played it just right. Teasing her, then leaving it alone. Of course, he had no intention of actually leaving it alone, which was why he remained awake and thinking the situation through.

No matter what his instincts told him, he'd be remiss not to consider the fact that he didn't really know the adult Liliana. People change. People make poor choices and bad decisions, sometimes based on desperate circumstances. He'd known her when she was a child. All he really knew of her life now was a rare mention by her brother in response to an ordinary "How's your family?" query by Brick from time to time. He'd seen her what . . . twice . . . three times . . . in the past ten years? For all he knew, she could have developed a larcenous streak or let herself be taken in by a con man. Maybe she didn't embezzle two hundred thousand dollars. Maybe she'd stolen 2 million.

Yeah. Right. And maybe he'd catch a great white shark when he went fly-fishing on a Rocky Mountain stream tomorrow.

He knew the Howe family. They were good, solid people. Maybe a little more book smart than street-smart, but good folk. Honest folk.

So who had put the wounded-doe look in her eyes? He wanted the story — the whole story — told without interruption, which meant changing his plans for his day off. Before extending his invitation to Liliana, he had planned to hike the Devil's Ridge trail, which was a strenuous six-hour effort. After careful consideration, he decided to take her up to the waterfall on Branch's new acreage.

Over the past few months, it had become

one of Brick's favorite places. They would fish a little, have a picnic lunch. She could tell him her story without interruption.

It was a perfect place to do it. Not only was it private property, but that part of the mountain had no cell phone service. *Maybe afterward, we can neck a little bit.*

Whoa, whoa, whoa. Put the brakes on there, boyo. She's Derek's little sister.

The same little sister whose kiss packs a punch.

Okay, no necking. A little bedtime fanta-sizing wouldn't hurt anything, would it?

He recalled the flash of long, shapely thigh when her skirt swished when he spun her on the dance floor. Those mermaid eyes. The faint pattern of freckles across her nose.

And her mouth. That mouth of hers could make a man howl at the moon. Her nervous habit of nibbling at that full lower lip made Brick want to do some biting of his own.

His thoughts pleasantly drifting toward the carnal, he had drifted off to sleep. To dream.

He awakened with an itch that needed scratching — and the knowledge that he had no business having sex dreams about his best friend's little sister.

Because no matter how much Brick would enjoy hooking up with her, it was never going to happen. He respected his friendship with Derek more than to go down that road.

Even if Brick and Liliana started out on the same page, the chances of staying there were slight. In his experience, casual relationships with women never stayed casual. No matter how clear he made himself in the beginning, invariably the *s* word eventually came up.

Brick didn't do serious. Not anymore. Never again. That's why he'd drawn his three-date line. More than that, and females got to thinking. He didn't need that.

He got along just fine as a single man. He had more family than he knew what to do with as it was. Whenever he got a hankering for kids, he spent time with Nic and Gabe's hoodlums or took a quick trip to Texas to hang with Dad and Annabelle's brood. In the summertime, Brick couldn't walk down a street in Eternity Springs without running into a Callahan. In fact, the first of the family was due to arrive next week. By the Fourth of July, the entire clan would be here.

The last thing he'd need would be for his busybody kin to take an interest in his sex life, which was one of the reasons he didn't sleep with any of the women he'd dated in Eternity Springs. When he wanted to get laid, he took a road trip.

It was bad enough that Aunt Nic kept a close watch on who he dated and when. If she got wind that he was interested in Liliana? Trouble. Nothing but trouble. Add Aunt Maddie, Aunt Torie, and Annabelle into the mix and he'd have one miserable summer.

Hell, he might just end up married.

Brick shuddered at the thought.

He could admit that the bitterness he harbored toward love and romance had grown stronger since Tiffany contacted him a year or so ago. He didn't appreciate being used in the divorce war she'd had going on with her banker-husband. But Brick had dealt with the situation. Dealt with her. And reminded himself he had plenty of reasons not to get involved.

Since thoughts of Tiffany managed to pour cold water on the lingering effects of his dreams, Brick rolled out of bed and readied himself to satisfy his curiosity and be a friend to his friend and said friend's little sister.

And he wouldn't think about skinny-dipping with a mermaid anymore.

Today, anyway.

Lili awoke the following morning in desperate need of a glass of water and a painkiller. Next time she went out barhopping, she'd limit herself to beer.

As she popped two ibuprofens and drank three glasses of water, the events of the previous night drifted through her mind. Had she really told Mark Christopher about the accusation against her?

No, I told Brick Callahan.

And he believed me. Believed in me.

A faint smile hovered on her lips until she remembered Brick's invitation. Her gaze flew to the clock. Twenty minutes to eight. "Oh, man."

She bolted into her RV's tiny shower. On days when she planned to wash her hair she made use of the camp's shower house, because she liked the extra space for all of her products and her hair dryer, but with only twenty minutes to work with she'd make do with her own little shower and a ponytail.

She wished she'd thought to ask him for a few more details. Primarily, the length and difficulty of the trail. Her first hike up the hill behind the campground had convinced her that yoga and her twice-weekly spin class hadn't prepared her for physical exertion at this altitude. And he'd said the high country, hadn't he?

"And me with a hangover," she muttered as she pulled on the hiking pants she'd bought in town at Cam Murphy's outdoors store, Refresh. She'd be huffing and puffing for sure. *This could be really embarrassing.*

"Ya think?" she muttered. Of course it would be embarrassing. He was going to want to hear the whole ugly story.

She opened the drawer that held her shirts. Maybe she shouldn't go. She hadn't actually told him she'd go, had she? She could beg off.

Except she wanted to go. Hiking some of the trails around Eternity Springs was on her Colorado bucket list. This was beautiful country, and she wanted to see more of it. Since Brick was a local, bet he knew of some great places to hike. She chose a rose-colored long-sleeved shirt, then sat on her bed to don socks and her hiking boots.

She ate a couple pieces of peanut butter toast and had just finished pulling her hair into a ponytail when she heard a knock at her door. Lili checked her watch. Eight o'clock exactly. The man was punctual.

She inhaled a deep, bracing breath, pasted on a smile, and opened the door. Oh, holy cow. He looked deliciously outdoorsman. The man hadn't shaved. He wore a green shirt that matched his eyes, a ball cap with the Stardance Ranch logo, and had a pair of sunglasses hanging around his neck.

"Good morning," Brick said. "How's your head?"

It shows? Great. "It's just a little naggy. I'm fine. I only had two and a half drinks the whole night."

"It's the double A — altitude and alcohol. It sneaks up on you." He gave her a quick once-over. "Are you drinking lots of water?"

"Yes, Dad," she drawled. "I'm wearing my sunscreen, too."

He laughed. "Good. So, you ready to go?"

"Yes, except you didn't say how long we'd be gone. Do I need to bring a sandwich?"

"We're not on a time clock, but I have lunch covered. You might want to bring a change of clothes, though. It rained yesterday where we're going and mud can be a problem."

"Okay." After adding shorts and a T-shirt to her backpack, she slung it over one shoulder, stepped outside, and locked her door. Turning, she spied the trailer hitched to Brick's truck. "A four-wheeler? I thought we were going hiking."

"We *will* hike. I didn't know how much of a hike you'd be up to, so I thought we'd split it up. Besides, riding a four-wheeler is fun. Have you ever done it?"

"No."

He walked around to the passenger door and opened it. "Then hop in, Liliana. I'll take you for a ride."

In my dreams, she thought, climbing into his truck as she stifled a rueful smile.

Lili braced for the expected question about embezzlement as he turned out of the RV camp and took the road toward town. Instead, he asked, "Do you have a fishing license with you?"

"Yes. I did some shopping at Refresh, and Cam Murphy convinced me I needed one. I've never been fishing before."

"Seriously? I know your family went to Lake Texoma a few times."

"Dad and Derek used to go fishing. Mom and I never went with them. She wasn't much of an outdoors person."

Brick glanced at her. "What does she think about your new residence?"

She doesn't know about it. "Let's just say she's not a fan."

"Well, maybe you can convince her to give Stardance River Camp a try. I'll take you over to it sometime soon. You can snap some pictures and send them to her."

Lili wasn't about to turn down the chance to see Brick's luxury camp. "I saw flyers for it at Refresh. It looks fabulous."

A slow smile spread across his face. "It's getting there."

"Tell me about it."

"You want the long version or the short version?"

"How far is our drive?"

"Forty minutes, give or take, until we reach the trailhead where we'll park the truck and trailer. It's the other side of Sinner's Prayer Pass."

"Let's hear the long version."

"How much do you know about my Callahan family?"

Lili thought back to the time that Derek had come home with startling news about his best friend. "I know that there was some sort of family estrangement drama and your birth father thought you were dead. That's about all I recall."

"Yes, my dad's family went through some very rough times after my grandmother died, and my dad and his three brothers ended up separated from each other and my grandfather for a number of years. By the time everyone kissed and made up, my uncle Gabe was living here in Eternity Springs. I visited and fell in love with the country. I knew I wanted to live here; I just had to figure out a way to make a living." As he started up a winding mountain road, he darted her a look and added, "Independent of them."

"I understand that," Lili said.

He nodded, obviously pleased with her response. "Did you take that basic money management class in high school?"

"From Mr. Stone?" When he nodded, she shook her head. "My parents thought the curriculum was too basic."

"It was." Brick shrugged as he negotiated a switchback. "But Mr. Stone liked to talk stocks. I took his advice and invested half my graduation gift money in tech stocks. It gave me my stake to get started with the RV park. More important, it provided the leverage I needed to negotiate an equitable partnership deal with my grandfather when he purchased the prettiest piece of valley ranch land in Colorado."

"Aren't you smart."

"Lucky. Very, very lucky."

Lili's ears popped as they climbed in altitude. The shoulder on the narrow two-lane road was nonexistent in places and the drop-off was straight down. "Tell me you're a good driver."

"I'm an excellent driver. And Liliana, I'm happy to have you lean on me, but that's really not going to help the truck stay on the road."

"What? Oh." Embarrassed, she realized that she was, indeed, leaning away from every curve — and into him. Seeking a distraction from her mental vision of a blown tire and sudden plunge off the mountain to certain death, she returned to the subject at hand. "So why luxury camping?"

"It's an underserved market segment. Urbanites, especially, are attracted to the idea of communing with Nature in a relatively isolated environment, but they do like their creature comforts. And face it, tents and tree houses are romantic."

Lili smirked. She almost said something about seeing him take Tiffany up into his tree house, but she absolutely didn't want to bring the Queen of Mean along on their hike. "I've seen pictures of the tents. They look huge."

"They are big. Big and sturdy. They're made of cotton duck canvas with a metal frame and erected on a six-hundred-forty-square-foot wooden platform. It's big enough for a king-sized bed, two nightstands, a sofa, rocker, desk, and chair. We have a gas stove on a thermostat and an en suite bathroom with a six-foot soaker tub and shower. Double sinks, heated towel racks. Right now we're using spa products that Savannah Turner created for Angel's

Rest, but eventually we'll have our own line of custom scents."

"Sounds fabulous. Like the opposite of 'roughing it.' "

"That's the plan."

"So what about the tree houses?"

"Different fantasy. Similar setup. They're a lot more expensive to build, so we'll go slowly when it comes to expanding our numbers there. The bigger priority is to renovate the ghost town so we can move from a May to September calendar to something year-round."

"Ghost town? What ghost town?"

He flashed her a smile. "That's part of today's surprise."

Lili started to ask more, but she was distracted by the view as they approached the summit of Sinner's Prayer Pass. "Oh, wow. Look at that valley view. How gorgeous. And doesn't the town look like a cute little happy, all-American place? I stopped at one of the scenic pull-offs the day I arrived, but it was farther down, I think. And the drive had me too nervous to truly appreciate it."

"I think the best spot to view the valley is just around the next turn," Brick said. "Want to stop?"

"Please."

A few moments later, he pulled off the road and onto a wide shoulder marked Scenic Viewpoint. Lili opened the passenger door and stepped cautiously toward the edge of the mountain. "I'm going to stop driving past scenic viewpoints. I need to put that on my list. Look at what we miss by not getting out to appreciate the scenery! You're right. This is a fabulous spot."

"It is. This is the place where I fell for Eternity Springs."

Carefully, Lili leaned forward and gazed down at the significant drop below. "Not literally, I hope."

He laughed. "No. Though I'll admit I started out in such a distracted funk that I could have been careless enough to accidentally miss a turn on a switchback. Luckily, Celeste was driving. It was the first time we met."

"Ah, a Celeste story. It seems like everyone I meet in town has one."

"You know, I've never really thought about that, but I do think you're probably right. In this case, I'd spent Christmas at my grandfather's ranch with the Callahan clan. I had some . . . stuff . . . going on in my life and, like I said, I was in a mood. So, my aunt Nic and uncle Gabe convinced me to come home with them for a visit."

171

"It was your first trip to Eternity Springs?"

"Yep. We were on the other side of the pass just as the road begins to climb when we came across a woman about to change the flat tire on her Jeep."

"Celeste."

"Yes. By this time I'd driven fourteen hours with the twins. Don't get me wrong. I love those girls, but I was thrilled to have an excuse to get out of my uncle's car. I volunteered to change Celeste's tire and she offered to drive me home. She pulled off the road at this spot and asked me what I saw."

Lili smiled. "Knowing Celeste, I'll bet she had a particularly insightful point to make."

He pursed his lips and nodded. "There was snow on the ground. It was bitter cold. I told her I felt like I was looking at Bedford Falls."

"Bedford Falls?" The name sounded familiar to Lili, but she couldn't quite place it.

"*It's a Wonderful Life.* Jimmy Stewart?"

"Oh yeah. Ringing bells and angel wings. I'll bet that answer made her happy."

"She did laugh, but then she said that Bedford Falls was an imaginary place, but Eternity Springs is very real. She asked me to step out of the car and give it another look. I did what she asked and . . ." Brick shook his head. "It was eerie, Liliana. It had been snowing on us on the way up the mountain. Bitter cold and gray and I was in a bitch of a mood."

"Had something bad happened?"

He waited a long moment before answering. "Do you remember the girl I dated in high school?"

Who could possibly forget Tiffany? "Tiffany?"

"Yeah. We dated all the way through college, too. We'd had a rough patch . . . nothing I thought we wouldn't eventually work our way past . . . but then she up and married another guy. It was a few weeks before Christmas."

The words to tell Brick that she'd seen him scoping out the church on Tiffany's wedding day hovered on the tip of her tongue, but Lili bit them back. Nor would she mention Tiffany's new job. Now was not the time.

"Anyway, like I said, it was a gray and gloomy day that perfectly matched my mood. But when Celeste and I got out of her Jeep and stood here, I felt this sudden sense of anticipation. Sure enough, after just a minute or two, the clouds cleared, the sun came out, and starting about there." He pointed above them toward the summit of the mountain, then moved his arm, drawing an arc toward town. "And ending about there . . . about where Sarah's bakery sits . . . were not one, but two, rainbows."

Lili tried to envision it. Bet it had been a gorgeous sight to make such an impression on Brick Callahan. Lightly, she said, "I wouldn't argue against Sarah's cinnamon rolls being the pot of gold."

"True, that. But Celeste's take was a bit loftier than leprechauns. What's seriously weird about it is that the moment is burned into my memory. I remember it as if it were yesterday. She told me that the road over Sinner's Prayer Pass is like life — full of ups and downs, potholes, rough patches, and blind spots."

"So, the town is what? A road crew who fixes potholes?"

"According to Celeste, the town was going to be the answer to my prayers. The symbolism of the moment couldn't have been any plainer. A double rainbow that began on Sinner's Prayer Pass and ended in town. She said that was God slapping me up the side of the head and I darn well shouldn't ignore it. Mind you, at the time I'd been neglectful toward prayerfulness and rainbows never had much spiritual symbolism for me, but then sunbeams hit the snow and Eternity Springs sparkled like diamonds. I decided I liked that sunshine. In that moment, I decided I'd stay here for a little while. A little while turned into a year and then another and so on."

"You are happy here."

"I am." He motioned to the truck. "Ready?"

"Yes."

They didn't speak when they returned to the truck and continued up and over Sinner's Prayer Pass. About one-third of the way down, he turned onto a dirt road and followed it for a few miles stopping before a gate marked Private Property.

"Do you know the owner?" she asked.

"My grandfather. These five hundred acres came up for sale after we closed on the Stardance River Camp property. There is nothing Branch Callahan likes better than adding acreage. I'll open the gate. Would you slide over into my seat and drive through?"

"Okay."

Brick hopped down, opened the gate, then motioned toward where he wanted her to park. "Grab your pack. We're on the ATV from here."

Lili eyed the fire-engine-red machine with

oversized tires and a big box strapped to the back a bit warily. "I remember how you used to jump that motorcycle you had in high school. Promise me you've never run this thing off the side of a cliff?"

"Only twice," Brick said cheerily. He removed two helmets from the toolbox in the back of his truck and handed one to her. "Don't worry. I gave up my death-defying ways ten years ago."

Lili's fingers shook a little bit as she fastened the chinstrap. Not from fear, but with excitement. Never in a million years would she have thought she'd be about to climb onto a four-wheeler behind her high school heartthrob.

Too bad there were handholds at the side of her seat so she didn't have an excuse to wrap her arms around his waist. She could pretend she hadn't noticed them, but that would cross the line she'd drawn for herself. It was one thing to score a bucket-list kiss but something else entirely to flat out chase the man. That she would not do. She had more pride than that. And since she saw little of Oklahoman Mark Christopher in Coloradan Brick Callahan, she couldn't use bucket-list kiss number two as an excuse.

Besides, he might be acting all nice and friendly now, but she had to be realistic.

Guys like him didn't go for girls like her. And she'd had enough humiliation in her life of late, thank you very much.

But you had two good-looking guys flirting with you last night. Don't forget that.

True. But she was also the only woman below the age of fifty who wasn't their sister in the place, too.

"Ready?" he asked.

"As I'll ever be."

"Here, let me help." He took her hand and elbow and steadied her as she climbed up and onto the ATV. He settled onto the seat in front of her and a moment later the engine roared to life. He glanced over his shoulder. "Hold on to my waist, Liliana."

"But the handholds . . ."

He reached around, grabbed her wrist, and wrapped her arm around him, saying, "Hold on!"

The ATV lurched forward and Lili's other arm naturally came around his waist. Moments later he started up a steep trail that had him sliding back against her.

Lili held on. Hard.

She bounced. She lurched. She laughed. She squealed and buried her face against his shirt. She smelled fabric softener and a spicy-scented deodorant. And, yes . . . Armani. Briefly, her mind returned to high school and her hunt through the men's fragrances. *When the man finds something he likes, he doesn't let it go.*

He drove through a mountain stream and splashed icy water on them both. Lili shrieked in surprise, then laughed like an idiot when he exited the trail, increased his speed, and sped across a high alpine meadow.

She didn't anticipate the tight turn he made, and as a result when the back tires started to slide she gasped and hugged him even tighter. She heard the rumble of his laughter and snuggled up against the heat of his body. Then, almost before they came to a stop, he switched off the engine and pulled off his helmet. As Lili's hands dropped away from him, he made a flourishing gesture and said, "Ms. Howe, welcome to paradise."

Lili's mouth dropped open and she let out a little, "Oh."

Hot-pink wildflowers framed either side of the mountain stream that spilled over a rock edifice some forty feet high and fell into a pool. Rainbows painted clouds of mist that billowed into the air. Droplets of water sparkled like diamonds in the sunshine. Beside the pool sat a rustic picnic bench. It was a bucolic feast for the eyes.

A mountain chickadee's call soared above the muted rush of the waterfall, and when Lili removed her helmet, gave her ponytail a shake, and drew a deep breath she smelled Christmas in the air — spruce trees wet with the morning dew.

"What a spectacular spot," she breathed.

"As Celeste likes to say . . . a little piece of heaven in the Colorado Rockies." Brick flipped the locks on the storage box on the back of the four-wheeler. From inside he removed a box sporting the Mocha Moose logo. "This is just about my favorite spot within a two-hour drive, so I keep a supply crate in that stand of trees. I have a couple of fly rods, tackle, waders if you want them."

"Is the fishing good here?"

"Honestly, it's not as good as it is other places, but other places don't soothe my soul quite like this one." He pulled a small red cooler and a backpack from the four-wheeler's storage box and added, "I thought it would be a good place for you to tell me how you came to be an embezzler."

CHAPTER TEN

Liliana turned her face away from the breathtaking vista and met his gaze. "Any chance we can pretend I never mentioned that little detail?"

"Sure. Though I'll just ask Derek about it next time I talk to him. That was quite a conversational hand grenade you tossed out, Liliana."

"Stupid umbrella drinks," she muttered, her expression glum.

She looked so miserable that Brick took pity on her. "Want to fish a little first?"

Her eyes went warm with gratitude at the reprieve. "Yes, please."

"All right, then. Now for the hike part of the hike. Follow me."

He led her up a rocky trail, pointing out elk tracks in the rain-softened ground along the way. The hoofprints caught her attention, and she kept her gaze sharp, looking for more. When they'd climbed about halfway to the lake she called, "Here's another one. Look, Mark. What is it?"

Mark. Damned if he didn't like hearing his real name on her lips. He retraced his steps and peered down at the tracks. The sparkle in her eyes had him pursing his lips and teasing, "Hmm. Looks like grizzly."

Sparkle morphed into alarm, and Brick laughed. "Just kidding. Those are cottontail tracks."

Her brows arched. Her eyes flashed. "A bunny? It's a bunny and you said a bear?" She punched his shoulder. "No wonder you and my brother were such good friends. You have the same mean streak."

"Ow," he said, rubbing his shoulder despite the fact that he'd barely felt it. She rolled her eyes and he grinned.

Lili trailed behind him as he led her to the storage box he'd moved up here as soon as the snow melted. After setting down the lunch supplies, he unlocked the box and removed two sets of fishing gear. He explained that the stream they'd be fishing was shallow, so full waders weren't needed. They both put on waterproof boots, and he spent a little time instructing her about the basics of fly-fishing. He had her make a few practice casts before leading her to the stream.

They climbed up above the waterfall to a meadow where the gentle, grassy slope of the creek bank allowed easy access to a fishing hole that had proved fruitful in the past. Brick led her to the spot. "See how the bend in the creek creates a pool beside the more swiftly moving water? That's where lazy rainbows like to wait for that perfect bug to float by. So you want to drop the fly above the pool and let the water carry it to him."

She quickly got the hang of casting, though Brick had to remind her to keep her rod tip up and wait out the drift.

When they'd fished for ten minutes without a single strike, she observed, "I've heard that the sandwiches at the Mocha Moose are very good."

"They are. But don't worry. We'll catch something. You just need to be patient."

"You don't know the half of it. Impatience is what got me into this mess."

He glanced her way. She stood chewing on her lip again, staring blindly at the bubbling water. Her fly had drifted to the bank, but since she had the look of someone about to spill her guts, he didn't want to interrupt her.

So when he sensed the bite at his own line, he purposefully neglected to set the hook.

"It happens more often than you'd think. Theft, fraud, embezzlement, I mean. Small businesses are especially vulnerable because they usually have few controls in place and employees whom they trust. More often than not, the thief doesn't set out to steal. Maybe she gets in a tight spot and she sees a way to borrow from the company, meaning to pay it back on payday. Only something else comes up and she doesn't pay it back and she doesn't get caught and thus faces no consequences. It's easy to justify, too, if she feels she's being underpaid for the job she's doing. Then before you know it, something else comes up. It's rinse and repeat."

Brick shot her a sharp look. This explanation sounded personal, but he didn't think she was talking about herself.

"It's a criminal charge, of course. Once the police get involved, there's no going back. More than once I've seen the situation where the thief thinks it's okay for her to steal because she has personal knowledge of something wrong the business owner has done. Like cheating on his taxes. They try to bargain with the prosecutors, but by then it's too late."

"Who did you try to help, Liliana?" he asked, taking a stab in the dark.

She shook her head. He'd guessed wrong. "A division of our firm does financial planning. I did a stint in that division before I focused on tax, and I got to know a few of our clients. A lot of them are retirees. Nice people. They trusted the firm. I'd see some of the people I'd worked with from time to time, and I started hearing about a great, safe investment we'd put them in. Bringing thirteen percent returns. People were thrilled."

"In today's financial climate, I bet they were."

"It sounded fishy to me, so I started doing some checking. I couldn't find much of anything about it. Little pieces here and there that didn't add up. It bothered me. Maybe I pursued it longer than was strictly necessary, dug a little deeper than I needed to dig, but I was trying to do a great job. I was on track to be the youngest partner in the history of the firm."

Of course you were. "You're a Howe."

A spasm of emotion crossed her face. She looked like she had sucked a piece of sour apple candy. *Holy crap. Her family is part of this trouble?*

"I found just enough to concern me, but then I ran into a wall. So I asked a founding partner at the firm, my mentor, what he

184

knew about it. He asked for my files and said he'd look into it. He reassured me all would be well, and then he gave me a huge project to do and dangled the partnership bait. I let it go." She paused a long moment, then repeated, "I let it go."

"It was a scam?" Brick asked.

"Yep. After turning over my files to my mentor, I trusted him to take care of it. I didn't hear any more about it and I really didn't think anything about it. I worked all the time and April fifteenth was roaring down on me and I was drowning. Everyone worked late, but I was there by myself a lot. It was just after two in the morning when I went to put a file on my mentor's desk. I was tired and careless, and I knocked a stack of files onto the floor. While I was picking them up, I saw the file I'd given him. It was much thicker than before."

Liliana noticed then that her line had drifted onto the rocks. Holding her rod exactly as Brick had instructed with her right hand, she guided the line through her left, drew her rod up, and flicked an excellent cast.

Brick watched the yellow fly float downstream, perfectly positioned to drift across a placid pool where he'd bet his left nut that a trout waited. Liliana wasn't actively fishing. She had retreated into the past.

"First, I couldn't believe that the file was on his desk. It had been three . . . almost four . . . months. Second, some of the names had changed, and the numbers had changed. But then I thought I must have been remembering wrong. I'd worked with a lot of clients, a lot of numbers. I must have been remembering wrong. Except . . . I knew that wasn't it. I'm good with numbers."

Brick shifted his gaze from the fly to Liliana's frowning face, then back to the drifting fly. "I'm sure you are."

"But I'm terrible with people. Reading them. Knowing who I can and cannot trust. It never occurred to me to make copies. To protect myself. I was the Queen of Naïve."

Brick could see where this was going. "Someone set you up to take the fall?"

She whipped her head around and met his gaze. "Yes! How did you guess?"

He started to say he'd left naïve behind decades ago but decided that sounded mean. "I watch a lot of movies. So, who was the culprit? Your mentor?"

"He was in on it. In on the cover-up. The actual thief was his partner's son."

"Ah," Brick said. "You know, one of my grandfather's favorite rants is how often the second generation destroys a family business."

"Well, Carlton Harbaugh certainly did his part. He appropriated the pristine reputation of the firm his father had spent his entire professional life building to set up a pyramid scheme and bilk unsuspecting retirees of their savings."

"He preyed upon seniors? What a scumbag."

"I thought he was a great guy. I really liked him. He's exhibit A for my lack of good people-judging skills."

"So what's the bottom line, Lili-fair? Are you in legal trouble?"

"No. And neither is Carlton Harbaugh. His father made restitution, so according to the firm, no harm, no foul, and the matter was over. Nobody even knew it had happened. Nothing prevented Harbaugh from doing it again. That was wrong. It was criminal, and I stewed about it. I finally worked up the nerve to broach the subject with my mentor."

"And he threw you under the bus."

She nodded. "They'd anticipated my protest. They reconstructed everything only using my name and employee number. They said they'd use it if I took it any further."

"It can't hold up. A forensic accountant

surely —"

"Yes. Probably. That's why they set me up with a DUI."

Brick did a double take. "They what? How?"

"A dirty cop. It's costing me my license."

"Your driver's license?"

"My CPA license."

"Whoa . . . whoa . . . whoa. They are taking your career away from you?"

"Yep."

"That can't happen. You have to fight it."

Her mouth twisted and she waited a long minute before replying. "I had thought to do so. My parents convinced me to go another direction."

"What direction?"

Her genuine smile caught him unaware. "Colorado."

"I don't understand. How does — Strike, Lili! Good-sized fish, too. Rod up. Set it."

She let out a yelp and yanked her pole up. The rod tip bent toward the water. "What do I do? What do I do?"

"Keep your rod tip up. He's running the show right now. Let him fight you and wear himself out."

"Do I reel him in?"

The rainbow on her line looked to be about eighteen inches. A good fish. He breeched the water and Lili let out a squeal.

"But work him real slow, Lili-fair. Mainly you want to prevent him from getting into the rocks and cutting the line."

"He's heavy! This is hard."

"He's a good fighter. You're doing great. Rod tip up. Up!"

"Oh no. It's gone slack. Did I lose him?"

"No. He's still there. He's resting. Work him a little now. If you can get him a little closer I'll net him."

It took her another couple of minutes, but Lili landed the trout. She bubbled with delight, and when Brick asked if she wanted to have her catch for lunch she shook her head. "No. We have sandwiches, and besides, he's too pretty to eat."

Brick carefully removed the barbless hook from the fish's mouth. When the rainbow disappeared back into the bubbling stream, Brick bent and washed his hands. Rising up, he discovered Liliana with her bright eyes and infectious smile standing right there beside him.

"Thank you, Brick. This is something I've always wanted to do." She went up on her tiptoes and aimed a friendly kiss toward his cheek.

But Brick still hummed with the effects of last night's erotic dreams, so he didn't have the strength or desire to fight his natural instincts. He turned his face and met her mouth with his.

He knew the moment his lips touched hers that it was a mistake. She tasted of spearmint and smelled of sunshine and she brought the theme song from the Rodgers and Hammerstein musical to his mind. "Oklahoma."

She was . . . home.

He loved his life in Colorado. Loved his Callahan family. But the house and neighborhood where he grew up, and the family who'd cared for him since toddlerhood, would always be home.

He was lonely for home.

His free arm went around her and clutched her tight, but then her boot slipped on the wet rock and she lost her balance, falling into him. Brick shifted his weight, almost managed to steady them, but he was a man and therefore attempted to protect the expensive fly rods, too.

He took two steps back toward the bank. His foot slipped; she stumbled. They were going down.

With a grimace and a prayer, Brick flung the fifteen-hundred-dollar-apiece fishing rods toward the bank and at the same time clapped Lili's head against his chest in order to protect her from the rocks.

He hit ass first against a large, relatively flat rock. One of his shoulder blades banged against something sharp, but the other landed on packed dirt. Liliana's forehead whacked against his chin and her knee just missed his jewels.

All in all, not a bad landing, Brick thought even as icy-cold water soaked him from his knees down.

"You hurt?" he asked.

She sucked in a breath. "No. I'm okay. You cushioned my fall."

He'd done that, all right. Now her breasts lay pillowed against his chest and her crotch was snuggled up against his thigh. She wiggled like the rainbow and Brick's rod reacted.

Liliana tried to climb to her feet, but Brick was an experienced fisherman. He knew just how to hold her.

He rolled her onto her back and kissed her again.

Brick's kiss was as hot as the mountain stream was cold. When his hands cupped her butt and shifted her, pulling her tight against the ridge of his arousal, Lili wondered if this counted as getting down and dirty.

Then his mouth trailed down her neck, his teeth scraped at her sensitive skin, and she quit thinking at all.

They made out like high school kids beneath the bleachers. At least, Lili guessed that this was what making out beneath the bleachers would have been like. She'd never had the experience. But this fit what she'd always imagined it would be. Long kisses. Deep kisses. Exploring kisses. Explosive kisses. Exquisite kisses. It was sexy and sensual and sinful, and Lili lost herself in the pleasure of a fantasy come true.

She was making out with Mark Callahan and one of his work-roughened hands had found its way beneath her shirt. Beneath her bra. He cupped her and kneaded her and stroked her nipple. Sensation arrowed straight to Lili's core and she moaned into his mouth.

He answered with a groan and the warmth of sunshine on her skin finally penetrated her senses. When had he unfastened her bra? The man's moves were smooth, but then, practice makes perfect and, heaven knows, he certainly had plenty of that.

And she was going to enjoy his expertise. Learn from it. Revel in it. That's what her trip to Colorado was all about, wasn't it?

So she allowed her hands to explore. He

was hard and broad. Slick with mud. Deliciously dirty.

He rolled her onto yellow wildflowers with sticky stems. She might have preferred to have a blanket beneath her, but she wasn't about to complain. His tongue laved her nipple, and when his mouth closed over the tip of her breast she arched her back and shuddered. This was the most exciting, spontaneous, erotic adventure of her life!

Until she moaned out his name . . . his given name. He froze and rolled away from her. He lay breathing heavily, his forearm covering his eyes, for the count of five.

Then he cursed a streak as blue as the sky above.

"Well," Lili said, insulted. She sat up and straightened her clothes. "That's flattering."

"I'm not trying to flatter you!"

"Obviously." She scrambled to her feet and went hunting for the waterproof boot that had slipped off during her fall.

Brick let out a few more curses, then explained, "I'm sorry that happened, Liliana."

I'm not.

"It was inexcusable."

She rolled her tongue around her mouth. "Careful there, Callahan. My self-esteem is fragile. You're liable to damage it."

He shifted his arm enough for one eye to glare at her. "Don't be stupid. There's nothing fragile about you, and even if there were, better your self-esteem be dinged than my legs both be broken."

"Your legs? Did I hurt you?"

"No." Brick rolled up to a seated position. "But your brother would if he knew I'd been rolling around in the mud with you."

"Oh, for crying out loud. That's ridiculous."

"No, it's really not." Frustration hummed in his voice as he added, "Guys have rules, Liliana. *I* have rules, and for some reason whenever I'm with you I have trouble remembering them.

"Rules?"

"I don't mix business and pleasure. Ever. Which means I don't seduce customers. That's a terrible business practice. Neither do I hook up with sisters of my friends. That's a real good way to destroy a friendship."

"And of course you would never do more than 'hook up' with a woman," she replied, unable to keep the scornful note from her tone.

He climbed to his feet and rinsed the mud from his hands. "That's correct. And I'm up-front about that with the women I date.

If the lady is on the same wavelength as me, we'll play around a time or two. But I don't do relationships, period."

Lili gave him a long look. "She really did a number on you, didn't she?"

Brick didn't meet Lili's gaze as he bent to pick up the fishing rods and inspect them for damage. "You know my history better than most. I'd be lying if I denied it."

"She got my partnership."

"What?" He looked up from the fly rods. "What are you talking about?"

"She joined the firm after her divorce. She's not a CPA, but she is Queen of Contacts. They created a special position for her. I suspect they recently made her a partner."

"Tiffany? You're talking about Tiff?"

Lili nodded.

"You work with Tiffany."

"Not anymore. And I never really worked *with* her."

Brick stood up straight and speared Lili with a look. "Was she part of the scam?"

"No. I can blame her for a lot, but not that. They played the scam strictly need-to-know. Keeps the sword they hang over my neck sharper."

"Evil people," Brick muttered. "What are

their names? Do I know them from the old days?"

"I doubt it." She identified the two senior partners and the son who'd caused her so much trouble. "We weren't exactly part of their social circle."

"No. Never heard of the bastards." Brick shook his head and changed the subject. "You had enough fishing, Oklahoma? Those roast beef sandwiches are beginning to call my name."

She cleared her throat. " 'Oklahoma'?"

Brick shrugged. "You prefer 'Freckle' — ?"

"No!" she interrupted with a shriek. Then, after a pause, she added, "I do like 'Lili-fair.' "

"So do I," he said softly. "I like her very much. And dammit, I'm trying to stop that from becoming a problem."

They didn't speak as they climbed down to the picnic spot beside the waterfall. Lili grabbed her backpack and went around behind Brick's storage shed to change her clothes. When she returned, he had taken his muddy shirt off and he was sorting through the backpack.

Liliana's mouth went dry. She'd seen a shirtless Mark Christopher many times before, because her parents' house had a backyard pool and his had not. He'd been a star stud athlete in high school whose numerous hours spent in the weight room made him pretty to look at. Lili had spent a fair amount of time peeking past her bedroom curtains doing exactly that. She'd thought the teenage Mark Christopher was a hunk.

The all-grown-up Brick Callahan made her weak at the knees.

He pulled a Denver Broncos T-shirt from his pack and shoved his arms through the sleeves. He lifted the shirt over his head, and her gaze swept across broad shoulders, a smattering of dark hair covering a chest corded with muscle and narrowing over six-pack abs toward his low-hanging jeans and his groin.

She really wished he hadn't stopped what they'd started beside the stream. He'd left her achy and needy and wanting. It really wasn't very gentlemanly of him.

Maybe she should tell him so. The old Lili wouldn't dream of it, but she was a Tornado Alleycat now. She could be bold.

She eyed him speculatively. She could respect his rule against sleeping with his customers, but that wasn't the reason why he'd stopped. Honestly, he had no business bringing Derek into the creek with them.

Lili was working up the nerve to voice her

protest as Brick called, "There's a quilt in the storage shed. Want to get it and pick a spot for our lunch?"

"Okay." While she fetched the quilt and spread it atop a patch of white wildflowers she tried to decide whether she was happy to have a reprieve or not. Maybe it was better that things hadn't gotten out of hand. The last thing she needed was to fall for Mr. Three-Dates-and-You're-Out.

She took a good look at the covering she'd placed atop the wildflowers. "This is a beautiful quilt, Brick. I've always loved the kaleidoscope pattern. It belongs on a bed or hanging on a wall. I hate to spread it on the ground."

"Aunt Torie made it. We have dozens of them. The woman loves to quilt and to picnic. She has quilts and blankets stuck all over the place."

Brick carried a large brown bag bearing the Mocha Moose logo and the small cooler just big enough for a half-dozen cans. He launched into a story about a special item his aunt Nic had requested at the Mocha Moose when she'd been expecting her son. "Peanut butter and bananas I get. But add pickles and that's just disgusting. What's funny is that we have so many pregnancies in this town and the sandwich got so popular that the Moose went ahead and put it on its menu. Don't worry, though. Today we have roast beef."

He set down the bag of sandwiches and the cooler and sat cross-legged on the quilt. Opening the lunch sack, he handed Lili a sandwich and asked, "So how do you plan to fight them?"

"Fight what?" She glanced around the quilt. Had she set it on an ant bed or something?

"The asshats at your firm."

Her sandwich halfway to her mouth, Lili paused.

Brick continued, "You're not going to let them get away with this. What's your plan? Have you hired a lawyer?"

Deliberately, Lili took a bite of her sandwich. She knew the roast beef didn't taste sour. Her taste buds had reacted to the topic he'd introduced. *Appetite killer.*

She chewed her food thoroughly and prepared to present her arguments out loud for the first time. She was confident in her decision. Well, more confident than doubtful at this point. Say, 60/40 percent confident.

She swallowed, took a sip from the can of sparkling water she'd chosen from the cooler, and said, "No, no lawyer. I decided not to pursue it."

He frowned. "Legally, you mean."

"Legally. Personally. Publicly. I'm letting it go."

"Why? I don't understand."

Her chin came up. "It doesn't really matter if you understand or not. It's my problem. My fight. My choice not to fight."

"That's bull." He unfolded his legs and stretched them out. "These people stole from you. They blackmailed you. They're criminals. You can't just ignore that. You can't run away from it."

"That's not what I'm doing. I'm making a choice not to pursue the issue."

He took another bite of his sandwich and chewed it slowly, studying her. Lili reached for a single-serve-sized bag of potato chips that she didn't want just to have something to do. "Then why are you keeping it such a secret? You only told me about it because the word 'embezzled' slipped out of your umbrella drink."

She shrugged her shoulders. Ate a salty chip.

"You haven't mentioned it to any of the Alleycats or anyone in town. I would have heard."

He polished off the rest of his sandwich, licked his fingers, then said, "Derek doesn't know, either, does he? That's why you didn't want me to tell him you're here. You're afraid. Afraid of losing your reputation. Afraid of losing people's respect."

The observation triggered her fury. She blurted, "So what if I'm afraid?"

He leaned over to search through the basket. Pulled out another sack of chips. "I never thought I'd live to see the day. What happened to that girl who sneaked into my backyard and climbed into my tree house to put a garter snake in Derek's sleeping bag?"

"Wait. You knew about that?" *Wonder if he knows about the blue bra, too?*

"Or the young woman who, when put in an untenable situation on a bus, lifted her chin and squared her shoulders and walked like a queen into the fast-food restaurant."

"You really didn't just bring that up." Lili shut her eyes and her cheeks flushed with embarrassment. "I can't believe you brought that up."

"I can't believe you're running away."

"I didn't run away! I joined the Tornado Alleycats! And it's nobody's business why I left Oklahoma."

"Sure it is. Those people committed a crime. You might be the only victim this time, but what about next —"

"I'm not a victim. I'm making a choice. I

201

have a plan. I'm going to change."

"Change what?"

"Me. I'm going to change me. I'm done being the dutiful daughter and a gracious coworker and dedicated professional. I'm done with being a good girl."

"Why do I think I don't want to hear this?"

She rolled up onto her knees. "Then put your fingers in your ears, because I'm going to shout. I'm going to live, Mr. Callahan. Live with a capital *L*. No more sitting on the sidelines because that's what good girls do. What is that saying, 'I'll be hanged for a sheep as for a goat'?"

" 'Lamb.' I think it's 'hanged for a sheep as for a lamb.' "

"Well, I'm not a lamb. I'm going to be the GOAT. The GOAT bad girl."

"What are you talking about?"

"Not up on your slang, Callahan?" She gave her ponytail a toss. "*G-O-A-T.* Greatest Of All Time. My plan is that from this time forward I am going to be a Life GOAT. Patsy is a Life GOAT. A girl I went to college with is a Life GOAT. She was born with a genetic disease that gives her a life expectancy into her thirties. She did more living during our four years in college than I've done in my entire life. She was brave and courageous and daring. She wasn't afraid to let a guy pick her up in a bar and take her to Paris for a weekend."

Brick drew back at that. "She should have been afraid of doing that."

"I've never been to Paris. Certainly never on a whim. I've never had a one-night stand. I want to pick up and go to Paris and Rome and Vienna. I want to pick up a stranger wearing a three-piece suit in a bar and be picked up by a biker wearing leathers."

Brick yanked open the sack of chips. "Sounds like what you need to do is retrace your steps until you find your wits. Obviously, you've lost them."

"I think I finally found them. It took me long enough, don't you think? I'm almost thirty."

"I'm serious."

"So am I." She shoved to her feet. "This is *my* career crisis. It happened to me, so I get to deal with it the way I want. And I *don't* want to be an accountant anymore. I don't want to waste time and effort and energy and money trying to reclaim something that was never right for me to begin with. I'm not wasting another minute of my life."

"I understand that, Liliana. Honestly, I

do. But you're talking about picking up bikers in bars!"

He sounded so appalled that laughter burst from Lili's mouth. Expressing her secret desires made her feel empowered. Expressing them to this particular man made her feel invincible. "It's not just about men. It's about living. I want to break free from 'dependable' chains and live my life with abandon. People who do that — they're happy. They don't have regrets. They live! It's about time I had some adventure in my life, don't you think?"

"Not that kind of adventure." He climbed to his feet and braced his hands on his hips. "Go hang gliding or shark watching. Go bungee jumping! But picking up guys in bars is dangerous, Lili."

"And shark watching isn't?"

"At least you're in a cage. The shark can't stick something in your drink when your back is turned. Besides, you're not that kind of girl."

"I'm evolving."

"There's evolving, and then there's being stupid. One-night stands aren't safe or smart."

"I just said this wasn't all about men! Yet you're bound and determined to go there. And besides, you're one to talk. Are three-night hookups any better? I've heard about you, Brick Callahan. You've dated every unattached woman in town three times. Exactly three times."

"That's not true."

"Oh, isn't it?" She folded her arms and lifted her chin in challenge.

A gust of wind blew across the meadow and sent an empty bag of chips blowing. Brick stooped to snatch it up. "Not *every* unattached woman. And it's not like I sleep with every woman I date, either."

"No. Just those on . . . how did you put it? A similar wavelength?"

A muscle worked in his jaw. A full thirty seconds passed before he grumbled, "Okay, fine. You have a point."

She pressed the momentary advantage. "Times have changed, Brick. Ganders and geese have equal rights."

"I know that. I'm not denying your right to sample the sauce. I'm just afraid you don't know what you're getting into. Deny it if you want, but you did grow up in Norman, Oklahoma. You are naïve."

"Maybe. But I'm strong, too. Having an average of four tornadoes blow through town every year builds character."

"I won't argue that. But you're like my little sis —" He bit the word off. "Friend.

You're my friend, Liliana. I don't want you to get hurt."

Yes, well, I'm glad he doesn't roll around creek banks feeling up his sister.

"The neighborhood where we grew up is a nice little bubble of good-hearted, caring, salt-of-the-earth people."

Yeah. Right. Two words. Tiffany Lambeau.

She folded her arms. "Do you think I've done no living whatsoever since middle school? I did go off to college. I may look like a nerdy, number-crunching virgin, but I have had *some* experience. I don't live with my mommy and daddy."

"You don't look like a nerd. Definitely don't look like a nerd. As far as being virginal, well, the world isn't *full* of stupid guys."

She choked back a snort. Barely.

"You get anywhere near water and all I think about are mermaids."

She wanted to take a moment to preen but decided she'd best make her point while she could. "Here's the thing, Brick. I get it that living adventurously can be dangerous, but recent events have taught me that life in a safe little bubble can be just as perilous. Cruelty doesn't have geographic boundaries."

He crushed the empty chip bag in his fist

and shoved it into a sack of trash. "Promise me you'll be careful out there. The mountains attract some . . . characters."

Lili's lips twisted. He really did sound like Derek. All big brotherly. Lili told herself that was fine with her and tried to believe it. He did have a point, after all. Knowing that she'd hooked up with him, be he Mark Christopher or Brick Callahan, would drive her brother insane.

"You are a nice guy, Callahan."

"No, I'm honestly not. This is killing me." He gave her a slow, hot once-over. "You do it for me, Lili-fair. It's all I can manage not to jump you right this second and finish what we started earlier. But you're a line I can't cross."

"The rules."

"Yeah. The rules."

With his admission of her appeal, Lili's appetite returned. She knelt back down and happily took another bite of her sandwich. "The Mocha Moose's sandwiches are as delicious as advertised."

He looked as if she'd thrown him a lifeline with the change of subject. "I recommend their egg salad, too."

As the conversation turned to the culinary offerings in Eternity Springs and the surrounding area, a part of Lili's thoughts drifted to her bucket lists. She'd had fun catching that fish. She wanted to do it again. But as much as she'd enjoyed netting that eighteen-inch rainbow, after this morning she thought she might set her sights on landing something bigger.

When she returned to Stardance Ranch RV Resort, she would add a blue marlin fishing trip to Cabo San Lucas to her life bucket list. As far as her Colorado list went . . . well . . . fishing had long been a secret desire of hers. Today Brick Callahan had given her a taste of the activity, and she wasn't ready to let him off the hook.

Lili was a Tornado Alleycat now. Her goals and aspirations had changed. Yes, there were lots of fish in the ocean, but she could think of no reason why she shouldn't go for the prize.

Brick Callahan. Three-date-limit, Mr. I-Have-My-Rules, Camp Director Dreamboat. What he didn't realize was that she had a unique bait for her line. She knew Mark Christopher. Mr. I-Never-Met-a-Rule-I-Won't-Break.

She wasn't looking for a relationship, either. She had too much living to do first. Lili polished off her sandwich, then licked her fingers. Slowly. One by one.

Liliana Howe, Tornado Alleycat, had

decided she was looking to cast her line and try a little catch and release.

CHAPTER ELEVEN

By the third week of June, Stardance Ranch RV Resort was rocking the summer season. The number of Tornado Alleycats camped at the resort continued to fluctuate as members arrived and departed, more of the former than the latter. Not a meal went by that somebody didn't invite Brick to join them, and almost every night the activity center rocked with laughter.

These ladies were the craftiest bunch of folks he had ever run across. Scrapbooking. Painting. Sketching. Coloring. Quilting. Knitting. Every time he turned around someone was dragging him into her RV to show off her latest creation. And don't even get him started about the name tags. He'd never dreamed that so much time and effort and expense could be involved in creating name tags for every special event they held — and they held something almost every night.

He liked the Alleycats. Friendly and fun, they were for the most part laid-back, undemanding, and easy to please. The kind of people he'd hoped would choose Stardance Ranch when he'd decided to open the RV resort. The kind of people he enjoyed having in his life.

The exact opposite of those who right at this moment were making his life miserable.

In the camp office, Brick tossed his phone onto his desk and scowled. "Glamping, shmamping. Whose stupid idea was it to open River Camp?"

"That would be yours, boss," said Josh as he restocked the moose head Pez dispensers on the pegboard beneath the registration counter.

In her second week as his newest employee, Courtney looked up from her computer and spoke to Josh. "Is he always this cranky in the morning?"

"He was out late last night."

"Are you my brother or my mother?" Brick asked with a scowl.

"I'm thinking somebody needs to be your keeper. Seriously, Brick, you can't keep burning the candle at both ends. Not this time of year. We are completely booked today. We have two washers on the fritz, three broken boards on the fishing pier, and four clogged toilets. Plus, it's pizza night and Wendy called a few minutes ago and said they're all down with a bug. We need to either fill in and man the oven ourselves or cancel."

Brick shook his head. "We can't cancel. They'll riot."

"Yep."

"I'll call into town and see if I can't rustle up another pair of hands or twelve to help out. Who is scheduled to work happy hour at River Camp tonight?"

Josh rattled off the names. Brick nodded. "Good. Remind Suzy to double-check the preference lists and labels before she pours. Our guests in Wilson swear they were poured something other than the Macallan last night."

Brick had named the tents at Stardance River Camp after some of the fourteeners in Colorado — mountain peaks with elevations over fourteen thousand feet. Wilson currently was occupied by a couple from Boulder, winners of this week's PITA award.

"Seriously?" Courtney folded her arms and leaned back in her chair. "That's a crock. I watched your bartender break the seal on the Macallan myself. Is that why you're grumbling about River Camp?"

"No, I know that guest is full of it. Tom is

an excellent bartender and as honest as the day is long. The pretentious SOB is just trying to impress his lady. That type of guest I can handle. It's the twinkles that make me crazy. Particularly the one coming the end of the month."

"Twinkles?" his sister asked.

Without looking up from the box of Pez dispensers, Josh clarified, "Celebrities."

Courtney's eyes went round. "A celebrity is coming to River Camp? Who?"

Brick shook his head. "I don't know. All I have is a code name."

"You're kidding."

"Nope. A code name and a basket full of troubles. Now I have to order in a supply of bottled water from some little town in Italy. The only good thing is that their deposit arrived in today's mail. Which reminds me, Courtney, you can pay the stack of vendor bills underneath the bear paperweight."

His sister nodded. "What about the ones beneath the hula girl?"

"Nope. Those are going to have to wait until the Alleycats pay this week's rental."

"The purchase orders we discussed yesterday?"

"Put them through."

"What about the Pikes Peak paperweight stack?"

213

Brick looked at the small mountain of bills and sighed heavily. It was his fault for having fallen so far behind on bookkeeping after Donna Barton moved away. Josh had helped, but Brick had piled way too much on his plate. They'd both fallen behind. Courtney's decision to move to Eternity Springs had been a lifesaver. "If any twinkle deposit money is left after the bear bills, take a run at Pikes Peak. We should be able to blow it up completely soon since I'm requiring full payment of twink upon arrival."

"What sort of code are you talking in, CDD?" came Patsy Schaffer's familiar voice from the doorway.

Brick dipped his chin toward his chest. "Am I ever going to convince you to quit calling me that?"

"Probably not."

"That's unfortunate." Brick gave her a rueful smile, then added, "Can I help you with something, Patsy?"

"I hope so. Do you have time to take a little walk with me? We've a situation I'd like to discuss."

"Sure." Brick glanced at his brother and sister. "Josh, will you follow up with our maintenance guy and make sure he tackles those toilets?"

"Of course."

Courtney stopped him by asking, "Can you give me a few minutes first, Brick? I need you to sign some checks and paperwork if I'm going to make it to the post office before they close."

He nodded as Patsy said, "No rush. I'll be outside doing my stretches."

A few minutes turned into almost fifteen as Courtney gave him a stack of checks and purchase orders and the office was suddenly slammed with phone calls and check-ins. When Brick finally managed to tear himself away, he gave his sister a hug. "I'm so glad you decided you liked Eternity Springs."

As he left the office, he reflected on what a difference Courtney had made at the Ranch in the short time she'd been there. She was quick with numbers, quick on the computer, and willing to pitch in with whatever he asked. He was oh, so glad to have her and Josh in his corner this summer season. And he was bummed by the realization that neither one planned to make their stay in Eternity Springs permanent.

"Wonder what it'd take to change their minds?" he murmured to himself as he glanced around the campground, halfway expecting to see that Patsy had given up on him.

He spied her over by the playground where one of the Alleycats pushed a granddaughter, visiting for the weekend, on the swing. He headed in that direction. "Sorry for the delay, Patsy."

"No problem at all. I've been enjoying myself listening to a little girl's giggles. It's a lovely day to be alive, isn't it?"

"That it is."

"Shall we walk up toward the wishing bridge?"

"Sure." After a moment's hesitation, he asked, "Where's the wishing bridge?"

Patsy laughed and took his arm. "We've dubbed the bridge over the creek that leads to the kid fishing hole the wishing bridge."

"Oh. That's cool. I should have a sign made."

"Don't bother. We're planning to make one in our wood-burning class next Tuesday night."

"I swear, Patsy. You are a wonder. Is there any craft your group doesn't know how to do?"

"Actually, Celeste is coming out to help us with that lesson."

Brick couldn't help but grin and shake his head at that. "Are you sure you and Celeste aren't secret sisters?"

Patsy got a gleam in her eye. "Some things

are simply not meant to be known, my dear."

She asked about the rumor going around camp that pizza night was to be canceled and followed it up with a question about campsite plans for the Fourth of July. Brick sensed that neither topic was what had brought her to the office, and he was afraid he knew what subject was on her mind.

"So," Patsy finally said. "About Lili."

Bingo.

"She told me that she ran into you a few nights ago at Murphy's Pub. And twice at the Bear Cave's happy hour."

"Yes, well, I've been thirsty."

"And at a church fund-raiser the night before last."

"I support local causes."

"And at the Stargazer's Club meeting last night."

He shoved his hands in the back pockets of his jeans. "She was meeting one of those motorcycle gang members!"

"Yes," Patsy drawled in her southern, sweet-tea voice. "The dastardly one who had his Harley towed in from Lake Tahoe for a ride with fellow members of his bar association."

"Well, she met him in a bar. That's just a

little too much bar association for my comfort."

"I don't disagree with you, Brick."

"Just because some guy has money and a two-hundred-dollar haircut doesn't mean . . . wait." His head swiveled toward her. "You said you *don't* disagree?"

"That's correct. While I don't believe that going stargazing with the Lake Tahoe lawyer was dangerous, I am worried about her."

"Me, too. She's acting reckless."

"And that's not like her. I fear our Liliana is headed for trouble if she continues on this path. She's a kitten playing with tigers."

"I know." A wave of relief washed over Brick. Finally, someone else who recognized that Miss Party Central was out of control. "She's acting totally irresponsible. It would be one thing if she focused on local guys, so at least we know something about them. She's not doing that. She avoids flirting with locals and sets her sights on the guys just passing through. I don't understand her. She doesn't know what she's doing."

"Actually, I think she knows exactly what she's doing. I'm afraid I've inspired her in a manner I didn't intend."

Brick cast a sidelong look toward Patsy and noted the worried purse of her lips. "She did mention something about living her life like you've lived yours."

Patsy sighed. "Like so many do, I'm afraid she's focused on the sex. I have admitted to having a colorful sexual history, but like we say in the South, Lili is turned different from me. If she were meant to walk on the wild side of life, she wouldn't be so entrenched on the straight and narrow."

"Not anymore. You should have seen her night before last. She wobbled all over the place. And I only saw her drink two beers."

"Yes, her tolerance for alcohol is low." Patsy repeated her sigh, more heavily this time. "In all honesty, I agree that Lili can use more sexual experience. It's been entirely too long since she's gotten laid."

Brick almost tripped over his own feet. *Did she just say that? She* didn't *say that!* He didn't just hear that! He could feel the tips of his ears growing warm from embarrassment. He shifted his hands from his back pockets to his front ones.

"But sex isn't why I encouraged her to join the Tornado Alleycats."

A good thing, since it's an all-female club and Liliana is straight.

"Lili tries too hard to please her family."

"Not anymore, Patsy. From what I've observed . . . from what she's shared . . .

she's actually doing the exact opposite of that."

"Nonsense. She's *hiding* from her family. That's what worries me. She's taken one step forward and two steps back. Leaving Oklahoma City was huge. Don't get me wrong. But she's lost it in the follow-up. Lili has the sweetest heart of just about anyone I know, but she's a pushover."

Brick frowned in annoyance. "No, she's not."

Patsy proceeded to tick off five separate instances in which Liliana had proved to be precisely the pushover she claimed. Still, Brick felt compelled to defend Liliana.

"The Liliana I knew when we were kids has never been a pushover. If anything, she was a determined pest who followed along behind us every chance she could. Her brother and I used to go to great lengths to avoid her. I can't tell you how often we failed. And she's been just as stubborn in my dealings with her here in Eternity Springs."

"I know! Isn't that wonderful? There's something about you, Brick, that trips her trigger. She's strong around you. We need to encourage that. She's going to need her strength in the days to come."

That roused Brick's suspicions. "Why do

you say that? What do you know?"

"I know that Liliana is alone. Alone with a capital *A*. Most of her friends in Oklahoma she knew through work, and they have certainly let her down in the wake of that horrible DUI business. Why, you'd think she had a contagious disease the way they've kept their distance. She's making friends here with the Alleycats, but frankly, she's the youngest among us and while many of us act like we're still in our twenties, we're not. She needs to make friends her own age. And she needs to reconnect with her family. They do love her, you know."

"Her parents didn't stand by her. What kind of love is that?"

"Complicated, I'd say. I suspect that the Howes have their reasons for acting the way they did. Lili caught them by surprise with her news, and then she ran away and hid. That's fine for a period of time, but don't let her drag it on too long."

"Me? What do I have to do with any of it?"

"You'll have to reach out to her brother."

Brick halted. "Oh no. I'm not telling Derek where she is. She asked me not to. She'd kill me. Besides, I don't break my word."

"She wasn't being truthful with you when

she asked for that word. That gives you an out. She'll be angry, true. And that anger will stand her in good stead. She'll need it."

Brick knew he was missing a piece of the puzzle. "What is it you're not telling me?"

Patsy patted his arm. "Listen to what I am saying, dear. It's obvious from your recent behavior that you care about Lili."

"Hold on. It's not like that," he defended. "I'm just trying to watch out for her."

"Yes, you keep telling yourself that, CDD. I firmly believe that Liliana is destined to become a strong woman. She will learn to protect her gentle heart without changing its essence. Since you care about her, I know that you will want to support her on her path. That's why you need to keep those two things I've mentioned . . . well, make that three things . . . in mind. She needs friends. She needs family."

"And the third thing?"

"She needs to get laid."

Brick raked his fingers through his hair and his voice climbed half an octave as he said, "Why in the world are you telling me that?"

Patsy splayed her hand against her chest and spoke with exaggerated innocence. "You have declared yourself her protector, have you not? You're playing her white knight?"

"I'm not playing anything. I'm just . . . filling in for her brother. And believe me, Derek would not go around facilitating his sister's hookups."

"No, I don't imagine he would. I've never met Dr. Howe, but Lili has spoken of him often."

Patsy stopped walking and Brick realized that they had reached her RV. Apparently, their walk — and thus their conversation — was over. He didn't know if that made him feel better or worse.

"Thank you for joining me, Brick. I do feel better about things now."

Why? I sure as hell don't. "Patsy, she's my best friend's little sister. I'm not going to . . . to . . ."

She patted his arm. "Just remember what our friend Celeste likes to say. 'Love is what gives an angel's wings lift.' "

She disappeared inside her RV long before Brick found his voice. He spoke to her closed door in a low voice. "Love isn't on the table, Patsy. Not now, not ever.

"And I'm damned sure not an angel."

"You look like an angel."

Rather than roll her eyes like she wanted to, Lili smiled at the doctor from Denver and wondered how often his lines worked for him. Actually, she wondered if he truly was a doctor from Denver. Denver she could believe. Something about the hazy gleam in his eyes made her wonder if the closest he came to a hospital was a dispensary.

"Aren't you sweet," she said, purposefully brightening her smile because her self-appointed bodyguard had just entered the bar. With a beautiful brunette.

His date.

Lili's stomach sank. So much for her fishing acumen. Brick Callahan was being painfully uncooperative. Catch and release? *Hah.* Two weeks of trolling with bait fish on the line and so far she'd been skunked. Not even a nibble from the prize.

All she'd gotten from Brick was the stink-eye.

No more hot looks. No more stolen kisses. No more touches of any kind. On the rare occasions when he spoke to her, he called her Lili or Liliana. No more mermaid or Lili-fair.

The burst of self-confidence that she'd experienced the day of their fishing trip had fizzled. The last ember died out when she saw him place his hand at the small of the brunette's back and lead her toward a booth.

Lili brightened her smile a little bit more and managed not to lose it when the Denver dude gave her a wink.

She hadn't even wanted to come out to the Bear Cave tonight. She'd had every intention of attending this evening's Alley-cat activity. But when word got around the Stardance Ranch laundry that Brick had a date tonight, her pride wouldn't let her stay home, even though it meant missing the second wood-burning lesson.

Lili had wanted to be there for that. She had her trailer canopy welcome sign half-done. Everyone else would have theirs finished and on display tomorrow, and her poor little trailer would look even more naked than it already did.

The majority of the club had been decorating their campers for years. And redecorating. And decorating some more. They all had a basic theme, and then a theme on top of that theme, and sometimes yet another on top of that.

Lili's trailer didn't even have a name. She needed to do something about that. She'd been working on it, but so far nothing she'd come up with seemed right. She wasn't one for personification. No Molly's or Maribeth's or Mabel's. But at the same time, she couldn't come up with a decent concept, either.

"So, Lili," said the doctor. "Do angels' dreams always come true?"

Oh, brother. She really, truly didn't want to hear the follow-up to that come-on question. So when a seasonal ranch hand from the Bar L tapped her on her shoulder and asked her to dance again, she gratefully accepted.

Billy Bodine was tall and wiry and actually kind of cute. A terrible dancer, though, she'd discovered earlier tonight after he stepped on her feet as often as he missed them. He was also seven years younger than she and head over heels for a hometown girl, the daughter of a farmer in Pampa, Texas. Billy planned to formally ask for her hand in marriage when she visited him for the Fourth of July weekend.

"Thanks for dancing with me again, Lili. I know I'm lousy at it, but I'm trying real hard to learn. I know Leah wants dancing at our wedding, and she'll be wearing white shoes. Could be a disaster."

Lili laughed, her first genuine response since Dr. Denver had approached her. "You'll get the hang of it, Billy."

"I sure hope so."

They both winced when he stepped particularly hard on her left instep during a twirl. "Sorry."

"Not a prob— Whoa." She tripped over his feet and stumbled into him. His arms wrapped around her as he steadied her.

She caught a glimpse of Brick's stormy expression right before Billy released her, and suddenly she was tired. Tired of casting her line. Tired of reeling it in empty. Tired of making a fool of herself.

So much for fishing for marlin. If she truly wanted to find her inner Alleycat, she needed to change course. Change bait. Forget about fishing for a trophy.

"Guppy, anyone?"

Billy gave her a puppy dog grin. "What's that?"

"Nothing. Never mind." Despite her efforts to avoid looking at Brick, she spied him striding toward the men's room. Suddenly free from his judgmental stare, she took the opportunity to relax. This time, it was she who misstepped. The heel of Billy's boot came down on her hard.

She gasped and yanked up her hurt foot, hopping on the other. Did she just hear something break?

"Oh no," Billy said. "That was bad. Wasn't

it? Can you walk? You don't need to walk. Here."

He scooped her up into his arms. "Shall I take you to your table? Want to go outside?"

She hurt. She really hurt. She wanted to whimper a little bit and let the tears fall. Her heart hurt just as much as her foot. "I think I'm done for the night. I rode here with Sharon. Would you mind taking me back to Stardance, Billy?"

"I'll be happy to."

By now they'd caught the notice of other people in the bar. Sharon hurried up to them. "Lili, what's this? Are you okay?"

Out of the corner of her eye, she saw Brick return to the barroom. She acted on instinct. Throwing her arms around Billy's neck, she said, "I'm fabulous, Sharon. I'm leaving with Billy. I'll find my own way home."

Sharon cast a glance from Lili to Brick. Brightly, she said, "You go, girl. Have fun!"

"I plan to." She rested her head on Billy's shoulder and lowered her voice to a tone only he could hear. "Get me out of here now, please."

"Are we trying to make somebody jealous?" he asked, whispering in her ear.

"No. Yes. Well . . ."

"Then let's make a grand exit, shall we?"

He slowly twirled her around as he headed toward the exit, graceful now that he no longer had another set of feet to worry about. At the door, he hesitated, bending his face toward hers as though he intended to kiss her but positioning them both so that no one inside could see for sure. He swept her outside into the cool night air, lifted his head, and asked, "So, who is he? Callahan?"

"I'm that transparent?"

"No." Billy gave a little laugh. "*He* is. I've noticed before. He watches you like a hawk."

"Not a hawk," she replied glumly. "A brother. He's my brother's friend, so he's decided he needs to fill in for him."

"Oh. Funny, the way he looks at you isn't exactly brotherly." Billy's brow lowered in a frown. "So, is he going to come out to the Bar L tonight wanting to pound on me?"

"No." She didn't think Brick would do that. But then, she didn't really know what Brick would do. Probably nothing. Because even though he'd kept a close eye on her, he had yet to interfere. Obviously, her ploy had not worked. "If he does anything, it'll be pounding on my door and giving me grief."

Billy carried her to the passenger side of a red Chevy pickup and set her carefully on the ground. "How's the foot doing? Do you think it's broken? Do I need to take you by the clinic?"

"No, it'll be fine. Just take me . . . ," she trailed off. She didn't want to go back to the RV camp. What if Brick did come knock on her door to scold her? What if he didn't come back to camp at all tonight? After all, he was with a beautiful woman. He certainly hadn't rushed out of the bar to prevent Lili from leaving, had he? He'd probably spend the night with the brunette. Or bring her back to his tree house.

Lili absolutely, positively wasn't in the mood for that.

". . . not to Stardance, Billy. Please, take me to Angel's Rest. I'll soak my foot in the hot springs and rent a room if they have one available. I could use a little break from life in the trailer park."

"I'm sure sorry to cause you trouble, Lili. I'm just such a clumsy oaf."

"No, you're not. This one was my fault. Now, tell me more about this girl of yours. You say she likes to ride?"

"Loves it. That's the common interest that brought us together." He shared details about his Leah all the way to the front door of Angel's Rest. "I'm going to go in with you, make sure you're walking okay and can get a room."

"You're a gentleman, Billy."

"It's the way my mama raised me."

Lili did manage to walk, and she was delighted when the desk receptionist told her they had two available rooms. She thanked Billy, promised she'd dance with him again sometime, then hugged him good-bye.

"The first room is in a newly opened section of the resort," the friendly teenager said as Lili handed over her credit card. "Have you heard about the cave?"

"No."

"It's awesome." The girl's pretty eyes brightened. "Celeste got the idea to build it after she saw what Brick Callahan has done with the springs at Stardance River Camp. Our building is built over a hot springs, and there's a natural cave and hot pool that acts like a sauna and hot tub all in one. It's fabulous."

The last thing Lili wanted tonight was a reminder of Brick. "I'm sure it is, but I'm afraid this was a last-minute visit. I don't have a swimming suit with me. I just want to relax and take a bubble bath. Where is your other available room?"

"It's upstairs here in the main house."

A familiar figure entered from the kitchen,

a wide smile on her face. "Lili," Celeste said. "How lovely to see you. I missed you tonight."

"I wish I'd stayed for the lesson."

Celeste waved dismissively. "I'll be back next week. We didn't get a lot accomplished, I'm afraid. The girls got to telling me tornado stories, and then Josh wandered into the room to fix the icemaker and before it was done he'd opened up some about his history. Such tragedy he's faced. I hope Eternity Springs is able to work its magic on him."

Lili knew the facts about Josh's bad weather luck, but she didn't know details. Before she could ask, Celeste addressed the desk clerk, "Which room do we have open, Melissa?"

"Number nine."

Celeste wrinkled her nose. "No, that won't do. Liliana needs a luxurious soak in the bathtub. We had a late cancellation and our honeymoon cottage is unoccupied tonight. Give her that — at the same rate as number nine."

Honeymoon cottage? All by herself? Could anything be sadder . . . or more appropriate?

But she couldn't refuse the offer. Not with Celeste looking so pleased with herself. And shoot, at the rate she was going, this might be the only opportunity she'd ever have to spend the night in a honeymoon cottage.

Feeling a little sorry for yourself, Howe?

Sure am. Just stick a fork in me; I'm done.

"You will absolutely love it, Lili, dear," Celeste continued. "It's the perfect place to pamper yourself. As much as I love my little canned-ham trailer, I will admit that it's always nice to come home and have room to stretch out."

"Thank you, Celeste. Where do I — ?"

"It's isolated, of course. I'll take you over in the golf cart." She wiggled her fingers and the teen handed over an old-fashioned metal key on a white satin ribbon. "Follow me."

Having surrendered, Lili did as she was told. Celeste led her to a golf cart painted gold and sporting the Angel's Rest logo in celestial blue. The innkeeper drove the vehicle like a madwoman. Lili was glad that the near-full moon illuminated the path because she really didn't want to be the reason why a guest got run over while on a nighttime stroll across the grounds of the healing center and spa.

Along the way, Celeste chatted constantly. She talked about the Alleycat meeting and her book sales and asked if Lili had an interest in playing baseball while she was in the area. "Our adult league has grown enough to field three teams, but we are desperate for subs, especially as we head into the busiest weeks of the summer season. Many of our small-business owners simply don't have time for recreation in July. Claire Lancaster owns Forever Christmas. She has missed the last two games. Brick told me yesterday that he'll probably have to quit altogether."

In that case . . . "I can probably sub from time to time, Celeste."

"Excellent. I'm so glad. It's a wonderful way to enjoy our lovely summer weather and make new friends."

"You can never have enough friends, I guess."

"Exactly. Now . . . here we are." Celeste braked to a stop in front of a dollhouse of a cottage.

Yearning washed through Lili. What would it be like to be arriving at a place like this with the man she loved, the man she'd married, at her side?

I'm lonely.

The realization weighed heavily on Lili's shoulders as she climbed out of the golf cart and followed Celeste inside. It was true. Lili had great new friends and if their interests were sometimes different from hers . . . well . . . she couldn't complain. She might not have grandchildren to go on about and as a rule she didn't find talk about blood pressure and cholesterol levels all that interesting, but hey, had she ever laughed any harder than she had at last night's pole-dancing lesson?

And I can always get a dog. She could get a dog tomorrow, in fact. Nothing was holding her back from that.

Celeste showed her how the lights worked, where to turn the gas fireplace on and off, and how to operate the lighting on the outdoor in-ground hot tub. Then she handed Lili the key, saying, "You'll find a bathrobe in the closet and towels are out by the hot tub. Like I said, we had a very late cancellation, so there is champagne on ice, a cheese tray, and fruit. They are included in the price of the room, so enjoy yourself."

"Thank you, Celeste."

The older woman patted Lili's hand, then surprised her with a kiss on the cheek. "Don't despair, my sweet. Throughout history, the men and women who make a world a better, brighter place — the teachers and the talented, the firemen and philanthropists and physicians, the artists and, yes, the accountants — have been people who had to build a bridge over a river of challenges and cross it in order to find the angel inside of them. Only after they discovered that inner angel did the universe open up to them. They dreamed, and achieved those dreams. They grew their wings. They learned to fly.

"The thing you must remember is that each and every angel is an individual. Her talents are her own. Each angel has her own flight plan. Embrace yours and sail."

Uncertain how to respond, she said, "Angels seem to be a theme tonight."

"I speak of them quite a lot. I do like to empower my friends with the discovery of their inner angel. You have the tools to build your bridge, Liliana. Make it a priority and allow her to lift you out of the quicksand of perceived limitations. Allow yourself to love like an angel. That's the secret to happiness and joy."

For some weird reason, Lili got a lump in her throat.

"I'm going now. If you need anything, just call the office. I hope you sleep well, dear."

"Thank you. Thank you for everything, Celeste."

"My pleasure."

Lili shut and locked the door behind her hostess and then wandered around the cottage, looking in drawers and closets, exploring the basket of soaps and lotions in the bathroom and the collection of lotions and oils beside the oversized bed. It was a luxurious place, a comfortable place, a sensual place.

"I might as well relax and enjoy it," Lili said aloud, drifting toward a bookcase full of books, hardbacks and paperbacks, thrillers, mysteries, and romances. She chose a historical romance and flipped the switch to light the fire. She opened the champagne, poured herself a glass, and carried it and the cheese tray to the table beside the recliner in front of the fire.

She switched on some soft instrumental music, settled into her chair, and prepared to be swept away by a pirate story. Instead, her mind kept returning to the stormy look on Brick's face when Billy carried her out of the Bear Cave.

Brick didn't want her, but he didn't want anyone else to want her, either. How fair was that?

She took a long sip of champagne and decided she needed to put him out of her mind. She needed to move on. Maybe she should find another RV camp. Maybe find another camping club.

But that would mean leaving Patsy and

the new friends she'd made, and she didn't want to do that. Neither did she want to let Brick drive her away.

One thing these last two weeks of trolling had taught her: She could get a legitimate date if she wanted one. Maybe that was the most important thing she needed to do — start dating seriously and actively. Forget playing the barfly routine. She didn't enjoy it. Neither did she want to tell her future children that she met their father in a bar.

"If I ever have any children," she grumbled, refilling her champagne glass and toasting her little pity party.

She ate a bite of Brie and tossed the pirate romance aside. Standing, she began pacing the room. She'd gone out of her way to avoid meeting local single men, but it was time for that to stop. Eternity Springs was as good a place as any to attempt to meet someone. She had nothing to return to in Oklahoma City. She could always sign up on one of the online dating sites. She wouldn't mind driving a little ways to have a real date.

Maybe before she did that she should see about getting a real job.

Nothing in numbers. Maybe she could get a teaching certificate and teach school. Or open a flower shop. She loved flowers and she was excellent at arranging them. Did Eternity Springs have a florist? She couldn't recall seeing one. Maybe she could open a flower shop here in Eternity Springs. She liked this little town. She enjoyed — *No. No.* This was Brick's hometown. She couldn't.

Or could she? What was it Celeste said? Build a bridge over a river of challenges and on your deathbed you'll find total consciousness. *Gunga, gunga lagunga.*

Lili closed her eyes, knowing that Celeste had somehow gotten mixed up with *Caddyshack.*

Not consciousness, then. Happiness. And not on your deathbed, but when you build your bridge over troubled water. Or something like that.

Lili let out a giggle. Ordinarily, she wasn't one who giggled, but the champagne had gone to her head.

The bottom line was that this was still America, Danny, to quote *Caddyshack,* and she could live in Eternity Springs if she wanted. If she managed to build her bridge to the not-giving-a-flip-about-an-old-crush shore, then she could arrange flowers here if she wanted.

Celeste's voice echoed through her mind. *Love like an angel.*

Sudden tears filled her eyes. Her throat got tight and her chest physically hurt. Giggles to tears in fifteen seconds. *Welcome to my world.* "I'm so tired of being alone."

Needing a change of scenery, she grabbed the champagne bottle and stepped outside. She switched the lighting in the hot tub to a faint blue and decided she might as well soak her feet. They both hurt.

She kicked off her sandals, sat on the coping of the spa, and sank her feet into the blissfully hot water. It felt divine.

At some point during the next hour, she drank half the bottle of champagne. At some point, she lay back upon the wood decking and gazed up at the moon and stars. They spun a little bit. Twice she thought she saw one shoot across the sky, but that could have been the alcohol. Or her angel.

Celeste's voice brushed through her thoughts as gentle as an angel's wing. *Only after they discovered that inner angel did the universe open up to them. They dreamed, and achieved those dreams. They grew their wings. They learned to fly.*

Liliana fell asleep and she dreamed. In her dreams, she learned to fly.

CHAPTER TWELVE

Brick didn't sleep worth a damn, and it wasn't because he was better occupied.

When he'd made reservations at the Yellow Kitchen for his second date with Jennifer, he'd had every intention of trying to romance his way into receiving an invitation back to her house at the end of the night. Ever since his conversation with Patsy, he'd been unable to banish the idea of getting laid. Yes, she'd been talking about Liliana's dry spell, but Brick was working on one of those of his own.

The date certainly had started off well enough. Jennifer had answered the door dressed to kill in a little black number and do-me heels. She'd entertained him through dinner with amusing stories about some of her real estate clients and listened attentively when he talked about his abbreviated baseball career. When, at the end of the meal, he asked if she'd like to go somewhere for a drink and dancing, he'd sincerely intended to take her out to the new dance hall at his family's compound on Hummingbird Lake. The Callahans' arrival had been delayed, so he'd have had the place entirely to himself and Jennifer.

Just how they'd ended up at the Bear Cave instead he couldn't say.

All right. That was a lie. Jennifer had asked to see River Camp, so he'd given her a tour. On the way back, he'd made a sweep through the RV camp to show her some of the vintage trailers they'd discussed at dinner and he'd timed it just right — or wrong, depending on your viewpoint — to see Liliana emerge from her trailer wearing a sexy little number of her own.

Red. Clinging, Christmas red. The kind of wrapping that makes a man think about tearing it. Off. She'd climbed into a car with Sharon. The same Sharon who had given the Alleycats a pole-dancing lesson recently!

He couldn't get the woman in red out of his head.

He lost interest in getting the woman he was with into bed.

However, he'd been too much a gentleman to dump Jennifer and go running after Liliana when she left the Bear Cave with that double-left-footed cowboy. By the time

242

Brick had managed to finesse his and Jennifer's way out of the bar, Lili was long gone and Jennifer wasn't very happy with him.

No lights had glowed in Liliana's trailer when he'd returned to the RV resort and her curtains had hung open. She always closed her curtains when she went to bed.

She wasn't home yet.

Okay, he hadn't really expected her to be back. During the last week or so when she'd gone out at night, she'd closed the bars down.

Brick had told himself he wouldn't wait up for her. It wasn't his place. He'd gone straight to bed, but unfortunately, he'd been unable to fall asleep. He'd kept listening for the sound of cars returning to Stardance, and whenever he'd heard one he'd crawl out of bed to see who'd arrived.

Eventually, he dosed. When he heard an unusual noise around 3:00 a.m. he felt honor bound to check into it. If they were getting nighttime visits from a bear, his people needed to know about it. Never mind that the wildlife motion-sensing camera setup caught everything.

He did a security circuit of the camp in his golf cart. Lili's curtains were still open. She still wasn't home.

He braked the golf cart hard. The tires

slid on the gravel. He sat staring at her moonlit trailer, his fingers drumming on the steering wheel, and told himself that maybe she'd come home tipsy and just forgotten to close her curtains.

Or maybe she'd brought someone back with her. Maybe *he* liked to sleep with window curtains open.

Don't be an idiot. Her truck was the only vehicle in her parking lane. That cowboy certainly hadn't carried her all the way home.

She's not here. That trailer is empty. She didn't come home tonight.

She'd gone and done it. Damned if she hasn't gone out and hooked up with that cowboy and had her one-night stand.

Brick's grip tightened around the steering wheel. His jaw went hard. He jerked his gaze away from the window above her bed and . . . focused on a soda can lying on the road two trailers down from Liliana's. Scowling, he wrenched himself out of the golf cart and marched toward the can. He scooped it up and shifted course, headed for the Dumpster.

Exactly why he was picking up trash at three o'clock in the morning he couldn't say. Maybe because he'd lost his mind?

Maybe because I'm jealous?

244

Maybe because my feelings are hurt?

"You pansy-assed wuss." He drew back his foot and kicked a stone the size of a baseball. Hard. It sailed harder and farther than he'd anticipated, and it banged loudly against the metal Dumpster. He winced, as much from the sound as the pain radiating from his toes.

He was acting downright ridiculous. He had no claim on Liliana. For the past couple of weeks, he'd gone out of his way to establish that. She had every right to sleep with whomever she wanted, whenever she wanted. He knew that.

He just hadn't realized how much it would bother him.

In that moment, fatigue hit him. He needed to get back to bed, back to sleep. He was on the early shift in the morning.

He tossed the soda can into the Dumpster, then returned to his golf cart. He drove home, went to bed, and eventually, fell asleep.

The alarm sounded way too early, but he made it to the office by the scheduled opening at seven. He checked out three campers in the first half hour but sat alone in the office drinking a strong cup of coffee when the sound of a car door caught his attention. He glanced out of the window to see the van belonging to his friend and town veterinarian, Lori Timberlake, pulling away from the Stardance Ranch entrance.

And Liliana Howe was striding toward her trailer, barefoot, head held high, seemingly not a care in the world, swinging her sandals by the straps. Wearing last night's dress. Her grass-stained dress.

His Lili-fair was making the walk of shame.

Be Brazen.

It was the next item Lili intended to add to her Colorado bucket list. Brazen through the hangover. Brazen through the embarrassment. Brazen though the confrontation she fully expected to have with Brick.

Her luck wouldn't allow it to happen any other way.

She'd lain sleeping . . . okay, passed out . . . in the honeymoon cottage's backyard until about 2:00 a.m., at which point she went inside, swallowed two ibuprofens, and drank four glasses of water. She soaked in the luxurious bathtub for almost an hour until she felt sleepy again and climbed naked into the great big lonely bed.

Sunshine on her face had awakened her. She'd still been a little tipsy when she'd crawled into bed, and she hadn't thought to pull the bedroom curtains all the way closed. She lay there snuggled in luxury, her head aching, taking stock of her situation. That nobody had been there to witness her full-blown pity-party meltdown filled her with gratitude.

The question she'd pondered this morning dealt with the next four hours. How did she want to play this? Should she call Patsy or Sharon or one of the other Alleycats and request a ride back to Stardance Ranch? Should she try to get someone from town to drop her off? If she weren't wearing heeled sandals, she'd walk.

That wasn't happening. Her feet were swollen this morning and those shoes had been tight to begin with.

And exactly what was she going to tell Patsy or Sharon or one of the Alleycats? It was a sure bet that word of how she'd left the Bear Cave had swept through camp before she made it back. She'd be the hot topic of gossip during the morning dog-walking circuits.

They wouldn't *all* think that she'd had a hookup with Billy, but some of them would. Considering he'd made no secret of his fiancée, the very idea of that rumor going around made Lili feel bad for Billy and herself. So she wouldn't lie to anyone. She'd tell the truth. She'd tell them she had rented a room at Angel's Rest because she'd been in the mood to soak in a bathtub. The Alleycats would understand that.

Nobody needed to know just what room she'd rented. That's where she drew the pity-party line.

Of course, some of those people wouldn't believe her. She couldn't say she'd blame them. After all, she had been acting slutty of late.

Which brought her to the big question of the morning. How did she want to play this with Brick?

Unless she tried to sneak into camp like a teenager late for curfew, she figured her chances of returning to Stardance without encountering him hovered somewhere between slim and none. He might not be standing there waiting for her arrival, but he'd darn sure make his presence known pretty darn quick. It would crush her soul if he knew she'd spent last night crying over him. Lili had her pride.

So she wouldn't lie to him, either, she'd decided. Not to his face, anyway. If he made false assumptions about her based on what he saw . . . well . . . that was his fault.

And that's how Be Brazen got added to her bucket list.

That's why she accepted Celeste's invitation to join her and Lori Timberlake, the town's veterinarian, for breakfast in the Angel's Rest dining room. Celeste asked about Lili's night. She raved about both the bed and the bathtub and, in doing so, managed to convey her reason for renting a room for the night.

"I totally get it," Lori said. "I'm a soak-in-tub girl myself."

Despite feeling less than 100 percent, Lili did enjoy the breakfast, the company, and the conversation. Toast and tea were all she could manage, but they did help steady her stomach, and her head didn't pound quite so hard. Also, she liked Lori Timberlake very much. She was around Lili's age, friendly, down-to-earth, head over heels in love with her new husband, and an outspoken proponent of pet rescues.

When Celeste offered Lili a ride to the RV park, Lori explained that she had an appointment out beyond Stardance that morning and said she'd be glad to drop Lili off on her way. "Thank you," Lili said. "I appreciate that. Maybe during the drive you can tell me about any small dogs in the area available for adoption."

Lori's eyes gleamed. "You're in the market for a pet?"

"Just thinking about it. I'm not ready to commit yet."

"Fresh meat!" Lori teased, speaking to Celeste from the side of her mouth. Then she patted Lori's hand. "Be assured. I will find you the perfect companion."

"In that case . . ." Celeste's blue eyes twinkled and the slow molasses of the South hung in her voice as she said, ". . . I think you should concentrate on introducing her to some of the two-legged variety before moving on to four."

Lori shared an amused look; then Celeste reached across the table and patted Lili's hand. "Next time you spend the night in our honeymoon cottage, you should have one of those with you. It's much more fun that way."

Lili's blush didn't fade until she climbed into Lori's van for the short trip to Stardance Ranch. At that point she turned her concentration toward getting her brazen face on.

They did talk dogs on the drive. And Lori asked if Lili had met her brother Devin yet. "No," Lili said. "I don't believe so."

"I wasn't sure. He's in and out of town all the time these days on some sort of business he's secretive about. However, when it comes to the two-legged variety of companionship, I have to say that Devin is down-right fine. He'd like you. You're adventure-some."

Complimented, Lili smiled. "Do you really think so?"

"Absolutely I do."

"Thank you very much, Lori."

It was just the thing that Lili needed to hear as they arrived at the RV resort and she prepared to run her personal gauntlet. The next few minutes were bound to be an adventure. For a short time, she'd see how the wicked girls lived.

Somewhere between the day Brick took her fishing and now, she'd figured out that she wasn't cut out for one-night stands. She wasn't her old roommate. Lili never would fly off to Paris with a man who had picked her up in a bar. That wasn't her. She still wanted to get a life, but she needed one that suited her. Not one that she *thought* should suit. Or one somebody else thought should suit. *No, Mom and Dad, I don't want to be an accountant.*

However, since she did have that slutty item on her bucket list, she'd do a little role-playing and allow it to count. She was the boss of the list. She could do that.

But first she had to take off her shoes. They were killing her.

She slipped out of her high-heeled sandals just as Lori pulled her work van to a stop. Lili picked up the red leather wristlet containing her phone, credit card, and spare trailer key and said, "Thanks again for the ride."

"My pleasure."

Lili drew a deep, bracing breath, opened the van's door, and stepped out into the cool mountain morning air. "Brazen," she murmured, squaring her shoulders and lifting her chin. "Act like you haven't a care in the world."

She took one step forward and halted. *Except stepping on a sharp stone.*

She eyed the path before her more closely in order to avoid hazards, then continued. She spied both Patsy and Mary-Ellen out watering their potted plants. Sharon sat on her yoga mat on the grass beside her trailer. Brick's sister Courtney climbed down the outdoor staircase from the apartment above the office where she'd slept since moving to town. Channeling her inner actress, Lili pasted on a sunshine smile and gave them all a little wave.

As she'd expected, Brick stepped outside the office, a mug of coffee in his hand and an unreadable expression on his face. *Of course he's here. I knew he would be.*

Why couldn't I have been wrong?

He watched her, deliberately sipping his coffee, but he didn't speak as she walked past. Lili began to breathe easier. She might have even strutted just a little bit. Brazen. *Yep, that's me. I'm the GOAT. I'm the brazen GOAT. Brazen and doing the walk of shame. Halfway there. A piece of cake.*

She got too confident just a little too soon.

"Why, Liliana Howe," Sharon called out, a smirk on her face. "You naughty girl."

Courtney added, "Those look like grass stains on your dress. It's obvious you had fun last night."

Lili spied dismay on Mary-Ellen's face and she worked to keep her smile from slipping. *And this is real embarrassment. I am so not cut out for sluthood.*

She might have given up the charade, dropped her sandals, and dashed for her door had Brick's gaze not rested so heavy on her shoulders. Because it did, she had no option but to continue to be brazen.

"Did you get a chance to try out what you learned at pole-dancing class?" Sharon asked.

The *thunk,* then *crash* of a coffee mug against the porch decking on the office brought Lili's attention back to Brick. His expression was easily readable now. The man was torqued.

He looked down at the broken mug, then up at her. In a dry year, his glare could have started a forest fire. Suddenly he whirled around and disappeared back inside the office.

With Brick gone, beneath Mary-Ellen's disappointed stare Lili's brazen faltered. She picked up her pace, ignored the discomfort caused by rocks and debris against her bare feet, and dug her key from her wristlet long before she reached her door.

When she finally escaped inside, she shut the door behind her, leaned back against it, and whooshed out a breath. "I did it. It's over. I'll explain to Mary-Ellen and Patsy later."

First, though, she needed out of this dress and into yoga pants and a T-shirt. And sneakers. In fact, maybe she'd go for a run.

Just as soon as she shook this headache.

Lili changed clothes, popped two more painkillers, and crawled into bed for a nap. She slept an hour and forty-five minutes and awoke feeling like a new woman.

Now what she needed was that run.

He didn't follow her.

Okay, so, maybe he did follow her.

But he'd been planning to go for a run

himself. Hadn't he asked Josh to come in an hour early to cover him? Hadn't he already changed into running shorts? He honestly had planned to go running.

After his nap.

But then he saw her leave and he knew the route she took when she ran — the mountain bike circuit that took her around the kid fishing hole and past the tent camping section to the footbridge over the river. It was a comfy little two-mile run. Something he sometimes did as a warm-up.

Without really thinking it through, he put on his shoes and headed out, going the opposite direction from her. He figured he'd go at a nice, slow pace and meet her at about the halfway mark where a picnic bench sat between the riverbank and a stand of aspen.

He didn't figure on the extra speed that his anger gave him. He ran the mile in record time, then, winded, knelt beside the river and splashed cold water in his face.

He couldn't believe she'd let that left-footed cowboy pick her up. Not Liliana. Not after she'd spent two weeks trolling him.

At least, he'd thought that's what she'd been doing. He'd sent her mixed messages that day up at the waterfall, and he'd thought she'd been trying to tempt him, to seduce him. Liliana had been . . . cute . . . about it. A little awkward. Obviously inexperienced, something he found endearing. Trying to make a man jealous was a tried-and-true weapon in a woman's bag of wiles, and she'd simply been . . . innocent . . . about it.

Until last night.

Boy, had she had him fooled.

He hadn't believed she'd been serious about that nonsense she'd spouted up at the waterfall. Her and her ridiculous Life GOAT idiocy. He'd thought the entire rant had been a reaction to the mixed messages he'd sent her by kissing her senseless, then pushing her away.

Life GOAT. What a stupid idea. Stupid series of ideas. Pick up a biker. Pick up a banker. She'd never said a single word about a cowboy half her age.

And Brick had never believed she'd actually go through with it. *She's a Howe. Howes aren't stupid. Howes aren't hos.*

So maybe it was something else. This behavior reeked of payback. Of manipulation. He wouldn't have thought that of Liliana. That was Tiffany's M.O., not Lili's. It was exactly the sort of thing that Tiffany would have done. Hell, the sort of thing she *had* done. Dammit, he'd thought Liliana was different. He felt . . . betrayed.

Hell, Callahan. She's a woman. What did you expect?

Standing, he gave his head a shake, sending the water droplets flying. Maybe he wasn't being fair about the woman part. He knew plenty of good, decent, nonmanipulative women. His mother, for one. Annabelle. All of his aunts. Half the women in town. Before the events of last night, he'd have included Liliana in that company.

Now . . . damn, he was pissed.

He heard the crack of brittle leaves and the rattle of dislodged stones. He turned toward the path, his hands naturally lifting to rest on his hips.

She ran with a smile on her face, her long blond ponytail swinging from side to side. She looked fresh and energetic and beautiful. She looked happy.

While Brick was tired, achy, and cranky. He moved onto the path. Liliana saw him and abruptly stopped.

With scorn in his tone, Brick said, "Goats are barnyard animals."

She blinked. "Excuse me?"

"Life goat? I thought you were all hormonal and making up stuff. I didn't think you meant it. And you never said anything about a teenage cowboy."

Liliana folded her arms. "Billy is not a teenager. He's a college senior."

"Well, whoop-de-do."

She closed her eyes and softly counted to five. "What are you doing out here, Brick? Does the word 'stalker' mean anything to you?"

"It's my property. I can go wherever I want."

"Now who's the teenager? Check that. I mean eight-year-old."

"Are you proud of yourself, Liliana Howe?"

She advanced on him, her eyes flashing fury and her cheeks flushed. "Beyond your capacity as the lizard from whom I'm renting space for my fifth wheel, you have no say in what I do or who I do it with. You are not my brother, my lover, my mother, or my priest! You're not my anything."

"I'm your friend!"

"You're everybody's friend! I get that now. Heaven knows I've heard it enough from everybody in town. Brick Callahan, Eternity Springs' Ambassador of Friendship."

"No need to be snotty, Liliana."

"I'm feeling snotty."

"Oh? I thought that was 'slutty.' "

She sucked in a breath as the arrow landed. "You jerk." She pushed past him, ready to continue down the path. "Here's a news flash, Callahan. I don't need friends like you."

He caught her arm. Held her. "I'm sorry. Sorry. That was mean."

She flattened her lips in a grim smile. "Yes, it was."

"I'm just . . . I wish . . . dammit, Liliana, I didn't think you'd go that far. It shouldn't have happened. If I'd known you were going to go that far I would have . . ."

"You would have what?"

He set his teeth, biting back the words that, once spoken, had the potential to change everything. And Brick wasn't ready for that kind of change.

When he failed to answer her question, Liliana sighed. "Look, Callahan. You can quit beating yourself up over failing in your self-appointed guardianship duty. It didn't happen. I wanted to soak my feet in a hot bubble bath, so Billy dropped me off at Angel's Rest. I spent the night there. Alone. Now, if you'll excuse me . . ."

"A bubble bath?" The relief that washed through him was way too strong for his peace of mind. She tried to pull away, but he tightened his grip.

"My trailer only has a shower. Your shower rooms only have showers. I wanted a bath."

"But this morning . . . you acted . . ."

"Brazen. It's harder than it looks. And, frankly, less fun than I anticipated. After I finish my run, I'm going to take another look at my lists. Probably do some editing."

"Oh." Brick rubbed the back of his neck. He didn't know what to say to her. He didn't know what he wanted to say.

Was he disappointed that he could no longer begin to justify finishing that unspoken observation? *If I'd known you were going to go that far I would have asked to be your hookup.*

"Liliana . . . look. I understand that you desire changes in your life. Those asshats at your firm shook your world. But I don't think that the way you've gone about trying to make your changes is necessarily healthy."

"You're wrong. The last two weeks haven't been about my job or the firm or anything but my inability to let go of old dreams. I'm glad they happened because I've learned something about myself. I've been focusing on the wrong thing. It's not about sex. I'm not cut out for one-night stands. Trust me, I could have had a couple in the last weeks. You were right. It's not me. I still want to be a Life GOAT, but I have to make that life one that is right for me. I still want that spur-of-the-moment trip to Paris. Only not

260

with a man I've just met. I want a relation-ship, Brick."

Crap. He'd known that. Hadn't he known that? "I don't, Liliana. Been there, done that."

"I know that, Brick." Regret softened her eyes. "We all have our issues to overcome. Mine is trying to please my parents. Yours is . . ." — she hesitated a moment before finishing — ". . . something different."

Not something. Someone.

Tiffany.

"The sad thing is, I said I didn't want regrets anymore. I regret that you won't re-alize that not all women are like Tiffany Lambeau. I think you're a great guy, even when I'm irritated with you. It's a shame that you're living with her shadow looming over you."

Brick released Lili's arm. She gave him a sad little smile, then jogged off toward the kid fishing hole.

He watched her go, feeling helpless. When she disappeared around a bend in the path, Brick experienced a sense of loss he knew was going to pain him for a very long time.

CHAPTER THIRTEEN

Lili took three days to reevaluate her list and formulate a plan for moving forward with her life. She quickly realized that the bucket-list approach wasn't working for her, so she scrapped it. Analytical by nature, she did better with decision trees and spreadsheets.

She spent a considerable amount of time with Patsy and the other Alleycats asking questions about their lives and loves. Because they were on average thirty years older than she, they had a wealth of experience to share. She also talked to Celeste, who had a way of offering sound advice and soothing counsel. At Celeste's suggestion, once Lili felt like she'd done her research, she took the journal covered in lovely angel wing fabric that Celeste had given her and went up to the inspiring scenic overlook, Lover's Leap. Looking out at the expansive vista of mountains and valley and heavenly blue sky, she spent half a day not actively thinking, but more absorbing.

Then she put pen to paper and let her feelings flow. She began with the moment she realized she'd been set up to take the fall and wrote until she'd filled half the pages. She cried a little bit but laughed some, too. When she finally reached the point where she recorded the confrontation with Brick during her run, she was exhausted and emotionally drained.

She slept like the dead that night, the best sleep she'd had in months. The following morning, she took her coffee and computer outside and, in half an hour, had her plan.

Lili identified three primary areas she needed to address in her quest for happiness and fulfillment: career, friendships, and romance. While she abandoned her bucketlist approach, she kept the Life GOAT concept, only tweaked.

From this day forward, Lili intended to work toward accomplishing GOHLs. Not the Greatest Of All Time, but the Greatest Of Her Life. She would live her life in such a way that she'd have the greatest job of her life, make the greatest friends of her life, and have the greatest romance of her life.

Neither Brick Callahan nor one-night stands would be part of it.

If she felt a little pang in the vicinity of her heart, well, she was simply going to ignore it.

"You look pleased with yourself," came Patsy's familiar voice.

Lili glanced up from her computer screen to see her friend striding toward her. This, she thought, was the prototype she would use for her friendship GOHL. Despite the difference in their ages, she and Patsy had bonded since the moment Lili answered her ad for a garage apartment tenant. What they'd lacked prior to this Colorado trip was spending time together. It was a lesson Lili would keep in mind going forward. Smiling, she gestured for Patsy to join her. "I *am* pleased with myself. I've been thinking about how lucky I am to have you as my friend."

"Well, honey child, that's a sweet thing to say."

"It's true. You and the Alleycats have changed my life, Patsy. Joining you up here is the best decision I've ever made."

Patsy's look turned knowing. "Despite the blast from the past?"

"Yes." Lili realized she could say that without hesitation and her smile widened. She had told all the Alleycats about the truth behind her night away from Stardance

Ranch. However, Patsy was the only Alley-cat with whom Lili had shared the real reason behind her sudden desire for a bubble bath. "Now that it's behind me, I can admit I learned a lot about myself during the past couple of weeks. I know now that I can test my wings and still survive if I fall. That's good experience, don't you think?"

"Oh, sweetheart, it's excellent experience. I'm so happy to hear that you haven't allowed this bump in the road to send you running."

Bump in the road? Like roadkill? "I'm not running," she confirmed. "Honestly, I feel better about my life than I have in a long time. I finally have a plan."

"So all the questions you've been asking have paid off? You've figured out what you're going to do about a job when the summer is over?"

"No." Lili decisively shut her computer. "But I've decided that even if I were to fight for my license and win, I definitely will not go back to accounting."

Patsy pursed her lips in a frown. "You've been saying that all along."

"True, but this is the first time I believe it. I think I want to do something that allows for a little creativity. That's as far as

I've gotten, but I have time to figure it out. It's still June."

"For two more days." Patsy waved at two Alleycats out walking their dogs. "I can see you doing something creative, Lili. You obviously enjoy the Alleycats' craft activities. I like that you are thinking outside the box."

"I'm done with boxes."

"Fabulous. In that case, I hope I'll be able to talk you into accompanying me on a bit of an adventure this afternoon?"

Lili eyed her friend warily. She wanted to immediately agree to anything Patsy asked, but experience had taught her to beware of Patsy's definition of adventure. "Does it involve any kind of jumping?"

Patsy gave her eyes an exaggerated roll. "No ropes. No harnesses. No sails of any type involved today. But I do think you should reconsider the parasailing. It's quite a different sensation from zip lining. I know that wasn't particularly your favorite. But no, this will be a laid-back adventure. A little walking, picnic, just you and me. I have something I'd like to discuss with you."

"A picnic sounds wonderful. We could go up to Lover's Leap. I was there yesterday and it was simply fabulous."

"Actually, I have another place in mind. This is where it comes in handy for me that you aren't running from Brick."

Lili's smile faltered. "Brick. This adventure involves Brick?"

"He had planned to take me fishing today up at some special place on his private land. I've heard about the waterfall and want to see it. He offered to take me up this afternoon because he needs to drop something off at Stardance River Camp and it's apparently just over a ridge from the picnic spot. He said he doesn't think you could find your way on your own, but he can point out landmarks on the way up so that you'll be able to lead us home."

"So he won't stay with us."

"No. You may not have noticed that he's been away from Stardance the past few days. He's been occupied at River Camp almost constantly. I think he has a special guest up there."

Lili hadn't seen Brick since their confrontation. She'd assumed he had been avoiding her on purpose. Or maybe spending time with his brunette.

"He'll just lead us there and we'll be on our own. That should be all right with you, shouldn't it? Since you're not running."

"You've boxed me in nicely, Patsy."

"No, I haven't. You're done with boxes, remember? Think of this as another chance to test your wings. I understand that four-wheeling is a lot of fun. We'll each have our own. Cam Murphy is running a half-day rental special, so I've reserved one for each of us."

"I'll get to drive," Lili said, intrigued. Now that she knew what to expect from the four-wheeler experience, the idea of driving excited her. Besides, she needed to face Brick sometime. Might as well be today when she was feeling so good about herself. "Sure, Patsy, I'd love to go with you. It's a beautiful spot and I've wanted to go fishing again. What can I bring for our picnic?"

"If you'll bring something for dessert, I'll cover the rest. We're to meet him at noon at Refresh. Want me to pick you up?"

Lili considered a moment, then shook her head. "I have some shopping to do. I'll meet you at the sporting-goods store."

Lili took extra care while getting dressed because she intended to stop by Savannah Turner's soap shop, Heavenscents, and Sage Rafferty's art gallery, Vistas, and Maggie Romano's B and B, Aspenglow. She wanted to make a good impression on these Eternity Springs entrepreneurs. She told herself that the fact that she'd see Brick later had nothing to do with it.

It was almost true, too. Almost.

At Heavenscents she took her time making her selections and waited for Savannah to finish assisting the other customers in the store. When the shop emptied but for the two of them, Lili introduced herself and added, "Celeste suggested I talk to you about running a small business. Do you have a few minutes now, or could I make an appointment? Take you to lunch later this week, perhaps?"

"I can talk now." Savannah wore her long blond hair in a braid down her back. "Celeste told me you might be stopping by. So, you are searching for your destiny, are you?"

"Destiny?" Lili shrugged. "I don't know that I'd put it that way exactly, but yes, I need to decide on a new career. I'm exploring what I like and what I think I could be good at. I think Heavenscents is one of the most appealing shops in a town full of appealing shops. How did you decide on handmade soaps?"

Savannah shared how she'd learned soap making from her grandmother and then told a fascinating tale about a stint in prison, her reinvention, and her romance with the Eternity Springs sheriff, of all people. "I will tell you it's difficult to make an excellent living in Eternity Springs because we still don't have much of a winter tourist season. My Internet business grows every year, though. Primarily reorders from tourists who made their first purchase here in the store."

"Quality matters," Lili observed.

"In niche retail, definitely."

The door chime sounded and a man sauntered inside. A lock of thick brown hair fell rakishly onto a forehead above gleaming blue eyes that focused on Savannah such love that it took Lili's breath away. This must be Zach Turner.

"Hey, Peach," he said.

Quality always matters, Lili concluded.

Savannah greeted her husband and introduced Lili. They discussed Stardance Ranch a few minutes; then Lili thanked Savannah for her time and information and took her leave. She made her way to the Vistas art gallery, where she discussed creative occupations with Sage Rafferty until her husband, Colt, arrived with their children.

Lili had an hour before she needed to meet Patsy — and Brick — so next she made her way to Maggie Romano's bed-and-breakfast. Lili already knew that Maggie was the mother of Lucca Romano, the retired professional basketball player and current high school basketball coach. She didn't know until she mentioned that she'd just come from Heavenscents where she'd met both the soap maker and the sheriff that Maggie was Zach Turner's mother, too.

"It's a long story and I really need to be drinking wine to tell it. Celeste told me she'd asked you to come by. I can't tell you how grateful I am. I don't know what I've done to mess my records up so bad. Nothing balances. I think I must be categorizing things wrong. I truly am an intelligent person and I'm an excellent innkeeper, but I hate numbers. I truly hate them. I've been lost since Donna Barton moved away. I know that it's insulting to ask CPAs to do basic bookkeeping, but I'm happy to pay your ordinary hourly rate and Celeste said you wouldn't mind."

Celeste hadn't said word one to Lili about looking at Maggie Romano's books when she suggested Lili visit Aspenglow.

"I'm happy to look at your stuff, Maggie, but only as a friend. I no longer have my license to practice accounting. And honestly, I came here seeking your advice because I'm considering opening a bed-and-breakfast myself. It wouldn't be right for me to dig into your figures."

"Oh, that's lovely news. Eternity Springs can use another B and B. I hate having to turn people away. It looks to me like we could be of great help to each other."

"I'm only just beginning to explore the idea," Lili warned. "I want to get my career right this time. I won't make any decisions quickly."

"Good. You know, you should also talk to my daughter, Gabby Brogan. She changed careers. Went from being in law enforcement to being a glass artist who runs a retail shop."

"Whimsies is your daughter's store? I've shopped there. It's a fun store. And the gallery next door . . ."

"That's Cicero's work. He's a serious artist. Gabby likes to make people smile with her creations."

Lili checked her watch. "I have to meet my friend in forty-five minutes, Maggie. Would you like me to see what I can do with your bookkeeping issues in that amount of time?"

"God bless you."

Quite capable of multitasking, Lili asked Maggie to share her likes and dislikes about being an innkeeper while she tackled Maggie's mistakes in her bookkeeping program. While Lili didn't have time to work through everything, she did manage to clear up a couple of errors and identify a common mistake Maggie continually made. "If you go back through the last few months and correct that error, I bet you'll be able to get this account to balance."

"You are a goddess, Liliana," Maggie Romano said. "I can't thank you enough."

"I'm glad to help."

It was true, she realized as she departed Maggie's B and B and made her way toward Refresh. Maggie Romano was a delightful woman and Lili was happy to help her. She'd also given Lili a lot to think about regarding a possible future as an innkeeper.

Maybe she would talk to Gabby Brogan, Lili decided. *It would be nice to —*

Lili lost her train of thought the moment she caught sight of Brick. He stood talking to Cam Murphy, gesturing wildly and with more than a little frustration. He looked tired and unhappy. Harried, too.

Maybe going on this waterfall trip wasn't such a good idea.

Then he saw her and his first reaction was to smile, which brought a smile to her face in return. If both smiles were a little sad, well, that was still better than mutual scowls.

Cam said something else that grabbed Brick's attention, and when he turned away from her Lili glanced around for Patsy. Thank goodness the older woman was coming up right behind Lili. She wouldn't have to greet Brick by herself.

"I'm so excited about our adventure today," Patsy said. "Thank you so much for agreeing to come with me. I think that . . . oh, dear . . . Brick doesn't look happy, does he?"

Without waiting to hear Lili's response, Patsy strode up to the men. "Nothing like two pretty men standing in front of a place of business to make me want to patronize it. That said, your frowns almost spoil the view. Is something wrong?"

"Not really. Just a little mix-up with my credit card. I'll get it taken care of later."

Cam said, "Patsy, I got a new shipment of flies in yesterday. I picked out a few for you. Shall I add them to your order?"

"Yes, please. Brick assures me that there are at least half a dozen fish in that stream with my name on them today."

"It's his fishing hole. He knows what he's talking about." Cam flashed an easy grin at Lili. "How about you, Lili? Do you need any supplies?"

She glanced at Brick. "Do I?"

"It never hurts to have a few extra flies."

She nodded and said to Cam, "I'd like a fishing hat, too, please."

"Come inside and I'll get you fixed up." He glanced at Brick and said, "Need help loading the rentals?"

"Nah. I've got it handled."

Inside the sporting-goods store, Lili discovered that Patsy had already paid for the rental of both four-wheelers and she sighed. This was becoming a bad habit of Patsy's. Lili might be living off her savings, but she wasn't destitute. She could pay her own way.

Though if she wanted to start a business things could be a little tight for a while. While she hadn't intended to live in her trailer when she bought it, she could do it if necessary. Who knows, maybe she'd find another little town like Eternity Springs somewhere in America and sink her roots. Or park her tires and hook up her electricity. Establish a business. Make friends. Fall in love.

Surely Eternity Springs wasn't the only special small town in this country. Spying a familiar figure riding a mountain bike, Lili waved and murmured, "Hmm . . . wonder if Celeste has a sister somewhere."

"Here you go, Lili," Cam said, handing her the hat she'd chosen with her newly purchased flies fixed expertly to the bill. "Now you'll look like a pro. Good luck out there today. Hope you land a big one."

Lili lifted one side of her mouth in a crooked smile. "I'm not worrying about the size of the fish anymore. My GOHL is to enjoy the experience."

"There you go. That's an excellent goal for a fisherman to have."

When she joined Patsy and Brick outside, the trailer was loaded, hooked up, and they were ready to go. She climbed into the back of the extended-cab pickup and didn't try to join the conversation on the way up to the four-wheeler part of the trip. Although Brick and Patsy talked about town events during the upcoming Fourth of July holiday, he seemed a bit subdued to Lili. Since she couldn't help but think about events that had occurred between them during their last trip up this mountain, she wondered if that was the reason for his preoccupation.

She couldn't have been more wrong.

CHAPTER FOURTEEN

The last time Brick remembered being this grumpy, he'd been on his grandfather's ranch outside of Brazos Bend, Texas, and stepped into a mess of fire ants.

He'd almost rather lie down in a fire ant mound and roll around than deal with the viper who had rented out Stardance River Camp for the next three weeks.

He had to find a new code name for this type of celebrity. "Twinkle" was simply wrong for this piece of work. Hell on wheels, that's who she was. He'd charged her an arm and a leg for the rental. For what he had to put up with, the price was way too cheap. Should have added a kidney, too. Maybe a lung and a liver.

In the years since his dad had come into his life, Brick had grown accustomed to people with money. His grandfather had oil and ranching money. His dad and uncles had made a killing in the dot-com boom.

Some of his friends here in Eternity Springs were downright wealthy. Inventor Flynn Brogan owned his own island in the Caribbean.

Brick had friends who were famous, too. Cicero was a glass artist who regularly dined in the homes of Silicon Valley moguls, and painter Sage Rafferty had students studying her work in art programs in college. Then there was Claire Lancaster. She was both wealthy and famous, having made a bajillion bucks off a children's Christmas story she wrote and turned into a franchise. A second movie was in the works.

And every last one of them was a decent human being.

Unlike the Wicked Witch of the West Coast.

And if she and her retinue weren't enough to deal with, now Cam had informed him that he apparently had credit card issues.

And Liliana Howe was in his backseat smelling like sunshine and lavender — which brought up a whole other sort of cranky.

"So your entire family comes up for the holiday?" Patsy asked.

Glad for the distraction, Brick replied, "Yep. Ordinarily some of them are already here, but my Oklahoma parents went on an

Alaskan cruise with friends and won't show up until the morning of the Fourth. Most of the Callahans stayed in Texas for a wedding last weekend, but they'll start arriving today."

"I'm looking forward to the party at Hummingbird Lake. It was nice of you to invite all the Alleycats."

Brick gave one of his first real smiles of the day. "Hey, y'all make a party fun. Fair warning, my mom and stepmom and aunts are liable to drop hints for invitations to join your club. I've told them you've capped your membership, but they're persistent when they want to be. And they're intrigued. They've been looking for some activity to offset the Callahan men's fishing trips, so this is right up their alley."

Patsy's expression settled into a pleased smile. "I suspect we could make that happen."

Throughout the drive, Brick remained conscious of Liliana's presence behind him. He'd thought about her often the last few days, but he'd not seen any way to reconcile the basic difference in their goals. His reluctant conclusion was that it was best for both of them to halt things now before they got in any deeper.

That didn't mean he didn't still want her.

Didn't still dream about her and wake up hard and aching.

One more reason for his lousy attitude.

He was glad when they reached the trail. He left his windows cracked because he worried that otherwise her appealing scent would haunt him every time he climbed into the truck.

Patsy bubbled like a schoolgirl with excitement. This was her first time on a four-wheeler, so he gave both women a quick lesson on basic handling. "I'll lead the way and we'll take an easy pace. Don't try to pass me, Patsy. I've heard that you're a speed demon."

"Now who told you something like that?" she responded with false offense.

"Most everybody in town who witnessed the ride you took with Celeste on her Gold Wing."

All three of them laughed at that.

Brick led them to the waterfall and nodded with agreement and satisfaction at Patsy's heartfelt wonder at the beauty of the site. Sensing Liliana's stare upon him as he unlocked what he considered his toy box, he glanced over his shoulder. Their gazes met and held.

He pictured how she'd looked and felt beneath him here the day of their picnic, and he mourned what might have been. When she turned away from him, he sighed and continued to unload fishing supplies from the locker. Once that was done, he could think of no good reason to delay his departure any longer.

"I need to get going. Liliana, now that you've made the trip again, are you comfortable finding your way back down to the truck?"

"Yes."

He looked at both women. "Have confidence operating the machines?"

Lili nodded and Patsy said, "They're not nearly as difficult as they look. Besides, I see youngsters on these things all the time. I'm young at heart, so I'll do fine. Thank you, Brick. This is exactly what I needed today. You don't know how much."

"Glad to share, Patsy. This is my favorite place in Colorado." *Even if Liliana will probably haunt me here for the rest of my life.* "I unhooked the trailer from the truck. Just leave the four-wheelers nearby, and Cam's guys will load them up before they haul them back to town. They'll be up this way about five thirty to pick them up. The extra key to the truck is in the storage compartment of your ride, Patsy. If you have any trouble, you can get cell service up above the waterfall and down by the truck. So, any questions?"

The two women shared a look, then Patsy said, "We'll be just fine, Dad."

"I'm sure you will," Brick said with a laugh. He slung his leg over the seat of his four-wheeler and started the engine. "If you catch dinner, I expect you to share."

"It's a deal." Patsy picked up one of the rods he'd left leaning against a tree and tested its give.

Brick met Liliana's gaze once more and the image of the woman he was on his way to meet flashed into his mind. The witch was drop-dead gorgeous with the exotic kind of beauty that lasted throughout a woman's life. Much like Tiffany.

Liliana was the fresh-faced girl next door. Infinitely more appealing.

Why the hell hadn't he noticed it years ago?

Lili and Patsy ate the sandwiches Patsy had brought and decided to save the dessert for a midafternoon snack. Then Lili pointed out the fishing spots Brick had shown her and they went to work. Lili caught six — count 'em, six! — trout. Patsy landed three, all of them bigger than Lili's, before putting her fishing pole away. "That was fun. You know, before my husband got sick, we had planned a fishing trip to Cabo. We wanted to catch a blue marlin."

Lili's lips twisted in a crooked smile. "Trophy fishing. I had that dream, too, for a while."

"I really wish we'd gone," Patsy said, her tone wistful and a little sad. "I'm tired, Lili. I'm going to take a little nap, I think."

"All right."

Patsy stretched out on Brick's quilt, and while she slept Lili hiked up above the waterfall, where she sat for a time thinking about her morning visits with Savannah Turner, Sage Rafferty, and Maggie Romano.

Would she like working retail? she wondered. One could adjust to working weekends. While the B-and-B idea did appeal to her, she didn't know if she'd ever adjust to cooking breakfast every morning. Not that either was a choice for her anytime soon unless she cashed out every investment she owned. Still, it was fun to think about, especially because it kept her brain occupied with something other than Brick while Patsy slept.

"Quarter for your thoughts."

Lili grinned at her friend. She'd been so preoccupied that she hadn't noticed Patsy had made the climb. "Why the extra twenty-four cents?"

"Inflation."

"I'm thinking about the future."

"Well now, that's handy. The future is one of the reasons I asked you to join me this afternoon.

"You know, I had a feeling that this was about more than a picnic." Lili wondered if her friend was about to offer her a job of some sort, though she couldn't imagine what it would be. More likely, Patsy might offer to bankroll whatever career move Lili decided to make next. She couldn't forget that when Tiffany Lambeau went to work at her firm and Lili whined about it over a bottle of wine one Friday night Patsy had offered to finance Lili's return to school if she wanted to pursue another career.

Lili had appreciated the gesture then and she would appreciate it now. However, she wouldn't take Patsy up on it. Fall or fly, Lili wanted to do it on her own.

"What's up, Patsy?"

The older woman handed Lili a bottle of water from her backpack and gestured toward the trail Brick had taken earlier when he left them. "Feel up to a bit of a hike? I'd like to see what's on the other side of that ridge."

"I'm game." Maybe during the hike she'd

find the right words to refuse Patsy's offer without hurting her feelings.

Patsy led the way and took it slow, so the climb to the apex of the trail took twenty-five minutes. Patsy was audibly winded when she took a seat on the trunk of a fir tree that had fallen beside the trail. She took three long sips from her water bottle, then said, "I'm so glad you joined the Alleycats, Lili."

"I am, too."

"This summer is a special time for me, and you're making it all the more meaningful by being part of it."

"That's a nice thing to say. Thank you. It's a special time for me, too."

"I never was blessed with children, but I've come to think of you as family, Lili. You're the daughter . . . okay, the granddaughter . . . I've always longed for. I want you to know that I love you."

"I love you, too, Patsy." *But I can't take your money.*

"I know you do, honey, and that's why this is hard. I can't in good conscience keep the news to myself any longer."

Lili straightened her spine. The conversation had just taken a turn she hadn't anticipated.

Patsy drew in a deep breath, then exhaled

with a murmur of pleasure. "I adore the forest. Being surrounded by trees, with the absolute stillness broken by the sounds of breezes moving the branches and leaves, with the scents. I've always loved the fragrance of Douglas fir— slightly citrus with a hint of floral. It's the gift of Christmas to me. That message of love, hope, and forgiveness. I find a forest to be one of the most relaxing, peaceful places on earth. That's part of the reason I chose the mountains for the Alleycats' summer trip."

"I can't say I've seen you relaxing very much, Patsy."

"No, but I have made peace with what's to come."

What's to come? Wariness fluttered through Lili like aspen leaves in a breeze.

Patsy reached out, took Lili's hand, and squeezed it. "Liliana, I'm on my last campout. I have pancreatic cancer. In April, the doctors told me I probably have six months to live."

The mountain beneath Liliana's feet seemed to quake. Her knees turned to Jell-O and suddenly she was sitting on the ground, her head between her knees. "Breathe, honey," Patsy said, patting her back. "Calm breaths. In and out. There you go."

"Patsy . . . ," Lili said when she could speak again. "You're not sick. You don't look sick. You don't act sick. You're not sick."

"No, I'm not sick because I opted out of the poison pills and for the open road. I'm not going to spend the time I have left in a hospital. I'm not doing chemo. Not doing radiation. I'm going to enjoy my life for as long as the good Lord allows."

"You're not getting treatment?"

"My life. My choice. Don't dare try to tell me I'm not fighting it. Believe me, sunshine, I fight every single day. But I've made the choice to spend these last months living instead of dying and I'm good with that. I'm well and truly having the time of my life."

Lili covered her mouth with her hand. She blinked back tears. "No, Patsy. No."

"I'm going to ask you to keep my confidence. I know I can trust you to do that. It's important to me. I want this summer to be a celebration, not a long-drawn-out death watch."

"You haven't told the other Alleycats?"

"No, I haven't. I probably will at some point. I think that's only fair, but I'm hoping to make it to the end of the summer without needing to do so. I hope to have our big end of summer party, return to our homes, and then I'll send letters. I have no desire to basically attend my own funeral, which is how it would be if I announce it here."

Lili had to work to get the words past her throat. "Why did you decide to tell me?"

"Two reasons. You've become my family, Lili. The way I look at it, that gives me a little say in things. Now, I fully understand that you might not agree. You might even resent what I'm going to do. But, since I'm the old dying hardheaded, manipulative woman, I'm going to do it anyway."

"Oh, Patsy, you're not —"

"You're my family," she interrupted. "Which brings us to the second reason. I've made you my heir, Liliana."

Lili drew back. "Patsy, I don't want your money."

"Then you're a fool. What have you been doing these past few days, child? Exploring your options. Don't you think I've been watching? Don't you think I know you well enough to identify what appeals to you?"

"I don't . . . I don't know what I want yet, Patsy."

"Sure you do. You want to be your own boss."

Lili opened her mouth, then shut it without speaking. Patsy was right. That's why the idea of teaching didn't appeal, the reason why Lili wasn't pulled toward a corporate job in finance.

Patsy patted Lili on the knee. "The thing about starting any business is that you need working capital, and thus you need investors. Of course, then the investors can pull your strings. This way the only person pulling your string is a dead woman — a guaranteed onetime pull."

Lili shoved to her feet and covered her ears with her hands. "No. No. I don't want you to say that. I don't want to hear this. Oh, Patsy. This is just too much, too fast. Back up and tell me about the cancer. Are you certain of the diagnosis?"

"Yes, dear. I did get a second opinion. Actually, I got three opinions and three treatment plans. I did all my research and made a choice that I am totally comfortable with."

Now that she'd absorbed the shock, Lili couldn't hold back her tears. Soon they streamed down her face. Patsy went to her and held her in a comforting hug. "It's okay, honey. I've had a long and wonderful life. I believe in the hereafter and the promise of heaven. I look forward to seeing my darling again."

"But I don't want to lose you. I love you."

"I know, baby. I love you, too."

Patsy shushed her and wiped at her tears and brushed her hair away from her face. "I'm going to ask something of you, Lili. You are going to have to be very strong for me, because I need about seven more weeks of silence from you. No hangdog looks. No sad sniffles. You need to get all your tears out now, because I don't want to see them again. Not over me. Do you understand?"

"I'm not done crying yet."

"Okay. That's okay. It's just the two of us up here. However, I need to do something or I'm going to start crying, too, and I really don't want to do that. Are you up for hiking a little further?"

"I can, but are you sure you are —"

"Stop right there," Patsy said sternly. "I won't be treated as an invalid. I know my own limits and I respect them. You need to trust me."

Lili swiped away her tears with the back of her hand. "Yes, ma'am."

"All right, then. Let our adventure continue. Brick said this trail leads to his River Camp. What do you say we sneak down and check it out?"

"Uninvited?"

"If he's still there, he won't care. If he's not, we can pretend to be tourists who took a wrong turn on the trail and got lost. I want to see these tents of his. And the tree houses, too. They're supposedly something special. Do you know he charges over fifteen hundred dollars a night for them?"

In the process of taking a sip from her water bottle, Lili choked. Coughing, she said, "For one night? In a tent? Fifteen hundred dollars to sleep a night in a tent?"

"With a three-night minimum, I understand."

"Oh my. That's criminal."

"So don't you want to see the tents?"

"Oh yeah. I want to see them. But Sharon told me Brick's sister said he has some high-profile guest. Perhaps we should wait."

"Perhaps. But I don't know that I'll make it up here again. I do so want to see them. We could go partway, survey the scene, and then make a decision?"

Lili found that she couldn't deny Patsy anything at this particular moment. "Let's do it."

The hike down the ridge was challenging at times, and Lili scouted for a walking stick to help Patsy. Then she found one for herself, too.

They were halfway down the mountain when they heard the growl.

CHAPTER FIFTEEN

Brick briefly considered lifting one of the cuticle sticks from the manicure table and stabbing it into his eye. Or, better yet, through the actress's long, lovely throat.

Too bad he wasn't a masochist or a murderer. As the owner/operator of Stardance River Camp he could do nothing except stand there and let her slice him up, down, and sideways with the stiletto she used as her tongue.

When she finally ran down a bit, he ventured, "I assure you, our masseuse is highly trained and he comes to us with fabulous references. He's worked at the Olympic Training Center in Colorado Springs."

"I don't care if he worked at the White House. He's unacceptable. I don't like his hands. I'll expect someone new for my four o'clock massage."

Brick closed his eyes and counted to three. He cleared his voice before he spoke in a modulated tone. "Blake is the only male masseuse I have available. I do have a female who could possibly take your appointment today."

He'd probably have to pay Gina triple her usual rate plus babysit her two kids to get her up here today. She usually worked at the Angel's Rest spa, but she'd taken the summer off to stay home with her elementary-school-aged children. However, Brick knew the kids were in vacation Bible school this week, so maybe she'd take pity on him.

The actress gave a dismissive wave and a disgusted sigh. "Never mind. I'll fly my Tomás in from Beverly Hills, but I will expect some accommodation in my bill. Really, this is just intolerable."

You're telling me.

"We've replaced all the soaps, lotions, and shampoos with the Heavenscents fragrance you requested yesterday." Never mind that the stuff he'd replaced had been imported from France at her demand.

"Well, that's something. I will say the items my assistant has been able to find in town are quality. Perhaps you could arrange an after-hours shopping trip for me? Of course, I'd need signed confidentiality affidavits. And heaven knows, no teenage clerks. Shop owners only."

"I'll see what I can set up. Is there a particular day you'd like to go?"

"I think tomorrow."

"I imagine our businesses would need a little more lead time than that. This is our summer season."

She wrinkled her nose and sniffed. "Try."

Brick managed to keep his expression neutral as he asked, "Anything else before I leave?"

"Yes. Double the number of cinnamon rolls for our breakfast. Broderick particularly likes them."

"Will do. If you think of anything else, you have my number." Brick tipped his hat toward the actress, then used long, fast strides to escape to River Camp's office, where his managers waited to speak with him. *Please, God. Don't let them quit.*

It was touch-and-go for a bit and he had to spend a lot of time listening and soothing feathers and apologizing, but he managed to talk the married couple, both former managers for Marriott, into staying. When he climbed into River Camp's limousine used to ferry guests to and from the airport, he desperately wanted to grab a beer from the bar in the back. Instead, he called his dad.

"Where are you?" Brick asked when Mark Callahan answered the call.

"My brood arrived at the North Forty about twenty minutes ago. It was Luke's turn to bring your grandfather and you know Branch."

"He had them on the road before daylight?"

"You guessed it. They're settled in and the girls are already fishing."

"What about Matthew?"

"They're behind us a way. How about you? You are coming to dinner tonight, right?"

"Wouldn't miss it. I'm driving in from River Camp now, but I need to make a couple stops and a handful of phone calls before I call it a day. Look for me around five thirty, I'd guess." About the time Cam's guys were picking up the four-wheelers. *Wonder if Liliana and Patsy caught any fish? Wonder if they struck out and gave up and were already back at the RV camp?*

Guess he'd see when he got there.

"The dance hall looks great, Brick," his father added. "You did a fine job finishing it out."

"Not me so much as Jax Lancaster. The man does good woodwork for a nuclear engineer. So what's for dinner?"

"Do you really have to ask?"

Brick grinned and in that moment felt better than he'd felt in days. "Branch killed the fatted calf?"

"More than one of them. Dry-aged prime beef. I think a couple of rib eyes have your name on them."

"There is nothing better than the day when Texas comes to Colorado. Looking forward to seeing y'all, Dad."

"We're anxious to see you, too."

"Tell Annabelle I'm bringing dessert."

"Oh yeah? What?"

"It's a surprise." He'd sweet-talked Maggie Romano into making one of her Italian cream cakes for the Callahan family's first-night dinner. A beep signaled an incoming call. Josh's number. Brick said, "Gotta answer this, Dad. I'll see you later."

Brick pushed "accept call" on the limo's screen and when the call connected said, "What's up, Josh?"

"Where are you, boss?"

"Headed your way. Ten minutes out."

"Is Courtney with you, by any chance?"

"No."

"She didn't show up for her shift. I went and knocked on her door, but she didn't answer. Her car's not here, either."

Brick grimaced. *What next?* "Great. Just great."

"Want me to call in one of the teenagers to cover the desk?"

"Yes. I was going to do that anyway. I planned to ask Courtney to make an airport pickup this evening."

"Another guest at River Camp?"

"The Wicked Witch of the West Coast is bringing in her own masseuse from Hollyweird. She doesn't like Jenkins's hands."

Josh muttered a curse. "I'm getting real tired of that lady, boss. Want me to make the run for you? I heard your family is in town."

"She's no lady. And thanks, but I'll find someone else. You're family, so you're invited to dinner, too."

"I appreciate that, but I'd rather wait until Paul and Cindy arrive. It's a Callahan night. You take tonight with them. I'll go pick up your Californian."

"Thanks, Brother."

"You're welcome. Just bring me back a rib eye from Texas north, would you?"

"How did you know that's what's for dinner?"

"Your uncle Gabe told me when he stopped by earlier to invite me and Courtney to join y'all."

"Ah." At the mention of his foster sister, Brick frowned. "Wonder what's up with her? It isn't like her to just not show up."

"Maybe she just got her days mixed up. She's probably in town shopping or something."

"Yeah." Brick pulled the limo into the entrance to the campsite and glanced toward his normal parking spot. The truck wasn't there. Patsy and Liliana weren't back yet. Maybe those new flies Cam sold 'em had brought them a lot of luck.

Steak for supper. Italian cream cake for dessert. Maybe some trout for breakfast. Things were looking up.

Or so he thought.

"Is that a bear?" Patsy asked.

"No, I don't think so."

"Maybe a mountain lion, then?"

"Doesn't sound like a cat." Lili lifted her walking stick from the ground and held it like a club. "Maybe a . . . coyote?"

Grrrrrrr.

"But you're sure it's not a bear?"

Lili couldn't say much of anything. She was shaking in her boots. How stupid was this to take off hiking in the mountains without a weapon of any sort?

Well, other than a walking stick. She could

use this nifty walking stick to defend herself and a dying woman from a rabid coyote or wild hog. "Do they have wild hogs in Colorado like they do at home?"

"I don't know."

Grrrrrr. . . .

"That's not a snort. Hogs snort. That's definitely a growl. There are wolves in Colorado. Someone in town was telling me a story about this family who —"

Patsy's nervous chatter broke off when the bushes began to move. Lili stepped forward, moving between Patsy and the threat. Softly, she said, "Slowly back away, Patsy."

"Lili. You, too."

"I will. Just —"

A snout pushed forward out of the brush. Long and narrow, white-gold fur on a black nose. Big brown eyes gazing up at Lili with a glazed combination of pain and weakness.

"That's no wolf. Look, Lili. That's a dog." Patsy walked around Lili and approached the dog. He growled menacingly.

Lili put out her hand to stop Patsy. "He could be rabid, Patsy."

"Look at those eyes. They're not wild looking. They're filled with pain. This dog is hurt."

"Yes, I think you're right." Carefully, Lili leaned forward and attempted to peer into the bush where the dog lay hidden. *Poor baby.* She saw matted fur and dried streaks of brown that might have been mud or blood. "Hello, boy," she said in a calm, gentle voice. "Or girl. Can't tell which. Do you need some help? We'd like to help you."

The animal's growl softened to a whimper.

"I think she's a golden retriever. Look at all the gray on her snout. She's not young." Patsy's voice hardened as she added, "An old dog. I wonder if somebody brought her out to the wilderness and dumped her. It happens, you know."

"I know. People can be horribly cruel. Do you have any water left in your bottle?"

Pasty handed it over, and Lili went down on her knees. She poured a little into her cupped hand and carefully held it out to the dog. He lapped it up as if he were dying of thirst.

Lili poured him more and most of the tension left her body. "That a boy. Good boy. You were thirsty, weren't you?"

"I don't think we need to worry that he's rabid. Here, Lili, I have a protein bar. It's one of those made with meat. See if he wants that."

Patsy unwrapped the bar and handed it to Lili. She broke off a piece and the dog wolfed it down. Lili rose back to her feet and extended her hand with another piece, attempting to lure the dog out of the shrub and onto his paws.

He tried, but the women quickly realized he was a she and had something wrong with at least one of her hind legs. "You poor girl. Here." Lili gave her the rest of the protein bar. "Well, what are we going to do, Patsy? Should one of us stay here with her and the other go for help?"

"She looks to be mostly fur and skin and bones. Any chance you could carry her?"

"If she'll let me. But I don't know that I could carry her all the way down to the truck. And I don't see managing her and a four-wheeler."

"We won't go to the truck. We'll go down to Brick's River Camp and ask for help."

Lili's teeth chewed at her bottom lip. "I don't like the idea of trespassing, but this is an emergency."

"A matter of life and death."

"People will tell us we're stupid to get involved with an injured stray dog this way."

"I quit worrying about what other people say fifty years ago," Patsy replied with a dismissive wave.

Lili knelt beside the dog once again. "Okay, sweetheart. Patsy and I are going to try to help you. Will you let us? No biting, now. Sweet puppy dog." She reached out a hand and gently stroked the dog's head. "You're a sweet thing, aren't you? Good girl. Good girl."

Lili spent almost five minutes petting and crooning to the dog before she judged her comfortable enough to attempt to pick up. The dog let out a yelp of pain, but she didn't snap at Lili.

"Good girls," Patsy said. "Both of you. Good girls. How heavy is she?"

"Not heavy enough for a dog with her frame. Maybe forty pounds?"

"She's been on her own awhile." Patsy took a better look at the dog's legs and shook her head. Pulling her cell phone out of her jacket pocket, she said, "She's tangled with something. Another animal, I'll bet. Her wound is obviously infected. The vet in town . . . what's her name?"

"Lori. Lori Timberlake. Her business is the Eternity Springs Veterinary Clinic."

"I'll call her as soon as we have a signal. Now, let me lead the way, Lili. I'll watch the trail and warn you of the tricky spots."

"Sounds like a plan."

The hike down the mountain to Stardance River Camp proved challenging in a couple of different ways. Twice a split in the trail left them unsure of which path to take.

Luckily, signs of the recent passage of a four-wheeler provided the clue of where to go. Once Patsy had to sit and slide to negotiate a particularly steep section of trail. With her longer legs, Lili was able to make her way down by walking sideways. The dog whined and whimpered, but she proved to be a trooper. Lili talked to her almost non-stop.

Finally, the trail twisted around a bend and gently sloped another twenty yards to a meadow. Patsy got a cell signal and called the vet clinic. Lili got her first good look at the collection of tents that lined a bubbling mountain stream. Under other circumstances, she'd have stopped and marveled at their size, but right now her back ached and she wanted to sit down.

The last thing she needed was to be accosted by a big, brawny man wearing fatigues and carrying a gun.

Brick sat next to his dad on the tailgate of his uncle Luke's pickup, a cold beer in his hand and a grin on his face as he watched the Callahan cousins play tag along the lakefront and listened to them laugh. Bacon-wrapped stuffed jalapeños sizzled on two of the outdoor kitchen's grills. Texas Red Dirt music drifted from speakers located strategically across the property.

"So, you want to tell us what had you so worked up when you got here?"

"Not especially."

His father and all three uncles gave him the hairy eyeball. Brick sighed. "Just a pesky bookkeeping problem. I need Courtney to help me figure it out, but she wasn't at work today. It'll keep until tomorrow."

"I was hoping she and Josh would come to dinner tonight," said his stepmother, Annabelle, as she stepped between Brick and Mark and wiggled her butt so that the two men would scoot over and make room for her on the tailgate. "It's been a long time since we've seen Josh, and I'd like to meet your sister."

"I'm sure they'll both be here for the Fourth."

"What do you hear from Paul and Cindy?" his father asked. "Are they enjoying their cruise?"

"Judging by her Facebook posts, Mom certainly is. I'm getting tired of looking at dessert pictures, though."

A shout from behind them had everyone's heads turning. Branch Callahan, the patriarch of the family, drove his motorized wheelchair toward the spot where his sons, daughters-in-law, and eldest grandson were congregated. "Hey, boy. I drive all this way to see you and you don't come inside the house to say hello?"

"I did. Figured I'd kiss your ring later, though, because you were on the throne."

Branch broke out in a loud guffaw as Brick slid off the tailgate and strode toward him. When the octogenarian showed no sign of slowing down, Brick held up his hands palms out. "Jeez, Branch. You gonna put the brakes on before you hit the lake?"

"I like to stir me up some dust."

He did just that and once he'd stopped, rather than shake his hand, Brick leaned down and gave him a hug, not too hard, because age had whittled away at the once-brawny man. Still, Branch remained far from frail. "It's good to see you, Granddad. You're lookin' good. Like the fishing shirt."

"You don't have to tuck it in. That's the style. I'm told I'm fashion-forward."

"You're a lot of things, Branch."

"Truer words were never spoken," Matt Callahan drawled.

Branch ignored his son's comment as he surveyed the company. "Where's John Gabriel and his family? Why aren't they here to greet us?"

Luke's wife, Maddie, said, "Nic has the baby at a doctor's appointment. The twins are with Gabe up at the Rocking L camp delivering our Callahan Fourthfest T-shirts to the kids. They'll all be here by time we put the steaks on. Would you like a glass of lemonade, Branch?"

"You know better than that, girl. It's cocktail hour. I'll have a bourbon and branch." He turned a narrow-eyed gaze on Brick and added, "I need to talk to you, boy. You have sorely disappointed me."

Brick grinned and sipped his beer. Hearing this old, familiar lecture was like coming home.

"I'm dying, you know. A heart attack waiting to happen."

As one, his three sons snorted. Branch Callahan had been "dying" from "heart attacks" for years.

"You are selfishly denying me the chance to meet my first great-grandchild before I pass to my reward. What do you have to say for yourself, young man?"

"The same thing I always say, Granddad. When I meet a woman who is Callahan quality — as beautiful as Annabelle, as sweet as Aunt Maddie, as special as Aunt Torie, and as loving as Aunt Nic — I'll snap her up in a heartbeat." Even as the words left his mouth, Brick felt a wave of unease. *Holy crap.*

For the first time in all the years he'd been using that excuse with Branch, he couldn't deny having met that woman.

Branch harrumphed. "I'll give you that such women are rare, but they're out there. I expect you to get off your butt and find one."

"Yessir."

"Okay, then."

Just then three honks of a horn sounded, car doors slammed, and two girls came running. "We're here! We're here!"

Gabe and Nic Callahan's twin daughters, Cari and Meg, dashed to greet their cousins, aunts, uncles, and beloved Grandpa Branch. The already-celebratory atmosphere raised another notch as the family embraced the reunion that never got old — that of John Gabriel Callahan, his father, and three brothers.

For a number of years that had come close to destroying the family, Branch and his three elder sons had believed that John Gabriel was dead. Brick would never forget that Christmas when his cousin opened the front door of Branch's house in Brazos Bend, Texas, to reveal a miracle, the return of the man who took their broken family and made it whole.

After life dealt him a series of horrific

blows, the youngest Callahan brother had gone to Colorado to die. Instead, Eternity Springs had worked its magic on him and he'd found a reason to live. Nicole Anderson and a dog named Clarence helped his heart to heal, and he'd made a new life for himself. But by the time he'd worked up the courage to return home to Texas, it had almost been too late. Branch lay on his deathbed — legitimately, for once — and the family had gathered for a funeral. Gabe's knock on the door had been the Callahan family's Christmas miracle. He'd brought a little bit of Eternity Springs' healing magic with him to Texas, and with his family reunited Branch had rallied.

Now years later, Brick still choked up at the memory.

So intent was he on watching the five men he admired most in the world greet one another in the way of men with backslaps and jibes and insults that he almost didn't notice that his phone was ringing.

He didn't recognize the number, so he let the call go to voice mail. Almost immediately it rang again. Same number. As he watched his dad swing Cari Callahan around and Uncle Luke do the same to Meg, he gave in and answered. "Callahan."

"Hey, Brick. Zach Turner here. I need you

to come by the office ASAP."

Brick's thoughts immediately went to Courtney. The smile on his face slowly died and his knees went a little weak. He leaned back against his uncle's truck for support. "My office? The RV camp?"

"No," Zach replied. "My office. There was trouble up at your River Camp. I have some women here in jail and I need you to help sort things out."

"Excuse me? What did you say?"

Zach's sigh was long and put-upon. "Just get over here, Callahan. And if you happen to run into your aunt, send her this way, too. We have a seriously injured dog, and Lori is up at the Rocking L lecturing the kids on one of Celeste's nature hikes. This dog needs attention fast."

Whatever had happened, Brick knew one thing for sure. The Wicked Witch of the West Coast had struck again. "All right, Zach. Nic is with me. We'll head that way."

"Sooner the better. It's ugly around here."

Brick disconnected the call, his mouth set in an angry line, and he went to join the family who were still in the process of greeting Gabe and Nic. "Sorry to do this," he interrupted. "I just got a call from the sheriff and I guess I have some trouble. He needs me at his office. I have to go now."

The Callahan brothers shared a look. Uncle Matt said, "We'll come with you."

"No, *I'm* not in trouble. Something happened at River Camp. Only thing I know is that it involves a dog." Brick glanced at Nic. "Zach asked for you to come, too. Lori's out-of-pocket and the dog is seriously injured."

"Sure," Nic said. "Let me get my bag."

"Do I need to take you by your house for it?"

"No. I always carry it with me in the car."

Brick started toward the Stardance Ranch Jeep he was driving since Liliana and Patsy still had his truck when he'd left for the North Forty. He called over his shoulder, "I'll bring her back ASAP. Save me some steak!"

It was a ten-minute drive from the Callahan property to the sheriff's office in town. Brick wasn't the least bit surprised to see another of the family vehicles following him. In many respects, trouble was the Callahan family business.

"Can you tell me anything else about the dog, Brick?" Nic asked. She'd been the town's only veterinarian until her protégée, Lori Timberlake, graduated from vet school and took over Nic's practice. Nic was a contented stay-at-home mother now, though she did fill in for Lori during circumstances like today.

"No," Brick replied. "All Zach said was that it's seriously injured. He didn't mention breed or size of what type of injury."

"I guess I'll find out soon enough."

They drove in silence for a couple of minutes before Nic said, "Your grandfather looks good."

"He does. It's like he went into reverse-aging mode on that first Christmas when Gabe brought you to Brazos Bend."

"Gabe needs to get back to Texas more often than he does. That fifteen-hour car ride is a killer with the kids. But JG will be walking soon and that will make traveling easier."

"How does Clarence travel? He's getting up there in years himself." Gabe's dog was an integral part of their family. They never traveled without him.

"He does great. Ten times better than the twins. Hmm . . . maybe the thing to do would be to board the girls and take Clarence and JG with us."

Brick's smile faded as he made the turn onto Cottonwood Street and spied the crowd gathered outside of the sheriff's office. "Oh, man. This doesn't look good."

"Who is up at River Camp right now, Brick?"

"I can't say. I've signed every legal document known to man and will have to give her my left kidney, right lung, and firstborn if I so much as whisper her name."

"Firstborn?" Nic piped up. "Does that mean there's one on the radar?"

"You are such a female relative," he grumbled as he pulled his truck into the parking lot across from the sheriff's office. "If this costs me the rental fees, I may have to sell the kidney she doesn't take."

They climbed out of the Jeep and Nic grabbed her physician's bag. They crossed the street and wouldn't have made it through the throng if the deputy guarding the doorway hadn't directed the crowd to let them through. As they climbed the steps to the front door, Brick asked the deputy, "What's going on?"

"Zach will brief you. Glad to see you, Dr. Nic. I have a soft spot for dogs and this old girl is just pitiful."

"Where is she?"

"The breakroom."

Familiar with the sheriff's office, Nic headed for the breakroom the moment they stepped inside. Brick scanned the room for the sheriff. Zach Turner sat with a hip propped on his desk, his eyes closed, rubbing the bridge of his nose as he spoke into the phone.

"I understand, Governor. . . . Yes. . . . Yes. . . . No." He listened for half a minute, his mouth settling into a grim line. "No, sir, I won't do that. I don't care who she is. This isn't Washington, D.C. This is Eternity Springs, Colorado. Nobody is above the law here."

Zach listened a few more minutes. He quit rubbing his brow and began rubbing his neck. That's when Brick noticed that the sheriff had a black eye.

Brick's phone rang. He checked the number. Didn't recognize it, so he ignored it. It rang three more times in the next minute — three more numbers he didn't recognize — so he switched it off.

"Yessir," Zach said. "I will do that, sir. Yes, Governor."

Brick's father and three uncles stepped into the sheriff's office as Zach finally returned the desk phone receiver to its cradle. Brick didn't give him a chance to take a breath before he asked, "Zach, what the hell is going on here?"

Zach sighed heavily, slid onto his feet, and gestured for Brick to follow him. He led the way into the section of the jail that contained the holding cells. Brick wasn't the least bit surprised to see the Wicked Witch of the West Coast in one.

Discovering Liliana Howe in another left him speechless.

CHAPTER SIXTEEN

Lili sat as still as a mannequin seated in a department store display window. Only her eyes showed any life. They burned. Shot flaming arrows of rage. Her clothes were filthy and her hair a mess. She never took her gaze away from the woman incarcerated at the opposite end of a row of four jail cells. Not even when Brick stepped into the hallway.

The witch came to her feet with a screech. She wore a thick white towel wrapped around the same white sundress she'd worn when he saw her earlier this afternoon. Her formerly styled hair was a damp rat's nest and she had mascara running down her cheeks.

"This is all your fault, Callahan," she screamed. "Your security sucks. I'm going to sue you for everything you own."

Brick looked from the witch to Liliana, whose stare remained locked and loaded, then to Zach. "Sheriff?"

"I'm hoping you can play peacemaker here. It's in everybody's best interests if we settle this without getting the governor any more involved than he already is."

"The governor?"

The witch gave her wet hair a toss. "He's a personal friend."

This just kept getting better and better. "Would someone please explain what happened?"

"Despite all your assurances that it wouldn't happen, not to mention the exorbitant amount of money I paid for privacy, those two women trespassed and wouldn't leave."

Two women. Patsy. Brick turned to Zach. "Where's Patsy?"

"Had too much of a catfight going on in here, so I put her in the breakroom with the dog."

Brick had most of what must have happened figured out. Odds were that Patsy and Liliana had come across an injured dog and taken him to the river camp, looking for help. The witch, being the witch, must have given them a hard time. How she'd ended up drenched he couldn't discern from the information he'd been given.

"Catfight!" the witch exclaimed, shifting

her fury to Zach. "Listen, mister, you're already on thin ice here. You disrespect me one more time and I'll have your badge."

Brick had opened his mouth to ask Zach to step into the front office so they could speak without interruption when Patsy's perky voice drifted from that direction. "Sheriff, may I speak with you, please?"

Without a word to the witch, Zach returned to the front office. Patsy stood in the breakroom door. "Great news. Nic says our four-footed friend should recover in a week or two. She's done what she can here, and now she intends to take her to Lori's office and finish treating her there." She glanced toward Gabe, who was stretching to peer into the back room, and asked, "Gabe, will you take her?"

"Of course." Gabe Callahan looked at his brother. "Matt, can I use your truck?"

Matt handed over the keys. "Don't worry about bringing it back. There's room for everybody in Mark's truck."

"Okay, Nic and I will see you back at the lake."

Patsy glanced from one Callahan man to another and beamed a smile. "Well, who do we have here? Callahans, obviously. Brick is the spitting image of . . . hmm . . . all of you. My goodness, you're a fine-looking bunch of men."

Getting his first good look at Patsy, Brick stopped short. She had a cut on her cheekbone, a tear in her shirt, and her jeans were filthy. "Patsy. What happened to you? Did the dog do that?"

"Oh, heavens, no. The dog was sweet as can be, even when she was in pain. Lili carried her halfway down a mountain and she didn't complain once." Wrinkling her nose, she added, "That's more than I can say about your other visitors, Brick. Look."

She pushed up her sleeve to reveal a ring of bruises around her arm and Brick's temper went cold. Quietly, he asked, "Who did that?"

Patsy hooked a thumb toward the back room. "Ms. Precious in there's muscleman bruised my arm, but she's the one who pushed me down the mountain."

"I did *not* push you down a mountain!" the witch shrieked. "You quit saying that or I'll sue you for slander."

"You must have a whole truckload of lawyers, sweet-cheeks," Patsy fired back, her tone remaining cheerful. "You throw that threat around often enough."

"I need a beer," Zach Turner mumbled softly. "Ms. Font—"

"Do not use my name!" demanded the witch.

The front door opened and three more women slipped inside — Annabelle, Aunt Torie, and Celeste, who carried an Angel's Rest shopping bag. "Zach, I have the items you requested from our boutique."

"Thank you, Celeste." Zach's mouth lifted in a rueful smile as he surveyed the now-crowded front office space. "Maybe I didn't make it clear enough just which Callahans I needed?"

Torie offered up a shameless grin. "You know our family, Sheriff. One for all and all for one. Just be glad we didn't bring Branch."

"Maddie drew the short straw. She stayed home with him and the kids," Annabelle added. "So, what happened?"

"That's what I'd like to know," Brick said testily.

Celeste reached into the shopping bag. "I brought our newest T-shirt design for you, Patsy. I know you told Zach you didn't need anything, but it's a sample, so I won't put it out on the rack. You'll be doing me a favor if you'll wear it. Presales, you know."

"Why, thank you, Celeste." Patsy held up the shirt and said, "It's darling. I don't believe I've ever worn angel wings before."

319

She winked at Brick and added, "I've always been more devilish."

"Excuse me!" shouted the witch. "What is going on out there? Where is my lawyer? I demand to speak with my lawyer! He's going to hear of this cruel and unusual punishment. Leaving me in wet clothes is against my constitutional rights."

Zach rolled his eyes, took the package Celeste offered, and disappeared into the back room. Keys jangled, hinges squeaked, and a moment later the sheriff escorted the witch past the crowd and down the hallway to the department's shower and locker room. "You can't lock the door, but I'll ensure your privacy, ma'am. You have my word on it."

When the door closed behind her, Zach stood in front of it, arms crossed, head down and shaking slowly back and forth.

Annabelle and Torie shared a round-eyed look. Annabelle asked, "Was that —"

"Don't say her name!" Brick and Zach exclaimed at the same time.

"Don't think it's gonna matter," the deputy said. "A tourist recognized her and snapped some pictures. They're already trending on Twitter."

Zach mouthed a series of curses that would have earned a scolding from Celeste if he'd given them voice.

His patience razor thin as he saw his financial security go up in tweets, Brick said, "Would somebody please tell me what happened?"

"I will," Patsy said. "But part of it is Lili's story to tell. Zach, would you let Lili out of her jail cell so we can talk?"

Zach shook his head. "No way. Only one of them out at a time. I don't trust either one of them to act like an adult."

Patsy clicked her tongue. "Really, Zach. Don't you think you're being a little harsh? Liliana was provoked."

"How?" asked every Callahan in the room.

"Fine." Zach sighed. "Y'all can all go back. The other cell doors are open. Make yourselves comfortable. Maybe you can get Liliana to explain in such a way that I can understand what went down. So far, I'm clueless."

Brick held out his hand and wiggled his fingers. "Gimme the key, Sheriff. And your first-aid kit. I'll lock myself in with her. Did you notice the scratches on her neck? She needs first aid. I don't doubt the witch could give her rabies."

As Zach handed over the requested items to Brick, Patsy led the Callahans into the back section of the sheriff's office.

Upon seeing the newcomers, Liliana's eyes went wide and she went from a slouch to sitting with perfect posture on the metal bench. Patsy introduced Lili as an old friend of Brick's from Norman, and then the Callahan family introduced themselves.

Brick entered Lili's jail cell, sat beside her, and with a tender touch began to clean the scratches on her neck. Taking care to maintain a calm note to his voice, he demanded, "Somebody start talking."

"It all started with me, I'm afraid," Patsy said.

Brick wasn't one bit surprised by that.

"I relayed some news to Lili that she found particularly disturbing. Afterward, we both needed to move around, so I suggested a hike down toward Stardance River Camp, Brick. We never intended to actually trespass. But then we found Sugar."

While Brick dabbed antibiotic cream gently at Liliana's scratches, Patsy explained about finding the injured dog and their lack of options in seeking care for her. "Even half-starved, she's still a big dog, Brick. Lili carried her all the way down the mountain. Then out of nowhere, Mr. Big and Brawny was pointing a gun at us. I didn't care for that one bit, and I'm afraid I caused a bit of a ruckus."

Brick paused in his ministrations and glanced over at Patsy. "Ruckus?"

Liliana drawled, "She was carrying a walking stick. She hit him with it. Between his legs. Put him down."

All five men in the room winced.

Patsy lifted her chin. "Just the fact that somebody wears the word 'Security' on his jacket doesn't give him the right to point a gun at a girl when all she is doing is asking for a little help."

Torie Callahan crossed her legs, rested her elbow on her knee, her chin in her palm, and leaned forward. "So how did Ms. Hollywood end up soaking wet and in the calaboose?"

Patsy smiled at Lili. "Do you want to pick up the story there, Liliana?"

Lili shrugged. "I don't know if should say anything without a lawyer present."

In the middle of dabbing at one particularly deep scratch, Brick said, "A lawyer? Do you really think you'll need one?"

"I'm in jail, aren't I?"

"What did you do, Lili?"

Patsy clicked her tongue. "She lost her temper."

"Why? If the security man was down . . . did the witch kick the dog or something?"

"Ms. Hollywood claimed to be afraid of

Sugar, which is ridiculous. The poor thing could barely move, much less attack. But what set her off was the exception she took to my response to having a gun pointed at me. When she came after me, Liliana set Sugar down and stepped in. It was quite something to see, I will tell you."

"She had no business putting her hands on you." Liliana's eyes went stormy once again. "She's at least forty years younger than you. I don't care if she's the Queen of Hollywood or the Queen of Sheba, she had no right to lay a hand on you. Just because she slaps people in the movies and on TV doesn't give her the right to do it in real life."

"She slapped you?" Mark Callahan asked Patsy.

"That's how you got the cut on your face?" Brick added.

"Yes. She got me once, but that was only because I was watching the security guy and Liliana was slow because her arms were full of dog. After Lili took care of Sugar, she made sure Queenie didn't get anywhere near me."

"So you were defending Patsy," Brick said.

"She was. And that she-devil is persistent. I'll give her that. Like the Energizer Bunny of wackos. She kept coming back and coming back and coming back for more." Patsy lowered her voice and added, "I think she's on something. Zach should have her tested. She's also cranky because her boyfriend didn't show up when he promised. While we waited for Zach to arrive, one of the servers told me that she'd been on the warpath until someone told her a hiker had been spotted on the mountain. She thought her fellow was surprising her. Instead, it was us."

"I know about this chick," Torie said. "She starred in her first movie the year I traded in my long-range lens for a Callahan. She was already a piece of work back then."

Matt explained to Patsy and Lili, "My wife was a paparazzo back in the day."

"You were?" Patsy asked. "How fascinating. I'd love to hear more about it. Who did you —"

"I'd like to hear the rest of this story first," Brick interrupted. He finished doctoring Liliana's scratches. "She came after you with her claws?"

"Yes." Her tone sour with disgust, Lili added, "She fought like a girl."

"Pitiful. You ought to ask Nic to give you a distemper shot, just in case." As Lili laughed softly, he lifted her hands to examine them. "You have scrapes on your knuckles. Did you pop her?"

"Yes. Twice." Lili looked down at her hand. "I don't regret it. She deserved it. I can't stand bullies."

"How did she get wet?"

Lili's lips twitched. "I pushed her into the river."

"You, Liliana Howe . . ." — he kissed the bruised knuckles of first one hand and then the other — ". . . are my hero."

From the corner of his eye, Brick saw Annabelle and Torie exchange glances, and he knew that he'd be in for an inquisition. When Annabelle elbowed his dad, Brick figured said inquisition would be sooner rather than later. So he was happy to see Zach move to stand in the doorway.

Hopefully, Brick asked, "Do any of you ladies have any makeup with you?"

The five women looked at one another and shook their heads. Celeste said, "I should have dropped by the spa to pick some things up when I gathered the items from our boutique. It would have been easy to do."

Zach sighed. "Some days this job truly sucks."

Patsy smiled helpfully. "One of our Alleycats sells Mary Kay. She always has her sample kit with her. Would you like me to call her?"

"Yes, please. Ask how quickly she could get here." Zach rubbed the back of his neck and explained, "My guest knows this has hit social media."

"Crap," Brick muttered.

"No. Believe it or not, I think it's a good thing. She hasn't tossed around the word 'lawyer' in at least five minutes." He glanced at Brick. "She wants to know where your limo is."

Brick checked his watch. "If her masseuse's plane was on time, it should be twenty minutes or so away from town now."

"Call him. Tell him to come here and park across the street." Zach glanced toward his deputy. "See whose cars are parked there. Need two spaces. Track 'em down and sweet-talk them into moving them. Then, cone it."

"We're parked there, Zach," Matt Callahan said.

"Finally. Something goes right."

The deputy scowled at his boss. "What about your black eye, Zach? You gonna let her get away with that?"

"I'll let her blacken the other one if she'll leave me and my town alone. The governor called a second time." Glancing at Brick, he added, "I sure hope you get a better brand of clientele up at your fancy camp next time."

"You and me, too, brother."

Patsy finished her phone call and said, "Marilyn is on her way with her kit, Sheriff."

Zach closed his eyes. "Thank you."

When he returned to the front part of the office, Torie spoke into the sudden silence. "Well, now. This has simply been too much fun. It always amazes me just how entertaining Eternity Springs proves to be each time we visit. So, Liliana, you knew our Brick back before he earned his nickname?"

She glanced at Brick. "Yes. He and my brother were friends."

"*Are* friends," Brick said more than a little grumpily. "You've heard me talk about Derek."

Annabelle snapped her fingers. "Yes. The doctor, isn't he?"

"Heart surgeon."

"So, Liliana." Torie Callahan's eyes gleamed as she leaned forward. "Tell us something about Mark Christopher that he won't have told us and his parents didn't know about."

Lili blinked in surprise, then glanced for a second time toward Brick. He knew the futility of fighting when the Callahan wives took to interrogation.

His uncle Matt, God bless him, made an effort. "Come on, girls. Give the woman a break."

"Ignore them," Annabelle said to Lili. "Believe me when I tell you that Brick has this coming. In spades. You wouldn't believe all the grief he's given us over the years."

A glimmer of amusement lit Liliana's eyes. "Actually, I probably would. Hmm . . ." She pursed her lips and considered. "You probably haven't heard about the time he didn't get around to studying for a calculus test because a baseball game went into extra innings. Lots of extra innings. So rather than pull an all-nighter, he went home and raided his mother's spice cabinet and made a sneezing powder. He made sure to be the first person in the classroom before his calculus class, and he spread the powder on all the desks — including the teacher's. He threw pinches of it in the air all around the room and tossed some onto the blades of the fan."

The men in the room started to grin. "A chip off the old block, for sure," Luke observed.

"So what happened with the test?"

Brick lifted his head toward the ceiling at the memory. "I flunked it. Lili's brother was pissed at me because I hit into a double play and we lost the game, and he could do calculus in his sleep, so he ratted me out to the teacher. Everybody else got an extra day to study. I had to take the exam that day."

"Without wiping off your desk, as I recall," Lili said.

Brick shot her a narrow-eyed look. "You were three years behind me. You weren't in that class, were you?"

"I took algebra and geometry in middle school. I've always been good at math."

"Figures." He scowled at her; then it melted into a grin. "Sure were some red, runny noses in that classroom. The teacher included. Fun times. Fun times. Almost worth bombing the test."

"Genetics are an interesting thing," Luke observed. "I seem to recall a sneezing-powder incident in grade school."

"Only because Branch always bragged about putting it into the vents at school," Mark fired back.

"So you're telling me three generations of Callahans played sneezing-powder pranks?" Annabelle asked. She turned to Torie and said, "We need to be frightened. Very frightened."

Torie nodded sagely. "Seriously strong genes. So, Liliana, tell us another one."

"Enough," Brick insisted. "Shouldn't you

all go home and check on your kids? It's really not fair of you to leave Maddie with the burden of all of those children — and Branch — all by herself after a long drive from Texas."

"Hey, she drew the short straw," Annabelle said.

"And she sure wouldn't rush home," Torie added.

"Dad?" Brick pleaded.

Mark Callahan simply smirked, but Celeste took pity on Brick. Rising, she said, "I happen to own a building across the street, and the angle of the second-floor windows provides an excellent view of this office's front door and the parking spot for the limo."

"That's tempting," Torie said.

Luke pushed to his feet. "Oh, give the boy a break. He doesn't need our help or our interference. I'm getting hungry. Let's go home and put the steaks on."

"I'm not a boy," Brick protested, pouting like a . . . well . . . a boy.

Luke continued, "Brick, bring your young woman to supper tonight."

"Oh, I'm not —" Lili began.

"She's not —" Brick said at the same time.

Matt interrupted, saying, "Celeste, I hope you and Patsy will join us, too."

"Thank you, dear, but I already have plans," Celeste said, showing her familiar winsome smile.

"Me, too," Patsy added. "Lili is free, though."

"I am not. I'm in jail!"

"Zach is going to spring you as soon as the Wicked Witch of the West Coast leaves," Brick said. "You might as well tell them you'll come, Liliana. They won't give up."

"I thought you were the one whose head was hard as a brick."

"Genetics," Torie and Annabelle said simultaneously.

From the front room came the sounds of a new arrival, interrupting the debate. A woman's crisp, businesslike voice said, "Patsy said you have an emergency?"

"You can't even begin to guess," Zach said.

With the makeup source on-site, Brick began to hope that the worst part of today's event might be over. When Zach announced that the limo had arrived and the Callahans took their leave, a wave of relief washed over him. He might not survive today financially, but at least the immediate turmoil was almost behind him.

Or so he thought.

Looking naturally beautiful and wearing a

flattering sundress in a red poppy print with matching heeled sandals, Brick's nightmare swept into the back room. Brick expected her to announce her immediate departure from River Camp and demand a refund of her rental fees. Instead, she requested changes to the following day's menu before giving Liliana a scathing once-over look. "I trust I will never see you again?"

"Count on it," Lili responded. "As long as you leave my friends alone, that is."

The actress turned on her high heels and glided out of the room.

Crowd noise buzzed in the street. Brick heard people call her name and request to have pictures taken with her. He heard her famous laugh. "Life throws some strange curveballs along the way, doesn't it?"

He was totally unprepared when Liliana's eyes filled up with tears and silently overflowed. "Hey, now. Hold on a minute. What's this about? Lili-fair, don't cry. Why are you crying?"

"Curveballs," she said, then leaned her head against his shoulder. The tears continued to fall.

Brick felt a little panicked. This wasn't like the Liliana he knew. "Talk to me, sweetheart. I don't understand."

"I can't. I promised. Oh, Brick, my heart

is broken."

"Why, Lili-fair? Why?"

Movement in the doorway caught his attention. Patsy stood watching Liliana with a sympathetic expression on her face. He asked, "Patsy?"

"You can tell him, Lili. Brick will keep our secret and he has a nice broad shoulder for those tears. I'm catching a ride back to Stardance Ranch with Marilyn. You'll bring Lili home, Brick?"

"Sure."

For the next few minutes, he held her, rocked her, patted her back, and smoothed his hand down her silky blond hair, shushing her, murmuring soothing words, offering what comfort he could. After Patsy's comment and seeing the look on her face, he had a bad feeling about what Liliana had to tell him.

Zach came to check on them and Brick waved him away. He left, returned with a box of tissues he fitted between the bars of the cell, and said, "Office is all yours. My deputy and I are going to Murphy's. Don't worry about the phone. It's forwarded to my cell."

"Thanks, Zach."

Brick set the tissue box on Lili's lap and she grabbed a handful, wiped her eyes, blew her nose, and finally managed to dry her tears. "Talk to me, Liliana."

"I'm sorry. It just all hit me. I was so sad and so angry and I just lost it. Today was one of those days."

"What happened?"

First she explained how the camo-clad security guy had marched them into camp at gunpoint. "You'd have thought we were at some Central American drug kingpin's hideout."

"That chaps me," Brick said. "There's absolutely no reason to pull a gun on two women and a dog. He's private security she brought with her, but I'm gonna find a way to get rid of him. I'm probably liable for anything he does."

"He marched us over to . . . that woman . . . and before we even got a word out, she launched into attack mode. I've never seen anything like it, Brick. She said horrible, ugly things. Unnecessary things. Patsy may be right about her being on something at the time."

"Wouldn't surprise me one bit."

Lili's mouth twisted in a crooked smile. "However, the situation only escalated because Patsy went all Southern Belle on her and blessed her heart. Patsy's mistake was reaching out to pat her cheek. That's when it got physical and it was my turn to go ballistic. I was already so upset because of what Patsy told me, and then the dog was hurt and mewling and the dog and Patsy sort of got mixed up inside my head. I was so angry. Beyond furious. When that woman shoved Patsy to the ground . . . well . . . I lost it. I went after her. Threw a punch or two and shoved her into the river."

Brick had plenty more questions, but he focused on the central one. "What had Patsy told you?"

Liliana drew in a deep breath, shuddered, and teared up again. Brick handed her another tissue and she, in fits and starts, told him about Patsy's diagnosis and decision to forego treatment. "Oh, baby, that's terrible news. I'm so sorry."

"I love her."

"I know you do. She's a lovable woman."

"I don't want to lose her. I want her to fight. I want her to get treatment, and I realize I only want that because I'm a selfish person. That makes me mad at myself. I mean, how hypocritical am I? I won't fight for myself, and my fight is only for a job, not my life. And I want her to fight when her odds of winning are long and the battle would tie her down and make her sick on many of the days she has left."

"Don't beat yourself up, Lili-fair. What you're feeling is natural."

She shrugged and leaned her head back against the wall, her eyes shut. "What a lousy day."

He laced his fingers through hers and brought them to his mouth for a kiss. "Did you catch any fish?"

Her mouth quirked. "Yeah. We both did."

"And you saved a dog."

"True.

"So not all bad, right?"

"Not all bad. Did you see the dog?"

"No."

"She's really pretty. Looks like a golden retriever to me. If no one claims her, I think Patsy would like to. Those two bonded. But she worries about it being fair to Sugar, she's named her Sugar, because of . . . well . . . she doesn't have much . . ." — Liliana's voice broke on the word — ". . . time."

"I think Sugar is meant for Patsy. Believe me, Lili-fair, I've lived in Eternity Springs long enough to become a believer where the dog population of this town is concerned. Have you heard the story about how a stray dog literally saved Uncle Gabe's life and brought him and Nic together?"

"No."

"Ask him about it. He loves to tell the

337

story. And then there's Bismarck. He is truly a miracle dog. Saved Gabby and Flynn Brogan from pirates. And when Chase Timberlake was in a bad place after his . . ."

Brick's voice trailed off when he heard footsteps and the sound of hushed giggles in the outer room. What now? If Annabelle and Torie came back for more nosy interference he might just be the one who blew.

But the people who peeked into the holding cell section of the sheriff's office were strangers.

With cell phone cameras.

CHAPTER SEVENTEEN

The weather forecast for the Fourth of July predicted morning showers that would continue through mid-afternoon. Celeste assured the worried organizers of the inaugural Eternity Springs Independence Day parade that skies would clear off by the time the event was due to begin at ten.

The sun came out at nine thirty, and by quarter to ten the sky was a bright, heavenly blue.

The Eternity Springs Community School band led the parade playing John Philip Sousa and behind them filed anyone who wanted to participate. Locals and tourists, campers from the Rocking L summer camp, Stardance Ranch RV Resort, and nearby national parks joined in to march, ride bicycles, scooters, skateboards, and horses. Participants walked dogs, pushed baby strollers, drove motorcycles, golf carts, four-wheelers, and scooters. The Chamber of

Commerce entered a float celebrating the town's history and Angel's Rest sponsored one featuring red, white, and blue angels.

"Go figure," Patsy said to Liliana when she spied it. "Whoever would have guessed Celeste would do angels?"

Because Celeste was scheduled to ride on the Angel's Rest float, she asked Lili to do her a favor and drive her Caddie and Shasta in the parade. Delighted at the opportunity, Lili agreed. The vintage trailers paraded by Tornado Alleycats members were bound to be a big hit, but she expected the Murphy family businesses entry, the Fresh and Refresh float, to win the parade's first prize. Who could compete with cute little kids throwing cellophane-wrapped cookies to the crowd from a deck boat on a trailer?

Lili took her place in line at the end of the vintage trailers. Celeste brought Nic Callahan and her twin daughters by to ride in the classic convertible with her. "We need wavers," Celeste explained. "Can't have a car in a parade and not have somebody in the backseat waving."

"I'm glad to have the company," Lili replied.

It was true. The Callahan twins were dolls. At eight years old, Meg and Cari wore patriotic T-shirts and shorts, with red, white, and blue ribbons tied around their ponytails. They sat on the car's backseat and giggled while they practiced their "princess" wave — hand cupped, fingers together, movement back and forth rather than up and down.

Nic sat up next to Lili and grilled her like a hot dog.

"So, the day before yesterday was interesting. I didn't know that you and Brick had become so close. How long have you two been dating?"

Lili shot her a look. "We're not dating. It's not like that."

"It sure looked like it to me."

Frowning, Lili kept her gaze on the trailer in front of her in line. "I don't recall seeing you at the sheriff's office. I thought you went straight to the breakroom to work on Sugar."

"Oh, I did. I saw all the Twitter pics. The YouTube video, too."

"Mommy! Mommy!" Meg called from the Caddie's backseat. "You're not waving. You need to wave, too."

"Oh. Sorry." Nic offered the crowd lining Spruce Street a wave.

The girl continued, "You don't have to wave, Miss Lili, because you're driving."

"Gotta be safe," Lili said, glad for even a

temporary interruption.

Quite temporary, she realized when Nic focused her laser-eyed attention back on Lili. "Well?"

"Brick and I are just friends."

Nic shook her head knowingly. "Brick is everyone's friend. But he doesn't look at everyone the way he looks at you. No, Liliana. You mean something to him."

Thankfully, the inquisition ended when the noise level surrounding them increased due to fact that the Bear Cave Bikers pulled in behind them on their motorcycles.

Liliana completed her participation in the parade without further interrogation, and the squeals and giggles from behind her combined with the happy excitement of the crowd and the chance to drive such a splendid . . . land yacht . . . made for an enjoyable morning. The activity helped her forget about the stresses of the previous two days.

When they finally left the sheriff's office Brick had wanted to take her to dinner with his family, but she'd begged off. He'd dropped her back at the Ranch, where she'd checked on Patsy, eaten a bowl of cereal for supper, showered, and gone to bed. Yesterday had been an exercise in avoiding her cell phone, e-mails, and even knocks on her trailer door by paparazzi and tabloid reporters and bloggers.

The news that had arrived last night that Hollywood's newest heartthrob had been spotted in Aspen with the wife of a professional football player ended Lili's fifteen minutes of fame. She couldn't have been happier.

Following the parade, she joined Patsy and the throngs of shoppers taking advantage of the three hours that retail shops and restaurants would remain open before closing for the official town festival out at Hummingbird Lake.

It was a bittersweet time for Lili. She made a point to enjoy shopping with Patsy, but when the older woman went a little crazy in Forever Christmas buying gifts for all the Alleycats Lili had to fight back tears. She was glad when the time came to migrate out to the lake for the canoe races.

She'd registered in the female-only race, assuming she'd be paired with one of the Alleycats. Instead, she discovered she was slated to partner with Maddie Callahan.

Wow. This was her week to mingle with celebrities.

She'd known from local gossip that Brick's aunt Maddie was the infamous Baby Dagger, daughter of rock royalty Blade.

"Hello, partner," Maddie said, waving the pairing sheet and smiling brightly. "How lucky am I to get you on my team! We're going up against Torie and Lori. You have to watch out for my sister-in-law. She may be tiny, but she's strong as an ox. I really want to beat her because of what's at stake."

"You care about the trophy?" Lili asked.

"Well, sure. Although what really matters is loser washes pots and pans tonight. We do mostly throwaway stuff, but the pile is still high. I'm not a fan of dishwater. Besides, I like to win."

Waiting to board the canoe for their race, Lili caught her first glimpse of Brick since he'd dropped her off at her trailer the night before last. Based on gossip going around the campground yesterday, he had spent the day at River Camp smoothing things over with his guest, fielding phone calls, and basically doing damage control. According to Sharon Cross, matters at the RV camp weren't running so smoothly, either.

Sharon had walked into the office yesterday and overheard Josh on the phone quarreling with Courtney. He'd acted seriously upset until he spotted Sharon, ended the call, and pretended nothing was wrong.

Brick didn't appear to be concerned about anything as he sauntered toward Maddie with his father — or was it his uncle Luke? The two men were twins.

Luke, Lili deduced when the older Callahan said, "Red, how about a kiss for good luck?"

Then he bent Maddie back over his arm and kissed her senseless.

"Daddy, stop it! You're embarrassing us again."

Another set of identical Callahan twins — a dominant family trait, apparently — who were a little older than Gabe and Nic's girls and redheaded like their mother squealed in disgust. "He's always doing that," the girl dressed in white said.

"It's humiliating," the one in blue added.

"Hush, urchins," Luke Callahan said. "I want to introduce you to Ms. Howe. Liliana, these are our daughters, Samantha . . ." — the girl in white wiggled her fingers — ". . . and Catherine."

"Nice to meet you," Catherine said.

"Hello." Samantha beamed a smile toward Lili, winked at Brick, then smiled innocently toward her mother. "You're right, Mom. She *is* pretty. I'll bet Brick's in luuuuv."

Brick lowered his sunglasses and studied his cousin. "So, Sam, you still crushing on that boy who —"

"What boy?" Luke demanded.

"Nothing, Dad," Samantha was quick to say, shooting Brick a glare. "You better get in your canoe, Mom. The race is about to begin and you don't want to give Torie a head start."

Brick smirked at his cousin, then helped Luke steady the canoe as Lili and Maddie took their places. When they lifted their paddles and pointed toward the starting line, Luke called, "Good luck, beautiful ladies."

"He is such a flirt," Maddie said with a sigh. "They both are."

Lili couldn't argue against that.

"So, how long have you and Brick been dating?"

Again Lili protested the assumption, and when Maddie dismissed her much like Nic had she seriously considered diving over the side of the canoe. She wasn't even surprised when Matt's wife, Torie, asked her the same question after taking the seat beside Lili at the children's concert.

So later that afternoon upon arriving at the North Forty for the Callahan cookout and the fireworks show, she decided to take matters into her own hands. She tracked down the last Callahan wife, Annabelle, and said, "I've been secretly dating Brick since I was nine years old. His tree house was the bomb. I gave him my virginity there and have since borne him three sets of twins."

Annabelle looked up at her and grinned. "I knew I'd like you, Liliana. But that's not the question I was going to ask."

"It wasn't?"

"No. I was going to ask you how long you've been in love with my husband's son?"

The question took Lili's breath away. It was a question she'd never had the guts to ask herself. Nevertheless, she answered it honestly. "Since the day he offered me his high school letter jacket."

Brick greeted his mom and pop with bear hugs. Cindy and Paul Christopher looked rested and relaxed after their Alaskan cruise, and as always Mom got teary eyed when she saw Brick. "Oh, Mark. You get more handsome every time I see you. Look at you." She reached up and played with the ends of his hair trailing below his collar. "I like the longer hair."

Mom was the only person who'd never given in to his nickname. "I'm a mountain man, now. It keeps me warmer than the military cut."

They discussed the flight from Seattle and the drive from Denver. Then Mark and Annabelle spied the new arrivals and came over to exchange greetings. Watching the friendly exchange between his two sets of parents, Brick was struck once again about how lucky he'd been when it came to families.

Families. That reminded him. He began looking around the grounds for Josh and Courtney. He knew Josh was here. He'd spotted him down by the fishing pier earlier. Come to think of it, he didn't think he'd seen Courtney all day.

Then as if his mother was reading his mind, Cindy Christopher asked, "Where's your brother? And Courtney? I'm so looking forward to seeing her. It's been years."

"Honestly, I don't know. Every time I see Josh he's on the opposite of the compound from me. And I don't know what's up with Courtney. I haven't seen her in a couple of days."

Annabelle spoke up. "Josh was in the dance hall a few minutes ago. I suspect he's still there. A few of the Alleycats were giving a pole-dancing demonstration."

Brick's brows winged up and she added, "Kidding. Just kidding. I heard they give lessons, though. Quite an interesting bunch. Anyway, we're almost ready to serve dinner. Josh is up there helping."

"That's no surprise. He always was good

about helping in the kitchen," Cindy Christopher said, slipping her arm through Brick's. "Do you have any surprises for your parents, Mark? A new girlfriend perhaps?"

Playfully, he thumped Cindy's nose. "It's nice to know I can always count on you, Mom, and that some things never change."

The look in her eyes went from teasing to serious. "I want you to be happy, Mark. That's all I've ever wanted. But I think you need that special someone in your life for you to find that happiness."

"I love you, Mom." It was always the best dodge that he could throw out, Brick knew. "Let's go track down Josh and Courtney. You can pester them about their love lives."

Cindy asked him what he knew about his siblings' love lives as he led his parents toward the dance hall where volunteers manned the buffet line serving the Callahan family's traditional Fourth of July feast — smoked brisket, chicken, and sausage, beans, grilled corn on the cob, mac and cheese, potato salad, coleslaw, fresh watermelon, and more salads than Brick could count. For the younger crowd and others so inclined, they had metal skewers and a tray full of hot dogs ready to roast over the fire pit.

Josh Tarkington spied the Christophers

and a wide smile broke across his face. "Well, the world travelers have returned."

The trio exchanged handshakes and hugs and spent a few minutes catching up before Branch Callahan rang the dinner bell and, like ants at a picnic, children began to swarm into the room. They'd serve the Rocking L campers first, then guests, then family. "I need to man my spoon," Josh said to Paul. "Y'all save me a spot at your table, would you?"

"Sure," Paul said.

"What about Courtney?" Brick asked. "Where is she?"

Josh glanced toward the door and his brow furrowed. Unease fluttered through Brick. "Josh?"

The man gave his head a slight shake, then gestured toward the line already twenty kids deep and stepped away without answering. *What the hell?*

Josh took up his place behind the potato salad and mac and cheese. Brick decided he'd go assist with the baked beans, right next to his brother, but just as he took half a step forward Uncle Gabe called his name. "Wienies are proving popular. Will you help me supervise the skewers?"

Brick nodded, gave his brother one more puzzled look, then followed his uncle outside to the fire pit.

For the next nerve-wracking hour, he supervised children aged two to twelve with sharp metal skewers and fire. By the time everyone had been fed, he needed a beer. Badly.

He grabbed one along with a plate of food and made his way down toward the lake to the picnic tables where his family invariably congregated. He joined Chase Timberlake, Jax Lancaster, and Devin Murphy at a picnic table to enjoy his beer and brisket and talk baseball while watching the children's games that were about to begin.

Liliana had pitched in to help there, he saw. She, Claire, and Lori had organized a game of tag divided into age groups. Soon the property rang with shouts and laughter and giggles and the barking of happy dogs. After tag they played other schoolyard games and at some point someone broke out footballs and Frisbees and some of the older children — Brick included — joined in the play.

And as the evening progressed, everyone waited for fireworks to begin.

In the dance hall's bathroom, Patsy Schaffer coughed one more time, then reached for another tissue and wiped her mouth.

The bright red staining the white of the tissue wasn't lipstick, unfortunately.

Sighing, she leaned toward the mirror and studied the whites of her eyes. Were they more yellow than yesterday? Probably. The pain in her gut was definitely worse.

"Well, you knew to expect it," she said to her reflection. Didn't mean she had to like it, though.

She stuck her tongue out. "Cancer, you suck."

She drew an enameled pillbox from the back pocket of her jeans and tossed back two small white pills. Then she pulled her red lipstick from the other pocket of her jeans, painted her lips, and pasted on a smile. She stopped beside the five-gallon jugs of beverages and filled a disposable cup with lemonade. So sweet. So delicious. Definitely a moment to savor.

Five minutes later when Celeste waved her to a circle of lawn chairs where she sat with Cindy Christopher and the Callahan wives, she gave no one any reason to think anything was wrong.

Taking the empty seat next to Celeste, Patsy observed, "What a beautiful evening, isn't it?"

Celeste beamed a smile. "That it is."

"I'm looking forward to the fireworks, but

I'll be honest. I hate to see this day end."

"Every day is a gift."

"So very true." A slight smile played about Patsy's lips as she added, "Some gifts are easier to appreciate than others."

"That is our challenge, is it not? We must climb those mountains and conquer those hurdles that prevent us seeing the gift of each day."

"I have a confession to make. Some days I don't have the energy to climb and jump. Some days I want to lay down and surrender."

Celeste reached over and patted Patsy's knee. "May I offer a piece of advice?"

"Of course."

"When the gift becomes difficult to recognize, look to your inner angel and accept the guidance she has to offer."

"I don't know, Celeste." Patsy sipped her lemonade and considered her friend's advice. "I reflect on all the mistakes I've made and . . . well . . . sometimes, my inner angel seems to be missing in action."

"Then you are looking in the wrong place. You will find your angel not in worldly deeds, Patsy. You'll find her when you focus on the accomplishments of your soul. Allow her to guide you, to be your support during those final climbs and jumps that will lead you back to the heart of your heart — the love and faith and goodwill that will be your bridge to heaven."

"It's an intimidating journey."

"Only if you think you are making it alone. You're never alone, Patsy. Don't forget that."

Patsy focused on the sunset beginning to paint the sky in hues of brilliant gold and vermillion, purples and pinks. "God's promise."

"His promise."

"I'll remember, Celeste. Thank you."

"Thank you, my friend. Your friendship has been a gift to me and to many of us here tonight." Celeste patted Patsy's knee again, then gave her hand a comforting squeeze. "And speaking of friends and gifts . . . I'm reminded that different kinds of alone exist."

She gestured toward the lawn where Liliana was in the process of diving in front of Brick to intercept a Frisbee Lori had thrown. "I believe those two are being blind to the gift in front of their noses."

"I couldn't agree more," Patsy said. "I don't know who is more stubborn, Brick or Liliana."

At mention of the Callahan name, Cindy, Maddie, Torie, Annabelle, and Nic broke off their conversation about the roses blooming in front of Branch's cabin and turned their heads and attention toward the older women. "Who is more stubborn?" Annabelle repeated. "That's easy."

"Brick," the Callahan wives and Cindy said as one.

"I don't know," Patsy said. "My girl is quite the hardhead herself."

"I don't remember a lot about her," Cindy admitted. "I do know that the whole Howe family is a determined lot. They're good people."

That ruffled Patsy's feathers a bit. "Well, they haven't treated Lili very well through this work-related fiasco."

"That I can't explain. I'm surprised at Derek, though. He always doted on his little sister."

"That I *can* explain," Patsy admitted. "Lili is in the midst of a bit of a rebellion where family is concerned. High time, if you ask me. The girl is a pleaser who up until now has denied her dreams. She hasn't told her brother what happened. She doesn't think her parents shared the news with him, either."

Celeste added, "She's a dear, dear girl. She wasn't born with wings, but she's working hard at growing some. Brick probably isn't aware of it, but he has been helping her in that respect."

"So what's the deal with them?" Torie asked. "The look he gave her the other day at the jail was absolutely steamy."

Nic bent over and plucked a dandelion from the grass at her feet. "All I know is that I've watched him circle dozens of women since he moved to Colorado and this one is different."

"He's different for her, too," Patsy said. "She's let enough things slip. I think he's owned a piece of her heart since childhood."

"A piece of her heart . . . as in the *l* word?" Cindy sat up straight. "Does your Liliana love our Mark?"

"Yes, I think she does. I've watched them both. I think he has real feeling for her, too."

"I agree," Celeste said.

"Hmmm . . . ," said the Callahan women, and for the next few minutes the group of females studied the game of Frisbee taking place.

Annabelle said, "He's so much like his father that it's scary."

"Has there a Callahan man ever born who didn't fight falling in love?" Maddie wondered. "Even Branch will say that he and Margaret Mary didn't have smooth sailing at first."

"Hookups aside, Brick hasn't been in a boat in years," Torie said.

Eventually, Annabelle voiced the question that, based on appearances, the family members all were thinking. "Could it be that Brick is finally getting over She Who Will Not Be Named?"

"From your mouth to God's ears," Maddie said with a sigh.

"He's always listening," Celeste offered.

"In that case, I wish He'd give them both a swift kick in the . . ." Nic's voice trailed off. "Wait a minute. . . ."

Annabelle met Maddie's and Torie's gazes. "She's got that look in her eyes. Do you have an idea, Nicole?"

"I'm just . . . remembering." She looked at Celeste. "Do you recall the night that Gabe and I got trapped together in your basement?"

"Of course," Celeste said, preening. "That was one of our early romantic successes."

Torie leaned forward. "Nic, I've never heard this story. Do tell."

Nic waved it away. "Later. Then there was the time at Lori's roommate's wedding."

Celeste's eyes twinkled. "Her estranged parents got trapped inside Mistletoe Mine. It led to their reconciliation."

Maddie looked at Annabelle. "Didn't you

and Mark get trapped in a closet in Hawaii and —"

"We hid in a closet."

"But it did kick-start your reconciliation, didn't it?"

Annabelle considered a moment, then nodded. "Yes."

Patsy surveyed the Callahan wives and said, "I like you girls. You should consider joining the Tornado Alleycats. You, too, Cindy. You'd all fit right in."

"I thought your membership was full?" Nic asked.

Patsy waved her hand. "That's the good thing about being the one who makes the rules. I can change them when I want."

Celeste rapped her knuckles on the aluminum arm of her chair. "Let's stay on task, ladies. Is the proposal on the table to trap Brick and Liliana together someplace overnight tonight?"

"So fast?" Maddie asked.

"There's no time to waste," Patsy declared. "Every day . . . and night . . . is a gift."

"There you go, girlfriend," Celeste said. "So, the question is where and how?"

"Hmmm . . . ," six voices said as one.

"What about your little vintage trailer, Celeste?" Nic asked.

Maddie shook her head. "A big man like Brick wouldn't be able to turn around."

"Or roll around," Patsy added.

"I have a thought," Celeste said. "Isn't this summer's Callahan family project supposed to be the completion of a tree house?"

"Now there's a thought," Patsy said. "Lili has told me she's been intrigued by tree houses ever since Brick and her brother built one when they were kids."

Torie pursed her lips. "I like the idea of it. Our tree house is huge, but it isn't nearly finished. They just have the base, the walls, the roof, and the sky deck."

"Sky deck?" Cindy asked. "Mark's tree house in our backyard had one of those for his telescope. He loved it."

"Our tree house also has a temporary ladder," Annabelle said. "One that can be removed."

"Hmmmm . . ."

A slow grin spread across Maddie's face. "A pile of blankets. A bottle of wine."

Torie shook her head. "No. Champagne. Matt and I have a bottle of good stuff on ice in our room that I'm willing to sacrifice to the cause."

"You are a generous aunt, Victoria," Cindy Christopher said.

"I am, aren't I?"

"But how will we lure them up there?" Annabelle asked.

"Hmmmm . . ."

Maddie suggested, "A dog? A kid?"

Torie waved a dismissive hand. "We will think of something. We always do."

Cindy asked, "You don't think they'd try to climb down, do you?"

The women focused on the game where Brick swooped in on Lili, wrapped his arm around her waist, and lifted her away and to the side, enabling him to snatch the Frisbee from her grasp. The couple both laughed.

Celeste shook her head. "I think both of them are ready to fly."

CHAPTER EIGHTEEN

Lili couldn't remember a holiday she'd enjoyed so much.

Playing with the Rocking L campers warmed her heart and made her feel like a kid again herself. The children, all of whom qualified to attend the camp because each had suffered a significant loss of some sort, reminded her that in the big scheme of things her problems weren't bad at all.

Shoot, in the *little* scheme of things she didn't have anything to whine about.

The game of Frisbee had evolved into another game of tag. That ended when twilight fell and the Callahan men broke out sparklers for the children. Lili watched Brick tease and joke with his younger siblings, cousins, and campers, and her heart gave a little twist. *If only . . .*

"He's awfully good with children," Annabelle Callahan said, slipping her arm through Lili's. "Better than with Hollywood starlets, for sure."

"That woman is not a nice person."

"No, she's not. Although you have to admire the way she's capitalized on the publicity. By the way, you sure looked cute in that picture on the front of yesterday's *Star.*"

Lili winced. At least the photo had been small and she'd been wearing her sunglasses. "Oh. Don't remind me."

"Brick said his phone rang off the wall yesterday. He's booked halfway through next season. He owes you. At the very least he should give you a free vacation at Stardance River Camp."

Liliana grinned. "I might take that."

A shriek of squeals and laughter interrupted them, and they turned to watch Maddie's daughters being chased by Nicholas Lancaster's dog. Annabelle said, "It's noisy here. Will you walk with me a bit, Liliana? There's something I'd like to show you."

"Okay."

Lili thought Annabelle Callahan's voice sounded just a little too casual. She hadn't missed the speculative looks the group of women had been giving her earlier. She hoped Brick's stepmother didn't plan to serve grilled Lili for dessert.

Lili sensed Annabelle could do it if she wanted. The Callahan wives were impressive. Beautiful, strong, and obviously devoted to their families — and their men had eyes only for them.

Yearning pulled at Lili. She wished . . .

Annabelle's next comment surprised Lili. "Mark and I are so proud of the life Brick is building here. I know that you are aware of his background, his family, and how he came to know that Mark was his dad. When I first met Brick, he was almost a grown man. Ready to head off to Hawaii for college. He'd been raised with love and was strong enough to take on the world — and he did. Mark was so proud of him. We wanted him to settle in Texas, but he knew what he wanted. He's always known what he wants."

Tiffany. Lili didn't think she said the name aloud, but maybe she had, because Annabelle went there, too. "Of course, like anyone, sometimes he wants something that isn't good for him. That's when it's difficult to be a parent." She gave Lili a sidelong look and said, "Brick's father couldn't stand Tiffany Lambeau."

Me, either, Lili wanted to say.

"There was just . . . something . . . about her. Something manipulative, and when the breakup finally happened none of us were surprised. Frankly, I was relieved. But I was sad that she broke Brick's heart."

"She recently went to work at my firm," Lili shared. "Believe me, he's better off without her."

"I'm sure. But enough about her." They both looked up as a bright red cardinal flitted from a fir tree to a spruce. Annabelle continued, "The thing I've learned about Callahan men is that when they love, they do it with their whole hearts and without reservation. They may all be big, strong, powerful men, but when their hearts are wounded, it takes them a long time to heal. And young love — first love — is especially binding.

"John Gabriel almost grieved himself into a grave over the loss of his first wife. Mark took years and years to put the loss of Brick's mother behind him. And Branch . . . that cantankerous old dear . . . his heart still bleeds for his Margaret Mary."

A string of firecrackers exploded and both women glanced over their shoulders to see the Callahan men with punks in their hands and maniacal grins on their faces. Lili smiled and said, "They're acting like boys now."

"They do so love the Fourth. And family.

The journey here has been a long and hard one for my husband, his brothers, and Branch. That's part of the reason why they appreciate it so much. They came so close to losing it forever."

"It's wonderful that Mark was able to find his son."

"Yes, isn't it? What is fascinating — and a bit scary to be honest — is that despite an eighteen-year separation, Brick and his father are so much alike."

She looked at Lili as she said, "Mark likes to think that if he'd been around, he could have nipped the Tiffany thing in the bud. I disagree. I think Brick needed that experience to make him the man he is today."

Mr. Three-Dates-and-You're-Out?

"I know he's relationship shy. Another thing about Callahan men is that they have a tendency to learn things the hard way. With Brick you have to add in the fact that he's so, well . . . brick headed. I fear he's the most like his grandfather in that regard, heaven help him. Makes him a challenge. Makes him a lot of work."

Lili wouldn't argue that.

"But like anything else in life, if it was easy, anyone could do it. It takes a strong woman to love a Callahan man. It takes a patient woman to earn his love in return. I have to tell you, Liliana, it's more than worth the effort."

Lili had to ask her question past the lump in her throat. "Why are you telling me all this, Annabelle?"

"You love him, don't you?"

That left Lili speechless. She'd only recently figured it out herself. She'd loved him since she was nine years old, but fear had kept her from admitting it now at twenty-nine.

When Lili didn't respond, Annabelle continued, "Here we are. This is what I wanted to show you. Our men always have one special project they work on together here at the North Forty. After the dance hall, which turned out to be a much bigger project than they had planned, they chose something smaller. This was Brick's idea. It's not finished, of course, but it's pretty spectacular even now. Don't you think?"

A tree house. Lili's lips lifted in a smile. "It's a real tree house. Not like the fancy things up at his River Camp. It reminds me of the one he and my brother built in his backyard. You know, I wasn't allowed in that tree house."

"Because it wasn't safe?"

"Because I was a girl."

Annabelle frowned in disgust. "Those

dogs. Well, Liliana Howe, you *are* allowed in this tree house. In fact, I'm inviting you to watch the fireworks from here. I promise you a beautiful view."

"That sounds like fun," she replied, meaning it. "Thank you. I'll do that."

Annabelle gestured toward the ladder. "Be our guest, Lili. Be courageous. Welcome to our world."

Lili climbed the ladder, expecting Annabelle to follow her. But when she poked her head through the opening in the tree house floor and spied the items stacked in one corner, she suddenly understood. Quilts. Champagne. Condoms.

How weird was this? His mother!

And yet the fact of Annabelle Callahan's approval both warmed her heart and encouraged her. Lili repeated, "Be courageous."

She drew a deep, bracing breath and climbed the rest of the way into the tree house.

"Do I have to?" Brick whined.

"Oh, for crying out loud," Aunt Torie said. "You sound just like Benny."

Matt and Torie's Benjamin was eight years old.

Nevertheless, Brick didn't want to leave

367

the lakefront and go retrieve the binoculars his aunt had left up in the tree house. He still had a few more aerials to shoot off before the professional show started, and he needed to find Liliana. Call him a fool for torturing himself, but he wanted to sit beside her to watch the fireworks.

As Brick bent over to peer into his sack of fireworks, his grandfather kicked his ass. "Do as your aunt asks, whippersnapper."

"Yessir. Just one last Spider."

He set out the shell, set the punk to wick, then stepped back when sparks began to sizzle. *Thwump!* A white trail of sparks wiggled up into the sky and exploded into fast-burning legs of red, white, and blue. Brick extinguished his punk, glanced around once more for Liliana, then hurried toward the tree house.

It had been a great day. Ever since his family had purchased the property on Hummingbird Lake and begun spending the Fourth in Eternity Springs, the holiday had eclipsed Christmas in his enjoyment. Nothing like having both his families together.

That thought reminded him of his Oklahoma siblings. Courtney never had shown up today, and his parents hadn't been able to hide their disappointment. It teed Brick off. No wonder Josh had tried to dodge him all day. He wondered what excuse she'd given their brother for having bailed on the family get-together. Whatever it was, it wasn't good enough. Paul and Cindy Christopher had been nothing but kind to Courtney — just like they'd been to all of their foster children.

Something was up with Court. Probably that asshat ex-boyfriend in Denver. Brick wished she'd confide in him so he could help.

Thinking about that situation threatened to totally ruin his good mood, so Brick chose to put it out of his mind for the rest of the holiday. As he approached the tree house, the patriotic strains of "The Stars and Stripes Forever" sounded from the outdoor speakers stationed about the property and the first percussion explosive launched into the sky.

He climbed the ladder quickly and had just stepped onto the tree house floor when a huge golden Peony burst above him and momentarily illuminated the inside of the tree house. He identified the shadowed figure immediately. "Liliana," he said. "Here you are."

"Here I am."

"Aren't you smart to grab the best viewing spot on the property? Except . . ." He folded his arms and teased in an accusing tone, "Some things don't change. You shouldn't be here. No girls allowed."

Wryly, she drawled, "Tell that to your stepmother."

"Annabelle?" Brick's delight at discovering her in the privacy of the tree house suddenly faded to wariness. "What does Annabelle have to do with it?"

From below, he heard interfering Annabelle's familiar voice call, "I invited her."

Immediately it clicked. He knew what the wives were up to. Brick moved toward the ladder but proved to be half a step too slow and the ladder slipped below his reach. He stared down into the darkness toward the ground, twelve feet below. "Seriously?"

"Enjoy the fireworks," Aunt Maddie called.

"Bet they're all down there," he grumbled. "I should have known." Raising his voice, he called, "I can climb down, you know."

Aunt Nic's voice drifted up. "Only if you're stupid."

He knew his aunt wasn't referring to the possibility of falling and breaking his neck.

"What's the matter, Callahan?" Aunt Torie asked. "Scared of the dark? Good thing you have . . . protection."

The women cackled. Darned if he didn't

hear Mom's voice saying something about hot rockets, too.

Feeling a bit like a caged mountain lion, he whirled on Liliana and demanded, "Did they put you up to this?"

"I'm innocent. Honestly. Annabelle said she wanted to show me something. I didn't expect a thing until I saw the champagne."

"Champagne?"

"In the corner."

His eyes adjusted to the added darkness of the tree house, and he was able to identify the bucket and blankets in the northwest corner of the tree house.

"We're missing the show. I'm going up."

"Up" was the platform attached to the tree house's roof designed for cloud watching on a summer day. While Chrysanthemums and Horse Tails burst in the sky above, he considered his options. It was true. He could climb safely to the ground, replace the ladder for Liliana, and go on his way. This attempted manipulation by matchmaking meddlers rubbed him the wrong way.

But at the same time . . . champagne and a beautiful woman and the night sky? Fireworks? He'd wanted to watch the fireworks with her, hadn't he?

In public. Around his family. Around the

children.

Not in private.

With champagne. And . . . "Oh . . . no. Tell me they didn't."

Protection.

He looked closer at the supplies in the corner. Boxes. Three boxes of condoms. For the first time in longer than he could remember, Brick sensed the heat of a flush of embarrassment on his cheeks. What sort of parenting was this? *I'm selling everything and moving to Alaska. And I'm not leaving a forwarding address.*

But despite his misgivings, Brick couldn't stop himself from reaching for the champagne. The pop of the cork blended with the boom of rockets. Moments later, carrying two glasses of a fine sparkling wine, he climbed the staircase to the platform and Liliana.

She lay atop a blanket, her hands cradling her head, watching the fireworks show. He sat down beside her. "I brought champagne."

She levered herself up and accepted the glass. "Thank you."

He held his out for a toast. "To . . . freedom."

"To freedom," she repeated.

They clinked glasses, sipped the champagne, and watched the sky. A full five minutes passed before he said, "My family drives me crazy."

"I love your family. My parents wouldn't have done this on a bet."

"They're a bunch of busybodies. The guys are just as bad as their women. Sometimes worse."

"You're lucky to have them."

He sighed. "Yeah. I know."

"They love you very much."

"Yeah. I know. I love them, too. More when they're in Texas, but . . ."

She laughed and his body responded, his pulse pounded, almost keeping time with the patriotic music that was itself timed to the fireworks. It took all his discipline not to roll over on top of her and kiss her senseless.

When a particularly spectacular shell lit the sky and she purred with pleasure, he closed his eyes. "Why are you here tonight, Liliana?"

She waited until the glitter of a star's tail effect faded to respond. "To watch fireworks?"

Then she turned to look at him, as if to dare him to disagree. Her seafoam eyes were soft and slightly challenging, luminous and heated as a teal-green sunburst lit up the night sky. She wanted him.

"Is that all?" He let his hand curl in the waves of her hair, allowing a faint whisper of Heavenscents gardenia to envelop his senses.

This time a full minute passed before she answered his question. "I'd like more than three dates and we're done. I'd like tonight and the rest of the summer before I leave for romance. I've never had a summer romance. I'd like to have that with you."

He rolled up onto his elbow, reached out, and caressed her cheek. "I can give you romance, Lili-fair, but I don't know if I can give you anything else. Anything more."

He wished he could. If he had the ability to give anyone anything more, it would be her.

His heart pounded like a drum until she spoke.

"No strings, Mark. I'm here until summer's end. Can you give me a summer romance with no strings attached?"

It was an offer he'd be a fool to refuse. Brick was no fool. She wanted him, just him. No strings. No demands. Him, not all he brought with him. A summer romance. And yet the idea rested uneasily on his mind, even as he rolled over and kissed her. His voice low and rough, he said. "I can do that. I will be honored to do that."

She reached up and touched his face, moving her slender fingers over his skin. "Then take me down into your tree house, Mark."

He groaned deep in his throat. "Don't you want to wait for the grand finale?"

"Well . . . hmm . . ." She lifted her head and nipped at the lobe of his ear. "I'm sort of hoping that won't happen for hours yet."

With aerial explosions in every color of the rainbow lighting the sky, Brick leaned in and quickly caught her mouth with his own and then led Liliana down the steps to shelter.

With careful, almost reverent, attention, he stripped her clothes from her body.

And then the pyrotechnics began.

CHAPTER NINETEEN

When Lili awoke at dawn the following morning, naked and wrapped in Brick's arms, she felt deliciously sore. And uncomfortably sore. Next time she had tree house sex, she wanted it to be in one of Brick's tree houses that had a bed.

Tree house sex . . . and it hadn't even been on her GOHL list!

"Good morning," his deep, throaty voice rumbled in her ear, interrupting her inner gloat.

She stretched like a cat. "Good morning."

The golden glow of morning light spilled over his hard, naked body. His beard was rough, his eyes warm. "How did you sleep?"

"You mean for those whole ten minutes you let me sleep?

Grinning, he rolled over on top of her. "Look, my family left three boxes of rubbers. I didn't want to embarrass myself." He dipped his head and nuzzled her neck.

"Are you up for one more for the road?"

A wry smile lifted her lips and she wiggled against his obvious arousal. "Obviously, you are."

He nibbled her bottom lip, then kissed her. It was a different sort of kiss than any he'd given her before. Not the hot and erotic, demanding and thrilling kisses of last night, but a slow, tender, gentle kiss that for some reason brought tears to her eyes. She could get used to this . . . and that was danger with a capital *D.*

When he made love to her, it was different, too. His hands, his mouth, even the light in his eyes when he gazed at her made her feel . . . treasured. "You are such a siren, Lili-fair. My tempting little mermaid."

He took his time and made her feel cherished, and when they lay together in the aftermath, him drawing lazy circles on her stomach, Lili knew that while the summer would end, she'd remember last night for the rest of her life.

Eventually, sounds intruded. A door opening. An engine starting. Lili looked to see that sometime during the night someone had replaced the ladder. The thought of what that person might have heard made her blush from head to toes. "I can't believe your family."

Brick chuckled softly. "Fair warning, Lili-fair. They'll be a meddlesome lot until they return to Texas."

She shrugged. Since honesty caused her to admit that she liked the way they meddled, she couldn't exactly complain. "Do you think we'll be able to sneak out of here this morning? I don't know that I'm up to a walk of shame in front of two sets of your parents."

"Shame, Liliana? Really?"

She thought about it. "No. No, not ashamed. But I'm embarrassed to the tips of my toes."

"And lovely toes they are." Proving his point, he kissed his way down her legs to them — lingering long enough at the V between her legs to send her flying again — before finishing by tickling her toes.

She laughed and yanked her feet from his grip. He rolled to his feet and began gathering up their clothing, some of which they'd left up on the deck.

Lili put herself together as best she could, and as they descended the ladder to the ground she was almost afraid to look around. What if his family were all lined up waiting to see the results of their conspiracy?

Thankfully, the Callahan North Forty remained quiet. One of the brothers was down on the pier fishing and Lili was relieved that he didn't turn around as she and Brick made their way toward their trucks. "Patsy rode with me yesterday. I never even thought about how she'd get back to Stardance Ranch."

"Lots of people here were headed back that direction. I'm sure she didn't have a problem catching a ride."

No, but Lili could only imagine what Patsy might have told whoever offered her a ride. Somehow, she was in on last night's shenanigans, too. Lili would bet the farm on that one.

They approached the RV camp, and Lili asked Brick to take the back entrance and drop her off at her trailer.

"I'll drive through the main entrance and take you to you to your trailer and walk you to your door."

"No, Brick, I —"

His expression was fiercely protective and it stirred something in her chest. "We're not going to hide. I don't want to hide, and besides, we couldn't if we tried. Nothing is secret in an RV camp. You asked me for a summer romance, Lili. Let me romance you."

Seriously, she didn't know why she was being so nervous about this. These were the women who made ribald jokes every time CDD walked through camp. But they were her friends and what they thought of her mattered to her.

She couldn't forget Mary-Ellen's unvoiced but obvious disapproval the day of her fake walk of shame. *Well, like the saying goes, you made your bed.*

In a tree house. With the hottest guy in town.

Finally, for the first time in her life, Lili wasn't the wallflower. A smile played upon her lips. Aloud, she observed, "I'm brazen."

When he glanced at her, she noticed that his eyes looked tired. No, not exactly tired. More . . . satiated. Her smile widened.

"Brazen." He winked. "I like that about you, Legs."

"Legs?"

"Honey, after that last time this morning, I'm gonna be thinking about your legs all day long."

He turned into the main entrance and Lili was momentarily distracted when he said, "Huh. There's Courtney. Mind if we stop a minute, Liliana?"

"That's fine."

Brick's sister was walking from the camp laundry toward the office, a plastic clothes-basket in her hands. Brick rolled down his window as he pulled up beside her. "Where the hell have you been?"

A sheepish look crossed her face. "Hey, Brick. I'm sorry. I know I missed my shift a couple of times."

He waved his hand at the comment. "Josh and I were worried about you. You could have called. Mom and Pop are worried about you. You said you'd be at the picnic yesterday."

"I know. I'm sorry. I had something come up back in Denver. You're right; I should have called."

Lili could tell Brick wanted to ask about "something," but he chose not to do it, saying instead, "Yes, you should have."

"I'm really sorry, Brick. I thought I'd go see Paul and Cindy this morning, if you don't need me at the office." He didn't answer right away and she added, "If I still have a job?"

He sighed heavily. "Yes, you still have a job. Just call next time, would you? Let us know what's going on."

"I will. I promise." Courtney looked past him to Lili. "Good morning, Lili."

"Good morning."

Brick took his foot off the brake and the truck rolled forward. "Well, I'm glad to know she's safe."

381

The comment sent a shiver of guilt running through Lili. She'd done the same thing to Derek, hadn't she? He hadn't been in her parents' kitchen that day. He hadn't betrayed her. And she'd lied to him.

Well, I'm going to continue to lie to him. I'm darn sure not going to tell him that I'm sleeping with his best friend.

She stole a look at Brick, wondering if that particular thought had occurred to him yet this morning.

Then he turned onto the row of campsites where her trailer was located and saw Patsy throwing a tennis ball to Sugar. Across the street, Mary-Ellen sat beneath the black-and-white-striped canopy that matched her black-and-white trailer. Lili tried to keep the nerves from showing in her smile as they drove past the pastor's wife's trailer. Lili waved, and when her friend returned a wave wearing a genuine smile on her face the last of Lili's insecurity evaporated.

When her lover walked her to her trailer door and kissed her good-bye, she floated inside. *This must be what it feels like to have wings.*

And if the little voice inside her head whispered words of warning that Annabelle Callahan didn't know her stepson as well as she thought, well, Lili wouldn't worry about it. Not until the end of the summer.

And for the next few weeks, she didn't. She was too busy splitting her time between spending it with Patsy and being romanced.

She thought about this magical time as she dressed for the Tornado Alleycats Fifth Birthday Tea the first day of August. During the past three weeks, Brick had sent her flowers and left her little gifts at the door to her trailer. He'd taken her on dates and on nights they didn't spend together called her before he went to sleep.

They'd spent one night together in her trailer, but he was too tall for the bed and said never again. Lili had been glad. His tree house had been just about the most fabulous place she'd ever stayed — until the night last week when he asked her to meet him at the Bear Cave at 8:00.

"This is a little weird," Lili said as she pulled on the yellow sundress she'd worn the night she'd ended up at Angel's Rest. Brick still didn't like the Bear Cave very much, and this was the first time he'd asked her to meet him somewhere.

She walked into the bar at four minutes past eight and at first she didn't see him. He stood with his back to the door and didn't turn to identify the newcomer like everyone else in the bar. And he was wearing a suit. That confused her. And, frankly, alarmed her. She'd never seen him wearing a suit. Had somebody died?

She crossed the room to him. "Brick? Is something wrong?"

He turned toward her with a curious look on his face. "I'm sorry! Have we met?"

It took her half a minute to get it, but then she remembered her meltdown when she'd said she'd wanted to pick up a stranger wearing a three-piece suit in a bar. He was too funny. She slipped her arm around his and laughed. "Brick Callahan, you're funny."

"And you're beautiful. But I'm afraid you have me confused with someone else. My name isn't Brick Callahan."

Lili might have worried she'd stumbled into another Callahan twin thing, except for the gleam in his eyes. Was he into role-playing? Or was he trying to fulfill her dream? Either way, she was happy to play along.

"My apologies. I mistook you for someone else." She extended her hand. "My name is Liliana Howe."

"It's a pleasure to meet you, Liliana. I'm Hank Hammer."

She snorted a laugh at that. She couldn't help herself.

When they left the Bear Cave twenty minutes later, he'd taken her up to Stardance

River Camp for a night of unparalleled romance in one of his tents.

She'd been dizzy on their hike to the six remaining cabins of an old ghost town built on a hot springs. The altitude, he'd told her. Stardance River Camp was much higher than the RV resort. As they'd soaked in the hot springs and made love in an alpine meadow, Lili had known it wasn't the altitude but the man. The man and the oh-so-special moment.

If when their time together came to an end, Brick remained allergic to anything permanent with a woman, well, to paraphrase a movie, they'd always have Stardance.

Meanwhile, the clock continued to tick, growing louder every day. Almost like a bomb. As the sound grew so did her worry that she wouldn't be strong enough to maintain her resolve to be Ingrid Bergman and get on that plane to fly away and leave him behind.

She pulled on the costume she'd borrowed for the tea from the Eternity Springs summer theater, then pinned on the fascinator she'd made during one of the Alleycats' craft workshops. The costume was an 1880s-style walking dress in robin's-egg blue. The fascinator, a tribute to *The Wizard of Oz.* It included a little figure meant to represent the Cowardly Lion. Patsy would be wearing the Scarecrow. Sharon, the Wicked Witch. Mary-Ellen was wearing Dorothy; and Nic Callahan, Toto.

Celeste Blessing's fascinator portrayed the Wizard.

A glance at the clock showed Lili that she was almost ten minutes late. Getting ready had taken longer than anticipated. That's what she got for daydreaming. She needed to hurry. Picking up the little drawstring bag that matched the gown from her bedside table, she hurried to her trailer's door. In her rush, she almost tripped over the hem of the dress.

She picked up the gown and looped it over her left arm, then stepped down from her trailer and hurried toward the activity center until the sound of a familiar roar stopped her in her tracks.

Having delivered his surprise for the Alley-cats' fancy dress-up tea to the Ranch's activity center, Brick whistled "Viva Las Vegas" beneath his breath and climbed into the golf cart. He'd known his idea was a good one despite Josh and Courtney's lack of enthusiasm. Sharon had taken one look at the entertainment Brick had provided and begun howling with laughter.

"Knew I was right," he said to himself as he pressed the accelerator and steered toward the office. Something like this was right up the Tornado Alleycats' alley.

A few minutes later, he braked the golf cart to a stop in front of the office. He no sooner alighted from the cart than the office door was flung open and a figure rushed outside.

"You're sleeping with her? You asshole!"

Derek Howe launched himself at Brick and the two men went down in a heap.

Brick had figured this day would come. He'd even spent a little time thinking about what he might say to Derek when it did and how he might attempt to justify his actions. He'd come up with nothing.

He had no justification. All he could say was that he was sorry. Except that would be a lie, wouldn't it?

Especially after Derek damned near broke his nose.

Brick never would have thrown the first punch, but enough was enough. The men rolled in the dirt grappling and trading punches. Like old times, Brick thought, just before Derek landed one in his gut.

Meanwhile, Derek's mouth never quit running, the stream of invectives and insults showing the depth and capacity of his intellect and imagination. Finally, though, Brick had had enough. Besides, he worried about the talented surgeon hurting his hands. Bigger and stronger than his opponent, Brick managed to gain the upper hand. As he drew back his fist to land a forceful punch to Derek's jaw, a stream of cold water stopped him. "What the hell?"

"Get off of him!" Liliana screeched.

Brick could tell from the tone of her voice that it wasn't the first time she'd voiced the demand. He rolled off Derek, sat up, and felt his nose, testing it for a break.

"You're like a couple of fighting dogs," she continued. "Have to get the water hose to break you apart. Which one of you is Yankee and which is Kipper?"

Derek was sitting up, too, testing one of his teeth. He gaped at his sister, then looked at Brick. "Yankee and Kipper?"

"Those neighborhood dogs. The two that were always fighting. Boston terrier and a boxer."

"Oh yeah." Derek nodded. "Now I remember." Then he took a good look at his sister and observed, "This is bizarro world. What is that on your head, Lili? It looks like a lion." Turning to Brick, he added, "What the hell have you done to her, Christopher?"

Lili's eyes looked a little wild, fury in her tone. "Don't talk to him. Talk to me! What are you doing here, Derek? How did you find me?"

Even before the question was out of her mouth she'd turned a blazing gaze upon Brick. "You told him!"

Brick held up his hands, palms out. "I'm innocent."

"The hell you say," Derek fired back. He pointed toward the office. "That woman in there said you're fu—"

The ugly word didn't make it past his lips, because fast as a snake strike Brick popped him in the mouth. "Watch your mouth, Howe. I'll give you some latitude, but don't cross the line."

Brick rolled to his feet and dusted off his jeans. "Look, why don't we take this somewhere that's a bit more private."

"No." Liliana's chin came up. She stared at her brother with such disdain that Brick almost grinned. That costume she wore suited her. "I have a previous engagement."

"You look great, Lili-fair," he told her. "The hat's the bomb."

He couldn't quite read the emotion that flashed in her eyes. Gratitude or relief or despair? Maybe a combination of all three. "Thank you."

Like a nineteenth-century society maven, she nodded at her brother, then turned to leave. Brick could hardly tear his gaze away from the sway of her bustle.

"You have a helluva lot of explaining to do," Derek growled.

"Yeah. I know." Brick sighed and dragged his hand down his face. "But I have a few questions myself. Come with me to my place and we'll get a beer and hash this out."

"All right." Lili's brother dusted off his slacks and straightened his shirt. "Fair warning, though. I might still kill you."

"Yeah, well . . ." — Brick saw Lili disappear around the corner of a forty-one-foot Winnebago and realized his time with her might have just run out — "I might just let you."

CHAPTER TWENTY

Seated at her table in the Stardance Ranch activity center, Lili brought the china teacup to her lips with a trembling hand. The scone tasted like sawdust. The sweet raspberry jam struck her as sour. Derek was here. He'd discovered her lies. How? She believed Brick's denial. He'd met her gaze at that moment and honesty had shone clearly in his eyes.

Patsy. It had to have been Patsy. No one else knew her family.

Her gaze drifted toward Patsy, seated across the round table of ten.

Her first reaction was to feel betrayed, but almost immediately that emotion shifted to fear. Patsy must think that Lili needed advice or assistance from her brother. Or perhaps that her family now needed to know her whereabouts. Why would she think that? Lili could come up with only one answer.

The cancer.

Was Patsy running out of time?

Lili's cup rattled as she set it into the saucer. Needing something to do with her hands, she nibbled at a cucumber finger sandwich that she didn't want.

Seated next to her, Celeste leaned toward Lili. "Is something wrong, dear?"

"It's complicated. I had a bit of a surprise today. And I'm just . . . Does Patsy look all right to you?"

"She looks like she's having a grand time."

"Yes. She does. Doesn't she? I'm glad. Today is terribly important to her."

"Yes, that has been obvious."

Lili drew in a deep breath and released it on a sigh. It was true. Today was an extremely special day for Patsy, and Lili shouldn't risk ruining it with personal distractions or by dwelling on what-ifs. "I love her, Celeste. She's the grandmother I always wanted to have. The grandmother *everybody* wants to have."

"I know, dear. Here's something for you to remember. The sweet souls who inspire you, who cherish you, and who protect you dwell with you always — no matter where you both may be."

Lili gave Celeste a sharp look. Did she know something Lili did not?

Before she could ask, Sharon rose and

stepped to the podium. "Ladies, may I have your attention? Now that we've taken the edge off of our hunger with that fabulous tea provided by the Mocha Moose Sandwich Shop and Fresh Bakery, I have a special announcement to make. Our very own Camp Director Dreamboat was thoughtful enough to arrange some entertainment for our birthday tea. Ladies, allow me to present to you . . ." She made a flourishing wave toward the back door. "The King of Eternity Springs."

The door opened and an Elvis impersonator swept into the room singing "Happy Birthday, Baby," and when Patsy clapped her hands and exploded in laughter Lili forgot all about her brother. For the next little while, she devoted her attention to family.

The event relaxed her and grounded her and strengthened her, and when the birthday party wound down and Patsy stood to speak to the Tornado Alleycats Lili shed tears no more numerous than those of the other women in the room.

"My dear friends," Patsy said. "I want you all to know how much it's meant to me to have had you join me here in Eternity Springs this summer. Over the course of my long, interesting, and for the most part happy life, I've been blessed with some wonderful friendships. However, none of them have meant as much to me as those I share with you here today. You are — in every sense of the word — my sisters. You have brought joy and laughter and love into my world. You have opened my eyes to new adventures and possibilities and offered me hugs when I needed them. My new friend, Celeste Blessing, said something to me a few minutes ago that struck a chord with me. It's something I believe in my marrow. She said friends aren't coincidences. Friends are former strangers who are meant to come into our lives to teach us invaluable lessons and give us priceless memories. Each of you has done that for me. I believe each of you was meant to be a Tornado Alleycat."

Cheers and applause interrupted her. Smiling, she clapped her hands back at the crowd that had the activity center bursting at its seams.

"We love you, Patsy," somebody called.

"I love you, too," she replied. "Dearly. I've never had so much fun in my life. Thank you all for joining me on this summer's exceptional extended campout. Thank you for the happiness you've given me over the past five years. Thank you for the gift of your friendship. Now, let's all go get out of these long dresses, shall we, girls? I don't know about you, but I need to put on my loosies."

Alleycats all over the room wiped the tears from their eyes, and once again Stardance Ranch RV Resort's activity center erupted into applause and chants. "Patsy! Patsy! Patsy! Patsy!"

Laughing, she spoke once more into the microphone. "Loosies!"

Amidst laughter, the gathering finally broke up.

For an instant Lili wished she didn't know about Patsy's condition. But only for an instant. Were she unaware that time with her friend was limited, she might have spent more of it with Brick. While he'd given her no reason to think he'd changed his mind, at least that potential ending had some wiggle room. Patsy's situation didn't. No matter what happened with Brick, the time with her here in Colorado had been a gift.

A gift. Like sunlight slowly chasing the shadows of night from the sky, awareness dawned. This time Lili had spent with Patsy was a gift. So, too, had been the mess at the firm.

And the situation with her parents. If they hadn't turned their backs on her, she wouldn't be here now.

"Wow. Just wow." Everything truly did happen for a reason. It wasn't just a platitude.

Which means that Brick's presence in my life happened for a reason, too.

"Okay, then." Supported by this new realization, Lili exited the activity center and went in search of her brother. She'd expected to find him at her trailer. He wasn't there. She took a few minutes to change clothes — choosing yoga pants and a T-shirt since Patsy's "loosies" mention had put the idea in her head — and continued her search. Nor was Derek in the office or down beside the river or in the snack room or even the laundry. She asked Josh to check the men's room and showers for her, to no avail. Since Brick was nowhere to be found, either, she figured they must be together.

She decided to try his tree house next. Grabbing the bicycle she used to make the trip that was a good ten minutes from her trailer space, she pedaled there. When she dismounted at the base of the Z-shaped staircase that led up to the structure, she heard the rumble of male voices. She'd found Brick and undoubtedly Derek, too.

Lili climbed the staircase with all the enthusiasm of a condemned prisoner ascending to the scaffold.

The voices fell silent as they heard her on the steps. Just beyond view, she paused and took a deep breath, then knocked on the jamb beside the open door and stepped inside.

Shock left her speechless.

Brick sat at the foot of his bed, a bag of frozen peas against his nose. Derek sat in the wooden rocking chair, a bag of frozen corn against his eye.

Her mother and father sat at the kitchen table.

"Hello, Liliana," her mother said.

"Hi, little girl." Nerves showed in her father's smile.

She finally managed to get some words out. "Mom! Dad! What are you doing here?"

Brian and Stephanie Howe shared a significant look; then he said, "We've come to apologize, Liliana."

Her mother nodded. "We're so sorry we let you down."

It was too much. After the emotion of the birthday party, after the shock of seeing Derek prior to that, it was simply too much.

Liliana burst into tears.

Her mother came over to hold her, saying, "Hush now, honey. It's all right. Everything is going to be all right now."

Her mother's action only made her cry

harder. When was the last time her mother had held her? She couldn't remember. Her mother had never been much of a hugger.

Then Lili's father crossed the room and handed her his handkerchief. He always carried a handkerchief. Every year since she could remember, she'd given him a new box of handkerchiefs on Father's Day. She hadn't sent him his gift this year. The selection of fishing lures and a new box of hankies still sat in the backseat of her pickup. Guilt washed through her. She should have mailed the gift. Why hadn't she mailed it?

Lili cried harder.

She was vaguely aware of Brick excusing himself and stepping out onto the tree house's wraparound porch, leaving the Howe family alone. Her mother continued to hold her. "Don't cry, Lili. Please don't cry. We're sorry. Dad and I are so sorry."

"I hope you'll forgive us, pumpkin," her father added.

Pumpkin. When was the last time he'd called her pumpkin?

"Hush now. Hush. Here, let's sit down. Your father and I want to explain what happened." Stephanie Howe led Lili to the bed where Brick had been sitting, then sat beside her.

How weird was this? To be sitting here with her mother on Brick's bed where she'd had wild wanton sex not six hours ago! *My mom!* It was that realization more than anything that dried Lili's tears.

She wiped her eyes and blew her nose and gathered herself. "I'm sorry. It's been an emotional day."

"Yes, for us, too," her mother said. "We've been worried about you, Lili. This estrangement has weighed heavy on our hearts. Knowing that we'd finally have the opportunity to attempt to make it right has filled the day with uncertainty and stress. We are not of sure how you'll react."

Neither am I.

Her father moved one of the chairs from Brick's kitchen table near the bed. He sat and leaned forward, putting his elbows on his knees, winced, and immediately straightened. "The way we reacted when you came to us in trouble was inexcusable. That said, would you listen to us, Liliana, and allow us to explain why we failed you?"

She nodded.

He breathed a heavy sigh, rubbed his palms on his slacks, and began. "For a couple of weeks prior to your visit that day, I'd had a pain in my side. I went in for a sonogram and then an MRI."

All thought of wounded feelings evaporated. In her mother's arms, Lili stiffened.

"Shortly before you arrived that day, my doctor called. They'd found what appeared to be gallstones, but also a suspicious mass on my gallbladder."

Fear gripped her. She brought a hand up to cover her mouth. "Oh, Daddy."

"I'm okay," he assured quickly. "I had surgery and the tumor was benign."

Thank God.

Her mother said, "Lili, the timing was simply horrendous. Dad and I were reeling from the news when you arrived, trying to make decisions about surgeons and hospitals and worrying about the possibilities."

"Why didn't you tell me?" she asked.

Her parents shared a look, then her father said, "We should have. It's obvious in hindsight, but at the time . . . to be brutally honest, Lili, I wasn't concerned about you. I was scared."

She blinked. Her father was *never* scared.

"You know I watched both of my parents die from cancer. Following in their footsteps is my biggest fear."

"I was scared, too," her mother added. "I wasn't thinking clearly. All I knew at the time was that your father and I already had one fight on our hands and at that moment

I didn't have the capacity for two."

"I understand," Lili said. And it was true. She did understand. Seeing the importance Patsy placed on how and when to share the news about her cancer gave Lili insight into the motives behind her parents' silence that day. Horrendous timing, indeed.

Her father continued, "By the time we got our feet under us, you'd left on your vacation. We debated telling you then, but it was the first vacation you'd taken in so long, we didn't want to burden you with medical questions that had no answers. We decided to spare you until after the surgery when the lab results came back."

This was more difficult to understand. Her father had surgery and she hadn't known about it. He'd always been a private person, but she wasn't some stranger. She was his daughter.

But I'm not his son. She glanced toward her brother and guessed, "You told Derek, though."

"Well, yes," her father replied. "He's a doctor. He helped us interpret all the tests."

He had a point. Any jealousy she felt over that particular slight wasn't fair to her parents or Derek.

Her mother took up the telling. "The surgery took a couple of weeks to schedule

and then was a little more complicated than
we'd hoped. By the time he was home and
the pathology reports back, you were . . .
well, we didn't know where you were."

"I called you. You didn't say anything
about it."

"You didn't give us a chance. We could
tell you were hurt and angry with us. We
thought we'd give you some time."

"Time heals all wounds," her father
added.

"We weren't anxious until Derek told us
you'd confessed that you'd taken up with a
stranger and were traveling the country.
That has kept me up nights. It was such a
relief to learn that it wasn't so."

"How did that happen? How did you learn
where I was?"

Derek finally spoke. "Coincidence — or
maybe fate. I had a dentist appointment the
day before yesterday, and I was sitting in
the office twiddling my thumbs. I reached
for a travel magazine and an old tabloid
newspaper was beneath it. I saw a photo of
you sitting in a jail cell and thought you
had a doppelgänger."

"But that picture was on an inside page,"
Lili protested. "And they never published
my name."

Her brother shrugged. "It was folded

open. I read the article thinking I'd give you a hard time about it. Mark had told me about Stardance River Camp, so I recognized the name and took a closer look at the photo. I realized that the 'unnamed female' really *was* you."

Lili glanced from her brother, to her parents, then back to her brother again. "So you told Mom and Dad and you all decided to hop into a car rather than call me?"

"Actually, I flew," Derek said.

"It's awfully hot in Norman right now," her father added. "Supposed to hit one hundred and two today."

"You two," her mother scolded. She took both of Lili's hands in hers. "Sweetheart, your father and I believed we needed to make this apology in person. We are so very sorry for what those bastards at the firm did to you."

Lili's eyes widened. Her mother never used that sort of language.

"We are so very sorry for the way the way we failed you when you needed us. Will you forgive us?"

Lili blinked back fresh tears and swallowed the lump in her throat. "Of course I forgive you. I love you."

Tears misted her father's eyes, shocking

Lili yet again. Had she ever seen her father cry?

She didn't want to see it today. Misty eyes were one thing. Tears . . . no. "It's nice to understand what happened that day, and honestly, now that it's over, I'm glad I didn't have to worry about your pathology report results, Dad."

Both of her parents visibly relaxed. Her father nodded, then said, "Lili, I've spoken to my contacts, and there's not anything I can do about Ormsby, Harbaugh, and Stole. However, I did manage to take care of your dirty cop. The lie has been removed from your record, and your accounting license is and shall remain in effect. A check for the fines you paid arrived at the house last week." He paused and added, "You really need to change your permanent address, by the way."

"Daddy," she breathed, her head spinning at the news.

"That's not all," her mother added, her eyes bright with delight. "There's a job offer waiting for you from Kingston and Lear. You can come home, Lili!"

In the silence that followed, Lili heard the creak of a board that betrayed the fact that Brick stood near the window. *Eavesdropping, Callahan?* When he gave up any pre-

404

tense of giving the Howe family privacy by moving to an open window so that he could both see and hear her, Lili wanted to smile.

He cared. She could see on his face that he cared.

So, too, did her family.

"Thank you, Dad. Mom and Dad." She glanced at her brother and added, "Even you, Derek. I guess it's only fair you turned the tattletale tables on me."

"About damned time," he said with a tender smile.

"Dad, I don't care about the firm. I wouldn't have cared about the DUI except I have to buy auto insurance. Well, and the fines. That was a lot of money."

"It was," her mother agreed.

Lili continued, "I appreciate your going to bat for me. It heals a little wound on my heart. But as far as Kingston and Lear goes, I need to tell you something. I don't want to be an accountant anymore."

Brian Howe shook his head. "Now, honey. It's natural that you would have decided that while thinking you couldn't practice again, but things have changed."

"Not in this respect it hasn't. I don't like accounting. I never have. I never will." Her parents were shocked. Her brother, not so much. Brick gave her a nod and an approving grin.

"As far as going home . . . well . . . I'm going to remain in Eternity Springs at least until the end of the summer." She envisioned a pair of wings on her back and gave them a flutter for strength. Then she met Brick's gaze and declared, "Longer, I hope. I've fallen in love with Brick Callahan."

She could read nothing in Brick's expression but for the sudden heat blazing in his eyes.

Then her father asked, "Who the hell is Brick Callahan?"

She'd have introduced him, but the man had just disappeared from sight.

CHAPTER TWENTY-ONE

Telling herself that patience was a virtue, Lili showed her family around Stardance Ranch and introduced them to every Alleycat they encountered. Unfortunately, they never saw Brick. Her parents dined at the Yellow Kitchen that night, feasting on Ali Timberlake's fabulous red sauce. When dinner ended, her parents bid Lili an early good night and retired to their room at Angel's Rest since they planned to make an early departure the following morning. Derek hung behind and asked her to take him to a hot spot to have a beer. Briefly she considered taking him to the Bear Cave, but she knew his reaction would be similar to Brick's. So instead, they strolled over to Murphy's Pub and found a table for two out on the patio.

Derek didn't waste any time. "Are you sure about this, Lili?"

"Sure about what?"

"Mark. Brick. Whatever the hell you call him." He spun a paper coaster around on the table. "Tiffany did a real number on him."

"I know that." She took a sip of her beer. "He's a risk for me. I'm well aware that he might never get over her. But I'm also sure that if I don't give it a shot I'll regret it."

"You've changed, little sister."

"For the better, I hope?"

"Yes. Not that there was anything wrong with you before. You've . . . grown. You're confident. Strong."

Her mouth twisted in a wry and slightly sad smile. "It's all a front. I'm quaking in my shoes. He left and hasn't come back."

"That's Mark." Derek sipped his beer. "If you're set on having him, it's a good sign, too. For run-of-the-mill stuff, he makes his mind up fast, but if something is important, if it seriously matters, he has to chew on things awhile before he comes to a decision."

"I don't want him to love me with his brain," she grumbled. "I want him to love me with his heart."

"Well, that's easy. His heart is already there, Liliana. His head needs a little time to catch up."

"He told you this while you were pummeling each other?"

"Nah. I know him. He's my best friend. Which is why I know he's gone over you. No way would he have an affair with you if he wasn't already a little in love with you."

Little wouldn't cut it, Lili thought later as she delivered her brother to Angel's Rest. She hugged him good-bye and was about to get back into her truck when she heard her name.

"Isn't this a lovely coincidence?" the innkeeper said. "I intended to stop by Stardance Ranch tomorrow morning. This will save me a trip. Here, my dear. I have something to give you."

"Oh?" Lili asked as Celeste reached into her pocket and withdrew a small piece of jewelry. "What's this? How beautiful."

"It's the official Angel's Rest blazon awarded to those who've accepted love's healing grace. Your parents shared news of your reconciliation tonight. I'm so happy for you all, Liliana."

"Thank you, Celeste. I am, too." She looked closer at the silver medal. It looked familiar. "Nic Callahan wears one of these."

"Yes, she does." Celeste's blue eyes gleamed with pleasure. "Nic and Gabe both wear the blazon. Theirs was the first I awarded, in fact. Though the blazons aren't easy to earn, you will see quite a few of them around town. Now it's time to go to work to seeing that Brick earns his. I plan to get started on that first thing in the morning."

Lili wanted to ask her if she knew where Brick had gone this afternoon, but she didn't have the nerve. "This is a treasure, Celeste. I'll wear it proudly."

The two women visited a few minutes longer; then Lili took her leave. As she made her way back to the RV camp, her thoughts returned to the discussion with Derek. She'd like to think he was right, that she already owned a piece of Brick's heart, but if that was the case why had he run off? Had her honesty been a mistake? "TMI, Brick?"

Well, time would tell. One thing Lili knew for certain, being a little in love was okay for a summer romance, but not for a life-time.

Back at the Ranch, she went to his tree house. He still wasn't home, so she decided to wait for him. He didn't come home all night. At 7:00 a.m., she returned to her trailer.

If he was going to make a walk of shame — legitimate or fake — then she intended to be around to witness it.

He still hadn't returned by nine when

Patsy knocked on her trailer, Sugar at her heels. Lili took one look at Patsy's face and knew something was wrong. "What's happened, Patsy?"

"Lili, I need you to do me a favor."

"Of course. Anything."

Her friend handed her Sugar's leash. "I need you to take care of Sugar for me."

"I'm happy to babysit. You know I love her." Lili knelt and briskly scratched the dog behind the ears. "Who wouldn't love you, you beautiful girl?"

"Not babysit, sunshine. I mean permanently."

Lili's heart all but stopped. Slowly, she climbed to her feet. "Patsy?"

"I'm packing up. I'm afraid my summer is coming to an end earlier than I had hoped. It's time for me to go home."

Emotion lodged in Lili's throat. She would not cry. Patsy would not want her to cry. Nevertheless, her voice trembled as she asked, "What can I do to help?"

"I wouldn't mind an extra pair of hands. Maybe come by in an hour? Now I'm going to walk around camp and say good-bye to the girls." Her mouth lifted in a sheepish smile. "I considered sneaking off like a thief in the night, but that's not who I am. I've always met life head-on. No sense changing things now."

"No. No sense changing things now." Lili blinked hard, fighting back her tears. She was doing way too much crying of late. It had to stop. "I should come with you."

"Thank you, but no. This is something I need to do myself."

"Not now. I mean going home. I'll go with you."

As the dog wound between both women's legs, Patsy gazed at Lili with a tender smile. "And cut short your summer romance? I won't hear of it."

"But —"

"No. Absolutely not. For you to leave Eternity Springs now would be spectacularly bad timing. I won't be the reason your summer doesn't last forever."

"Patsy, I could —"

"No! Now, be a dear and get Sugar some water. She's the thirstiest dog I've ever known. You have a water bowl she can use, don't you? I should have brought that with me, but I packed everything up in a box — her bed, bowls, toys, and food. It's heavy, so I stopped in at the office and asked Josh to bring it over for us. He said he'd do it shortly. Poor man was fighting the computer over something. He looked to be at the end of his rope."

Yes, well. It can't help to have his boss up and disappear on him.

Patsy departed to make her rounds of good-bye. Lili filled a bowl with water for Sugar and the dog drank her fill. Then Lili sank to the floor, wrapped her arms around Sugar, and indulged in a good cry until a knock sounded at her trailer door. "Lili?" Josh asked. "I'm sorry to bother you, but would you take a look at something for me? I think Brick has some serious trouble."

Brick lowered his safety glasses, fired up his chain saw, and went back to work. After camping out at River Camp's ghost town, he'd been up working since dawn. A little demolition. A little repair. Nothing helped a man work out his aggressions like swinging a crowbar or hammer or running a chain saw.

Except for sex.

Don't go there.

He wouldn't think about sex. He wouldn't think about Liliana. Not anymore.

That's all he'd been doing since yesterday afternoon. Her voice wouldn't stop echoing through his brain. *I've fallen in love with Brick Callahan.*

He should have seen that one coming. Why hadn't he? Had he been blinded by

413

the sex? He clenched his teeth as he put the saw to wood. *Eyes wide shut. That's me.*

He'd cut a week's worth of firewood when he finally set aside his chain saw, yanked his work gloves from his back pocket, and pulled them on, then loaded his arms with firewood. He turned around and damned near dropped the logs.

Two pickup trucks were parked not fifty feet away. The tailgates were down and four men sat watching him work.

The Callahan brothers.

Well, hell.

"Didn't realize he's deaf as well as stupid," Matt drawled.

"Comes part and parcel with that hard head of his," Luke added. "You know, we really should have gone with 'Granite' for his nickname rather than 'Brick.' "

His father sighed theatrically. "Sometimes it's hard for me to believe that he is the fruit of my loins."

"What the hell is going on here?" Brick demanded.

Gabe explained, "It's what we call in Eternity Springs an intervention. Usually the women are involved, but we thought we'd cut you a break. Don't forget that you owe us."

"Brother," Brick grumbled.

"Brothers," Mark said. "Here to kick your ass."

Brick tossed down the logs and braced his hands on his hips. "What did I do?"

Luke slid off the tailgate. "Nothing. That's the problem. We had a visitor this morning."

"In Texas?" Nodding toward the three elder brothers, he added, "I thought you guys went home."

"We did." Matt slid down from the truck, too. "Our wives made us come back for the weekend. They have something going on with Celeste."

"So I have her to thank for this?"

"You should count your lucky stars," Gabe said, moving to stand beside his brothers. "You've been around town long enough to know that, too."

"I don't want or need a damned Angel's Rest medal to hang around my neck."

"What did I say?" Matt groused. "Dumb as a box of rocks."

He crossed the distance to Brick and used his index finger to poke him in the chest, punctuating his words as he spoke. "Hear my words, young man. You are a fool if you don't learn from the mistakes of others. I came within an eyelash of blowing it with Victoria because I was hard-headed, too.

415

Thought I had to go the road alone. Wasn't honest with her. I wouldn't admit that I loved her more than life itself. When I finally came to my senses, it was damned near too late. I had to set up this huge, wild-ass James Bond scenario to win her back. Believe me, you don't want to be parasailing in a tux and with a dog on your back. Be smarter than me, Mark Junior. Don't blow this."

Matt turned and walked to his truck. Luke sauntered over and took his brother's place. "You need to get the cotton out of your head. Liliana Howe is the best thing that's ever happened to you. Just like Maddie Kincaid was the best thing that ever happened to me. But I was a big, tough DEA agent. I thought I was the center of the effing universe. I thought I was the reason people lived and died, and when Maddie almost died I walked away from her. It took me way too long to come to understand that I didn't control the whole universe, that I'd given her my heart and I would never be whole again if she wasn't part of my world.

"Don't be the idiot I was. You have the opportunity to have something special with your Liliana. Don't let your stubbornness ruin your chances."

He got the shotgun seat next to his brother

and Gabe took his place. "Do you need me to beat you up, too?"

"Not necessarily."

"Good. Maybe that means you opened your ears. I do have something I want to say to you. I was about as low as a man could be when I first arrived in Eternity Springs. I haven't admitted this to more than a handful of people, but I was ready to put a gun in my mouth and end it all."

Brick gaped at him in shock. "You mean . . . ?"

"Yep. That day, I found my faith. I had a guardian angel on the mountain with me. Someday I'll tell you the whole story, but the point I'm trying to make today is that you shouldn't be dismissive of the possibility of having a guiding force in your life. Take the blinders off your eyes, Mark. Open your heart to healing. We do healing well here in Eternity Springs."

Gabe gave his nephew a guy hug, climbed into the backseat of the extended-cab pickup, and shut the door. Matt started the engine and put the truck into gear. Brick looked at his father. "You're not going with them?"

"Nope. I wanted to have my say with you in private."

"Oh, joy." But the sentiment was all

bluster. Brick was shaken by the advice his uncles had given to him.

Mark hooked his thumb toward the space on the tailgate that Gabe had vacated. "C'mere and sit. I'm too old to do this standing up."

"I repeat: Oh, joy." He did as his father asked and sat beside him.

"I know I've said this to you before, but it bears repeating. I'm so thankful that after your mother died you found a home with Cindy and Paul. You were raised by fine people, son. I couldn't have asked for better. Paul has been your father every bit as a much as I have. You were damned near an adult when I found you. As I tried to figure out my proper role in your life, I never wanted to step on his."

"You haven't."

"Well, I'm fixing to right now. You and I — from the beginning our relationship has been that of friends rather than father-son. You already had a father. That's the way it needed to be. But I think right now you need a dad. I'm going to give it my best shot."

Mark looked his son in the eyes and said, "I know you're scared. I get it. You truly loved Tiffany and she hurt you. It's no wonder you're gun shy. But dammit, son, it's gone on long enough. You've gotta get over that girl!"

"I am over her."

"Are you? Then why the hell are you trying so hard to screw things up with Liliana? Do you think Lili is out to manipulate you? Take advantage of your connections? Take advantage of your wallet?"

"No. Not at all. She's not like that."

"Then why treat her like she is?"

"I don't," Brick defended.

Mark arched a doubting brow at his son. "Tiffany was your first love. You lost her. That doesn't mean that your life should come to an end. It *doesn't* come to an end — if you don't let it. I will always love your mother, but I had to accept that she's gone."

"You're equating my mother with Tiffany, Dad. That's not right. It's not how I see it. My mother died. Tiffany jumped at a wallet. Two entirely different situations."

"Not to our hearts, it's not."

Brick raked his fingers through his hair. "To quote Branch, 'my heart doesn't know whether it's pitching pennies or playing shortstop.' "

"Your heart knows what it's doing. It's your head that's having a difficult time catching up. You gotta conquer your fear, Brick. You have to take a risk.

"It took me a while to figure out how, but once I did, I moved forward and built something real and something wonderful with Annabelle. I want that for you, and I believe that Liliana is the woman you've been waiting for. I've never seen you look at a woman the way you look at her. I've never seen a woman gaze at you with such obvious love in her eyes."

Mark pushed off the tailgate. "It's your life, Son. You have to live it the way you see fit. However, I think you'll be the biggest knucklehead on the planet if you don't get a ring on Liliana Howe's finger ASAP."

"A ring!"

"Yeah, a ring. I think she has all the right stuff to be a Callahan wife."

CHAPTER TWENTY-TWO

Sugar lay sprawled at Lili's feet while she worked with Josh. He brought her files; he provided passwords; he made phone calls and okayed her access to information. She took his suspicions and her expertise and knitted together the tale. The final tally made her stomach sink. She circled the number in red and handed the piece of paper to him without comment.

His complexion drained of color. "I can't believe this. This is going to kill Brick."

"Financially or personally?"

"Both." He rubbed the back of his neck. "I don't know that Stardance can survive the hit. The personal part will knock him for a loop, though."

"It's possible some or even all of the money is recoverable."

Hope lit his eyes. "How do we find that out?"

"We have to get law enforcement involved."

"Aw, jeez. I have to talk to Brick before we take that step." Josh dropped the paper back onto the desk and began to pace the office where they'd been working, laced his fingers behind his head, and gazed up toward the ceiling. "How could she do this to him, Lili? He gave her a job. He gave her a place to stay. He considers Courtney his sister!"

"So do you, Josh. She did this to you, too, Josh. You gave her your friendship."

"Yeah." He began to pace the room. "I can't believe that Brick chooses now to up and disappear on me. And not answering his phone? I swear, it would serve him right if I just walked out on him."

Lili couldn't stop herself from asking, "So he didn't tell you where he was going?"

"No. He rushed out of here like his shirt was on fire. Asked me to keep an eye on things until he returned. I didn't know to ask if it'd be anytime this year. Shoot, he could have run off to Texas for all I know. I can tell you one thing. He'd damn well better be back before Courtney returns from her day off tonight. I won't be able to look at her."

"Well, I can't help you there, Josh."

Sugar's tail began to thump the floor and

the office door opened. Patsy stepped inside carrying a tray of sandwiches. "You two have been working too hard. Take a lunch break. I have pimento cheese and tuna."

"I'm not hungry, Patsy," Josh said.

Sugar got up and walked to Patsy's side. Absently, the older woman petted the dog as she spoke to Josh. "Sit down and eat, young man. You worked awfully hard helping me pack while Lili worked on your bookkeeping problem. Any word from Brick yet?"

"No," Lili said. She glanced at the clock. "I don't know that you should wait much longer to say good-bye to him, Patsy. You don't want to be too late getting on the road."

"I said I'd wait until two o'clock, and that's what I'm doing. Besides, Celeste said she'd drop by around one thirty to see me off. I have to wait around until then."

"Well, you should at least go lie down. If you take a nap now, you won't be as tired if the day runs long."

"You are such a mother sometimes, Lili. I'll make a deal with you. You both eat a sandwich and I'll go lie down."

"Deal." Lili reached for a tuna sandwich and took a big bite.

"You, too, Josh," Patsy warned.

"Yes, ma'am."

Patsy turned to leave and Sugar moved to follow. Lili's heart broke a little when Patsy spoke to the dog. "Stay, girl. Go whimper at Lili. She'll probably give you a bite of her lunch."

Lili blinked back the tears that had hovered all day. *This waterworks needs to stop.*

Josh looked at her sharply and said, "What's up with her? This is more than simply cutting her trip short, isn't it?"

"Don't ask me, Josh. I can't say."

He studied her with a long look, then nodded. "This has been one helluva day, hasn't it?"

"Most definitely."

As Lili fed Sugar the rest of her sandwich, Josh asked, "Is there anything else we can do before Brick returns and I can give him the news?"

The office door opened before Josh finished his question. Brick stood holding the door for someone else. "Give me what news?"

Courtney Gibson walked inside carrying shopping bags from a boutique in Creede. Brick followed her and upon seeing the person to whom Josh had been speaking stopped short.

Lili couldn't read the look in his eyes as

he said, "Liliana."

Brick wasn't ready. He wasn't prepared. He'd expected her to be in her trailer or off on some activity with the Alleycats. Possibly waiting for him at his place.

He hadn't expected her to be here in the office.

He was rattled. He couldn't read her expression. She certainly hadn't lit up with a welcoming smile like he'd grown accustomed to. *Something is wrong.* "Tell me what, Josh?"

Courtney glanced from Josh to Brick and then to Lili. "Okay, um. Whatever is going on isn't my business. I think I'll just go on up to my room and put away my new shoes. If you all will excuse me?"

She headed for the staircase that led up to the office apartment that Josh had vacated for her, but Josh's voice stopped her. "No. You stay, Courtney. You need to hear this, too."

Brick tensed. *Oh, hell.* "Is it Mom and Pops? Did something happen to them?"

"What?" The question obviously caught Josh off guard.

"Something's obviously wrong!" Brick snapped.

425

"Oh no. It's nothing to do with Cindy and Paul."

That, at least, was a relief.

Josh continued, "I . . . um . . . well . . . you're right. Something has . . . um . . . happened. I . . . oh, damn. Patsy's leaving today. She just up and decided to go home."

Lili's expression revealed that she'd expected him to say something else. "Lili? What do you know?"

"She said it's time. She's been waiting to say good-bye to you." Lili looked at Josh and silently encouraged him. The man appeared downright miserable. When she reached out and rested her hand on his brother's arm, Brick had had enough. He needed to talk to Lili alone. Needed to make things right with her.

If Patsy was leaving early, was Lili planning to go, too? Was he too late? Had he screwed this up already? Just as his uncles and dad had warned him against?

He shouldn't have taken time at Stardance River Camp to shower and clean up. He should have just come straight here and thrown himself at her feet.

Well, he could do that now. She wasn't gone yet.

His brother and sister needed to be gone so he could talk to Liliana. "Just spit it out,

Joshua."

"Okay. Well. It's like this." Josh took hold of Lili's hand. He held her hand! "Lili and I spent the morning together and . . ."

Betrayal cut like a knife. He'd been here before, hadn't he? Was this the thanks he got for forgiving Josh for dating Tiffany after their breakup?

"There's a problem with your books."

Brick barely heard his brother. *Et tu, Liliana? Gotta get your payback in just like every other manipulative bitch.* Had they slept together? It must have been more than just "spending the morning" for Josh to look so miserable.

"Someone has been stealing from you, Brick. Almost eighty thousand dollars."

Wait. What?

Courtney dropped her shopping bags. "Lili did it!"

The accusation in his eyes pierced Lili's heart like a shard of ice and spread chilling pain throughout her body.

"I asked her for help," Courtney continued. "I gave her my passwords."

Josh glared at his foster sister. "You've been skimming, Courtney. Probably ever since you got here."

"That's a lie. It wasn't me. I'm innocent.

427

I wouldn't know how to skim. She does. She's the professional."

"She *is* the professional," Josh fired back. "That's why, for one example, she looked at the check for the taxes and realized something was wrong."

To Brick, he explained, "Courtney wrote the check to 'IRS.' Not the Department of the Treasury like it's supposed to be done. June's taxes haven't been received. The check has cleared. Deposited by Intrepid Resort Services."

"Wait." Brick shook his head, looking confused. "Repeat that."

Josh did as he asked, and at that point Brick's expression turned thunderstruck.

"I didn't do it!" Courtney declared. She pointed her finger at Lili. "She did. You just don't want to believe it because you're sleeping with her."

Lili never took her gaze off of Brick. She watched the comprehension sink in. She saw when he pulled his condemning gaze off of her and shifted it toward his sister.

Speaking to Josh, he asked, "How did we not know this?"

"She's been moving money around like a pro. Changed our address and telephone number with many of our vendors. Plus the biggest chunk of it came this week."

"You stole from me, Courtney? You stole eighty thousand dollars from me? Why?"

"I didn't do it! Your shack-up did it. She's in the office almost every day. She's been using my computer all summer because she doesn't have one of her own. Besides, I wouldn't know how to steal."

A series of different emotions flickered across Brick's face. Disbelief. Betrayal. Sadness. Finally, anger. A muscle working in his jaw and his green eyes blazing with anger, he spoke in a hard tone. "Josh, call Zach."

"Yeah. Tell him he needs to come arrest your girlfriend. Again."

Lili knew Brick well enough to tell that he wasn't buying Courtney's claims. That was something, she guessed. Nevertheless, that first reaction of his had been devastating.

That he could have thought she'd do that, even for only a moment, ripped her heart out.

He slowly shook his head. "Man, was I a fool. Courtney, I thought you had changed. But I guess that change was for the worse, not the better. What have you done with my money?"

"I didn't take it!"

"Bull. Like my grandfather likes to say, I might have been born at night, but it wasn't last night. So tell me, have you been stealing from your employers all these years or is this something you save for family? You stole a hundred and twenty dollars from me when we were in high school. Took it out of my stash in the closet. You lied like a rug and fooled Mom and Pop, but I always knew it was you."

"Your grandfather," Courtney sneered, her eyes blazing right back at Brick. Bitterness dripped from her words as she said, "You know, it wasn't enough that Cindy and Paul actually adopted you and you didn't get sent back and forth and back and forth to a stepfather who snuck into your bedroom at night. Oh no. You had a rich daddy come out of the woodwork. You got to have a big new happy family who have more money than God. So I took a little from you. Then and now. You can spare it."

Lili didn't believe that Courtney realized she'd just confessed to the crime.

Josh hung up the phone. "Zach is on his way."

Courtney fired off a string of curses, finishing with, "This is ridiculous. I'm not standing for it. Forget you both."

She turned and took three strides toward the door before Brick gripped her around the arm. "Oh no you don't. You're not going anywhere but to jail."

Courtney struggled, but Brick wasn't about to release her. When she began to spout seriously ugly epithets, Lili had had enough. Rising, she said, "I'll wait for Zach outside. Come on, Sugar."

Brick opened his mouth as though he wanted to speak to her as she passed. His foster sister interrupted the moment with more vicious accusations directed toward Brick. Lili and the dog escaped into the bright summer sunshine and clean, fresh air. Lili breathed a sigh of relief that failed to ease the ache in her heart.

Zach's sheriff's department SUV pulled up as Lili spied Patsy's truck and fifth wheel pulling out of her campsite spot. In that moment it was simply too much for her to bear. A mood similar to the one that had sent her running to Colorado swept over her. She marched up to Zach and her story poured from her mouth.

"You're going to want a statement from me, but if it's not against the law or anything, I'd like to do it over the phone. I can't stay here any longer, Zach. I told him I loved him and he ran away and came home and thought I'd stolen money from him. I've been down that road and was accused of drunk driving. Since I'm sober — not that I want to be, mind you — I'm going to drive Patsy home."

At what point the tears began falling she couldn't say. Zach pulled a handkerchief out of his pocket and handed it to her. "A handkerchief. You carry a handkerchief. Oh, Zach. I miss my daddy. I've never had a grandmother and now Patsy wants to go home. I want to go home. He keeps breaking my heart and I'm tired of being nine years old and kept out of the tree house. Can we do this over the phone? Please?"

"Honey, I'm sorry. I can't answer that. I'm not sure what we're doing."

She gave him a brief summary and her part in it, then offered a name and phone number. "You should call her right away. She's the best out there. If anyone can find his money, she'll do it. She'll be of great help to you. So . . . can I leave, Zach? Please? I don't know how much time Patsy has left."

"Sure. Go. I have your number. Good luck, Lili."

"Thank you." She started to leave, stopped, and returned his hanky, then hurried toward Patsy.

"What's wrong, love? What in the world is going on at the office? I saw Brick return, so I went to say my good-byes, but when I approached the office I heard Courtney yelling some vicious things."

"I'll tell you the whole story. Only in the truck. Sugar and I are going with you, Patsy."

"But Lili, I'm going home."

"I know. Me, too. Start the truck, Patsy. I'm going to get my purse and some dog treats and lock my trailer and go. My Stardance summer is officially over."

Following a lengthy interview during which Courtney proceeded to brag about how she'd duped Brick, Zach asked his deputy to take Courtney off to jail. To Brick and Josh, he said, "Your turns. Which of you wants to give your statement first?"

"You go," Brick said to Josh. "I need to go find Liliana."

Zach visibly hesitated before he flipped a page on his notebook. "I don't get paid enough for this job," he muttered before adding, "She's not here, Brick. She went home with Patsy."

Josh dropped his chin to his chest. Brick frowned at the reaction. "You mean she's gone to Patsy's trailer?"

"If Patsy lives in a trailer in Oklahoma then, yeah, I guess. She asked to make her statement by phone since she was returning to Oklahoma with her friend."

"You're saying Lili left. Eternity Springs." Brick stalked to the window. "That can't be. She left her rig."

"She said she was going to drive Patsy home."

"Patsy left, too?" Brick shoved to his feet. "So what is this? Tit for tat? I leave for a couple days, so she decides to pay me back?"

"Look, Callahan, I most certainly don't want to get involved in your love life, but the lady who left here was deeply upset."

"About?"

Zach closed his eyes and exhaled heavily. "I seriously don't get paid enough."

Then he told Brick as best he could recall exactly what Lili had said. "I think that's the important stuff. Honestly, I didn't follow all of it. Stuff about being nine and kicked out of a tree house. Women's tears give me the shakes."

"She was crying?"

"Oh yeah. She was definitely crying."

"Because she thought I believed Courtney. That really pisses me off. I never for a minute thought that! How could she have such little faith in me?"

"You did have a weird look on your face, bro."

"What do you mean?"

"The way you watched us when I told you about the money. Damn, Brick. Talk about if looks could kill."

"I wasn't even listening to that at first. She had her hands all over you. And she was looking at you all dewy-eyed."

"What?" Josh gaped at him. "Jeez, Brick. How stupid are you?"

"Okay," Zach said, flipping his notebook closed and standing. "I think we've done enough for now. Think I'll go visit my wife. Y'all look me up when you're ready to continue this."

Brick barely noticed Zach's departure. The news that Liliana had left was beginning to sink in.

"You didn't really think she and I . . ." Josh waved his hand, unwilling to put it into words.

"No." Brick grimaced. "No, of course not. I just . . . I went a little wacko there for a minute. I've had a tough couple of days. Got my ass kicked by my dad and his brothers. Learned that Lili was in love with me and then . . . aw jeez, Josh. I love her more than my life."

"I know you do."

"Really?"

"Yeah."

"How is it that everybody else knew it, but I didn't?"

"Because you have a brick for a brain?"

"I guess I can't argue that point since I just figured it out this morning. It knocked me off my game." Brick raked his fingers through his hair. "Why did she leave without talking to me?"

"Who the hell knows why women do anything? You're gonna have to ask somebody other than me. Why don't you go ask your aunt Nic or something?"

Brick dragged a hand down his jaw and considered it.

"All the wives are back for the weekend. I guess I could go talk to them. But I don't know that I have the energy for that. They won't settle for just kicking my ass. They'll skin me alive."

"Go talk to Claire, then. Or Lori."

"Actually . . . I have another idea." Brick rose and hurried toward the door. "Thanks, Josh. For everything. You saved my bacon. I owe you."

"Glad I could help. Wish I'd caught on sooner, though, and you don't owe me anything. It's the other way around."

As the door closed behind Brick, he heard Josh add, "You saved me. You just don't know it."

Under other circumstances, Brick would have turned around and demanded an explanation, but he was a man on a mission now. Ten minutes later, he pulled his car into the lot at Angel's Rest and he breathed a sigh of relief to see Celeste on her hands and knees in the rose garden, a trowel in her hand.

He parked and crossed the green grass toward the garden. "Celeste, mind if I interrupt you for a moment?"

She rolled back on her knees and smiled in welcome. "Not at all. Pull up a weed and join me."

"I can do that."

She returned to her weeding and asked, "So, what can I do for you, Mr. Callahan?"

"I screwed up. I need advice. I need your help. I need your prayers."

"Isn't that handy. I'm happy to offer all three. Tell me what's been happening."

So he did. He weeded half the bed as he poured out the whole pitiful story to her. When he finished, Celeste dug a dandelion from the dirt. "Yes, I know she left. She and Patsy stopped in to say good-bye on their way out of town."

"Was she still crying?"

"No. She'd moved on to the angry stage by then."

"Oh, man." He pushed up onto his knees. "What am I going to do, Celeste?"

"You messed up rather badly."

"I know. The whole stealing thing . . . it's her bugaboo. And, to be honest, the cheating paranoia is mine. Tiffany wasn't faithful to me."

"Oh, Brick." She clicked her tongue. "You won't win this battle if you don't put that woman behind you."

"I have. Honestly, I have."

"Then why that reaction?"

"Habit? A knee-jerk reaction? I haven't trusted in a very long time."

"But you trust Liliana."

"I do. Totally, I do." He paused a moment, then added, "I'm really angry at her, though."

"Because?"

"Because she left without talking to me. Because she didn't . . . oh."

"Trust you," Celeste finished.

"Well, we're a pair, aren't we?"

"You're both human. Humans make mistakes."

"So how do I fix it?"

"First, you have to forgive each other."

"I've got that one covered. On my side, anyway. But how do I get her to forgive me if she's in Oklahoma and I'm here? Do I go to Oklahoma immediately? Do I give her some time to cool down? What should I do, Celeste?"

"What do you want to do?"

"Marry her," he said without hesitation.

"In that case . . ." She set down her trowel. "Help me up, dear. Let's walk a bit. I do have an idea."

Brick assisted Celeste to her feet and tucked her arm through his as they began to stroll.

"She wanted a summer romance," Celeste said. "I think it's time you kick it up a notch."

"I'm happy to do that. But how?"

"Have you ever heard the story of when your uncle Matt proposed to your aunt Victoria?"

"He's mentioned something about a tuxedo and a beach."

Celeste stopped and smelled a rose. "I suggest you speak to him or Victoria and get the complete story. I will tell you, we've had some fabulously extravagant marriage proposals here in Eternity Springs. Definitely high romance."

An extravagant marriage proposal. Hmm. After a bit of consideration, Brick nodded. "I like it. I can do extravagant. And if you think it's a good idea, then I'm on board."

He hesitated a moment, then asked, "Where do I start?"

"Actually, I have an idea about that, too."

"I hoped you might."

They spent the rest of the afternoon making plans and arrangements. When everything was in place, he picked Celeste up, swung her around, and kissed her on the cheek. "Thank you, Celeste. You are my romance angel."

"I am always happy to help steer the course of true love."

Brick set Celeste on her feet and headed for the door. There he paused and glanced over his shoulder. "One last thing. Celeste, am I gonna get one of those angel necklaces?"

Her smile lit the room.

CHAPTER TWENTY-THREE

Off the coast of Cabo San Lucas, Mexico
"I feel like I'm flying when I stand at the bow. It's so relaxing to feel the wind in your face and hear the thrum of the engines. I could get used to this."

Now at the stern of the forty-six-foot Bertram yacht, Lili stretched out on a padded bench seat in the shade of a Bimini top. Relaxed and happy, she inhaled the briny scent of the sea.

She did love the ocean. Maybe she'd find a beach town to live in. She could run on the beach in the mornings. Swim in the afternoons.

A memory floated through her mind and she heard his voice. *You have a siren's alluring seafoam eyes, the kind that can lure a man to death. Just like a mermaid. You have mermaid eyes. Mermaid . . . attributes.*

Okay, maybe she wouldn't find a beach town. Perhaps she'd like the desert.

441

Patsy whirled the fighting chair around to face her, her eyes sparkling. "It is heavenly here, Lili. Hot as blazes, but heavenly. The scenery is breathtaking. The food fabulous. And the fishing! I've never had so much fun. The entire experience has been heavenly. What a dream come true this has been. Aren't you glad you let Celeste talk you out of twenty dollars for a raffle ticket before we left Eternity Springs? After today, I can die a happy woman."

"But not until we get back to Oklahoma. You promised."

"I did." Patsy scooted out of the chair. "Because I want to keep my promise, I think I'll go below and take a nap."

Lili's peaceful mood vanished. "Do we need to return to the marina? Are you — ?"

"I'm fine! I'm tired! We were up before dawn! Quit being a mother hen. You promised, too, remember."

"All right. Yes, ma'am. Enjoy your nap."

"Catch another big fish while I'm asleep, why don't you? That dorado you landed was nice, but I'd love for you to catch a trophy."

Yes, well, I tried. Didn't quite work out.

"I'll do my best. Enjoy your nap, Patsy."

Lili flipped a switch that turned on the boat's misters. Celeste had been right about the heat. It was brutal. But with the breeze and the mist and a little shade, this place truly was a little piece of heaven. Closing her eyes, she murmured, "Take that, Eternity Springs."

Almost a month had passed since she fled Colorado. She hadn't heard a thing from Brick. When she spoke with Josh about putting her truck and trailer up for sale, he'd not said one word about his brother. She tried to tell herself that she was okay with that. Lying to herself proved difficult.

She shouldn't have run. Not without talking to him first. Her only defense was the emotional turmoil of the day. She'd reacted defensively and acted cowardly by running. Maybe someday she'd work up the nerve to contact him and offer him an apology.

She'd stayed busy during the past weeks. Upon their return to Oklahoma City, Patsy had conceded to visiting her doctor, which led to a hospital stay. The source of her illness had been an infection unrelated to her cancer. Antibiotics cleared it up, and on the day Patsy returned home they'd received word from Celeste that they'd won the school's fund-raising raffle.

Lili barely remembered buying the ticket. She'd certainly not recalled the prize — an all-expenses-paid trip to Cabo including a fishing trip on a private yacht. Patsy remembered everything and she'd actually jumped up and down, clapping like a schoolgirl. "It's marlin season down there!"

So here they were. Between the two of them, they'd caught three dorado, six tuna, and a wahoo. Twenty minutes ago, after a thirty-minute battle, Patsy had landed her dream — a marlin. At 130 pounds, the fish had been on the small side for a marlin, but it was perfect for a woman in her state of health.

Lili was drifting toward sleep when she heard the ringing of her phone. "Moth-er," she whined, but she answered it. "Hello, Mom. What has Sugar done now?"

"Oh, she's just the sweetest thing. Dad and I took her to the dog park and she made friends with this little puppy. It was the cutest thing."

Her mother rattled on about the dog for almost fifteen minutes, and when they finally ended the call Lili no longer felt like napping. She couldn't get over how gaga her parents were over dog sitting. Imagine how they'd be if they ever got the chance to babysit a grandchild.

She startled when one of the crew jumped down from the flybridge. The captain throttled back the engine. "Have we hooked something?"

"No, ma'am," the young man said in heavily accented English. "Too long without a fish. Change the bait."

"Ah. Okay."

Lili had thoroughly enjoyed catching that thirty-pound dorado. Ugly fish, but fun to catch. She'd been thrilled that it had been Patsy's turn in the chair when they hooked the marlin, but Lili wouldn't deny that she'd like the opportunity to land one of those herself. All metaphors aside.

She expected the crewman to bait the hook with another tuna. Instead, he put on it an artificial . . . something . . . unlike anything she'd seen before. "What are we fishing for with that?"

"Big fish. Trophy."

Lili rose, intending to take a closer look at the bait, when the captain called to her from the flybridge. "Are you enjoying yourself, miss? Do you like the lunch?"

"It was fabulous, Captain. I'd love your wife's recipe for the *chilaquiles verdes.*"

"I have your e-mail. I'll make sure she sends it."

By the time they finished talking, the crewman had the line in the water. The captain pushed the throttle and the boat started forward. Almost immediately the outriggers snapped and began to hum.

Two crewmen hopped down from the fly-bridge. Lili jumped to take her place in the fighting seat. The two men fired a few sentences of rapid Spanish and grinned.

"Does that smile mean it's a big one?" Lili asked.

"Like nothing this boat has ever landed, I'm sure."

Lili took the rod. Tested it. There was something on the line, for sure, but this had a different feel than that dorado.

She was able to rather easily crank the reel. "Are you sure it's a fish? Not a tire or something from the bottom of the sea? This one's not fighting me."

Leave it to her to hook a piece of trash.

"It happens that way sometimes," the captain said philosophically. "Fish give up the fight on different timelines. Keep reeling him in, missy. You've all but landed him now."

"Okay." She couldn't help but be a little disappointed. This wasn't nearly as much fun as landing Patsy's fish had looked. "We haven't even seen him jump."

"Oh, he'll jump, missy," said a crewman. "They always jump. Keep reeling."

She kept reeling. Finally, she spied something in the water. Definitely big. Dark. The fish was almost to the boat, but he'd never jumped. Reeling him in hadn't taken much more than five minutes. Lili felt cheated.

"Put the rod in the holder, but stay in your seat now, missy." The crewmen reached over the stern and pulled something out of the water and onto the back platform. She leaned over and forward, trying to see. It looked like . . . metal? She *had* caught trash!

But then something moved. Black . . . arms. And a head . . . a mask. This wasn't a fish.

Hands braced against the platform and a body rose from the water. *What in the world?*

A ribbon of fear fluttered through her. This was drug-cartel-warring Mexico. Had she and Patsy inadvertently ended up in the midst of trouble? But almost before the thought formed, the diver removed his mask.

She recognized those green eyes that zeroed in on hers. *Green like the mountains in summer.*

Shock stole her breath. Her pulse started racing as her heart climbed to her throat. Without taking his gaze from hers, Brick unzipped his wet suit and took it off. He wore a Speedo beneath it. A Speedo and . . .

The first words Lili spoke to Brick in almost a month were an incredulous, "You're wearing a tie?"

"Uncle Matt wore a tux."

Okay, apparently that was supposed to make sense. It didn't. But Lili didn't really care. She drank in the sight of Brick even as she asked, "What is this, Brick?"

As he stepped into the boat, she heard the crewmen climbing the ladder to the fly-bridge. Brick asked, "Liliana, will you do a favor for me? I'd rather not do this when you're seated in the fighting chair. It's just bad karma."

Her mouth was dry. She climbed down out of the chair and moved to the middle of the boat. Brick's steady gaze never left her. The Bertram swayed beneath her feet from the gentle ocean swell, or maybe it was from her world being rocked.

Brick was here. For real. She wasn't asleep and dreaming.

"Lili-fair, I have a lot to say to you. Apologies and explanations and even a few old stories. But I want to start with the most important thing first. I love you. I love you to the depths of my soul and with every fiber of my being. I've waited all my life for you. You complete me. You excite me. You make me dream. You're the girl next door who waited for me to grow up, and for that I will always be grateful. Please tell me it didn't take too long."

"Brick . . . what . . . why . . . how did you get here!"

"You're gonna make me sweat, aren't you?" He took a step toward her so that they stood within arm's length. "How did I get here? I'm afraid I took the long route. Turns out all I needed to do was walk to my friend's house to the girl next door."

"What?"

He shook his head. "Never mind. First I drove, then I flew, then I boated, and finally, I swam. I'll crawl if that's what it takes, Lili. Tell me I'm not too late. Tell me I didn't blow it. Tell me you still love me. I need to hear it."

"You broke my heart."

"I know. I'm sorry. I was stupid. I'm a Callahan man. I'm afraid this won't be the last time, either. But I swear I'll try to keep it down to a minimum. I figure if the brothers have managed to keep it under control with their wives, then I should be able to do it with mine."

Wives! "What are you saying, Brick?"

"Tell me you forgive me. Tell me you trust me. Tell me you love me."

Her heart began to soar. A grin wanted to break out on her face, but she held it back. "You arranged this entire trip, didn't you?"

"Yes. Me and Celeste. Look." He moved

the tie and showed her the medal hanging around his neck. "I earned my wings."

"Congratulations." She gave up trying to fight off her smile. "That Celeste is something else."

Though he'd appeared completely confident, Lili hadn't missed the tenseness in his stance or the worry line between his brows. Her smile relaxed both. A grin began to play on his lips.

My, oh my, talk about wet-guy eye candy.

"Celeste is my angel," he said. "I went to see her the day you left. I'd known I'd screwed up by running away, but I didn't know how to fix it. I'm just a normal guy, Liliana. We make mistakes. We develop bad habits. That's what my whole relationship phobia was. A bad habit. My whole three-dates-and-good-bye rule had nothing to do with Tiffany. It's how I filled my time until I met you."

Lili's heart went all warm and gooey. "Celeste made you see that?"

"No. The brothers did when they tracked me down at the River Camp ghost town and kicked my butt because I was about to blow it with you."

He edged a little closer to her. "Liliana, you and I are so blessed. I don't know that it's been exactly fair of us to take a share of the Eternity Springs healing angel dust. What we've had standing between us is nothing compared to what many of our Eternity Springs friends faced. We haven't lost a spouse or a child or had one kidnapped. So a girl dumped me and bruised my heart? So your job treated you like crap? These are normal problems that people all over the country . . . all over the world . . . face every day. You pick up and you move on. That's what we do. But you're a girl and I'm a guy, so you figured it out before me."

"*That's* what Celeste taught you?"

"No. I had all that figured out before I returned to Stardance. Celeste played a more important role. She is my romance angel. She helped me plan this trip."

Lili laughed then, and he took it as a signal to close the distance between them. He put his arms around her and smiled down into her upturned face. "Give me the words, mermaid."

She'd give him the world if she could. "I forgive you. I trust you. I love you."

"Whew!" He pressed a fast, hard kiss against her lips. Lili wanted to pull him back down to her for something a little more satisfying, but he continued to talk. "First hurdle behind me. Now for the next."

Releasing her, he moved to the back of

the boat and opened the lid on the bait tank. Reaching inside, he felt around, keeping his back to her so that she couldn't see what he was doing. When he turned around, he appeared to have something concealed in his fist. *What in the world?*

Brick moved to stand before her. He went down on one knee and Lili caught her breath. In his hand, he held a sparkling diamond solitaire. "I want our summer to last forever. Liliana, will you do me the great honor of becoming my wife?"

Her eyes misty, she said, "Yes. Yes, I'll marry you, Mark. I've dreamed about it since I was nine years old."

He rose and lifted her left hand, and as he slid the ring onto her finger Lili asked, "Did you seriously hide my engagement ring in a fish tank?"

"I'm in a Speedo, Lili. I thought it was better there than with my jewels." His breath caressed her lips as he leaned in to kiss her. "Am I romantic or what?"

ABOUT THE AUTHOR

Emily March is the *New York Times, Publishers Weekly,* and *USA Today* bestselling author of over thirty novels, including the critically acclaimed Eternity Springs series. *Publishers Weekly* calls March a "master of delightful banter," and her heartwarming, emotionally charged stories have been named to Best of the Year lists by *Publishers Weekly, Library Journal,* and *Romance Writers of America.* A graduate of Texas A&M University, Emily is an avid fan of Aggie sports and her recipe for jalapeño relish has made her a tailgating legend.